# Tempting
# the Millionaire

## MAUREEN CHILD
## JACKIE BRAUN
## CASSIE MILES

Published in Great Britain 2014
by Mills & Boon, an imprint of Harlequin (UK) Limited,
Eton House, 18-24 Paradise Road, Richmond, Surrey, TW9 1SR

TEMPTING THE MILLIONAIRE © 2014 Harlequin Books S.A.

*An Officer and a Millionaire, Marrying the Manhattan Millionaire* and *Mysterious Millionaire* were first published in Great Britain by Harlequin (UK) Limited.

*An Officer and a Millionaire* © 2009 Maureen Child
*Marrying the Manhattan Millionaire* © 2009 Jackie Braun Fridline
*Mysterious Millionaire* © 2008 Kay Bergstrom

ISBN: 978-0-263-91196-1
eBook ISBN: 978-1-472-04491-4

05-0814

Harlequin (UK) Limited's policy is to use papers that are natural, renewable and recyclable products and made from wood grown in sustainable forests. The logging and manufacturing processes conform to the legal environmental regulations of the country of origin.

Printed and bound in Spain
by Blackprint CPI, Barcelona

# AN OFFICER AND
# A MILLIONAIRE

BY
MAUREEN CHILD

**Maureen Child** is a California native who loves to travel. Every chance they get, she and her husband are taking off on another research trip. An author of more than sixty books, Maureen loves a happy ending and still swears that she has the best job in the world. She lives in Southern California with her husband, two children and a golden retriever with delusions of grandeur.

To Desire™ Readers,
You've made all of this possible with your loyalty
and your enthusiasm for what we do!
Thank you all.

# One

Hunter Cabot, Navy SEAL, had a healing bullet wound in his side, thirty days' leave and apparently a *wife* he'd never met.

On the drive into his hometown of Springville, California, he stopped for gas at Charlie Evans's service station. That's where the trouble started.

"Hunter! Man, it's good to see you! Margie didn't tell us you were coming home."

"Margie?" Hunter leaned back against the front fender of his black pickup truck and winced as his side gave a small twinge of pain. Silently then, he watched as the man he'd known since high school filled his tank.

Charlie grinned, shook his head and pumped gas. "Guess your wife was lookin' for a little 'alone' time with you, huh?"

"My—" Hunter couldn't even say the word. *Wife?* He didn't have a wife. "Look, Charlie…"

"Don't blame her, of course," his friend said with a wink as he finished up and put the gas cap back on. "You being gone all the time with the SEALs must be hard on the ol' love life."

He'd never had any complaints, Hunter thought, frowning at the man still talking a mile a minute. "What're you—"

"Bet Margie's anxious to see you. She told us all about that honeymoon trip you two took to Bali." Charlie's dark brown eyebrows lifted and wiggled.

"Charlie…"

"Hey, it's okay, you don't have to say a thing, man."

What the hell could he say? Hunter shook his head, paid for his gas and, as he left, told himself Charlie was just losing it. Maybe the guy'd been smelling gas fumes for too long.

But as it turned out, it wasn't just Charlie. Stopped at a red light on Main Street, Hunter glanced out his window to smile at Mrs. Harker, his second-grade teacher, who was now at least a hundred years old. In the middle of the crosswalk, the old woman stopped and shouted, "Hunter Cabot, you've got yourself a wonderful wife. I hope you appreciate her."

Scowling now, he only nodded at the old woman— the only teacher who'd ever scared the crap out of him. What the hell was going on here? Was everyone but him *nuts?*

His temper beginning to boil. He put up with a few more comments about his "wife" on the drive through town before finally pulling into the wide, circular drive leading to the Cabot mansion. Hunter didn't have a clue what was going on, but he planned to get to the bottom of it. Fast.

He grabbed his duffel bag, stalked into the house and paid no attention to the housekeeper, who ran at him, fluttering both hands. "Mister Hunter!"

"Sorry, Sophie," he called out over his shoulder as he took the stairs two at a time. "Need a shower; then we'll talk."

He marched down the long, carpeted hallway to the rooms that were always kept ready for him. In his suite, Hunter tossed the duffel down and stopped dead. The shower in his bathroom was running. His *wife?*

Anger and curiosity boiled in his gut, creating a churning mass that had him moving forward without even thinking about it.

He opened the bathroom door to a wall of steam and the sound of a woman singing—off-key. Margie, no doubt.

Well, if she was his wife…Hunter walked across the room, yanked the shower door open and stared in at a curvy, naked, temptingly wet woman.

She whirled around to face him, slapping her arms across her naked body while she gave a short, terrified scream.

Hunter smiled. "Hi, honey. I'm home."

"Who—what—how—who—"

"Now, honey," he drawled the words out, completely enjoying watching the shock ripple across her features, "is that any way to greet your husband?"

"I—I—"

He had her nervous—that was for damn sure, he

told himself. Easy enough to see by the way her eyes darted from one side of the room to the other, as if looking for an escape route.

Well, there wasn't one. She wasn't going anywhere until he had some answers. But that wasn't to say he couldn't make her as uncomfortable as possible. No better than she deserved for pretending to be his wife, for God's sake.

The shower area was directly behind her, and steam twisted in the air like fog. A quick glance around the once familiar bathroom allowed Hunter to notice the jars and bottles of lotions women seemed to be unable to live without. Plus, the black towels he preferred had been replaced with navy-blue. Not to mention a vase full of flowers in the corner of the marble vanity counter.

Looked as though she'd made herself damned comfortable in his home, too. Which meant she'd been lying to his grandfather. Damn it. Fresh anger churned in his gut, and he had to fight to contain it. This naked, curvy, all-too-delectable woman had been lying to a lonely old man. Probably wormed her way into his affections and was no doubt stealing him blind to boot. Well, her game, whatever it was, was up. He didn't care how good she looked naked. Well, he cared, but not enough to let himself get sidetracked.

He took a step closer and caught the delicious scent of her. Jasmine, if he wasn't mistaken, and something inside him stirred. It had been a while since he'd had a woman. He'd been too busy with mission after mission and hadn't wanted to bother. But now, with a naked, wet, terrific-smelling woman within arm's reach, his body was snapping to attention despite the fact that he was as furious as he was aroused.

She was watching him as though she were a rabbit and he a cobra.

So, she was perceptive as well as a liar.

"What, no kiss?" he asked, moving in even closer. If she dropped one arm, he'd have another look at her high, full breasts. "Didn't you miss me, honey?"

She jerked a quick look behind her, saw no help there and whipped her head back around to glare at him. The action sent tiny droplets of water flinging from the ends of her dark red, curly hair, and they hit Hunter's face like raindrops.

"You just keep your distance, you…*pervert*."

"Pervert?" He snorted a laugh and wiped the water from his face with one hand. "I'm just a husband trying to greet his *wife*."

"There's no greeting going on here. At all." Sidestepping fast, she snatched a navy-blue towel off the closest rod and wrapped it around herself in the blink of an eye.

Too bad. Hunter had enjoyed the view and the glimpse of peaked pink nipples he'd had just before she'd covered up. If nothing else, his "wife" had a body designed to make a man want to spend some time exploring those curves.

Now, though, she was managing to look down on him even though she was a full foot shorter than he was. The ice in her emerald-green eyes was enough to give a lesser man frostbite. But Hunter had the fires of righteous anger on his side, so he wasn't moved. Meeting her stare with an icy glare of his own, he demanded shortly, "Who the hell are you?"

"Who am I?" She whipped her head to one side, and her soaking wet hair swung back and out of her eyes, spraying Hunter with another spill of droplets. Frantically, she tucked one end of the towel into the valley between her breasts. But she was breathing so hard, the terry cloth shield she was obviously depending on didn't look any too stable. "I'm in *my* bathroom taking a shower, minding my own business when— Oh, God." Her eyes widened. "You're…I can't believe I didn't recognize you right away. But you scared me and—"

He flicked another lazy glance at her now scantily clad body. "Babe, if I scared you, you had it coming. Imagine how it felt for me to find out from every-damn-body in town that I have a *wife.*"

"Oh, for heaven's sake…"

"That about covers it," Hunter snapped, taking another step toward her. His voice was deceptively quiet. "See, I've got a month's leave coming. Decided to head home, do some recuperating, check in with my grandfather…" He walked a small, tight circle around her and enjoyed the watchful look in her eyes as she slowly turned in place to follow his progress.

"Imagine my surprise when everywhere I go in town, people are telling me how excited my wife is gonna be to see me."

"Well, I'm not. Excited," she added, as if he'd missed that. "More like irritated," she said. "Annoyed, really."

"Now that's a damn shame." Hunter stopped directly in front of her and did his best to loom. Wasn't difficult. Since he was taller than his "wife," forcing her to tilt her head back to look up at him was all too easy. "You think *you're* annoyed?"

"Wouldn't you be, when a perfect stranger sneaks into your shower like a scene out of the movie *Psycho*? All that was missing was that hideous, screechy violin music."

If she had been scared, she'd recovered now, Hunter thought. "I'm not the one in the wrong here, babe. You're the liar. You're the intruder."

"Is that right?" She sniffed, plopped both hands on her towel-covered hips and started tapping one bare foot against the bathroom rug.

"Straight up, that's right. You know damn well we're not married, so why don't you tell me what your scam is? And how the hell did you convince my grandfather to let you into the house?" The more he thought about it, the angrier he became. "Simon's nobody's fool, so you must be the queen of con artists."

*"Con artist?"* She slapped both hands against his chest and shoved. He didn't even sway in place. But her towel slipped a notch. He had hopes of another good look at her.

"If you think you're scoring points by acting all outraged," Hunter told her, his gaze dropping briefly to the slippage of her towel, "you're wrong."

She fumed silently for a second or two, and Hunter could have sworn he actually saw the wheels in her brain turning, calculating, figuring.

"You're not supposed to be here," she muttered.

"Oh, that's a good one, babe. I'm the one who's not supposed to be here?"

"You didn't tell Simon you were coming." She scowled at him. "And stop calling me 'babe.'"

"I'll call you whatever I damn well please. And you're lucky I'm not calling the cops."

Her mouth dropped open.

"As for my not letting Simon know I was coming, I consider that a good thing," he told her, meeting those hard green eyes with a cold look that should have frozen her on the spot. "Hard to catch a liar and a cheat if she knows you're coming."

"I am not a—you're really a very irritating man, did you know that?" She cocked her head to one side, and her wet hair hung in a curtain behind her. "No one in town ever mentioned that part of your personality. But then," she added, "you're scarcely here, so they've probably forgotten."

"I'm here now," he pointed out, ignoring the slight twinge of something uncomfortable. No, he didn't get back to Springville very often. He spent most of his time on base or being shipped out for various highly secret operations. Was he supposed to take a rare weekend off and drive all the way upstate only to turn around and drive back down again? He didn't think so. Besides, how he lived his life was none of this woman's business.

"This isn't about me, *babe.*" He used the word deliberately and enjoyed watching her cringe at it. "Let's get to the real questions. What the hell are you up to? Why are you here? In *my* suite? Why are you telling everyone in town that we're married, and how the hell did you fool my grandfather into believing you?"

"Your suite," she muttered, inhaling so sharply she loosened the towel enough that it opened wide and swished silently down her body.

Hunter got one more good, long look at full, high breasts, perky pink nipples and soft brown curls at the apex of her thighs. His own body sat up and howled. Then she muttered a curse, grabbed the towel and wrapped herself up again.

"Your suite? That's a good one. I've been living in this suite for a year now, and, funny," she added with a touch of sarcasm, "but I don't remember seeing you."

Screw her snide tone. He was concentrating on the words. "A *year?* You've been pretending to be my wife, living in my house for a year?"

Had it really been that long since he'd been home? Damn, guess it had been. But he'd talked to Simon every couple of weeks over the last year, and the old man had never once mentioned the woman masquerading as Hunter's wife. Not one syllable. Not a noun. Nothing. What the hell was going on around here?

Had she done something to his grandfather? Threatened him in some way? Hard to believe. Simon Cabot was as tough as three old boots. But he was older now. Maybe…

Hunter moved in even closer, riding a tide of fury that had the edges of his vision blurring. He looked down at her and had to admire the fact that she didn't back up. She didn't cower, even though she was far smaller than he, not to mention naked and all kinds of vulnerable. Her eyes flashed at him as if daring him to try to hurt her. It was almost like watching a toy poodle transform into a pitbull.

But admiration aside, he had to know what she was up to. "Play time's over, honey. Whatever scam you've been running, you're done. And if I find out you've stolen so much as twenty bucks from my grandfather, your cute little ass is going to wind up behind bars."

Steam was slowly sifting out of the room, and the air was chill enough to bring goose bumps to her still-damp skin. If she was feeling the cold, though, she ignored it. Lifting her chin, she said, "I'm not going to continue this conversation naked."

"Well, you're not leaving this room till I get some answers."

"I should have known you were a bully."

"Excuse me?" He actually *felt* his glower darken.

"Is this a military thing? You barking orders and expecting us poor civilians to jump into line? Well, I don't take orders from you. And you should be ashamed of yourself."

"Ashamed of myself? You might want to back off, *babe*," he said, and it came out as more of a growl, "I'm not the one pretending to be something I'm not. I'm not the one living in someone else's home under false pretenses. I'm not the one—"

"Oh for heaven's sake, I'm not going to stand here and be insulted." She pushed past Hunter, giving him a straight-armed shove that caught him so off guard he actually stepped aside. He could have stood his ground, but then, he'd never been the kind of man to use his muscle against women.

His quick movement brought a twinge of discomfort from the still-healing wound in his side, and he automatically lifted one hand to it. Then he watched her storm out of the bathroom, somehow managing to look regal while wrapped in a towel. She left damp footprints on the thick, soft green carpet, which muffled the sound of her passage, and headed directly to *his* chest of drawers.

Wryly, he asked, "Going to be wearing some of my old boxers and T-shirts, are you?"

She shot him a surly look over her shoulder. "I moved your ratty old clothes to the bottom drawer a long time ago."

"Ratty?"

"What would you call T-shirts with more holes than fabric?"

"Mine."

She ignored him now, digging into an open drawer. Pulling out a pale blue lacy bra and a pair of panties to match, she hurried over to the huge walk-in closet, stepped inside it and closed the door behind her.

So he wasn't going to be watching her dress. Not that he wanted to. Fine. That was a lie. He wouldn't have minded another look at her figure. After all, he was human, wasn't he? And *male,* with an appreciation for a nicely rounded woman. And whoever the hell she was, he already knew she had some great curves.

Instantly, his mind filled with that last glimpse he'd had of her. Pale flesh, rigid pink nipples and a bottom that made a man want to grab hold and squeeze.

Scowling at the thoughts crowding his fevered mind, he shut them down resolutely. A Navy SEAL was nothing if not disciplined.

"Why are you here, anyway?" Her voice came from the depths of the closet.

"This is my home, babe. I belong here."

She snorted. That came through loud and clear. He also heard clothes hangers rattling and a hard thud followed by her muffled yelp.

"What're you doing?" he demanded.

"Breaking my toe," she snapped.

Hunter glowered at the closed door; then while he half listened to the sounds she made, he let his gaze slide around the room he'd grown up in. He'd been so distracted by the whole "wife" thing earlier that he hadn't really noticed how different the room was.

The walls were green, not beige. The carpet was green, not brown. There was a lacy quilt covering the king-sized bed he'd picked out himself at seventeen and a mountain of frilly pillows stacked against the headboard. Filmy white curtains fluttered at the windows that overlooked the garden at the rear of the mansion, and the French doors leading to the balcony boasted the same girly curtains as the windows.

How had he not noticed? He, whose very survival often depended on his observational skills? "What the hell have you done to this place?"

She stepped out of the closet then, and he whipped around to look at her. She wore a yellow T-shirt over a pair of worn, faded jeans that hugged every luscious inch of her and a pair of sandals that added about three inches to her measly height. Her green eyes were narrowed, her full mouth grim, and she'd somehow managed to fluff her wild mane of curly hair into a damp jumble of softness. When she folded her arms across her chest, his gaze locked on the wide, gold band on her ring finger.

Damn it.

Margie stared right back at him while she tried to ignore the rush of something hot and tempting inside her. His blue eyes were filled with suspicion he didn't bother to hide, and tension practically rippled off him in waves. Hunter Cabot was a lot…*bigger* than she'd expected. Not just tall. Big. His shoulders were wide, his chest and arms looked as though he spent most of his time lifting weights and even his long legs were thick and muscled beneath the black jeans he wore.

Impressive. And a little—no, a lot—daunting. But she wasn't about to let him know how nervous he made her. After all, she hadn't done anything wrong.

"Well?" He glared at her again. He really was very good at that. "Who the hell told you that you could move into *my* room and turn it into some female lair?"

The best defense, Margie had always believed, was a good offense. A lawyer she'd once worked for had taught her that, and she'd always found it to work.

"Your grandfather did," she answered with plenty of heat of her own. "You remember, the lonely old man you never visit?"

"Don't you start on me about my grandfather. You don't have the right."

"Really?" She marched right up to him, every step fueled by the anger she'd harbored for Hunter ever since she first came to work for his grandfather. "Well, let me tell you something, Captain Hunter Cabot, I earned the right to defend your grandfather the night he had his heart attack and *I* was the only one at his bedside."

He flushed. Anger? Or shame?

"Why were *you* at his bedside, anyway?"

Margie huffed out an impatient breath. She shouldn't be having to explain any of this. Simon had promised her that he would talk to Hunter before he came home. But this surprise arrival had thrown everything off.

"I'm Simon's executive assistant."

"His secretary?"

"Assistant," she corrected. "I was here. With him, when he had the heart attack. We tried to find you, but, big surprise, you were nowhere to be found."

"Just a damn minute…"

"No," she countered, stabbing her index finger at him, "you had your say; now it's my turn. You're never here. You hardly call. Your grandfather *misses* you, blast it. Why, I can't imagine—"

"That's none of your—"

"Not finished," she snapped, interrupting his interruption. "You're so busy running around saving the world you don't have time to be with your grandfather when he might have *died?* Like I said before. You should be ashamed of yourself."

# Two

There, Margie told herself as Hunter's mouth snapped shut and his blue eyes flashed. He might have had the upper hand since the moment he'd found her naked—oh, dear God—in the bathroom. But now, it was as it should be: him having to defend himself.

The room was so suddenly quiet that she could hear them both breathing. Sunlight streamed in through the open French doors and lay in a golden slash across the spring-green carpet. A slight breeze ruffled the curtains and carried with it the scents of roses and columbine from the garden just below her bedroom. Normally, she loved this room, found it peaceful, relaxing. Today, not so much.

"I've got nothing to be ashamed of," he said tightly. "I'm off doing my job, serving my country. I'm not the one here taking advantage of a lonely old man."

"You don't know what you're talking about." Her voice was stiff and so was her spine.

"I don't know," he mused. "Seems pretty clear to me. You were his secretary and somehow convinced him that we got married. How you did it I don't have any idea, but I'm going to find out."

"Oh, that makes sense," she said. "I just threw a ring on my finger, said, 'Guess what, I'm married to your idiot grandson,' and Simon believed me. Tell me, do you think your grandfather is really that foolish? You must, which means you're not letting logic get in your way at all."

"Logic?"

"Never mind, it's probably something you're unfamiliar with."

A long minute ticked silently past as they stared at each other, but Margie was determined not to be the one to speak first. Her patience finally paid off.

His mouth worked and his features tightened until he looked as uncomfortable as any man could be before he said grudgingly, "About Simon's heart attack. I suppose I should…thank you, for being with him that night."

"You think?"

"I was on a mission," he added as if she hadn't spoken, "I didn't find out about his heart attack until I returned. Then the crisis was over. I called him, if you'll remember."

"Very touching," she snapped, remembering the pleased look on Simon's face when his grandson had finally called to check on him. "A deeply personal phone call. Yet, you still didn't bother to come and see him."

"He was fine," Hunter argued. "Besides, my team shipped out again almost immediately and—"

"Oh, I'm not the one who needs to hear your explanation," she told him, "It's Simon you should be talking to. Besides, I didn't stay with Simon during his illness for *your* sake."

"Fine."

"Fine." It felt…odd, to be standing in the same room with the man she'd been legally married to for a year. Hunter Cabot had for so long lived in her mind only that having him here in person was more like a dream than the reality she'd been living with.

Strange, but in all the times she'd imagined her first meeting with Hunter Cabot, she'd never once thought they'd be embroiled in a huge argument right off the bat. But he'd started it, calling her a thief! So she didn't regret any of the things she'd said to him. His features were still tight, but there was something else in his eyes besides anger now. Something she couldn't quite read, and that was a little unsettling.

"Where is my grandfather now?"

"Probably in his study," she muttered. "He spends most afternoons there."

He nodded and left without another word to her.

Margie's breath whooshed out in a rush as soon as he was gone and she hurriedly walked to the bed to plop down on the edge of the mattress. Staring down at her hands, she looked first at the wedding ring she'd picked out herself, then noticed her hands were shaking. Not surprising, really. Not every day she had a huge, gorgeous, furious man walk in on her in the shower.

"Naked. He saw me *naked*." That really wasn't the

way she'd wanted to meet her husband for the first time. Especially because she still hadn't found a way to lose those ten pounds she didn't need, and her hair looked hideous, and she didn't have any makeup on and—she groaned and slapped one hand over her eyes.

"For pity's sake, Margie, it's not like makeup would have transformed you into supermodel territory anyway." She knew exactly what she looked like. Her mouth was too wide, her nose was too small and the freckles spattered across her cheeks defied all known foundations. She was not the kind of woman a man like Hunter Cabot would ever notice. "But then, it doesn't matter what you look like, now, does it? It's not as though you're really married to the man." Legally, yes. Really, no.

She flopped back onto the bed and stared up at the cool green ceiling. She hadn't planned to meet her husband for the first time until *after* his grandfather had explained the whole situation. And it would've worked out just like it was supposed to have done if Hunter hadn't shown up two weeks early, for pity's sake.

So if you thought about it, this was all his fault.

But as Margie blindly stared at the ceiling, she had to admit that that knowledge didn't make her feel any better.

Hunter moved through the familiar halls with a long, determined step, but no matter how fast he walked, he couldn't leave that woman behind him. Her voice kept time with the hard thumps of his boot heels against the floor.

*Lonely old man. Almost died. Ashamed.*

Muttering curses under his breath, Hunter silenced that voice and hit the bottom of the stairs. Slapping one hand to the newel post, he made a sharp right turn and continued down the carpeted hall toward the last door on the left.

He opened the door without knocking and stepped inside. This room at least remained the same. Unchanged. Dark paneling on the walls, polished to a high gloss, gleamed in the sunlight pouring through the windows. Dark brown leather armchairs and sofas were sprinkled throughout the room, and behind the wide, mahogany desk where his grandfather sat, floor-to-ceiling bookcases displayed everything from the classics to fictional thrillers.

But Hunter's gaze locked on the smiling old man slowly pushing himself to his feet. "Grandfather."

"Hunter, boy! Good to see you! You're early," he added, coming around the edge of the desk with careful steps. "Didn't expect you for a couple of weeks yet."

Hunter walked to meet the man who had always been the one constant in his life. When he was twelve years old, Hunter's parents died in a car accident and he'd come to live with his paternal grandfather. Simon had stepped into the void in his grandson's life and had always seemed to Hunter to be larger than life. Strong, sure, confident.

Now, though, Hunter noticed for the first time that the years were finally catching up with his grandfather. Something cold and hard fisted around Hunter's heart as he hugged the older man and actually felt a new frailty about Simon. He swallowed back the questions crowding his throat and demanding release, and he forced himself to be patient.

Stepping back, the old man waved one hand at a chair and said, "Sit, sit. Are you sure you should be walking around with that wound in your side?"

"I'm fine, Grandfather," Hunter said, reassuring Simon as he took a seat in the chair opposite him. He could wait for answers about the woman upstairs. For a moment or two, anyway. "Wasn't more than a scratch, really."

"They don't put you in the hospital for four days with a scratch, boy."

True, but he didn't want Simon worrying anymore than he could help. Hunter had caught a bullet on his last mission, but it had been more painful than life-threatening. Now all that remained was an ache if he moved too fast and a scar from the hastily maneuvered field surgery he'd had to perform on himself, since he'd gotten separated from his team members.

Smiling, he said only, "They don't let you out of the hospital after only four days if it's serious."

"That's good, then. You had me worried, boy."

"I know. Sorry."

Simon waved the apology aside. "Nothing to be sorry for, Hunter. It's your job, I know that."

He still wasn't happy about Hunter's decision to join the military, though. Simon had wanted him to take over the Cabot family dynasty. To sit behind a desk and oversee the many different threads of the empire Simon's father had started so long ago. But Hunter had never been interested in banking or any other kind of business that would tie him to a nine-to-five lifestyle. He'd wanted adventure. He'd wanted to do something *important*. Serving his country filled that need.

"Still," Simon was saying, with a touch of an all-too-familiar scheming note to his voice, "you're not going to be able to do this job forever, are you?"

Hunter scowled to see a calculating gleam in his grandfather's eyes. He hated to admit even to himself that he'd been thinking along the same lines lately. Frankly, since he was shot. Five years ago, it wouldn't have happened and he knew it. He'd have been quicker. Spotted the ambush sooner. Been able to get to cover fast enough to avoid the damn bullet that had nailed him.

But his career choices were not what he wanted to talk about. And since he couldn't think of an easy introduction into the subject at hand, he simply blurted out, "Forget my job for the moment. Grandfather, that woman upstairs is *not* my wife."

Simon crossed his legs, folded his hands together atop his flat abdomen and gave his grandson a smile. "Yes, she is."

"Okay, clearly this is going to be tougher than I thought," Hunter murmured and stood up. Rubbing one hand across the back of his neck, he reminded himself that the woman had had a year to worm her way into Simon's affections. It was going to take more than a minute to make him see the truth. "I've never *met* that woman, Grandfather. Whatever she's told you is a lie."

Simon smiled and followed Hunter's progress as he paced back and forth. "She hasn't told me anything, Hunter."

He stopped and shot his grandfather a hard look. "So you just let anybody who claims to be my wife move in and take over my suite?"

Simon chuckled. Probably not a good sign.

"You don't understand," the old man said. "She didn't lie to me about being married to you, because she didn't have to. I'm the one who arranged the marriage."

"You did what?" Hunter stared at his grandfather in complete disbelief. He didn't even know what to say. What the hell *could* he say? "You arranged—you can't do that."

"Can and did," Simon assured him, looking altogether pleased with himself. "The idea came to me after that heart attack last year."

"What *idea?*" Hunter walked back to his chair and sat down, his gaze pinned on the older man grinning at him.

Simon's white eyebrows lifted. "Why, the answer to my problem, of course. There I was, in the hospital. There you were, off only God knew where, and there was Margie."

"Margie."

"My assistant."

"Your—right. She told me that." Assistant turned granddaughter-in-law, apparently.

"Very organized soul, Margie," Simon mused thoughtfully. "Always on top of things. Knows how to get things done."

"I'll bet."

Simon frowned at him. "None of this was Margie's doing, boy. This was my idea. You remember that."

Hunter took a tight grip on his rising temper and forced himself to speak slowly and calmly. It wasn't easy. "What exactly was your idea?"

"I needed family here!" Shifting in his chair, Simon lifted one arm to the chair arm, and his fingers began to tap on the soft leather. "Blast it, decisions had to be made, and though I'd told Margie what I wanted, she didn't have the authority to make the doctors do a damn thing. Could have been bad for me, but I was lucky."

Instantly, Hunter's mind filled with images of Simon lying in a hospital bed, hooked up to machines that monitored his heart, his breathing, while doctors bustled and a short, curvy redhead tried to issue orders. He hated like hell that he hadn't been there for the old man when he'd needed Hunter most. But feeling guilt didn't mean he understood how he'd ended up with a wife!

"So, you could have given her power of attorney," Hunter said.

"Might have," his grandfather allowed, and his tapping fingers slowed a bit. "But I didn't. Instead, I convinced Margie to marry you."

"You—"

"It was the easiest way I could see. I want family around me, boy, and you're not here."

More guilt came slamming down on Hunter until he was half surprised he could breathe under the weight of it. Still… "You just can't marry me off without even mentioning it."

"I've got two words for you, Hunter," his grandfather said, "—*proxy marriage.*"

"Proxy? How can you even do that without my signature?"

"I got your signature," Simon told him with a sly smile. "And if you'd bother to read the Cabot financial papers I send to you for your signature, you'd have noticed the proxy marriage certificate."

Damn it. Simon had him there. Whenever the packets of papers arrived for him, Hunter merely signed where indicated and sent them back. The family business wasn't his life. The Navy, was. And he kept his two worlds completely separate. No doubt his slippery grandfather had realized that and exploited it. Admiration warred with irritation.

"Ah, good. You realize I'm right." Simon's fingers quickened, and the tapping on the old leather came fast and furious, belying the old man's attempt at a casual pose. "I stood in for you in the marriage ceremony. I knew that since you couldn't get home for my heart attack, you wouldn't have been able to get home for your own wedding—"

"—not that I was *invited*…"

"—my friend Judge Harris did the deed, and we kept it quiet. I sent Margie off on a week's vacation once I got better, and we put out that you and she eloped."

"Eloped."

"Worked out fine. Figured there was no rush in telling you."

"Especially since I didn't *want* a wedding."

Simon frowned at him and Hunter remembered being thirteen years old and standing in this very study, trying to explain why he'd hit a baseball through the study window. The same sense of shame and discomfort he'd felt then washed over him now. The only difference was he was no longer a kid to be put in his place.

"How'd she talk you into this, Simon?"

In answer, his grandfather pushed himself out of the chair, drew himself up to his full height and gave Hunter a look that used to chill him to his bones. "You think I'm some old fool taken in by a pretty face and a gold-digging nature? You seriously believe I'm that far gone, boy?"

"What else am I supposed to believe?" Hunter stood up too and met Simon's hard stare with one of his own. "I come home for a visit—"

"After two years," Simon threw in.

"—and you tell me you arranged to marry me off to someone I've never met just so you can have family close by?"

"You can watch your tone with me, boy. I'm not senile yet, you know."

"I didn't say you were."

"You were thinking it." Simon turned, walked to his desk and sat down behind his personal power center. From that very chair, Simon had run the Cabot family fortunes for more than five decades. "And I'll tell you something else. Margie didn't want any part of this. It was all my idea."

"And she went along out of the goodness of her heart." Sarcasm was so thick in Hunter's tone that even he heard it.

"'Course not. This was business, pure and simple. I'm paying her five million dollars."

"Five—" Hunter sucked in a gulp of air. "So she *is* in it for the money. And you said she's *not* a gold digger?"

"She damn well isn't, and you'll figure that out for yourself after you spend some time with her." Simon picked up a pen from the desk and twirled it absent-mindedly between his fingers. "Had to browbeat her into taking the money and doing this for me. She's a good girl and she works hard. She's done a lot of good for this town, too, and she's done real well by your name."

"How nice for me." Hunter shook his head at the sensation of a velvet-lined trap snapping shut around him.

"You should be grateful. I picked you out a wife who's a hard worker, and she's got a big heart as well."

"Grateful." Hunter moved in, leaned both hands on his grandfather's desk and ground out tightly, "What I'll be grateful for is a damn annulment, Simon. Or even a divorce. As soon as possible."

Disgusted, his grandfather muttered, "I should have known you wouldn't appreciate this."

"Yeah, you should've."

"If you'd open your eyes and see her as I do, you'd change your tune." Simon looked so damn smug, so self-satisfied that Hunter felt a surge of temper rise up and grab the base of his throat. For his whole damn life, Simon had been the one he could count on. The man who had taught him what *duty* and *honor* meant. The one who'd instilled in Hunter a sense of right and wrong. Now, he was blithely explaining how he'd set Hunter up with a marriage he didn't want all for Simon's own convenience.

"My 'tune' doesn't need changing," Hunter told him. "Just why the hell should I 'appreciate' having a wife I didn't want in the first place? One you're *paying*."

"I told you. She didn't want the money. Had to talk her into accepting it."

"Oh, yeah. I'll bet she was really hard to convince, too. Five million dollars? Damn it, Simon, what were you thinking?"

"You weren't here," the older man said softly. "I'm getting on, Hunter, and you weren't here. Margie is."

Again, he felt that soft, swift stab of guilt—then he buried it. "She's your secretary."

"She's more than that."

"Sure, *now*," Hunter allowed.

"You don't know her," Simon said, and his voice was whisper soft. "She came here to build a life for herself and she's done it. And she's been a good wife to you—"

"I haven't been here!"

"—and a good granddaughter to me."

All right, he could at least admit that much to himself, Hunter thought. Gold digger or not, the curvy redhead had at least apparently been good to Simon. When Hunter had finally heard about his grandfather's brush with death, guilt had gnawed him for not being there when the old man had needed him. But the nature of his job meant that he couldn't always be around. He lived and died according to orders.

So, knowing that Simon hadn't been alone during that frightening time in his life was good. And for that, he could be grateful. Not that he'd be telling that to the curvy redhead with the quick temper.

"Margie deserves your respect," Simon warned, lifting one finger to point at him.

"For marrying a man she never met to keep her boss happy." Hunter nodded sagely. "Yeah, that spells respect to me."

Simon scowled at him. "You never did know enough to listen to me."

"I listen. I'm just not interested in what you're

saying. I don't want a wife." All right, he'd been doing some thinking about his future lately. Maybe he'd even considered getting married, for about thirty seconds. But thinking about doing something and actually doing it were two wildly different things. And if he did eventually decide to get married, he'd be the one picking out his own damn wife, thanks.

"You could do worse," Simon grumbled.

"Yeah? I don't know about that. A woman who has to be *paid* to marry me pretty much sounds like the bottom of the barrel."

"Shows how much you know about anything," Simon said, and his fingers tapped restlessly again. "Margie's the cream of the crop."

"Not much of a harvest around here, then," Hunter murmured, then louder, added, "I won't stay married to her."

Simon blew out a breath. "No, I didn't suppose you would. Though you should know Margie feels the same way you do."

Hunter wasn't so sure. She may have had the old man fooled but not him. With five million dollars at stake, a woman might be willing to do just about anything.

"She's been good to me, and I won't have you embarrassing her."

"Oh yeah. Wouldn't want to embarrass anybody."

His grandfather sighed dramatically, then kept talking as if Hunter hadn't said a word. "She's planned a big party for my eightieth birthday, and I don't want anything spoiling that, either."

"A hell of a lot of demands flying around here," Hunter said under his breath.

"So, until the party's over, I expect you to act like the husband everyone in town knows you are."

"Excuse me?" He hadn't expected that.

"You heard me. People in Springville like Margie. They respect her. And I'm not going to stand by and watch you make her a laughingstock. You'll be leaving again, no doubt—" He paused as if waiting for confirmation.

Hunter nodded. "I have to report back in about a month."

Another frown. "Well, I'll still be here and so will Margie, hopefully, so I don't want her life ruined because you were angry."

Hunter's back teeth ground together. "No, wouldn't want Margie inconvenienced."

Simon went on again, ignoring Hunter's comments completely. "If after the party you still want the annulment—"

"—I will."

"—I won't stop you and I'm sure Margie won't. But until then, you'll do this my way."

Hunter looked at his grandfather and recognized the *set-in-stone* expression on the old man's face. There wouldn't be any budging him on this one. Once Simon Cabot made up his mind about something, nothing less than a nuclear strike would change it. Irritation swamped Hunter, and the uncomfortable sensation of being trapped came right along in its wake.

But Simon was an old man. And Hunter owed him. So he'd do this his grandfather's way. He'd be here for the party, and then before he went back to the base, he'd set annulment proceedings into action.

"Fine." Hunter tamped down the frustration bubbling

within and swallowed back the urge to argue. "When I'm in town, I'll act married."

"You'll act it here, too."

"What?"

"You hard of hearing all of a sudden? You should get that checked." A sly smile curved Simon's mouth briefly before he became all business again. "As long as you're home, you're a married man. I won't have the servants treating Margie badly. Everyone in this household knows you're married."

Hunter was still reeling from that piece of news when a soft knock on the study door sounded out. He turned around as the door opened, and there stood his "wife."

# Three

"Simon?" Margie asked, blatantly ignoring Hunter. "Is everything all right?"

"Fine, fine. I was just explaining the situation to Hunter."

"Good." Though judging from the look on the younger man's face at the moment, Margie thought he hadn't been too happy with his grandfather's explanation. Well, neither was she.

She hadn't wanted to marry Hunter, but she'd done it for Simon. And whether Hunter believed it or not, the five million dollars hadn't swayed her. What had convinced her to go along with Simon's plan had been the lost, *frightened* look in the old man's eyes that had convinced her to take part in what she'd recognized right away as a crazy plan.

And for the last year, she'd finally felt the sense of belonging she'd always wanted. She'd had a grandfather. A home. A place to call her own. People to care for—people who cared for her.

To Margie, that was priceless.

But she had to admit that being married to a Hunter who wasn't around was far easier than being married to the man in person. Looking at him now, he seemed too…big. His shoulders, his broad chest, his piercing blue eyes.

His scowl.

Frowning right back at him, she then shifted her gaze to Simon and said simply, "The doctor's here."

"Blast it." The older Cabot quickly picked up a sheaf of papers from atop his desk and busily started leafing through them. "Margie, tell him I'm too busy to see him today. Try me next week. Better yet, next month."

She smiled, since she was more than accustomed to Simon's frantic attempts to avoid his doctor. "There's no getting out of it, Simon."

"Is there a problem?" Hunter asked.

Margie reluctantly looked at him again, met his gaze and felt a bolt of something hot and wicked slice through her. The man had incredible eyes. Which, of course, meant nothing to her. Especially since great eyes did not make up for a crabby, arrogant nature. Still, he looked a little worried for his grandfather, and that was enough to touch Margie, so she hurried to reassure him. "No, it's just his checkup. The doctor comes here to see Simon every couple of weeks since Simon can't be trusted to keep an appointment in town."

"I'm a busy man. Too busy to go see a damn pill pusher," Simon muttered.

Hunter folded his arms over his impressive chest and asked, "Simon's all right, though? Healthy?"

Margie nodded and told herself not to look at that wide chest or the muscles so clearly defined beneath the soft fabric of his black T-shirt. "Yes, he's, uh…" She swallowed hard, cleared her throat nervously, then continued. "He's recovered completely. The checkups are just routine now."

"Routine," Simon muttered again. "What's *routine* about disrupting a man's life every time he turns around—that's what I want to know…"

"Good," Hunter said. "I'm glad everything's all right, but I'll want to talk to the doctor myself, of course."

"Why should *you* talk to him," Simon questioned. "He's *my* doctor and I don't need another babysitter," he added with a glare at Margie.

"Of course you will," Margie told Hunter as they both ignored the grumbling older man. Weren't they being polite all of a sudden, she thought. But she wasn't fooled. There was still something dark and smoldering in Hunter's eyes.

"Who's in charge here, I want to know?" Simon demanded.

"That would be me," a new voice announced.

Margie tore her gaze from Hunter's to see Dr. Harris striding into the room with a wide smile on his creased face. His wild gray hair was forever sticking up in odd tufts all over his head, and his soft brown eyes looked magnified behind his glasses. He walked straight up to

Hunter and shook his hand. "Good to see you back home, Hunter. It's been too long."

"Yeah," Hunter said, sliding a quick look at Margie, "it has."

"Wasted your time coming out here," Simon said, still shuffling papers. "Too busy for you today and don't need any more pills, thanks."

"Pay no attention to him, doctor," Margie said smiling.

"I never do." The doctor released Hunter's hand, then pulled Margie in for a quick hug. "Don't know what we would have done without your wife around here the last year or so, Hunter."

She stiffened as Hunter's gaze locked on her.

"Is that so?" he asked quietly.

"It is," Simon put in.

"The woman's a wonder," Dr. Harris said. "Not only sees that your stubborn old goat of a grandfather does what he's supposed to, but she also single-handedly helped us raise enough money to add an outpatient surgery annex to the clinic. Of course, she told us all how much *you* had to do with it."

"Did she?" One dark eyebrow lifted as he studied her, and Margie fought to keep from fidgeting under that stare.

"She did." Beaming now, the doctor added, "She let us all know that after Simon's heart attack, you wanted to be sure the clinic had everything it needed so locals didn't have to go into the city to be taken care of. Meant a lot to folks around here that you still think of Spring-ville as your home."

"Glad I could help," Hunter said, tearing his gaze from Margie's to look at the doctor.

"Simon always said how you'd start taking more of an interest in the town one day," the man said with a clap on Hunter's shoulder. "Seems he was right. So I just want to thank you personally—and not just for the clinic but for everything else you've done—"

"Everything else?" Hunter asked.

"Dr. Harris—" Margie spoke up quickly to cut the doctor off before he could say too much. "Didn't you have other appointments today?"

"True, true," the man was saying, still grinning his appreciation. "So I'd better get down to business. Just wanted you to know the whole town appreciates what you're doing, Hunter. It's made a difference. All of it."

"*All* of it?" Hunter's hard, cold gaze locked on Margie. "How much is *all?*"

"Aren't you here to plague me?" Simon snapped. "Or are you going to stand there and talk to Hunter all day?"

The doctor chuckled. "He's right. Why don't you two go off somewhere together while I examine this crotchety patient of mine?" He winked at Hunter. "Lord knows if I had a pretty little wife I hadn't seen in months, I'd want some alone time with her."

"Just what I was thinking," Hunter said, and Margie inhaled sharply.

She really didn't want any more alone time with Hunter at the moment. In fact, she was good. She could have waited days, or maybe forever, to be alone with him again. Unfortunately, it didn't seem as though she'd be getting that wish granted.

"Come on, *honey,*" he said, taking her elbow in a hard grip, "let's go get 'reacquainted.'"

She only had time to throw one quick look over her

shoulder at Simon before Hunter started propelling her across the room. Simon gave her a thumbs-up signal and a Cheshire cat grin—not much as life preservers went but better than nothing.

Hunter's legs were so long that she had to practically run to keep up with him, but Margie managed, barely. They slipped out of the study, and Hunter reached behind her to close the doors before he looked at her again.

Hard to believe, but there was both fire and ice in his eyes when he said, "You've got some explaining to do, babe."

"I told you not to call me that." If he thought she was going to simply curl up in a ball and whimper for mercy, he was sadly mistaken. He'd taken her by surprise when he'd shown up in the bathroom earlier, so she'd babbled too much. But she'd had time now to think. To gather her own sense of outrage along with her self-confidence. She hadn't done anything wrong. But Hunter Cabot couldn't say the same.

She took a quick look around the empty hallway, hardly noting the lavish furnishings that had, the first time she'd stepped into the castlelike Cabot home, completely intimidated her. How far she'd come, she thought idly, that she now felt at home here, with the rose-patterned Oriental rugs dotted on a gleaming wood floor. With the pale washes of color seeping through the stained-glass windows in the foyer. With the crystal vases holding arrangements of flowers that were nearly as tall as she was.

This castle had become her home, and she refused to let Hunter take that feeling away from her.

"I don't owe you anything," she said, keeping her tone calm and dispassionate, which wasn't easy.

His mouth curved in a smile that had nothing to do with humor. "Now see, that's not the right tack to take."

"How about this one, then? You're hurting me," she said, with a glance down to where his fingers were clenched around her elbow. Instantly, Hunter's grip on her elbow loosened. Not that he actually let her go, but the strength in his fingers eased up a bit.

"Sorry." He blew out a breath and glanced all around the empty hallway before dipping his head to speak to her again. "But after everything Simon just told me, I think you and I need to talk."

"Simon explained everything?" Thank heaven. He was supposed to have had this chat with Hunter *before* the man came home, and that would have made this situation a lot easier. But if Simon had told his grandson what was going on, what was left to talk about?

"Yeah, but that doesn't mean I'm cool with it, so like I said, start talking."

Now that he wasn't holding her so tightly, it was easy enough to pull herself free of his grasp. So she did, then took a step backward for good measure. "I don't know why I should explain myself to you when Simon's already done it."

"I can think of a reason. In fact," Hunter added, "I can think of *five million* reasons."

She blanched. "You don't seriously believe I'm doing this for the money?"

"Why wouldn't I?"

Margie sucked in a breath. "Why, you self-righteous, judgmental, arrogant son of a—"

His narrowed gaze flicked past her briefly; then he grabbed her, yanked her close and kissed Margie so hard she almost forgot to breathe.

Sensation raced through her bloodstream until every inch of her body was standing up and shouting *Yippee!* Her stomach dropped, her heartbeat thundered in her chest and her mind fuzzed out so totally, she couldn't have given her own name if asked.

Her whole world had come down to the feeling of Hunter's mouth on hers. His tongue pushing past her lips to sweep inside her warmth. His breath sliding into her. His arms wrapped around her like taut wire, binding her to his body, until all she could do was lift her own arms to hook them behind his neck.

She opened to him eagerly, hungrily, reacting solely to the passion he'd ignited. Didn't seem to matter that he was insulting, annoying and a bully. All that counted now was what he was making her feel. Never before had she reacted so completely to something so simple as a kiss. But then, this was no simple kiss, either.

There was heat and fire and lust and fury all rolled into one incredible ball of energy that felt as though it was consuming her.

Then it was over as quickly as it had begun. She staggered a little when he let her go. Not surprising, really, since he'd kissed her blind. "What? How? What?"

His lips quirked at one corner of his mouth before he again looked past her and said, "Sophie!"

*Oh, God. The housekeeper,* Margie thought, instantly feeling a flush of embarrassment.

But Hunter dropped one arm around her shoulders

and pulled her in close to his side as he greeted the older woman. "I was so busy getting reacquainted with my *wife*," he was saying. "I didn't see you come up."

How was he able to joke and laugh and speak coherently after what they'd just experienced? Margie looked up at him and couldn't believe that he was so unmoved by what had happened. How could he not have felt what she had? How could something that powerful be so one-sided?

"Oh, don't you worry about that," Sophie said. "It's good to see two such lovebirds canoodling."

*Canoodling?*

"I'm so glad to have you home again. Now you two go on upstairs, and we'll see you for dinner, all right? Cook's making all of your favorites, Mr. Hunter." Sophie gave him a quick hug. "We're all so happy to have you home again. Aren't we, Margie?"

Hunter finally looked down at her, and Margie saw the light of challenge in his eyes. "That right, babe? Are you happy to have me home?"

Margie still felt shaky from that kiss, but she didn't want to let him know how he'd affected her. Especially since that kiss had seemed to mean nothing to him. So she met his look with one of her own, then forced a smile she didn't feel. "Oh, *happy* doesn't even begin to describe what I'm feeling."

Dinner took forever.

Simon was at the head of the table acting like Father Christmas or something, and Hunter's "wife" was sitting directly opposite him, alternately ignoring him and sending him looks designed to set his hair on fire.

As for Hunter, all he could think was, he never should have kissed her.

Damn it.

Ever since tasting her, the only thing he wanted was another taste. And that couldn't happen. No way was he going to hook himself even deeper into this little fiasco his grandfather had arranged. For all he knew, his little "wife" was counting on seducing Hunter into making this a real marriage. Maybe that was her grand plan.

But how could it be her plan when it had been *his* idea to kiss her? Gritting his teeth, he avoided looking at the woman across from him and tried to draw his mind away from the memory of her mouth on his. Useless. He'd been trying for hours to forget exactly how he'd felt when his mouth had come down on hers. To brush aside the near electrical jolt of pure, white hot lust and desire that had threatened to crush him.

Hell, if it hadn't been for Sophie standing there in the hall, he might have pushed Margie up against a wall and...

*Way to not think about it,* he chided himself.

His body was hard and achy, and his mind was still spinning from the effect she'd had on him. She'd fit into the circle of his arms as though she'd been made for him. The taste of her lingered in his mouth, and the memory of the feel of her curves pressed along his body had kept him hard as stone for hours.

She wasn't at all the kind of woman he usually went for. So Hunter couldn't explain even to himself why he was suddenly so filled with the need to touch her again. To kiss her again. He should be thinking about strangling her for what she was doing here in this house.

Instead…

Damn it. Even as he looked across the table at her, wearing a shapeless blue dress with a high collar and short puffy sleeves, his mind was stripping away her clothes. Laying her bare on the fussy quilt that now covered his bed. In his mind, he was kissing every curvy inch of her, burying himself inside her and—

*And,* if he didn't turn his thoughts to other things, he'd never be able to stand up from this table without showing the world just how much he wanted her.

Grimly, Hunter fought for control. He looked at her again and tried to see past the softly curling dark red hair and bright green eyes. He shoved aside the memory of how she'd felt in his arms and instead tried to figure out how much of her "I'm innocent" act was for real. On the surface, she seemed to be exactly what she was portraying. A young woman doing a favor for a lonely old man. But for all Hunter knew, she was just a hell of a good actress. And if she was playing him, how much easier it would have been for her to play Simon.

They never had gotten around to having their "talk" earlier. After kissing her, Hunter hadn't trusted himself to be alone with her. So instead, he'd taken one of the horses Simon still kept and went for a ride over the property. Not that the long ride had done a thing for his sanity. Because images of Margie had ridden with him every step of the way.

"More wine, Hunter?"

Hunter looked at his grandfather and nodded. "Yeah, thanks."

But he knew even as more of the dark red wine was poured into his glass that there wasn't enough liquor in the world to ease the wild, churning thoughts running through his brain. Why her? he asked himself. Why this short, argumentative con artist? Hell, he'd just finished a relationship with Gretchen, a six-foot-tall model with the face of an angel and even she'd never gotten to him as deeply as this one tiny redhead had.

Gritting his teeth, he took another bite of the pot roast prepared just for him. It might as well have been cardboard. He'd been looking forward to coming home. Having a few days to relax and not worry about a damn thing. Well, that was shot, he told himself. Everywhere he went in the damn house, someone was winking at him or smiling knowingly.

Having every servant in the house treating him like a newlywed was annoying. Having his "wife" within arm's reach and untouchable was irritating. Hell of a homecoming.

The last mission he'd been on, Hunter had been wounded, cut off from his team, and he had had to find his own way out of hostile territory. Eight days he'd been alone and fighting for his life—and what he was going through now made that time seem like a weekend at Disneyland.

"There's a dance at the end of the week," Simon said, dragging Hunter gratefully from his thoughts. "To celebrate the new addition to the clinic."

"That's nice." He didn't give a damn about a dance.

"Now that you're here, you'll take Margie to represent the family," Simon said.

"I'll what?" Hunter looked at his grandfather and out of the corner of his eye noted that Margie looked just as surprised as he felt.

"Escort your wife to the town dance. People will expect it. After all, you and Margie are the ones who made it all possible."

"I didn't have anything to do with it," Hunter reminded the older man.

Simon bristled, narrowed his eyes on him and said, "As far as people in town are convinced, you did."

"He doesn't have to go with me," Margie said quickly, apparently as eager as Hunter was to avoid any extra amount of togetherness. Now why did that bother him?

"I'll just tell everyone he hasn't recovered from his injuries," she added.

Now it was Hunter's turn to scowl. Not that he wanted to go to the damned dance, but he didn't want someone else, especially *her,* making up excuses for him. The day he needed help—which would be never—he'd ask for it.

"Damn good at lying, aren't you?" he asked.

She turned her head to spear him with a long look. Then giving him a mocking smile, she admitted, "Actually, since I've had to come up with dozens of reasons why you never bother to come home to see your grandfather, yes, I have gotten good at lying. Thank you so much for noticing."

"No one asked you to—"

"Who would if I hadn't?"

"There was no reason to lie," he countered, slamming his fork down onto the tabletop. "Everyone in town knows what my job is."

She set her fork down, too. Calmly. Quietly. Which only angered him more.

"And everyone in town knows you could have gotten

compassionate leave—isn't that what they call it in the military?—to come home when Simon was so sick."

Guilt poked at him again. And he didn't appreciate it.

"I wasn't even in the country," he reminded her, grinding each word out through gritted teeth.

She only looked at him, but he knew exactly what she was thinking, because he'd been telling himself the same damn thing for hours. Yes, he'd been out of the country when Simon had his heart attack. But when he'd returned, he could have come home to check on the older man. He could have taken a week's leave before the next mission—but he'd settled instead for a phone call.

If Hunter had made the effort, he would have been here to talk his grandfather out of this ridiculous fake marriage scheme and he wouldn't now be in this mess.

With that realization ringing in his mind, he met Margie's gaze and noted the gleam of victory shining in those green eyes of hers.

"Fine. You win this one," he said, acknowledging that she'd taken that round. "I'll take you to the damned dance."

"I don't want—"

"Excellent," Simon crowed and reached for Hunter's wine glass.

"You can't have wine, Simon," Margie said with a sigh and the old man's hand halted in midreach.

"What's the point of living forever if you can't have a glass of wine with dinner like a civilized man?"

"Water is perfectly civilized." Apparently, Margie had already forgotten about her little war with Hunter and was focused now on the old man pouting in his chair.

"Dogs drink water," Simon reminded her.

"So do you."

*"Now."*

"Simon," Margie's voice took on a patient tone and was enough to tell Hunter she'd been through all this many times before. "You know what Dr. Harris said. No wine and no cigars."

"Damn doctors always ruining a man's life for his own good. And you," he accused, giving Margie a dirty look, "you're supposed to be on my side."

"I am on your side, Simon. I want you to live forever."

"Without having any damn fun at all, I suppose," he groused.

Hunter watched the back-and-forth and felt the oddest sense of envy. His grandfather and Margie had obviously had this same discussion many times. The two of them were a unit. A team. And their closeness was hard to ignore.

He was the odd man out here. He was the one who didn't belong. In the house where he'd grown up. With his grandfather. This woman…his "wife," had neatly carved Hunter out of the equation entirely.

Or, had he done that himself?

It had been a hellish day, and all Hunter wanted at the moment was a little peace and quiet. Interrupting the two people completely ignoring him, he said, "You know what? I'm beat. Think I'll head up to bed."

"That's a good idea," Simon agreed, shifting his attention to his grandson. "Why don't both of you go on up to your room? Get some rest?"

Silence.

Several seconds ticked past before one of them managed to finally speak.

"*Our* room?" Margie whispered.

Hunter glared at his grandfather.

Simon smiled.

# Four

"I'm not sleeping on the floor," Hunter told Margie.

"Well," Margie said from inside the closet, where she was changing into her nightgown, "you're not sleeping with *me*."

Good heavens, how could she possibly share a bed with the man who'd kissed her senseless only hours ago? If he kissed her again, she might just give into the fiery feelings he engendered in her and then where would she be?

"Don't flatter yourself, babe," he said, loud enough to carry through the heavy wooden door separating them. "It's not your body I'm after. It's the mattress. Damned if I'm sleeping on the floor in my own damn room."

She frowned at the closed door and the man beyond

it. Apparently, she didn't have anything to worry about. He had clearly not felt anything that she had during that kiss. Was she insulted? Or pleased? "Fine. I'll sleep on the floor."

"Help yourself," he countered.

Margie stopped in the process of tugging her night-gown over her head. "You'd let me, wouldn't you? You'd let me sleep on the floor rather than do it yourself like a gentleman."

"Never said I was a gentleman," he told her.

"Well, I'm not sleeping on the floor." This was her room now. Had been for over a year. Why should she be the one to be uncomfortable? And if he wasn't interested in her sexually, she should be perfectly safe. Right?

"Up to you."

"Just don't you try anything," she warned, telling herself to pay attention.

He actually laughed. "Trust me when I say you're safe."

Bastard. How easily he dismissed her. That kiss he'd given her clearly hadn't touched him at all. Even though her own lips were still humming with remnants of sensation. Of course it hadn't meant anything to him. Why would it? She'd known most of her life that she simply wasn't the kind of woman men like him noticed.

She was too short, too…round. He probably went for the six-foot-tall, ninety-pound type who thought a single M&M was a party. His kind of woman never had the last cookie in the box; she didn't *buy* cookies. His kind of woman didn't wear T-shirts; she wore silk. And her clothes hung on her as if she were a coat hanger. No bulges, no curves, no lines. His kind of woman didn't have to marry a man by proxy; she had men lining up at her door. And his kind of woman wouldn't have melted at a simple kiss.

"Oh God, how did I get myself into this?"

Being married to Hunter when he wasn't there had been so easy. So perfect. She'd made him into the ideal husband. Thoughtful, caring, loving. How was she supposed to have known that the real man was light-years away from the image in her mind?

And yet, this Hunter stirred something inside her that made her yearn for things to be different. Which was just a one-way ticket to misery and she knew it. The only way she would ever have a husband like Hunter was this way. A lie.

Still grumbling to herself, she stepped out of the closet to find her "husband" already ensconced in the bed. On *her* side.

"Move over," she commanded, waving one hand for emphasis.

"It's a king-size bed," he reminded her. "Plenty of room for both of us."

Oh, she thought, there probably wouldn't be enough room for her to lie down comfortably beside him if the bed were the size of the *county*. But she wouldn't let him know that she was feeling decidedly uneasy about this situation. Besides, she was going to have enough trouble falling asleep tonight, let alone having to sleep on the wrong side of the bed.

"You're on my side."

He looked around, then shrugged broad, bare shoulders. "Since I'm the only one lying on it, I figure it's *my* side."

His eyes shone with amusement in the pale wash of light from the bedside lamp. His bare chest gleamed like old gold, and when he shifted higher onto the pillows, the quilt covering him dipped, pooling at his hips.

Margie sucked in a gulp of air but couldn't quite stop herself from admiring the view. The soft, dark hair on his chest narrowed into a strip that snaked across his abdomen, then disappeared beneath the quilt.

He was naked.

Oh, God. She was never going to get to sleep tonight. Her stomach did a slow roll and pitch, and her mouth went dry. "Don't you have pajamas?"

He chuckled and she couldn't help noticing the dimple in his left cheek. Why did he have to have a dimple?

"No," he said, "I don't." Then his gaze swept over her, taking in her knee-length, long-sleeved cotton gown decorated with pale blue flowers. His eyes widened as he lifted his gaze to meet hers. "Don't you have something less…"

Margie felt his disapproval plainly, plopped both hands on her hips and dared him to finish that sentence. "Less *what?*"

"Less…*Little House on the Prairie?*"

She smoothed one hand over her comfy nightgown. Didn't she feel pretty? He couldn't make it any clearer that he wasn't experiencing the slightest bit of attraction for her. "There's nothing wrong with what I'm wearing. It's very cute."

One dark eyebrow lifted. "If you say so."

"And comfortable."

"Okay."

Margie huffed out a breath, finished doing up the buttons on the front of her perfectly sweet nightgown, then glared at him again. No doubt he was used to going to bed with women who were either naked or wearing bits of lace and silk. "Are you going to move over or not?"

"Not."

"You are the most insensitive, arrogant—"

He deliberately closed his eyes and snuggled his head into *her* pillow. "We've been over this already. How about we just put off the insult exchange until morning?"

"Fine."

"Fine. Now get into bed and go to sleep."

Muttering darkly under her breath, Margie walked around the wide bed to the absolute wrong side. It didn't bother him at all to share the bed with her. He'd already closed his eyes to dismiss her. He couldn't have made it any clearer that he was in no way interested in her. So why was she shaking and nervous? This was so not fair.

He'd tossed all of her decorative throw pillows to the floor, and she had to kick them out of her way as she moved. Before she could get into bed, Hunter reached over and flung the quilt back for her, incidentally providing her with yet another look at his long, tanned form just barely hidden by the strategically placed quilt.

And when she was finished admiring his leanly muscled body, she finally noticed the stark white bandage affixed to his left side, just above the hip. Somehow, she'd managed to forget during their argument that he'd been wounded recently, and for some reason she felt bad for harassing him in his condition.

"Are you—do you—" She stopped, blew out a breath and looked into his eyes. "Is your wound all right? I mean, are *you* all right?"

"I'm touched by your concern," he said, clearly untouched. "Yes, I'm fine, though not quite up to sexcapades just yet. So like I said, you're safe." His gaze dropped over her nightgown again and he shook his head. "Though even if I wasn't laid up, I'd have to say that your choice of nightgown is the best male-repellant I've ever seen."

Instantly, Margie regretted worrying about him at all. He was insulting, rude and arrogant, and she hoped his side ached like an abscessed tooth. And if she ever again felt those stirrings inside her, she'd squash them like a bug. "You're—"

"Insults in the morning, remember?"

"Fine." She swallowed back everything she wanted to say to the completely irritating, totally sexy man in her bed and turned instead to pick up the pillows he'd so carelessly tossed to the floor.

"What're you doing now?"

She didn't even look at him, just continued picking up the pillows and stacking them in a line down the center of the bed. When they were all in place, she smiled at a job well done. "I'm building a wall between us," she said. "As you pointed out, it's a king-size bed. Plenty of room for us *and* a wall."

"You don't need a wall, babe; you've got the nightgown."

"Maybe you need it," she told him, sliding onto the sheets and drawing the quilt up to her chin.

"Yeah?" he asked as he turned out the light and plunged the room into darkness. "Afraid you'll ravish me in your sleep?"

She closed her eyes and turned onto her side, giving him her back. "Afraid I'll murder you. Sleep tight."

The next morning Margie was back in the closet getting dressed when Hunter stepped out of the shower. Rummaging through his duffle bag, he pulled out a worn, faded pair of jeans and a dark blue T-shirt with the words *Navy SEAL* emblazoned across the front.

"I have to go into town this morning, see to a few details about the dinner dance," Margie called out from what had become her own private dressing room.

"Let me guess," he said. "You're in charge of that, too."

From what he'd been able to tell, Margie "Cabot" had insinuated herself into everything she could. What was the plan, here? Why would she be bothering with getting involved with the doings in Springville if she was married to him only for the five million dollars Simon had promised her?

Shaking his head, he ruefully admitted that he had even more questions about her than he had the day before. Starting with, why was he so attracted to a woman he probably wouldn't have noticed under normal circumstances?

"Why is it so hard for you to understand that some people actually *like* being a part of the community?"

"I just don't get why *you* want to do it." He shot a

look at the partially opened door and tried not to think about what she was doing in there. But images of her wet, naked, lush body kept filling his head. Plus there was the memory of her kiss and the soft, open eagerness she'd met him with.

His body went stiff and hard as stone almost instantly and groaning, Hunter adjusted his jeans. It didn't help much. Damn it, what he needed was a woman, not a wife. It had been a long two months since he'd been with a woman, and right now it felt more like two years.

Hell, it was a good thing he woke up early every morning, because that wall she'd built between them had come tumbling down sometime during the night. Hunter'd been surprised to find that he'd instinctively turned to her in the darkness, pushing those pillows aside and wrapping himself around her. Thankfully, she'd still been sleeping when he woke up and had the presence of mind to rebuild that stupid wall.

"Why wouldn't I want to contribute where I can?" she demanded, stepping out of the closet to face him.

Hunter stared at her for a long minute. Morning sunlight slanted in through the lacy curtains on the windows and shone down on his wife in all her frumpy glory. She wore a shapeless box of a black suit, the hem of which hit her knees. The white blouse under her jacket was buttoned to her throat.

And even with all that, he felt a short zing of something hot and dangerous. How the hell was she able to do that to him? Even the gorgeous Gretchen hadn't elicited a response like this.

Irritated that his own body was betraying him at every damn turn, he snapped, "Are you secretly a nun?"

"What?" She looked confused.

Hunter started for her and did a slow walk around, taking in the ugly suit from every side. "First your nightgown. Now, this thing."

She folded her arms under her breasts, giving them definition enough that he had to pause to admire them. Instantly, a memory of hard, pink nipples caressed by drops of water filled his mind and tortured his body a lot farther south.

"There's nothing wrong with this suit," she argued.

Except for the fact that it was hiding an amazing body. But if he had any sense, he'd be grateful for that fact, not so resentful.

"Nothing that a good fire wouldn't cure."

She inhaled sharply and Hunter admired the view. His slow smile told her that too, so she dropped her arms to her sides, and instantly the shapelessness of her clothes hid her physical charms.

"Seriously," he said. "Why do you hide that body?"

"Excuse me?" A faint flush of color filled her cheeks, and despite everything, Hunter was charmed. He hadn't known women could blush anymore.

He tucked one finger under her chin and lifted her face to his. Those eyes of hers fascinated him even while he knew that he shouldn't get even more involved with her. Wasn't it enough, he thought, that he was married for a month? Wasn't it more than enough that he was hot and hard and achy for her? But why shouldn't she feel the same discomfort he was going through?

"You forget, babe. I've *seen* that body of yours. I know it's got curves and valleys and some great…" He grinned and finished, *"hills."*

She pulled away from his touch, and Hunter rubbed the tip of his finger as if he could still feel the cool silk of her skin on his. "So why are you hiding it?"

"I'm not hiding anything," she argued, walking across the room to the dressing table. She took a seat on the padded stool, picked up a wide-toothed comb and dragged it through her long curls. "I just don't draw attention to the fact that I need to lose ten pounds."

Women. None of them were ever happy with their bodies, he thought wryly. Even Gretchen was constantly on a diet, and remembering her now, he realized that she was so damn skinny it was a wonder he hadn't cut himself on her bones when he'd held her. Sex with Margie, on the other hand, would be a lush experience. All those curves. All that soft, smooth flesh to explore and enjoy.

He grimaced as his body went even harder and felt more uncomfortable than before. Shaking his head, Hunter walked up behind her and leaned down to plant his hands on the dressing table. He was so close behind her that his chin rested on top of her head as his gaze met hers in the mirror.

"Don't you know covering up only makes a man wonder what's under all that fabric?"

As her gaze locked with his, he watched her swallow hard before saying, "As you just reminded me, you already know what's hidden."

A slow smile curved one side of his mouth as he realized she was embarrassed. Would a liar and a thief be so easily discomforted? Interesting thought. "And that body deserves better."

"Thanks for your opinion," she said and slipped out from underneath him by ducking under one of his arms. Then she grabbed her purse and stationed herself by the door. "I've got to go, so I suppose I'll see you later."

"I'll go with you."

"What? Why?"

He wasn't entirely sure himself. All he knew was that he wasn't ready for her to leave just yet. She was watching him warily, and in that oversize suit, she looked...vulnerable, somehow. Hunter had the urge to somehow protect her. Which was completely unreasonable and he knew it. She didn't need protection, he reminded himself sternly. She needed getting rid of. Which he would do at the end of a month. For now, though, she was his wife whether he wanted one or not, and they both might as well get used to it.

"I was going to go into town myself today. See some old friends."

"Oh."

"But I've changed my mind," he told her as he studied the ugly black suit she wore. "I think we'll go into the city instead."

"San Francisco?"

"That's the one," he said and walked to the side of the bed. Sitting down, he pulled on one boot first, then the other, and stamped his feet into them. Standing up again, he looked down at her as she asked, "Why?"

"To get you some decent clothes."

"I don't need new clothes."

"Now see, we're arguing again," he pointed out. "You won last night's round, but I'll win this one."

"Hunter—" She stopped and frowned slightly as if saying his name had actually felt odd to her. "There's no reason to buy me new clothes. What I have is perfectly serviceable."

"That's where you're wrong." He walked up to her, tipped her chin up again and smiled down into green eyes that flashed with irritation and suspicion. "See, babe, you're my wife. And my wife doesn't dress frumpy."

She blinked at him. "Frumpy? This isn't frumpy. This is a business suit."

"If you say so." He took her arm, turned her toward the door and started walking. What the hell did he care what she looked like? His brain was shouting at him, but apparently he wasn't going to listen. He wanted to see her in clothes that fit her, that showcased not just her body but the woman inside, too.

And just who was that, he asked himself as he stared into her eyes. Liar? Cheat? Or was she simply what she claimed to be? A woman doing a kindness for an old man? Hunter already knew she was strong. She stood toe-to-toe with him and never gave an inch, and he had to admire that almost as much as he admired the way she could set his body on fire with merely a glance.

"I don't want to shop."

He stopped dead, gave her a quick grin and said, "That may be the first time I've ever heard a woman say those words."

"You're not going to charm me into this."

"You think I'm charming now? Last night you threatened to kill me in my sleep."

"I didn't say you were charming," she corrected primly. "I said you were trying to use charm. Badly."

"Ah, there's the wife I know and loathe." The words

were out before he could stop them. And the instant he said them, he wished he hadn't.

She pulled free of his grasp, and he winced at the fury in her eyes. "I know you don't like me, but you don't have to be mean."

Hunter studied her eyes and finally saw more than her anger. He saw hurt in those depths too and regretted causing it. He'd been so busy concentrating on his own feeling of entrapment, the constant state of arousal, which he blamed solely on her, he hadn't really considered that she was as locked into their "performance" as he was. At least for the time being.

And he had the nagging feeling that maybe she wasn't the liar and cheat he thought she was. Even a practiced con artist would have a hard time worming her way into Simon's heart, which she had obviously done. Not to mention what she'd pulled last night.

Building that wall of pillows between them hadn't been the act of an adept thief. She'd behaved more like a vestal virgin trying to protect her virtue from a marauding horde. So what the hell was really going on? Who was she, really?

What if he was wrong about her? Well, he told himself firmly, for one thing, he didn't *want* to be wrong about her. It would make this so much easier if she was just what he suspected she was. In it for the money. But then, even if the five million dollars was her sole motivation, she was now faced with living the lie she'd built.

Couldn't be comfortable for her, either.

So did he give her the benefit of the doubt? Or did he continue to make both of them miserable for a full month? Neither, he decided. He'd give her enough rope, then stand back to see if she actually hanged herself with it. He could be patient. Hell, his training, his job, his *life* usually demanded patience. So he'd back off on the verbal attacks and see how she reacted.

"You're right," he said at last and had the pleasure of seeing surprise flicker across her face. "I'm sorry."

She studied him for a long second or two, obviously trying to decide if he meant it or not. But finally, she nodded. "It's okay. It's a weird situation. For both of us."

"Just what I was thinking." Interesting. Be a little more accommodating, and she was far less prickly.

"So. Truce?" she asked.

"Maybe," he said thoughtfully. "I'll let you know when we're finished shopping."

"Hunter…"

He shook his head. He wasn't going to let go of this one. "My wife doesn't dress like that," he said, waving one arm to indicate the hideous suit she seemed so attached to. "I'm not going to have everyone in town wondering why in the hell I won't buy you new clothes. You want to play the part of Mrs. Cabot? You'll do it looking a hell of a lot better than this."

She lifted her chin and glared at him, but whatever she was going to say remained unuttered.

"Good choice," he said with a brief nod. "You're not going to win this one."

Margie felt Hunter's hand on the small of her back as clearly as if it were a live electrical wire. Spears of heat as wild and unpredictable as lightning bolts kept shooting through her system, and it was all she could do to walk and talk despite the distractions.

Main Street in Springville was waking up after a winter that had been cold and gray and bleak. Now in springtime, the sun shone out of a brilliantly blue sky, a cool wind danced down the street and bright bursts of flowers filled the planters at the feet of the street lamps. Colorful awnings stretched out over the sidewalk in front of the stores, and clusters of neighbors gathered together to chat.

She loved this town. Had from the moment she'd first arrived two years before. It was like a postcard of small-town American life. A flag waved in the center of town square, moms with strollers sat on benches, laughing at toddlers wobbling around on the grass, and the scent of fresh bread baking drifted through the bakery's open door.

After growing up in Los Angeles, just one more face in an anonymous crowd, coming to Springville was like finding an old friend. She belonged here. She fit in. Or at least, she told herself with a sidelong glance at the man beside her, she *used* to.

Now, she knew that she wouldn't be able to stay once this month with Hunter was up. She'd have to leave this town, these people, even Simon, the grandfather she'd come to love. Because staying after the divorce would be impossible. She wouldn't be able to stand the pitying looks from her friends. She wouldn't be able to answer the questions everyone would have.

And mostly, she wouldn't be able to stay in the place where all of her lovely fantasies had died.

"Still say we should have gone to the city," Hunter murmured, then waved at someone across the street.

Margie shook her head. She'd agreed, finally, to shopping, but had insisted that they do their buying in town. "You're a Cabot," she said for the third time. "You should support the local businesses."

"You make me sound like a king or something. What does being a Cabot have to do with where I shop?" His voice was low, but she had no trouble hearing him. In fact, Margie had the distinct feeling that she would always be able to concentrate easily on the deep rumble of his voice.

In just twenty-four hours, she'd already become attuned to him. Oh, God. What a mess.

She smiled and nodded at an older woman they passed on the sidewalk, then muttered, "Your family built this town. The headquarters of your business is here. You employ half the people who live here."

"Not me," he insisted, "Simon."

"The Cabots," she reminded him.

"Oh, for—"

"Hunter!"

"Now what?" he muttered, stopping and draping one arm around Margie's shoulder.

They'd already been stopped countless times by people excited to see Hunter back home. The heavy weight of his arm on her felt both comforting and like a set of shackles, binding her to his side. And how was that possible? How could she feel desire for the very man who was making her life a misery?

A young couple, James and Annie Drake, holding hands as they hurried up the sidewalk, grinned at Hunter and Margie as they approached. The man had brown hair and thick glasses, and his grin was reflected in his eyes. "Hi Margie. Hunter, it's good to see you back."

"Good to be back, James," he said, and the tone of his voice was almost convincing.

Except that Margie knew he didn't really want to be here. So who, she wondered, was acting now?

"Annie, good to see you, too. How're the kids?"

"Oh, they're fine," the tall blond woman said, smiling at Margie. "Just ask your wife. She helped me ride herd on them during the last council meeting."

"It was no trouble," Margie put in, remembering the three-year-old twins, who were like tiny tornadoes.

"Is that right?" Hunter asked.

"Don't know what this town did without her," Annie said. "She's helped everyone so much. And she has so many amazing ideas!"

Margie gave her friend a wan smile and wished Annie would be quiet. She could feel the tension in Hunter's arm, and it was getting tighter.

"Oh, now that I believe," Hunter said with a squeeze of her shoulders. "She's just full of surprises."

"Oh, yeah," James added, "Margie's a wonder."

"So I keep hearing."

Hunter's arm around her shoulders tightened further, and Margie deliberately leaned into him, making his gesture seem more romantic than he meant it to be. The fact that the moment she was pressed to his side, heat spiraled through her system like an out-of-control wildfire was just something she'd have to keep to herself.

"Well, we know you're busy," James was saying. "We just spotted you and wanted to thank you personally for everything you're doing for the town. Folks really appreciate it."

"Yeah," Hunter said thoughtfully. "About that…"

Was he going to admit to these nice people that he hadn't had a thing to do with making their lives better? Would he tell them that Margie had been making up his involvement?

Annie interrupted him. "Just having the new day care center at Cabot headquarters has been a godsend," she said, slapping one hand to the center of her chest as if taking an oath. "Margie told all of us how important you felt it was that the mothers who worked for you be able to leave their kids in a safe place. Somewhere close where the moms could work and still be close to their children."

"Did she?"

Margie felt Hunter's gaze on her but didn't turn her head up to look at him, afraid she'd see anger or disgust or impatience in those cool blue eyes of his.

Tears swamped Annie's eyes, but she blinked them away with a laugh. "God, look at me. Getting all teary over this! It just means a lot to all of us, Hunter. I mean, I need the job, but having the kids nearby makes working so much easier on me."

"Good," he murmured. "That's real good, Annie, but the thing is…"

"See, honey," Margie said quickly, determined to stop Hunter before he could disavow himself of everything these people were feeling. "I told you, everyone in town is so pleased that you're taking an active interest in Springville."

"She's right about that," James said. "Why, the newly redone Little League field and all of the flowers planted along Main Street…" He stopped and shook his head. "Well, it just means something to know that the Cabots are still attached to the town they built, that's all."

"Hunter's happy to do it," Margie told them, smiling and leaning even harder into her husband's side.

"We just wanted to thank you in person," James said, tugging his wife's hand. "Now, we've got to run. Annie's mom is watching our two little monsters, and she's probably ready to tear her hair out by now." Nodding, he said, "It really is good to see you, Hunter."

"Right. Thanks." Hunter stood stock-still on the sidewalk as the happy couple hurried off, and Margie felt the tension in him through the heavy arm he kept firmly around her shoulders.

"Well," Margie said softly, trying—and failing—to peel herself off Hunter, "I suppose we'd better go on to Carla's Dress Shop now."

"In a minute," Hunter said, tightening his arm around her until she could have sworn she could feel every one of his ribs, every ounce of muscle, every drop of heat pouring from his body into hers. "First, I want you to answer something for me."

She swallowed hard, tipped her face up to his and found herself caught in his gaze. "What?"

"Why'd you do it?" he asked, features stony, eyes giving away nothing of what he was feeling. "Why'd you let everyone think that it was my idea to do all these things around town? Why didn't you just do whatever it was you do without dragging me into it?"

"Because I'm your wife, Hunter," she said. "It only

made sense that you be a part of all of the decision making."

"But I never asked for this," he argued, his eyes going icy as he looked at her. "I didn't—don't—want to be responsible for this town."

Margie shook her head and saw more than she guessed he would want her to. Whether he would admit it or not, he loved this place, too. She'd seen it in his face as they walked along the familiar street. She'd heard it in his voice when he greeted old friends. And she'd felt it from him as the Drakes offered their thanks for everything *he'd* done for them and everyone else.

"Don't you see, Hunter," she said softly and reached up to cup his cheek, voluntarily touching him for the first time. "It's not about what you want. It's about what they need. The people in Springville need to feel that they're important to the Cabots. And like it or not, you *are* the Cabots."

# Five

"Nonsense," Simon said. "There's no reason for you to leave, and I won't accept your resignation."

Margie sighed. She'd known that telling Simon she'd be leaving at the end of the month wouldn't be easy. But after spending several hours in Springville with Hunter, she'd realized that she'd never be able to stay once her "marriage" was over. How could she?

Once Hunter left, every time she went into town, she'd have to see pity on the faces of her friends. They'd talk about her and speculate about what had gone wrong in her "wonderful" marriage.

She just couldn't stand the thought of it. This place had been a refuge for her. A place where she'd found friends and a sense of belonging she'd never known before. She didn't want any of that to change. So to protect herself and her memories of this place, she had no choice but to leave.

"You have to accept it, Simon." Margie shook her head sadly. "I'll be leaving at the end of the month. I have to."

"No, you don't," the old man said, lips pinched as if he'd bitten into a lemon. "Hunter's not an idiot, you know. He'll open his eyes. See you for who you are. Everything's going to work out fine. You'll see."

If a part of her wished he were right, she wouldn't admit to it. Because her rational mind just couldn't believe it. She and Hunter hadn't exactly gotten off to a smooth start. "Simon, he thinks I'm a gold digger."

The old man barked out one short laugh. "He'll get past that fast enough. I told him I had to force the money on you."

"About that," she said, wincing inwardly. Margie had never wanted the five million dollars, but Simon had been adamant about her accepting it. All she'd ever wanted was an honest job and to be able to support herself.

She hadn't married Hunter for the money. She'd done it for Simon. And, she admitted silently, because she'd liked the idea of being married. Of being wanted.

Stupid, Margie, really stupid.

She should have known that she had been walking into a huge mistake.

"Don't you worry about my grandson, you hear me?" Simon said, pushing up from the chair behind his desk. He walked slowly toward her, linked his arm through hers and headed toward the door. "I've known Hunter all his life, and I'm sure he's going to do the right thing."

"According to him, the right thing is to have me arrested."

He laughed again and patted her arm. "Just trust me, Margie," he told her, ushering her into the hallway. "Everything's going to work out."

"Simon—"

"Not another word, now," he admonished, holding up one hand to still anything else she might have to say. "You just be yourself and let me worry about Hunter."

Then he closed the study door, shutting Margie out and leaving her to wonder if he'd even heard a word she'd said. Probably not. She'd learned in the two years she'd worked for Simon that his head could be every bit as thick and stubborn as his grandson's seemed to be.

For the next few days, Hunter suffered through oceans of gratitude. Stoically, silently, he accepted the thanks from people he'd known his whole life for things he hadn't done.

Margie had been right, he knew. The people in Springville did need to know that their jobs, their lives, were safe. And around here, that meant having the Cabot family take an interest. Be involved.

And his "wife" was the Queen of Involved. She was on a half dozen committees, spent some of her day with Simon, taking care of business matters, and then what time she had left, she devoted to being the Lady of the Manor.

Hell. Hunter rubbed one hand across his face and told himself to knock it off. Yes, he resented all of the time and effort she was putting into Springville, but this was mainly because he still hadn't figured out why she was doing it. And why was she giving him so much credit for everything she'd done? What the hell did she care if people in town hated or loved him? What did it matter to her if the Little League field had been re-planted and new dugouts constructed for the kids who would play there this summer?

Why was she so damn determined to carve a place for herself in this little town? And why was she dragging him along with her?

*It's not about what you want, Hunter. It's about what they need.*

Those words of Margie's kept repeating in his mind, and he didn't much care for it. He'd never thought about the town and his attachment to it in those terms, and a part of him was ashamed to admit it, even to himself.

"But damn it, I don't need a teacher. Don't need this woman who's not even my wife making me look good to a town I don't even live in anymore." He shook his head, glared out at the wide sweep of flowers spread out in front of him and muttered, "I didn't ask her to do it, did I? I didn't ask to be the damn town hero."

"You talking to yourself again, Hunter?"

His head snapped up, and his gaze locked on the estate gardener watching Hunter from behind a low bank of hydrangeas. How much had the man heard? How much did he know? This pretending to be some-thing he wasn't was driving him nuts. Just as being married to a curvy, luscious redhead he couldn't touch was beginning to push him to the edge of his control.

Sleeping beside her every night, waking up every morning to find himself holding her close only to jump out of bed and rebuild her damn wall before she could wake up and discover his weakness.

*Weakness.*

Since when did he have a damn weakness?

Taking a breath, he told himself to play the game he'd agreed to play. To get through the rest of the month and reclaim his life. When the month was over, he'd find a woman. Any woman, and bury his memories of Margie in some anonymous sex. Then he could get back to the base and do what he knew best.

"Just what planet are you on, Hunter?"

The gardener's voice came again and Hunter muttered a curse he hoped the older man couldn't hear. "Didn't see you there, Calvin."

Not surprising, since the man was practically hidden behind the massive pink and blue blooms dotting the rich, dark green leaves of the bushes.

"Don't see much of anything since you've been home, if you ask me," Calvin said, dipping his head to wield his pruning shears. The delicate snip of the twin blades beat a counterpoint to the lazy drone of bees dancing through the garden.

Hunter shoved both hands into the pockets of his jeans and walked toward the old man who'd been in charge of the Cabot gardens for nearly forty years. "What's that supposed to mean?"

"Hmm?" Calvin lifted his head briefly, shot him a glance and shrugged. "Just seems to me a man who's been apart from his wife for months on end would spend more time with her and less wandering around the estate talking to himself, that's all."

Hunter sighed. "That's all?"

Calvin's bristling gray hair wafted in the cool breeze, and his pale blue eyes narrowed on Hunter. "Well no, now that I think on it, maybe that's not all."

Hunter reached out, ran one finger along the pale pink petals of the closest blossom and slid a glance to the old man watching him. "Let's have it, then."

"You think I don't notice things? I'm old, boy, not blind."

"Notice what, Calvin?"

"How you watch that little girl of yours when she's not looking. How when she *is* looking, your eyes go cold and you look away."

Hunter scowled. Since when had Calvin become so damn perceptive? "You're imagining things."

"Now I'm senile, then? Is that what you're trying to say?"

"No," Hunter said quickly, then shoved his hand back into his pocket. Tough to be a hard ass with a man who'd known you since you were a kid. "It's just…complicated."

Calvin snorted a laugh. "You always did make bigger mountains out of mountains, boy."

"What?" Hunter laughed shortly as he tried to figure out what Calvin was talking about.

"No molehills for you. Nope. You look at something hard and make it impossible. Never could see what was right in front of you for staring out at the horizon. Always looking for something even though you wouldn't know it if you stumbled on it."

Hunter would have argued, but how could he? The old man was too damn insightful. Hunter had spent most of his life looking past the boundaries of this estate to the world beyond Springville. He'd wanted…more. He'd wanted to see other places, be someone else. Someone besides the latest member of the Cabot family dynasty.

And he'd done everything he'd wanted to, hadn't he? He'd done important things with his life. He'd made a difference. Shifting his gaze across the garden and the wide stretch of neatly trimmed grass that ran down to the cliff's edge and the sea beyond, he thought how small this place had once seemed to him. How confining. Strange that at the moment, it looked more welcoming than anything else. As if this place had simply lain here, waiting for him to come home.

Hunter frowned thoughtfully and wondered just why that notion all of a sudden felt comforting.

"Calvin?"

The sound of Margie's voice shattered Hunter's thoughts completely. He turned toward her and felt something inside him shift, like a bolt pushing free of a lock.

She stood in a slice of sunlight on the stone patio and Hunter's breath caught in his throat. She wore a green silk shirt with an open collar and short sleeves, tucked into a pair of form-fitting linen slacks. Her incredible hair was lifting in the wind caressing her, and it danced around her head like a curly, auburn halo. Her grass-green eyes were fixed on him as he stared at her and Hunter couldn't stamp out the hunger she was probably reading on his face.

Why the hell had he bought her new clothes?

Margie's heartbeat thundered in her chest, and her mouth went dry under Hunter's steady stare. Even from a distance, she saw him clench his square jaw as if fighting an inner battle for control. And somewhere inside her, she preened a little, knowing that just looking at her was in some small way torturing him.

At first she'd been uncomfortable wearing clothes that defined her too-voluptuous—in her opinion—figure. As if she were walking around naked or something. She wasn't used to people—*men*—looking at her the way Hunter was now. Always before, she'd sort of blended into the crowd. She'd never stood out, never been the kind of woman to get noticed.

For the first time in her life, Margie actually felt pretty. It was a powerful sensation. And a little frightening. Especially since Hunter didn't look too happy with whatever he was thinking.

Well, she reminded herself, it was his own fault. He was the one who'd insisted on buying out half of Carla's Dress Shop. He was the one who'd approved or vetoed everything she'd tried on. Which had really annoyed her until she'd gotten into the spirit of the thing and had pleased herself by watching his eyes darken and flash with hunger every time she appeared in a new outfit.

The arrogant, bossy man had, it seemed, painted himself into a corner of his own design.

"Did you need something, Margie?"

"What?" The voice seemed to come from nowhere. Hunter's gaze was still locked on her, and he hadn't spoken—she was sure of it. Tearing her gaze from the man who was her temporary husband, she saw the estate gardener giving her a knowing smile.

"Calvin. Yes. I mean, I did want to ask you something. I was wondering if you'd mind providing a few bouquets for the dance tomorrow night. No one's flowers are prettier."

"Happy to," the older man said. "Anything in particular?"

She shook her head. At the moment, she couldn't have discerned the difference between a rose and a weed anyway. "No, I'll leave that up to you."

"You're in charge of flowers, too?" Hunter grumbled.

"I'm helping." And why did she say that as if she were apologizing? She didn't owe him an explanation, and why did he care what she did anyway? In the few days he'd been home, he'd gone into town only that one day when they'd had their shopping expedition. The rest of the time, he remained here, at the house, as if he were…hiding?

Even as she considered that, she discounted it. Why would Hunter Cabot want to hide from the very town in which he'd grown up? He wasn't the kind of man to avoid confrontation or uncomfortable situations.

"Sure seem to do a lot of 'helping,'" he commented dryly.

"And it seems that you don't do enough," she countered, enjoying the quick spark of irritation she spotted in his eyes.

But she wondered why he was so determined to keep himself separate from the town and the people here. He would only be here another few weeks; then he'd be gone back to the Naval base, back to the danger and adventure he seemed to want more than anything. So why, then, wouldn't he want to spend what little time he had here seeing old friends?

She knew she'd be leaving at the end of the month, so Margie wanted to do as much as she could for the town she'd come to love.

So why didn't he love this place? He'd been raised here. He'd had family to love. A spot in the world to call his own. And he'd given it all up for the chance at adventure.

"Now," Calvin announced, interrupting her thoughts again, "I've got weeding to do." But before he left, he gave Hunter a quick look and said, "You remember what we talked about."

Then Calvin wandered off and Margie watched his progress through the lush, cottage-style garden. When the older man rounded the corner of the big house, she shifted a look to Hunter. "What did he mean by that?"

"Nothing." He muttered the one word in a deep, dark grumble. "It was nothing."

"Okay," she said, while wondering what the two men had been talking about before she'd stepped onto the patio. But one look at Hunter's shuttered expression told her that he wouldn't be clearing up that little mystery for her. So she said, "He probably thinks he's giving us a chance to be romantic in the garden."

"Probably," Hunter agreed and didn't look like he appreciated it.

"Calvin never stops to chat for long anyway," Margie said, coming down the stone steps to the edge of the garden.

"Yeah, I know. He's always preferred his flowers to people."

She stopped, bent down and sniffed at a rose before straightening again. When Margie saw Hunter's gaze lock briefly on her breasts, she felt a rush of something completely female and had to hide a small smile. Really, she was in serious trouble. She was beginning to enjoy the way Hunter looked at her, and that road would only lead to disappointment.

He didn't trust her. He made that plain enough every time they were together. But he did want her. That much she knew. Every morning, she woke up to the feel of his heavy leg lying across hers, his strong arm wrapped around her waist and pulling her tightly against his warm, naked body. And every morning, she lay there, quietly, enjoying the feel of him surrounding her, until he woke up, shifted carefully to one side of her and replaced the pillow wall between them.

Margie knew he didn't realize she was awake for those few brief, incredible moments every morning. And she had no intention of telling him, because he'd find a way to end them and she liked waking up to the feel of his body on hers. To that sense of safety she felt lying next to him.

Oh, God. She looked up at him saw those blue eyes go cool and distant and knew she was only making things more difficult for herself. There was no future here for her at all. Pretending otherwise was only going to make leaving that much harder.

"Why'd you come out here?" he asked, his voice low, his features strained. "Did you really want to talk to Calvin, or were you just following me?"

So much for daydreams. "Were you born crabby, or do I just bring it out in you?"

"What?" He scowled at her.

He probably thought he looked ferociously intimidating. But Margie had seen that look often enough that it hardly bothered her anymore.

"Crabby. You. Why?"

"I'm not crabby," he said and blew out a breath. "Hell, I don't know what I am." Shaking his head, he glanced across the garden and Margie followed his gaze.

The back of the house was beautiful. Late-spring daffodils crowded the walkways in shades from butter-yellow to the softest cream. Roses sent their perfume into the air, and columbine and larkspur dipped and swayed brilliantly colored heads in the soft wind off the ocean. It was a magical place, and Margie had always loved it.

"You really like it here, don't you?" he asked.

"I love it."

"I did too for a while." He turned and started along the snaking path of stepping-stones that meandered through the garden. Margie walked right behind him, pleased that he was finally talking to her.

"When I was a kid," he mused, "it was all good. Coming here. Being with Simon."

"Your parents died when you were twelve. Simon told me. That must have been terrible for you." She didn't even remember her parents, but she'd been told they'd died in a car accident when she was three. She'd give anything to have the few short years of memories of being loved that Hunter no doubt had.

"Yeah, they did." He tipped his head back to glance at the clouds scuttling across the sky before continuing on through the garden. "And I came here to live, and it was a good place to grow up," he admitted, now idly dragging the palm of his hand across a cluster of early larkspur. A few of the delicate, pastel blossoms dropped to the ground as they walked on. "The place is huge, so there was plenty of room for a kid to run and play."

"I can imagine." Though she really couldn't. Growing up in a series of foster homes, Margie had never even dreamed of a place like this. She wouldn't have known how.

As if he'd guessed where her thoughts had gone, he stopped, looked over his shoulder and asked, "Where are you from?"

"Los Angeles," she answered and hoped he'd leave it at that. Thankfully, he did.

Nodding, he said, "Coming from a city that size, you can understand how small Springville started to look to me."

"That's exactly what drew me in when I first moved here. When I answered the ad to become Simon's assistant, I took one look at Springville and fell in love." It was the kind of small town that lonely people always dreamed of. A place where people looked out for each other. A place where one person could make a difference. Be counted. But she didn't tell him all of that.

"I like that it's small. Big cities are anonymous."

"That's one of the best parts," Hunter said and gave her a quick, brief smile that never touched his eyes. "There's a sense of freedom in anonymity. Nobody gives a damn what you do or who your family is."

"Nobody gives a damn, period," she said quietly.

"Makes life simple," he agreed.

"Running off to join the SEALs wasn't exactly an attempt at simple and uncomplicated."

He laughed shortly. "No, I guess it wasn't."

"So, what were you looking for?"

"Why do you care?" He stopped, turned to look down at her and in his eyes there were so many shifting emotions that Margie couldn't tell one from the next. Then he spoke again, and she was too angry to worry about what he was feeling.

"Seriously, I get why you're doing this. Five million is hard to ignore. But why do you care when it's not part of the job description?"

She sucked in a gulp of air and felt the insult of his words like a slap. "I told you. I'm not doing this for the money."

"Yeah, you told me."

"But you don't believe me." That truth was written on his face.

"I don't *know* you," he countered.

Margie pushed her hair back from her face when the wind snaked the dark red curls across her eyes. Looking up at him, she found herself torn between wanting to kiss him and wanting to kick him. It was a toss-up which urge would win.

"Is it so hard for you to believe that I might love this place? That I might love Simon?"

"I just don't see what you get out of it beyond the money," he told her. "Unless it's hooking yourself to the Cabot name."

Understanding began to dawn as she noticed the tone of his voice. "Is that what this is about? Is that why you left? You didn't want to be a *Cabot*? Why? Is it so terrible to have a family? To be a part of something?"

His jaw clenched. She watched the muscle there flex as if he were biting back words fighting to spill out.

Finally he let them come. "In this town, yeah, it's hard to be a Cabot," he admitted. "Everybody looking to you to make sure they keep their jobs. Treating you like you're different. Figuring since you live in a castle, you're some kind of prince. I wasn't interested in being small-town royalty."

Margie laughed at that ridiculous statement. When he frowned, she held up one hand to cut off whatever he might say. "Please. I've heard plenty of stories about you when you were a kid, Hunter and in none of them did people talk about you like you were a prince. If anything, it was 'That Hunter was always into something.' Or 'Hunter broke so many of my windows I almost boarded 'em up.'"

A reluctant smile curved his mouth. "All right, I give you that. But…" He paused, looked around the postcard-perfect garden and then to the back of the castle, which seemed to glitter in the late-afternoon sun. "Simon wanted me to be the next link in the Cabot family dynasty. I wanted more. I wanted to be out in the world making my own mark. I didn't want to catch hold of the Cabot family train and ride on what my family's always done."

"So you walked away," she said softly. "From your friends. Your family."

She hadn't tried to mask the accusation in her voice, and he reacted to it. His spine went stiff as a rod, he squared his shoulders and looked down at her as if daring her to question his decisions. "What I do is important."

"I'm not arguing that," Margie said. "How could I? You risk your life for your country. For all of us. On a regular basis."

"Why is it I hear a 'but' coming?"

*"But,"* she said, accommodating him, "the smaller, less glorious battles are just as important, Hunter. The day-to-day work of building lives. Making people happy. Watching over the people you care about. That's no less honorable. No less significant."

"I didn't say that," he told her, his voice hardly more than a whisper of sound that seemed to slide over her skin like warm honey.

"Then why can't you see you're needed here?"

He shifted as if he were uncomfortable, and Margie hoped that she was getting through to him. As a Navy SEAL, Hunter knew his duty and did it, without question. Hadn't she listened to Simon talk with pride about the man Hunter had become? Hadn't she seen for herself since he'd been home how everyone treated him? The man was a hero. Now, she just had to make him see that this town—and Simon—needed their own hero back.

When she left, Simon would have no one again. Springville would slip back into the worry that without the support of the Cabots the town would die. Couldn't Hunter see that his family, his *home,* should now be taking precedence over his need for adventure?

He shifted his gaze from hers as if he couldn't look at her and say, "It isn't in my nature to stay."

Margie didn't believe that. She already knew he was a man who didn't avoid commitment. Hadn't he given everything to his country? "Then what is your nature, Hunter?"

"To protect." He said the words quickly. No hesitation at all. It was instinct. Turning his head, he gave her a hard, warning look, then added, "And I'll protect Simon from anyone trying to hurt him."

She knew exactly what he meant. He still believed that she was taking advantage of Simon. That she wanted only his money and whatever prestige came along with the name Cabot. He'd never understand that the love Simon had offered her had been far more valuable to her than dollars.

Suddenly she was tired of trying to make him understand. Tired of the veiled insults and the way he seemed to look at her with hunger one moment and disdain the next. If he was too hardheaded to see the truth, she'd never be able to convince him. And, since this farce would be over in a few weeks, why should she keep trying? Why should she keep beating her head against a stone wall when all she got for her trouble was a headache?

As he stood there watching her, waiting for her to try to defend herself yet again, Margie decided to take an offensive road rather than a defensive one.

"You want to protect Simon from anyone trying to hurt him? Like you did, you mean?" Margie's voice was quiet, but the words weren't. They seemed to hang in the air between them like a battle flag. "You left Simon alone, Hunter. You walked off to save the world and left an old man with no one to care about him."

His cool blue eyes went so cold, so glacial, that Margie wouldn't have been surprised to see snow start flying in the wind between them. "Didn't take you long to move in and correct that, though, did it?"

Anger swamped through her and rose like a tide rushing in to shore. Stepping in close, she lifted one hand, pointed her index finger and jabbed it at his chest. "I was his *employee.*"

He glanced down at her finger, then wrapped his

hand around hers and pushed it aside. "So, you were doing it for the money. Still are, aren't you?"

Margie pulled her hand free of his and shook her head at him sadly. As quickly as her anger had risen, it drained away again. What was the point? She stepped back from him because she needed the physical distance to match the emotional chasm spreading between them.

"It would be easier for you if that were true, wouldn't it?" she whispered, forcing herself to look into those hard, cold eyes. "Because if I'm staying because I love your grandfather, that makes you leaving him even worse, doesn't it?"

"You don't know what you're talking about," he muttered.

"Oh, I think I do. You're a coward, Hunter."

"*Excuse* me?"

She waved a hand. "Don't bother using that military, snap-to-attention tone of voice with me. I'm not afraid of you."

"Maybe you should be," he warned. "Nobody calls me a coward."

"Really? What else would you call a man who turns from the only family he knows because it's just too hard to stay?"

He didn't say anything to that, and when the silence became too much to bear, Margie turned and left him standing amid the spring flowers.

And because she didn't look back, she didn't see Hunter watching her long after she'd disappeared into the house.

# Six

The dance was a success.

But then it would have to be, Hunter thought. His "wife" wouldn't have settled for anything less.

To please his grandfather, Hunter was wearing his dress whites, and so he stood out in the crowd of dark suits and ties even more than he might have usually. Now, leaning one shoulder against the wall in a corner of the room, he tried to disappear as he watched the crowd assembled in a local church hall.

It was the only room except for the ballroom at the castle that was large enough to accommodate this many people. And from Hunter's vantage point, it looked as if most of the town had turned out for the event.

There were dozens of small round tables arranged around the room, with a long buffet line along one wall.

The dinner had been catered by a restaurant in town, and the tantalizing spices and scents of Mexican food hovered in the noisy air. There were helium-filled balloons trailing colorful ribbon strings bouncing against the ceiling, and Calvin's flowers decorated either end of the buffet table.

There was music blasting from someone's stereo at the front of the room, and several couples were on the dance floor swaying to the beat. But mostly, people wandered the room, laughing and talking as if they hadn't seen each other in years.

Then, there was his "wife," Hunter thought. His eyes narrowed on the redhead who'd done nothing but plague him for days. Since their conversation in the garden the day before, he hadn't been able to stop thinking about everything Margie had said to him, and that just irritated the hell out of him.

He didn't want to feel guilty. He didn't want her looking at him in disappointment as if he'd somehow let her, personally, down. He didn't want to remember her words and hear the ring of truth to them.

Oh, not the coward part. That he'd fight until his dying breath. He was no coward. He hadn't run from responsibility. He'd run *to* it. He'd wanted something different for his life. He'd wanted to leave a mark, to do something important. And he had. Damned if he'd apologize for that.

He straightened abruptly from the wall and felt a twinge of pain from his still-healing wound. And along with that ache came a whispering voice that asked, *Haven't you had enough of the adventure? Hadn't you already been thinking that maybe it was time to come home?*

Scowling out at the woman who'd made him think too much, remember too much, Hunter tried to brush her and all she stood for aside. But that was harder than he might have expected.

"You ought to be out there dancing with your wife," a deep voice said from somewhere nearby.

Hunter glanced to his left and smiled. "Kane Hackett." He shook hands with his old friend and said, "I don't dance. You should know that."

Kane grinned and slid a look across the room to where Margie was laughing and talking with a short blond woman. "A married man will do lots of things he didn't use to do. Take that gorgeous little blonde talking to your Margie…"

Hunter had hardly noticed the other woman. How could he be expected to see anything but how that strapless black dress Margie was wearing defined her lush body? Now, though, he forced himself to look at the blonde. "Cute."

"Damn sight better than cute," Kane corrected, taking a sip from the beer bottle he held. "That's my wife, Donna."

Staggered, Hunter looked at the man who had gone off to join the Marines at the same time Hunter had enlisted in the Navy. "You? Married?"

Hardly seemed possible. Hunter and Kane had both been keen on adventure, on seeing the world. Experiencing everything life had to offer and then some. Now Kane was married?

"Why sound so surprised?" His old friend chuckled. "You took the plunge, why not me?"

"Yeah, but—" Hunter's marriage was a fraud. "And you live here in town? Simon didn't say anything to me."

Kane shrugged. "Guess he was just waiting for us to bump into each other. And, yeah, I live in Springville. I'm the sheriff."

Hunter laughed now. "Oh, that's rich. You're the sheriff? After all the times we got hauled in for a good talking to, the people in this town elected you?"

Kane gave him a huge grin. "Guess they figured it took a bad boy to catch the bad boys."

Nodding, Hunter slid his gaze back to his wife as the music changed from classic rock and roll to a slow slide of jazz. "How long have you been back?"

"About a year and a half. Met Donna on my last leave. She knocked me off my feet, Hunt." He grinned and shook his head as if he still couldn't believe it himself. "Never saw it coming, but I'm glad it did." He paused then added, "So when my enlistment was up, I came home, ran for sheriff and married Donna."

"No more adventures for you, then, huh?" Hunter reached out, took his friend's beer and had a swallow.

"Are you kidding?" Kane laughed. "Every day with Donna's an adventure. Best thing that ever happened to me, I swear. But then," he said, reclaiming his beer, "I guess you'd know all about that."

"Yeah." Hunter watched Margie as an old woman stopped to talk to her, and his chest tightened as Margie gave the woman her complete attention along with a brilliant smile.

Briefly, he wondered what it would be like to actually

be married. To know Margie was his with the same surety that Kane felt about his Donna. Would he resent staying in Springville? Would he end up one day hating the town and the woman who had snared him?

Hunter frowned at the thought and had to ask himself if maybe Margie hadn't been more than a little right in everything she'd said to him the day before. Maybe he had been running from responsibility and disguising it with a different kind of duty.

"Well, good to see you," Kane was saying. "Stop by the station this week—we'll catch up. For now, I think I'll go dance with my wife."

"Right, right." Hunter nodded but barely heard his friend. He was too busy watching Margie as, one by one, everyone in the hall found the time to stop and talk with her, laugh with her, hug her. Something about that woman made her a magnet for people. Was it a con artist's gift, he wondered, or was it simply that she was a naturally kind person whom people wanted to be around?

"You know," Kane said, slapping Hunter on the back, "I really shouldn't even be speaking to you, all things considered."

"Huh? Why's that?"

"Because ever since Margie told Donna and some of the other wives about that honeymoon you two had in Bali…" Kane's eyebrows lifted and he huffed out a breath. "Well, let's just say, those stories made the rest of the husbands in town come in a sad second place to you in the romance department."

Bali, huh? So Margie was making up stories about honeymoons on tropical islands. And, painting him in a very romantic light, apparently. He smiled to himself and wondered just how detailed those stories had been.

"What can I say, Kane?" Hunter said with a slow smile. "I've always been good."

"That you have, Hunt." Kane slapped him on the shoulder again and walked past him. "You're missed around here, you know. It's good to have you back, man."

"Good to be back," he said automatically, but for the first time he realized he actually meant the words.

Margie felt Hunter's gaze on her as surely as she would a touch. Was he still angry about the things she'd said to him the day before? Not that he hadn't deserved it, she reminded herself while Jenna Carter babbled about the dessert tray. Margie nodded absentmindedly and remembered the way Hunter had looked at her when she'd called him a coward.

Even now, she cringed and wished that she'd found a better way to say what she'd meant. Yes, she thought he'd deserted Simon and the town that needed him, but she also knew he wasn't a coward. He was strong and sure of himself and brave and—*arrogant, bossy and irritating,* her mind added quickly before she became just a little bit too understanding.

After all, he hadn't exactly been kind to her. He was still convinced she was trying to scam Simon, for heaven's sake. At the thought of the older man, she shifted a quick look at him and spotted him sitting with his friends, laughing and whispering together. And men thought women gossiped.

Simon. She would miss him when she left. And God

help her, she would really miss Hunter. Somehow, that man had wormed his way into her heart, making her want him despite the fact that he thought she was a thief. *Margie, you are such an idiot,* she told herself.

Then Mrs. Banks murmured something about having a meeting the following month concerning the elementary school festival, and Margie only nodded. She wouldn't be there next month, and that knowledge was too painful to allow, so she buried that ache and let it simmer in the heat that Hunter's stare was causing.

How in the world was she going to make it through the rest of the night? Her insides were shaking, and her smile felt forced and wooden. She only hoped no one else could tell that her heart was breaking.

With Kane's words still repeating in his mind, Hunter left his corner and stalked the perimeter of the crowd. He nodded to those he passed, but he didn't stop. To stop meant being drawn into conversations, and he wasn't in the mood to talk. Not to old friends. Not to anyone. His thoughts didn't make him good company at the moment. Instead, he sought a darker corner, a quiet spot from which to watch and observe.

The music swelled around him, pulsing with an almost erotic beat, that slow, heavy sound of wailing sax that crept into a man's soul and wrung it dry.

He moved stealthily, using his training as a SEAL to help him slide almost unnoticed through a crowd so busy with their partying they didn't notice much of anything else. Across the room he spotted Simon— who'd decided to attend at the last minute—sitting at a table near the dance floor, holding court with some of his cronies. Old men gathered together to remember the past and plan for a future that most of them wouldn't see. A pang of something sharp and bitter sliced into him as he realized once again that his indomitable grandfather was old now. How much longer would he be here? How much more time could Hunter reasonably expect to have with the man who was his only family?

He clenched his jaw and deliberately shifted his gaze from Simon to Margie. As always, she was surrounded by a crowd, laughing and smiling as if she didn't have a disturbing thought in her head. But then, he thought, why would she? She'd dumped all of them on *him* the day before.

That he could acknowledge that just maybe he might have deserved some of her taunts only annoyed the hell out of him. His gaze fixed on her as she greeted all of the people who seemed to move in a stream toward her. She smiled, she laughed, she welcomed people into her warmth. People who weren't *him,* of course.

But when that thought scuttled through his mind, Hunter at least had the grace to admit that it was his own damn fault. He shut her out whenever his desire for her became too overwhelming—which was damn near every minute. He didn't want to care about her. Didn't want to want her. Didn't want to see beyond what he'd already seen. She was the manipulative woman he'd first thought her. She *had* to be because anything else was simply unacceptable.

They weren't really married. He'd made her no promises and didn't intend to, he reassured himself. When this month was over, he'd be leaving. Back to the Navy. Back to the next mission.

And who, his mind demanded, would be here to look after Simon?

The fierce scowl on his face that thought engendered was enough to convince most people to give him a wide berth, and Hunter was grateful for it. He was visited out. No more friendly chats tonight. All he wanted to do was survive this dance, get back to the castle and locate one of Simon's bottles of aged scotch.

At last, he found a slice of darkness, an alcove off the entrance, far enough away from the crowd that he could think without being interrupted by old friends. But close enough that his gaze could search out Margie. Damn it.

What was it about her that got to him? She was nothing like the women he was used to. She was…unlike anyone he'd ever known. God, when he compared her with his ex, it was as if the two women were from different planets.

Gretchen didn't want to think about tomorrow. She was the quintessential party girl. She was ready for adventure, good in the sack and beautiful enough to make a grown man whimper. But, he reminded himself, just two months before Hunter had hinted that he might be thinking about settling down. Maybe getting married— okay, no time soon, but someday. When he was too damned old to go out and get himself shot anymore. Gretchen had backed off like he was on fire and she didn't want to be singed by the flames. She'd broken up with him that night and taken off for a photo shoot in Peru, of all damn places.

Shaking his head, Hunter folded his arms over his chest, leaned back against the cold wall and watched

Margie. Unlike the gorgeous Gretchen, his temporary wife was all about the future. She was always planning tomorrows, looking ahead, dreaming dreams and finding a way to make them real.

Hell, she knew their marriage was a lie, yet she continued to pretend to everyone in town that all was well between them. She continued to do her best for a town that she was going to be leaving soon.

And she told sexy stories about him and a honeymoon that hadn't happened.

What the hell was he supposed to do with a woman like that?

Of course, he knew what he wanted to do. At least, what his body was clamoring for. But sex with Margie would complicate a situation that was already so twisted he couldn't see an easy way out. So he'd bury his lust and focus on getting through the next three weeks or so.

In the next instant, he wondered where Margie would go when she left Springville. What would she do? What would Simon do without her?

He rubbed one hand over his face and tried to wipe out the scrambling thoughts in his mind. But how the hell could he not think about her when she was there, in front of him, looking sexier and more desirable than ever?

"I never really believed Hunter was married to her," a woman said to her friend as she blithely walked past the shadowed alcove where Hunter stood silently.

"What do you mean?"

"Oh, come on." The first woman, a brunette who looked familiar to Hunter, laughed lightly. "I mean, when you look at Margie, do you really think…hmm, there's the woman for Hunter Cabot."

"I guess not," her friend said and shifted to look at Margie.

Hunter did too and frowned as the brunette kept talking.

"I knew him in high school, and even then he was the stuff dreams were made of."

He frowned and thought about moving out of the shadows so the women would know he was there. Then he second-guessed that idea. He'd learned long ago that a man could learn a lot with a little eavesdropping, so he held his ground and waited.

"I can imagine," the second woman said. "The man is…wow."

"Exactly. He's wow and she's…ho-hum. I mean, she's nice and everything—"

*Nice?* Margie was nice? Gritting his teeth hard, Hunter glared at the brunette. Margie worked continuously for this town, giving everything she had, and these two women felt comfortable standing in the shadows of the dance Margie had arranged and bloodlessly tearing her apart? Temper sparked and a protective surge like nothing he'd ever known before rose up inside Hunter.

"Completely," her friend agreed quickly. "Margie's a sweetie."

"But he's a…*god,* and she's a peasant. Never should have happened. And—" The brunette stopped, glanced at her reflection in a nearby window and smoothed her pinky finger over her bottom lip. Sighing, she said, "Until Hunter actually showed up here and claimed her, I never believed those stories she told all over town."

"Mmm," her friend said on a sigh. "Like Bali?"

"Yes…" The brunette shook her head, stared across the room at Margie and said, confusion ringing in her tone, "What the hell does she have that I don't have?"

"For one thing," Hunter spoke up and stepped out of the shadows, startling both women into gasping. "She's got *me*."

"Hunter—I—we—" The brunette threw her friend a desperate look, but that woman was already melting into the crowd, disassociating herself fast.

He looked down into the brunette's eyes and finally placed her. Janice Franklin. Cheerleader. Homecoming queen. And still the town's reigning bitch, apparently.

"Janice, right?"

She brightened, obviously pleased to be remembered. "Yes."

Hunter just looked at her for a long minute or two. She was still pretty, in a hard, sharp way. And clearly, she thought highly of herself if she figured he'd just brush aside everything she'd said about his "wife" without a second thought. Well, she was wrong. He wasn't going to stand there and let this woman—or anyone else for that matter—sharpen her claws on Margie's hide. Why it mattered to him so much, he couldn't have said. All he was sure of was that it did matter. He'd worry about the why of it later.

"Well, Janice," he finally said softly, chucking her chin with his fingertips, "let me tell you something else about my wife. What she has someone like you will never understand."

She blinked at him. "Well—I—"

"Do yourself a favor," Hunter told her as he left her babbling to herself, "don't say anything else."

Riding a wave of righteous fury on Margie's behalf, Hunter stalked through the crowd. His gaze locked on his wife, he was like a ballistic missile, focused solely on his target.

Who the hell did those women think they were, talking about Margie as if she were less than nothing? As if she wasn't good enough for him? Good enough? Hell, if she was everything she claimed to be, she was too damn good for him. What right did they have to say a word about his *wife?*

The fact that he was inwardly defending the woman he'd been complaining about for days didn't register with him. His only thought now was to get his hands on her. To make sure everyone here understood that they'd better treat her right.

Across the room, Margie looked up and saw Hunter headed right toward her. He was hard to miss, she thought, with an inward sigh. In his white dress uniform, with the rows of colorful ribbons and medals on his chest, he looked like every woman's fantasy. He was tall and strong and fierce and…headed right for her with an expression on his face that was a mixture of fury and determination.

What was wrong? A woman beside her was talking, but Margie didn't hear a word. Instead, she was caught up in the power of Hunter's blue gaze locked on hers. The people separating them seemed to melt out of his way, propelled by some invisible force. Margie's heart pounded and her breathing hitched as he came closer, never slowing down, never hesitating.

What was going on? She'd hardly seen him all evening, though she'd been aware of him. How could she not be, she wondered frantically. The man was inescapable. Just knowing he was in the room had kept her on edge all night—wondering what he was doing, what he was thinking—had had her own mind racing, questioning.

Now, he was only an arm's reach away, and the only thing she read on his face was a strength of purpose she couldn't identify.

"Hunter—" She spoke first as soon as he stopped in front of her. "Is everything all right? Are you—"

"Quiet." It was a command no less authoritarian for its whispered delivery.

*"What?"*

Then Hunter shook his head as if not surprised at all she hadn't been able to be quiet. His lips curved into a wicked smile that sent a jolt of something amazing staggering through her. And before she could recover, he grabbed her, swept her into a low dip, cradled her in his arms and kissed her, so long, so hard, so deep, that Margie forgot to breathe.

His mouth on hers was at first wild, aggressive, almost as if he didn't want to be doing what he was doing. But she responded to that hint of darkness instantly, as if the shadows in this man had reached out and found every dark corner of her own soul. There was fire here, a ferociousness she hadn't expected but thrilled to, in the deepest corners of her heart. In seconds, his kiss changed, shifted, became less brutal, more hot and hungry, more passionate. Margie sighed into his mouth and felt his body mold itself to hers as if he were trying to hold her so tightly she'd never be able to escape him.

She didn't know what had prompted this, and she didn't care. Since the first time he'd kissed her, days ago, she'd been dreaming about another one. And this kiss more than lived up to her fantasies. Her blood felt like champagne, bubbling into a froth that swam giddily through her veins. His tongue swept into her mouth, stealing her breath, filling her with a heat that felt over-whelming, mind boggling.

She gave herself up to it, and when her mind started whispering, she resented every taunting thought. *What was he doing? Why was he kissing her? Was it all a show for the townspeople? And if it was, why now? Why tonight? He hadn't seemed to care if anyone believed they were married or not. So what had changed?*

*And why do you care?* that voice murmured at last. Did she really have to question this? Couldn't she just, for once, enjoy the moment? Feel his arms around her and pretend, however briefly, that they were a real couple? Couldn't she just convince her brain to take the night off and let her body lead the way?

Oh, yeah.

Lost in sensation, she wrapped her arms around his neck and gave him everything he was giving her. And while she surrendered to the heat, she was only dimly aware of the thunderous applause rising up from the people surrounding them.

Margie couldn't sleep.

How could anyone be expected to sleep when the bodies were simmering at a high boil and sexual expectation was humming along at a gallop? Hmm. Mixed metaphors. Probably a bad sign.

Apparently her "husband" wasn't feeling any lingering effects from that kiss. His deep, even breathing sighed into the silence, telling her that at least one of them was going to get some rest that night.

Jerk.

With the pillow wall at her back, Margie tried to ignore the fact that Hunter had been ignoring her for hours—ever since that spontaneous kiss had ended. As if he somehow was blaming *her* for him kissing her. And wasn't that just like a man? Right back to Adam in the Garden. *It was all that woman's fault.*

She punched her own pillow and shifted position, trying to find a spot where the sheets didn't seem to be scraping sensitive skin raw. Where she could hear the sound of Hunter's breathing and not imagine that breath dusting her face as he loomed over her.

Moonlight sifted into the bedroom through the French doors and lay in a silvery blanket across the bed. In the dim light, she stared up at the ceiling and told herself she'd never fall asleep if she didn't close her eyes. But then every time she closed her eyes, she felt Hunter's mouth on hers again, so no sleep that way, either.

She folded her arms over her chest, pinning the sheet and quilt to her body and tried silently repeating multiplication tables. Maybe she could bore herself to sleep.

That's when Margie noticed Hunter's breathing pattern had changed. She listened harder, noticed the quickened tempo of his breaths, as if he were running in his sleep, and she went up on one elbow to peer over the pillow wall.

*He yanked a field dressing out of his pack and wrapped it around his side in an effort to stop the bleeding. Damn lucky shot, he told himself, fury at the situation spiking inside him.*

*Should have been a simple recon mission. But he'd been cut off from his team almost from the moment they entered the target area. They'd had to break for cover; then he'd been trapped, forced to hide while the others stealthily made a break for it.*

*The SEALs never left a man behind, and he knew his team would be waiting for him. They'd never evac the country without him, but it would be up to him to make it to the rendezvous point. Which would have been a hell of a lot easier if he hadn't been bleeding.*

*With pain his only companion, Hunter inched his way across a desert barren of any life but the enemy. He hid during the day, traveled at night. He rationed his water and was finally forced to dig the bullet out of his side with his own fingers. Days crawled past and tension, along with a fever, mounted. There were so many dangers, so many easy ways for him to die and be lost in this damn desert forever.*

*But he wouldn't go that way, he told himself. He'd find a way out. Get back to where things were green. Quiet. Where he didn't have to constantly expect the muffled explosion of a gunshot coming out of nowhere.*

*He wanted…*In his sleep, Hunter heard a whisper of something soft, something comforting, and he turned toward it, instinctively reaching. *Warmth surrounded him. A gentle touch smoothed his hair back from his face*

*and whispered words of comfort swam through his mind,
his heart. He reached for the source of that calm, for the
ease it promised, for the balm he so desperately needed.*

Gentle hands stroked his skin, and Hunter groaned
at the sensation. He was back, he was out of the desert.
It hadn't killed him, after all. And here he was, with a
warm, willing woman sliding her hands over his back,
tenderly across his face, and he wanted that touch more
than he wanted his next breath.

Coming up completely out of the dreamscape he'd
wandered through, Hunter heard that whisper again,
and this time, he recognized the speaker.

"It's okay, Hunter," Margie soothed, while her
hands stroked him tenderly. "You're okay. You're safe.
Come back."

He took a slow, deep breath and drew her scent of
jasmine deep into his lungs. His eyes cleared and he
looked up into her grass-green eyes and felt something
stir and shift inside him. The same something he'd
fought all night after kissing her at the dance.

Well, he thought, staring up at her, feeling her hands
on his bare skin, he was through fighting. He wanted
her. Had wanted her for days.

And now he was going to have her.

# Seven

Reaching up, he cupped the back of her neck in his palm and pulled her head down to his. The first taste of her inflamed him, jolting through his body like a zap from an electrical wire.

She stilled briefly, then groaned into his mouth and returned his kiss with an eagerness that staggered him. Hunter used one hand to shove the pillows separating them aside, then yanked her close, molding her cotton-nightgown-clad body tightly against him. Every curve, every luscious inch of her was molded to him; he felt her heat searing his skin, and he wanted more. He wanted *all*.

"Take this off," he murmured, moving his mouth a scant inch from hers.

"Yes, take it off. I want to feel you," she whispered,

her small, soft hands moving, constantly moving over his chest, his back, through his hair, scoring his scalp with her short, neat nails.

Every touch was fire. A blessing. A benediction. A compulsion. He wanted her skin beneath his hands. He wanted to trace every delectable curve with his fingertips, his mouth, his lips. He wanted everything she had to give, and then he wanted it again.

He raised himself up on one elbow, undid the buttons on that blasted gown—the very one that had been tempting him nightly—and then slowly, lingeringly, pulled the nightgown up and over her head. Her incredible hair fluffed out around her head as she lay back on the pillows, and he could think only about burying his face in the mass of curls, inhaling her scent, taking the tenderness she offered so openly.

Hunter had never felt anything like this. Such a wild, frenetic mixture of passion and gentleness. A driving need to bury himself inside her heat blended with the frenzied urge to watch her as she came. To push her higher and higher, to see desire flash and burn in her eyes, to hear her cry his name and feel her splinter in his grasp.

"You've been making me crazy for days," he muttered, dipping his head to take first one rosy nipple into his mouth and then the other.

"I have?" she whispered, then, "Ohh…"

"That nightgown of yours. Covering up what I knew was under there." He shook his head against her body, trailing his tongue around the edges of her nipple before nibbling gently at its peaked tip. "Ugliest, most seductive thing I've ever seen."

"I didn't know," she admitted, then arched up, pushing her breast into his mouth, silently asking, demanding more.

He gave it to her, sucking until she whimpered, while his hand swept down her lush body, sliding across jasmine-scented, soft, smooth skin, to the juncture of her thighs. He found her wet and hot for him and groaned himself as he cupped her, rubbing his hand over her center, loving how she lifted her hips into his touch.

"Hunter…"

Her breathy sigh filled the room and shuddered inside him. Hunter wanted her more than he'd ever wanted anything in his life. He'd never known such need, such all-consuming desire. And he wanted more.

Reaching quickly to the bedside table, he pulled the drawer open, rummaged one-handed inside it and came out with a condom. Quickly, he tore it open, tossed the foil wrapper and sheathed his aching body. Then he looked down at her, losing himself in her eyes. Moonlight played on her skin, making her flesh seem to shimmer in the pale wash of silver.

"Never get rid of that nightgown," he ordered, already imagining watching her wear it, knowing what was beneath it, being able to pull it off her, like unwrapping a much wanted present.

"Right. Never."

He grinned and slid closer, moving his mouth down now, across her rib cage, down to her abdomen to flick his tongue at her belly button. And still his hand worked her core. Fingers stroking, thumb pressing against the heart of her while she quivered and trembled for him like a finely played musical instrument.

He was the master, but she was the treasure. He touched her; she responded.

Her hands smoothed over his shoulders, her fingernails drawing light lines of sensation across his skin until he felt as if each one of her fingertips was a lit match head, singeing him down to the bone.

She carefully maneuvered around the bandage low on his hip and whispered, "I don't want to hurt you."

"You won't," he assured her, pausing for one kiss, then another. "I'm fine."

"Are you sure?"

The concern in her eyes touched him even more deeply than the flash of desire he read there as well.

"Let me show you," he murmured, and before she could speak, he had shifted position so that he kneeled before her, lifted her hips from the bed and covered her wet, slippery heat with his mouth.

He looked at her then, her green eyes wide with passion and dazzled with pleasure as she rocked into him, instinctively reaching for the release he didn't plan on giving her just yet. He took her to the edge again and again, working her flesh, driving her higher and higher. Her whimpered pleas became groans, and those became demands and still he wouldn't let her find satisfaction. He kept her on a razor's edge, even though he tortured himself as well.

His body hard, aching and unable to wait another minute, Hunter laid her down, covered her body with his and pushed himself deep into her heat. She was tight and hot and—gasping in shock.

"I don't believe it," he managed to say on a groan.

A long moment passed as he held himself still inside

her. He looked down into her eyes and saw pain melt into pleasure and forced himself to ask, "You're a *virgin?*"

She grabbed at him, her hands exploring his body so thoroughly he quivered under her touch. "Not anymore," she said.

"You should have told me." He was poised on the brink. So close to exploding that beads of sweat broke out on his forehead as he used every ounce of his self-control.

"Sex now, talk later," she told him firmly, then lifted her hips, taking him in deeper, farther, so that he had no choice but to lay final claim to her body. "I had no idea," she whispered, squirming beneath him. "This feels…amazing."

"It's about to get better," he said, damning himself. No way was he going to stop. Not when she so clearly wanted this as badly as he did. Besides, the damage was done. No going back now. But damned if he'd have her first time be so bloody quick. Easing back, he touched her center, where their bodies joined, and she jerked beneath him in surprise.

"That's it," he told her, watching as her eyes blurred, her mouth worked and her breath huffed in and out of straining lungs. Her hips moved beneath him and Hunter had to call on all of his discipline just to maintain. But he wanted her to explode first. He wanted to see it, to know that he'd touched her as deeply as she'd touched him.

He touched her, rubbed that one, most sensitive spot, with excruciatingly tender strokes, and when she at last surrendered to the power of her own climax, he took his hand away, gave a few hard, fast thrusts and erupted into a climax so powerful it left him shaking like a broken man.

When he collapsed atop her, he felt her arms come around him, cradling him to her. And wrapped in her tenderness, filled with her scent, Hunter dropped into a dreamless sleep.

"You should have told me," he accused when the first slice of sunlight slanted into the room.

Margie slowly opened her eyes, stretched languorously and looked up at the man hovering over her. "What?"

"About being a virgin," he ground out. "You should have told me.

Barely awake, her body still thrumming with the pleasures he'd shown her, Margie smiled. "Would you have made love to me if I had?"

He scowled at her. *"No."*

"Well, then," she told him, reaching to slide one hand across his broad, muscled chest, "I'm glad I didn't."

Of course she hadn't told him she was a virgin. It wasn't exactly something a twenty-nine-year-old woman would be eager to share. Especially since the reason she'd held on to it for so long was that she'd wanted to be in love when she had sex for the first time. Now *there* was something Hunter Cabot would have zero interest in knowing.

But it was enough for now that she knew. Margie was in love, despite the fact that there could be no happy ending in this for her. Her mind knew that she shouldn't fall, but her heart had taken the leap anyway. And there was no going back now. The deed was done. In more ways than one, she thought with an inner smile.

She could still feel Hunter's hands on her body, the smooth slide of his flesh joining hers. The taste of his mouth, the hard rush of his breath as he raced to join her in completion. It had all been so much more than she'd ever hoped. And well worth waiting for.

"Damn it, Margie." He caught her hand in his, holding it still. "Isn't this situation already complicated enough?"

She pulled her hand from his, pushed herself up onto her elbows and gave a quick glance down at her own body. She was still naked. Never had put her nightgown—that wonderful thing—back on. She felt slightly wicked, lying naked in bed beside a man who oozed sexuality from every pore. And that wicked thought produced a few others, tumbling through her mind with unrestrained glee. *Wow,* she thought, *unchain a virgin and then step back.*

But if she wanted more of what he'd shown her in the darkness last night, it was clear by the look on his face that she was going to have to do some convincing. With her newly discovered feminine power roaring to life inside her though, she told herself *no problem.*

"It doesn't have to be complicated, Hunter," she said, arching her back slightly, elevating her breasts with their hard, pink tips, closer to him.

His gaze darkened and his jaw clenched. Good signs.

"What're you—"

"We're *married,* Hunter," she reminded him, reaching out now to stroke her fingertips along his tight jaw until she felt that muscle relax under her caress.

Married. To the man of her dreams. The man who

would soon be leaving her, she reminded herself. Instantly, she shut down that particular train of thought. She didn't want to think about him leaving. She wanted to enjoy what she had now.

If there was one thing a foster kid learned early on, it was to live in the present. If you had a nice family, enjoy it while it lasted. If you had a present, treasure it. If you got an ice cream cone on a hot summer day, relish it. Because only God knew when—or if—something good might happen again.

"I'm your wife. You're my husband. Why shouldn't we…" She ran her hand down his neck, along his shoulder and down to one flat, male nipple. When she smoothed her fingertips across it, she was surprised—and pleased—to see him flinch at the sensation.

He trapped her hand under his, holding her palm to his chest, and Margie could have sworn she felt heat searing her skin from the contact. She loved touching him. Loved the feel of his hard, warm body under her hands. Loved knowing that she could push this incredibly strong man to the breaking point.

"It's asking for trouble, that's why," he told her, his gaze locked with hers, as if he could scare her off by looking especially intimidating.

It didn't work.

She lifted his hand, placed it on her breast and held it there. "It's not trouble I want, Hunter. It's you."

Margie watched him fight an inner battle and knew she'd won when his fingers moved on her breast, tugging at her nipple, rubbing the tip in quick strokes.

Shaking his head, he muttered thickly, "I want you, too. So God help us both."

He took her nipple into his mouth then and suckled her hard, deep, drawing on her breast as if his life depended on it. Margie sighed, arched into his mouth and bit down on her bottom lip as his mouth worked her tender skin feverishly. Her body trembled and quaked in eager response. She cupped one hand behind his head to hold him in place, loving the feel of his mouth on her. Loving what he could do to her with a kiss, a sigh, a touch.

Loving *him*.

Yes, she thought again, lowering her gaze to watch him suckle her, that was one thing she couldn't mention. And wouldn't. She loved him. This brash, arrogant, amazing man had stolen into her heart, and Margie knew she'd never get him out again. Knew she didn't want to.

Hunter wasn't interested in love, Margie told herself, even as his body and mouth took her back to that lush place of pure sensation. She knew he still didn't really trust her and was anxious for this month and their "marriage" to be over. A man like Hunter Cabot would never love a woman like her—their worlds were far too different for any kind of bridge to span them.

So Margie decided to do all she could to make the most of what time she had with him. She wanted all of the memories she could build in the next few weeks. She wanted to be able to remember with perfect clarity how it felt to have Hunter Cabot's hands and mouth on her.

She wanted the feel of his skin on hers imprinted on her mind so that it would never fade.

Reaching down, she curled her fingers around his

hard, thick body and felt a wash of heat fill her as he inhaled sharply. Sliding her fingers up and down his shaft, she felt the power inside him and wanted it inside *her*. How had she ever lived without knowing the feel of him. How would she ever live without him?

No.

She pushed that thought aside and reminded herself that now was the only important time. She squeezed gently, deliberately, and he hissed in another breath through gritted teeth.

"Now. Need you now," he murmured and pushed her over onto her stomach. His hands swept up and down her back, over her behind, cupping, kneading, and with every touch, Margie quivered like a too-taut bowstring about to snap.

Wicked, she thought wildly, turning her head on the pillow, feeling him slide his long, hard body over hers. Every caress fed the fires inside; every stroke of his fingers made her want more.

Then he lifted her hips, kneeled behind her and used his fingertips to open her for him. Her heat welcomed that first touch, and she whimpered his name as she closed her fists around the cool, silk sheets beneath her.

He pushed himself into Margie so deeply, so completely, that she gasped and shook with reaction. In this position, she felt so much more, felt him invade her higher and more fully than before. She pushed back against him as he rocked forward, and with every thrust, she felt him stake his claim on her more thoroughly.

Again and again, he pushed himself into her only to retreat and thrust harder the next time. She heard his breathing labor, felt his tension climb to the heights hers had reached, and still she wanted more of him. As he thrust into her, he leaned over her, braced himself on one hand and used the other to rub her center as his lips and tongue moved down her spine.

"Oh…my…"

When Margie's body shattered, dissolving into tremor after tremor of sensation, she cried out his name and was only dimly aware of him reaching his own release, while emptying himself into her depths.

Finally, Hunter rolled to one side of her, drew her in close and Margie snuggled into him, content in the circle of his arms. His breath dusted her hair, and she sighed, absolutely happy for the first time in her life.

"Better than Bali?" he asked.

Surprised, she tipped her head back to look up at him. "You heard about that?"

He grinned and her heart turned over. "Are you kidding? It's the first thing my friends ribbed me about."

"Oh, God. How embarrassing." She dropped one hand over her eyes, then peeked up at him from between her fingers. "At least I told everyone how good you were."

"Yeah." He chuckled. "Thanks for that. So, let's hear it. Was this better than Bali?"

He was teasing her. There was a light of humor in his eyes she'd never seen before, and Margie played along, enjoying this moment almost as much as she'd enjoyed the previous ones.

"Well," she said, "I'm not sure. After all, a man on his honeymoon goes all out. Now that you're just an old married man…"

He pulled her over to lie on top of him, then smoothed her hair back from his face with his hands. "You should know better than to challenge a Cabot."

An hour later, Margie was thoroughly convinced that Hunter Cabot was every bit as good in real life as he'd been on her fantasy honeymoon.

The next couple of weeks flew by.

Hunter slipped into a routine he hadn't seen coming and didn't really mind. He was used to being active and now that his wound was mostly healed, he saw no reason to change that.

Every morning before dawn, he tore himself from Margie's arms, left her sleeping in the bed that hadn't seen a pillow wall since that first incredible night together and went for a run.

The roads were familiar. He'd run them as a high school athlete, he'd run them to prepare for boot camp and he'd run them on those infrequent trips home since joining the Navy. He knew every field he passed, every house with lamplight just beginning to glow through the windows, every turn and curve in the road. It was all as familiar to him as his own face in the mirror.

In the silence, Hunter's mind was filled with thoughts he was normally able to dismiss or at least shove aside. But on narrow country roads, where his only company was the occasional bird sweeping across a brilliantly colored sky, there was too much time to think and no way to escape it.

He'd missed it here. For so long, he'd thought of Springville and the Cabot dynasty as a trap; he'd refused to allow himself to see the beauty of the place.

The near blissful *quiet*. He'd immersed himself in the adventure, the risk, the duty of a job he believed in, and had avoided all thoughts about the place that would always be home to him.

Now, though, this place was calling to him so deeply that the call to adventure was muffled inside him.

And time was almost up.

Soon, he'd be returning to base. Back to the job that had been his life for more years than he cared to think about. Since he was recovered, he would be assigned to missions with his team again, and as that thought registered, he waited for the rush of adrenaline-tinged expectation he always felt.

But it didn't come.

Frowning, he kept running, the sounds of his footsteps like a disembodied heartbeat thundering out around him.

It was Margie, he told himself. He'd allowed himself to be drawn into an affair he'd known from the first would be nothing but a mistake. And yet he couldn't really regret it, even now. Even knowing that he'd be leaving, a divorce would be filed and he would, most likely, never see her again.

His scowl deepened and his pace quickened. His breath charged in and out of his lungs, and sweat rolled down his bare back. Where would she go? What would she do? And how would he ever know if she was all right?

"Of course she'll be all right," he muttered, disgusted with himself. "She'll have five million reasons to be all right."

There. Reminding himself that she was doing this for the money made him feel less like a bastard for using her. Because, really, who was using whom?

He didn't even hear the car come up behind him until it paced him. Hunter didn't stop, just smiled at the man rolling down his window to talk to him. "Morning, Sheriff."

"Can take the man out of the Navy, huh?" Kane Hackett said with a grin. "Figured I'd find you out here running. You always did like this road for training."

Hunter kept going, sparing his old friend a derisive glance. "And it figures that you're driving the road, not running it. Out of shape, are we?"

One dark eyebrow winged up. "Not so's you'd notice."

"Then why are you here?"

"Have to go see Simon," Kane said, his smile fading into a worried frown. "Figured it'd be best if you were with me when I did."

That got Hunter's attention. He stopped running, bent in half and took a few deep breaths before asking, "What's going on?"

"There was a fire at the Cabot building in town last night," Kane said.

"Fire?" Hunter grabbed the edge of the car window. "Anyone hurt?"

"No." Kane shook his head. "The night cleaning crew went in; apparently one of 'em turned on a stove in the break room to make some tea. Left a towel too close to the burner."

"Damn it."

"That about covers it." Kane waved him over to the passenger side door. "There's damage to the first two floors, though, and I thought, well, Simon had the heart attack last year—"

Hunter was already moving. He climbed into the black-and-white SUV, buckled his seat belt and told his friend to drive.

"Well, how bad is it?" Simon wanted to know an hour later. The old man wore a faded blue robe, and his white hair was standing out around his head like cotton swabs on end.

"Kane took me by to see it for myself before he brought me back here to tell you," Hunter said, remembering that Kane had left right after delivering the news, leaving it up to Hunter and Margie to watch out for Simon's blood pressure.

Now as Margie poured Simon's coffee, Hunter watched his grandfather warily for any sign the old man was going to clutch his chest and drop like a rock.

"*And*…?" Not dropping. Instead, the old man wanted answers, not coddling.

Hunter gave him a wry grin. Apparently, Simon was a lot tougher than any of them knew. "And, it's a mess. The fire chief says no structural damage, but there's plenty of smoke and water damage to make up for it. Most of the files are on the upper floors, so that's good. We didn't lose much."

One corner of Simon's mouth tilted upward. "No," he said slowly, "I guess *we* didn't."

"Simon…" Hunter sighed. "That's not what I meant."

"Freudian slip, huh?" Simon looked pretty pleased for a man who'd just been told his company headquarters had nearly burned down.

Hunter hadn't meant "we" the way Simon had taken it. After all, the company wasn't his baby. He was a SEAL. But touring through the damaged building with Kane at his side, Hunter had actually caught himself thinking about the reconstruction. And what changes might be made. After all, if they were going to have to do some remodeling, there was no reason they couldn't do some updating as well.

Such as, for instance, making the break room larger. The area was so small now that it would comfortably hold only two or three people. The day care center Margie had instituted also had been ruined, since the room set aside for it was on the ground floor. Now that they were redoing it, he thought they should make it more kid friendly than the old room had been.

And the workers' cubicles that were now twisted and melted should simply be tossed. Why lock people away into separate little stalls? It's not as if cubicles gave people the sense of having their own little offices. All they really did was separate them from their coworkers, and what was the point in that?

"Hunter?" Simon prodded, "What're you thinking?"

What *was* he thinking? Scraping one hand across the top of his head, Hunter muttered, "Nothing. No thanks, Margie. No coffee." He put out one hand to stop the cup she held out to him. "All I want now is a shower."

Then he left the room fast before his own thoughts could start marching in time with Simon's.

"Well, well, well. Did you hear him?" Simon chuckled and took a sip of coffee that was mostly 2 percent milk.

"He doesn't want to stay, Simon," Margie told him.

"Nothing you can say will change his mind. You know that."

The old man's white eyebrows lifted high on his forehead and wiggled around like two worms on hooks. "It's not what *I* can say that'll keep him here, Margie, honey—it's you. I've seen the way he looks at you. And don't think I haven't noticed that you're looking *back*."

"Simon, don't play Cupid," she warned, not wanting the man she loved like a grandfather to be as heart-broken as she was going to be when this all ended.

He only chuckled again. "You'll see…"

She sighed, took a sip of her own coffee and slumped back into the chair closest to Simon's. Margie had seen the *hunted* expression in Hunter's eyes before he left the room and knew that he was already regretting getting as involved as he had in the fire investigation. He didn't want the life that was waiting for him here in Springville.

He didn't want her.

Not beyond the tumbled hours they spent together in his bed, anyway. There at least, she knew he wanted her. Felt it in his every touch, his kiss. In the way he held her during the night and the way he turned to her when nightmares plagued him. But she also knew that at the end of the month, he would leave and let her walk out of his life.

Just acknowledging that sent a spear of pain darting through her heart, and Margie didn't know how she would survive when that pain was her constant companion.

# Eight

Hunter didn't mind helping out, he told himself a few days later. After all, he was here, wasn't he? And there was just so damn much to do. There was the construction at the company headquarters to look after, and there was Simon's birthday party. Since Margie couldn't really be expected to do it all, and since he didn't have a clue about how to arrange a blowout party, Hunter had taken over the work on the building in town.

He met with the contractor, talked to the employees to get their ideas and helped to draw up plans for the remodeling. Now, sitting in Simon's study, with blueprints spread out in front of him on the desk, he asked himself how he'd managed to get sucked so far into the life of the town.

His grandfather was upstairs, taking a nap, Margie

was off in the kitchen talking to Simon's cook about the caterer's party menus and Hunter was sitting behind the very desk he'd spent most of his life avoiding.

"So, how'd you get here?" he muttered and poured himself a glass of scotch.

"We turned left into that freeway out front you call a driveway," a familiar voice said, answering the rhetorical question Hunter had posed.

"As long as you're pourin', brudda," another voice told him, "get two more glasses out."

Only one man Hunter knew used island slang in every conversation just to make sure people knew he was a proud, full-blooded Hawaiian. Hunter was grinning as he stood up to face two members of his SEAL team. Jack Thorne, "JT," his team leader, and Danny "Hula" Akiona were standing in the open doorway of the study.

"Where'd you guys come from?" Hunter asked as he came around the desk, hand out to welcome his friends.

JT was tall and blond with sharp blue eyes that never missed anything. Hula was just as tall, with black hair, black eyes and a smart-ass outlook on life. Damn, Hunter'd missed them both.

"We were on our way up to Frisco for a little R and R," Hula was saying. "Thought we'd stop and see how you were healing up. Didn't know we'd find you sitting in a mansion."

Hunter winced. Exactly why he'd never told his friends about his background.

Hula sniffed the air, then slid his gaze to where the decanter of scotch sat on the edge of the desk. "Hmm. Thirty years old. Single malt."

Hunter laughed. "How the hell do you do that?"

"It's a gift." Hula shrugged, looked around the immense study, then shifted a look back at his friend. "So how come you never told us you were stinkin' rich?"

JT frowned at him. "Nice. Real subtle."

"I don't do subtle," Hula told him and shifted a pointed look at Hunter. "Takes too long, life's too short. Gotta wonder why a friend keeps a secret like this, though."

Hunter blew out a breath. "So I wouldn't have to listen to you saying things like 'stinkin' rich.'"

"No offense, you know?" Hula glanced around the big room again, then slid his gaze back to Hunter. "Just surprising finding out one of our own is a gazillionaire."

"Shut up, Hula," JT said and walked into the study, his gaze also darting around the room, taking it all in.

"Have a seat," Hunter said, glad to see his friends despite the fact that they now knew his secret. He retrieved the scotch, got two more glasses and then sat down across from two of the men he routinely trusted with his life. They were looking around as if they couldn't believe what they were seeing, and he couldn't really blame them.

In all the time they'd been together, Hunter had never once mentioned that his family was rich. He hadn't wanted them or the others on the team to treat him differently. All he'd wanted was to be one of them. To be accepted for who he was, not what his family had. Now, though, he had to wince. Had to look to his friends as if he'd been lying to them for years.

Because he had been.

JT braced his elbows on his knees, stared at him and asked, "So why'd you never say anything?"

"Yeah, brudda," Hula said, his dark eyes flashing. "Seems you like to keep secrets, huh? What's wrong? Afraid I'll borrow money after one of our poker nights?"

Hunter sprawled in the chair, balanced his glass of scotch atop his flat abdomen and shot first one man, then the other, a hard look. "This is why I never said anything. You're both looking at me like I'm a rich sonofabitch."

"It's only the rich part that's new," Hula told him with a wink. "Seriously, man, why'd you hide it? If I had a great place like this, I'd be telling everybody."

"Yeah," JT said with a shake of his head. "We know. But then, you tell everybody you meet every minute of your life story."

"Well, I'm a fascinating man," Hula said with a smile before he took a sip of scotch. "Like the time I tangled with a tiger shark off the coast of Maui…"

"We already heard it," Hunter and JT said together.

Then the three of them grinned at one another like loons. And just like that, things were back on an even keel. The secret of his family's money was out, and his friends had put it aside already. Made Hunter wonder what the hell he'd been worried about for so long.

"I actually missed you guys," Hunter told them.

"Good to know," JT said, easing back into the leather chair. "When we didn't hear from you, I started thinking maybe you were reconsidering coming back to the team."

"I told him that was cracked," Hula said after a long,

appreciative sip of scotch. "No way Hunter doesn't come back, I said. Hell, Hunt *lives* for the buzz, man."

The buzz. What they called the adrenaline-laced rush they got just before a mission. What they all felt when they were given orders to complete and dropped behind enemy lines. What they celebrated when they were all back home safe.

The buzz had a hold on Hunter, and he couldn't deny it, but lately he'd been asking himself if the buzz was enough to live on. And how much longer could he do this job to the degree of perfection he expected of himself? He wasn't getting any younger, and already two or three of the guys he'd entered SEAL training with had retired or taken on stateside training jobs.

JT was rolling his glass of scotch between his palms and watching him quietly.

"What?"

"Nothing," his boss said. "You just seem…different, I guess."

"I'm not," Hunter assured him and wondered silently if he was trying to convince JT or himself. Because the truth was, everything had changed. In town. Simon. Margie. But had he? No, he told himself firmly, squashing the very idea. "Nothing's changed."

"Hunter?"

All three men whipped their heads around to face Margie when she entered the room. And then all three quickly stood up.

She was surprised and had stopped just inside the room. She wore a pale yellow, short-sleeved blouse over her favorite jeans and brown sandals on her small, narrow feet. Her hair was windblown into a tangled mass of curls that made a man want to run his fingers through them, and her green eyes were wide in embarrassment. "I'm sorry. I didn't know you had company."

"It's okay," Hunter said, glancing from her to the friends, who were looking at her with clearly admiring gazes. A flicker of irritation came to life inside him as he saw Hula give her a smile that had won him countless women over the years.

Hunter felt a stab of territorialism that surprised the hell out of him. But damned if Hula was going to make a move on his wife, right in front of him.

He didn't stop to ask himself if this was another secret he should keep. Why introduce her as his wife when he knew damn well there was a divorce hovering on the horizon? Because he didn't want Hula looking at Margie like a hungry man eyes a steak. Because she looked wide eyed and uncertain what to do and Hunter didn't want her to feel uncomfortable. Because, damn it, for right now anyway, she was *his*.

"Come on in, Margie. I want you to meet these guys." When she was close enough, Hunter draped one arm around her shoulders. "Jack Thorne, Danny Akiona, this is my wife, Margie."

JT grinned, clearly stunned. "Nice to meet you."

Hula coughed. "Your *wife?*" Shooting a look at Hunter, he said, "Man, what happened to Gretch—"

JT shoved him and said, "Sorry, Hula. I make you spill your scotch?"

Hula wiped the liquor off his black T-shirt and glared at his team leader. "No problem."

Margie looked confused, then smiled at both men.

"It's nice to meet Hunter's friends. Can I get you anything? Food? Coffee?"

"No, ma'am," JT said quickly. "Thank you, though. We just stopped for a quick visit. Then we're heading into the city."

"You sure you're his wife?" Hula asked, stepping away from JT before there could be another "accident."

Margie grinned. "I'm sure."

"That's too bad," he said with a slow shake of his head.

"Well." Margie backed up a step or two, turned for the door and said, "I'll let you visit. It was nice to meet you both."

Hunter watched her walk away, and despite his best intentions, his gaze dropped to the sway of her hips in those worn denim jeans she preferred. It didn't help any to finally look at his friends and see that Hula had been enjoying the same view. Irritation clawed at him.

"What the hell were you thinking bringing up Gretchen?" Hunter whispered when Margie was gone.

"Hey, man," Hula said in his own defense, "I was surprised is all. I mean, last time I heard, you were dating this Swedish goddess—now you're married to somebody else."

Hunter shot a look at the empty doorway and wondered if Margie had caught Hula's slip or if JT had managed to shut him up in time. And why the hell did he care if she knew about Gretchen? He and the model weren't together anymore. Besides, it wasn't like he and Margie were *really* married. He didn't owe her an explanation. So why, then, did he feel like a cheating husband who'd been caught in the act?

"So nothing's changed, huh?" JT asked.

"That's right," Hunter told him, knowing he didn't sound convincing. Hell, how could he?

"You know," Hula mused, "I like this one a hell of a lot better than Gr—" He stopped, covered his glass with the top of his hand to prevent spillage and stepped back from JT. "That other one, she was cold, man. Sort of empty. This one…" He smiled and nodded. "She's a different story."

Yeah, she was, Hunter thought, rubbing the back of his neck as he tried to ignore the rattle and clang of thoughts and notions running through his mind. Despite wanting to keep an emotional distance between him and Margie, she had gotten to him. She'd sneaked beneath his defenses and had managed to make him question the way he lived his life. Forced him to look at his decisions. His—

JT just looked at him for a long moment or two. Then thoughtfully, he said, "You know, you wouldn't be the first of us to choose to stay with his wife rather than risk his life every other day."

True. He'd seen plenty of other guys fall in love, get married and leave the military. But their situations were different. They were in love with their wives. He was deeply in lust. But he couldn't admit to more than that. If he did, too much in his life would be affected.

"I told you, boss," Hunter said tightly. "Not gonna happen. I'll be back. My…marriage won't stop me."

"Don't get me wrong, Hunt. I'm glad you're coming back, and we all know the buzz is good, man," Hula said quietly. "But you have a woman who loves you? That's a buzz, too."

Did she? Love him? He thought about that and wondered. Or, he asked himself, was she just enjoying him as he was enjoying her? Was she trying to make him need her? Was she hoping that he'd make this marriage a real one? And why was he thinking about all of this anyway? He knew what he had to do. What he always did. His duty.

"Not the kind I need," Hunter told him. "So why don't we quit talking about my wife and you guys tell me what's been happening while I've been gone."

They sat down again, and while his friends talked and filled him in on life on base, Hunter's mind drifted. He wasn't sure why. He should have been hanging on the guys' every word about the base and the other teams. Should have been eager to turn his mind back to his job, back to the world he'd sought and built. Instead, his gaze slipped to the doorway through which Margie had disappeared, and his mind filled with thoughts of her. How she looked, the scent of her, the sound of her laughter and even the soft whisper of her sighs.

She was more than he'd expected, more than he'd wanted, and playing this dangerous game of theirs was getting more complicated. Now he was lying to his friends about her, and they'd no doubt have questions when he and Margie got their divorce, too. He never should have agreed to this insanity.

Because there was a part of him that was buying into it. A part of him sliding almost effortlessly into the rhythm of married man. Of *Margie's* man. And that couldn't happen. Because his life wasn't here. No matter what Simon or Margie might want.

He'd be going back to the Navy because that was where he'd always felt he belonged. His friends, his team. The missions. He'd signed on to do a job and he would continue to do it. He'd given his word, and he knew what that entailed. He belonged to the Navy, not this little town.

But for the first time, that call to adventure seemed a little less compelling than it once had. For the first time, a part of Hunter felt that he would be leaving behind something important when he left.

Margie stood outside the open study doors and listened to the three men talk.

There was laughter and the rumble of deep voices, and she hugged herself as she picked Hunter's voice out of the crowd with ease. He sounded happy as he sat and talked about missions and danger and adventure, about the bonds that tied the men together.

This was something she couldn't fight. These men who were closer to Hunter than brothers had a hold on him that was so deep it couldn't be defeated. Even if she were trying to.

She knew that no matter how she wished things were different between them, Hunter would never stay with her. Even if he actually loved her—which he didn't—he still wouldn't stay. He was a SEAL, and she doubted that would ever change.

And just who was Gretchen?

A few days later, Hunter was feeling just as itchy as he had when his team members had visited. He felt as though he should be doing *something,* but he couldn't figure out exactly what. He worked out at the local gym, did his morning runs down country roads and in general tried to get back into shape for his return to duty.

But through all of it, a different kind of duty kept rearing its head, demanding he take notice. Over the last few years, when he'd come home to see Simon, he'd made fast visits, in and out and back to base. But this time, with his medical leave and Simon's precarious health and Margie, the visit had been a longer one. Long enough to remind Hunter that there was a world outside the Navy, that there were other duties every bit as important as the one he owed to his country.

And Hunter was having a hard time reconciling what he wanted to do with what he knew he *should* do.

"Hunter. Good. I was looking for you." Simon walked into the study, and his steps were slow and careful.

Hunter stood up to help, but the older man irritably waved him off. "I'm not helpless yet," he muttered, walking around the edge of the desk to pull out the bottom drawer.

His heart fisting in his chest, Hunter watched his grandfather and tried to tell himself that despite appearances, the old man was as tough as any SEAL recruit. There was steel in that old man's bones, he thought with pride. But even as he thought it, he knew that his grandfather wasn't as strong as he'd once been. That the years had taken a toll that Hunter had never allowed himself to notice before now.

Had he really been so selfishly determined to live his own life on his own terms that he'd avoided noticing how much Simon needed help? Was he really ready to turn his back on his grandfather? After all the elderly man had been to him? What the hell kind of man would that make him? Choose duty to country over duty to family?

Shaking his head, Hunter pushed away the thoughts crowding his mind, because he didn't have any answers. Instead, he concentrated on what his grandfather was doing. In the bottom drawer there were dozens of files, neatly arranged. While Hunter watched, Simon quickly thumbed through them all until he found the one he wanted. Then he set the file onto the desk and flipped it open. "I want you to look these over and sign them before you go."

Hunter lifted one eyebrow. "Getting me another wife?" he asked wryly.

"Wouldn't waste my time," Simon snapped. "You don't have the sense to appreciate the one I already got you."

The hell of it was, Hunter *did* appreciate Margie. Too damn much.

"Simon…"

"I'm not here to talk about Margie, boy. This is something else."

"What?" Wariness crept into his tone. Lamplight speared up from the desk, illuminating Simon's face from beneath, giving the older man an almost eerie look. Shadows crept over his eyes, and every line and crevice on his face was deeply defined.

Simon straightened up, looked his grandson square in the eye and said, "I'm turning over the family business to you."

"Damn it, Simon," Hunter said, lifting both hands as

if to ward the other man off. "Even if I wanted to take over, I've got seven more months on my enlistment. I won't be here."

"You can do most of the work through power of attorney, and I can keep an eye on things until you come back."

Hunter stood up, moved away from the desk and walked to the wide window that overlooked the acre of tidy green lawn and perfect flower beds. A colorful sunset was spreading across the sky and lengthening shadows from the row of trees at the edge of the yard. The road was lying beyond those trees, the road Hunter had taken so long ago when he'd made his bid for freedom. Strange now that the same road had brought him back. And wasn't he turning into a damn philosopher all of a sudden?

"That is," Simon added, "if you plan on coming back."

Hunter threw the older man a look over his shoulder and saw the expectation, the damn hope shining in his eyes even in the dim light of the study. And Hunter knew he couldn't fight it anymore. Knew that the only way he'd ever be able to live with himself was to accept the duty that had been waiting for him since childhood.

He knew too, at some deep-seated level, that this is how it was meant to be all along, what he'd been headed toward all his life, despite his attempt to avoid it. Maybe, he told himself, he'd had to go away to see where he really belonged.

"I'll come back, Simon."

A delighted smile creased his grandfather's face, and for one brief moment Hunter actually did feel like the hero he'd always wanted to be. Then reality crashed down. If he was going to be leaving the SEAL and coming home to stay, there were plans to set in motion, decisions to make. And he had to talk to Margie, he told himself.

The old man clapped his hands together and scrubbed his palms against each other. "I knew you'd do the right thing, boy. Eventually."

A wry smile curved Hunter's mouth. "Thanks. I think." Then he shoved one hand across the top of his head and rubbed the back of his neck. "I still have to go back to the base at the end of the month."

"Understood."

Hunter nodded, turned to face Simon and pulled in a deep breath. Finally, the tension in his chest had loosened. For days now he'd been torn about what to do. Questioning his own loyalties, feeling the tug of home and duty fighting with the call to return to the life he'd built. He'd been engaged in a silent battle within himself, and now that a decision had been made, he could breathe easy.

Yes, it would be hard leaving the Navy, but he was needed here. And, as he felt a slight twinge in his side, he reminded himself that he'd been thinking about the possibility of retirement ever since he'd been shot. So, maybe this was how it was supposed to be.

"What about Margie?"

Hunter focused on his grandfather. "What about her?"

"Well," Simon said, "if you're going to stay, there's no reason for her to go either, is there? You're already married. And I've seen the way you look at her, boy. I'm old, not blind."

He hadn't had time to consider all the options here. He'd just this minute decided to retire, for God's sake. It's not as if he'd thought everything through. But now that he did think about it, he wondered if Simon wasn't right. But, "We agreed to divorce."

"Damn hardheaded—"

Hunter wasn't willing to budge. He'd make up his own mind about Margie—without well-meant interference. "Simon, don't push it. Whatever happens between me and Margie is up to us, not you."

"She makes you happy, Hunter. Or hadn't you noticed that?"

Happy. With a wife he hadn't chosen. With a wife he'd suspected for too long was nothing more than a scam artist out for whatever she could finagle out of a lonely old man.

With a woman who set him on fire with a touch.

But damned if he'd let his grandfather run his personal life, too. "You can't screw with people's lives, Simon. You can't arrange everything the way you want it."

"Don't see why not, when I can see perfectly clear what should happen," Simon muttered.

"Because *you* don't get to decide my life, Grandfather. And you sure as hell don't get to decide Margie's." He loved the elderly man, but damned if he'd fall into line just because Simon demanded it. And if this was a sign of how things were going to be once he came home and took over the family business at last, then they were in for quite a few battles.

So, Hunter decided, it was best to stand his ground right from the get-go. "Back off of this, Grandfather."

"You look me in the eye and tell me you don't care for that girl," Simon challenged.

Well, that was the trouble, Hunter thought, as he deliberately looked away. He didn't know what the hell he was feeling at the moment.

# Nine

After leaving his grandfather, Hunter immediately made the phone call he never would have believed he'd be making. Punching in the numbers from memory, he dialed JT's cell phone and waited in the garden while it rang.

"Thorne," the voice on the other end of the line suddenly snapped.

"Boss, it's Hunt." Hunter stared up at the cloud-swept sky, tipped his face into an ocean breeze and closed his eyes.

"Yeah, I know. What's up?"

What isn't? Hunter took a breath, opened his eyes and stared out at the broad expanse of lawn and garden. This was his home. And though he'd avoided the knowledge for years, this was his *place*.

"I wanted you to know," Hunter said, his voice ringing

with the steel and strength of his conviction in the decision he'd made, "I'll be coming back to base, but when my enlistment's up, I'm going to be leaving the team."

There was a long pause and then a soft laugh. "If you're waiting for me to be surprised, don't bother," JT said at last.

Hunter laughed then, a short, sharp bark of sound. "Well hell, boss. It surprises *me*."

"It shouldn't, Hunt. You've got a life to go back to now. That wife of yours deserves better than a part-time husband."

Margie. She was a part of this decision, no doubt. How big a part was something Hunter hadn't let himself figure out yet.

"Yeah, I guess she does," he said because it was easy and it was a reason JT would understand. "Look, I don't like leaving the team in the lurch, so I wanted you to know so you could start looking into my replacement."

"Nobody's gonna be able to replace you, Hunt," JT told him. "But I appreciate it. We'll talk when your R and R is over, okay?"

Hunter scraped one hand across his face and nodded, though his friend couldn't see the action. "You bet. See you in a few days."

When he hung up, Hunter stood in the swath of sunshine and waited for regret to claim him, waited for the feeling that he'd made a mistake to slam home. But it didn't come. Instead, he felt a sense of peace he hadn't felt in a long time. Then he turned and looked up at the big house behind him. As if he sensed her presence, Hunter's gaze locked on the bedroom window.

"One more conversation to have," he told himself and stalked across the stone patio, determined to finish setting his life on its new course.

Margie was in the bathtub when Hunter went upstairs after getting off the phone. He saw steam wafting from the open bathroom door and heard the splash of water and her soft voice humming a little off-key. Even as his body went stiff and eager, his mind chided him, reminding him just what he'd come to see her about.

Now that he'd made the decision to take on the family responsibility, he and Margie had to talk. Damned if Hunter wanted to admit it, but Simon had a point. If Hunter was going to stay, there was no reason for Margie to go.

Nodding to himself, he stalked across the room, stepped into the bathroom and leaned one shoulder against the doorjamb. With her back to him, she sat in the dark blue, oversize spa-jetted tub, one arm draped across the edge of the tub, jasmine-scented bubbles floating on top of the water, caressing the mounds of her breasts. The tips of pink nipples poked through the water and his body reacted instantly. He had to shift position to ease the discomfort in his jeans—which only told him that continuing this "marriage" was a good idea. They'd already proven they were more than compatible in bed. She loved Simon and this town. Hell. She was happy here. Why wouldn't she want to stay?

Smiling to himself, he tore his gaze from the delectable sight of those twin nipples and said, "Margie?"

"Whoops!" She shrieked, slipped lower under the water and flipped her head around to stare at him, eyes wide. "God, Hunter! Are you trying to kill me?" She slapped one hand to her bubble-covered chest and added, "And if you are, could you *not* do it in the bathroom? Jeez, first in the shower, now in the bath. I really don't want to be found dead *and* naked."

He was smiling. Damn it, he usually ended up smiling around Margie. Hadn't really thought about it before this moment, but Simon was right. She did make him happy. When she wasn't making him crazy in bed. She was fun to talk to. Easy to be around. She'd made him realize there was more in his life to think about than his own ambitions. She wasn't afraid to stand up to him, either, and he liked that. He liked *her.*

Plus, the sight of her naked body turned him into a pillar of fire, burning up from the inside out. All good things.

Hunter watched as she pushed herself higher up against the back of the tub, and his gaze dropped to her breasts, almost completely exposed by the disappearing curtain of bubbles.

His body went even harder than it had been before, and Hunter fought down a groan. Hell, he told himself, get the talking with over—then he'd join her in that soapy water and show her a few things with the tub's jets.

"Is everything all right?" she asked, smoothing a wet washcloth up the length of her arm.

"What? Huh?" He blinked and shook his head. Talk. That's right. He'd come here to talk to her. "Fine. Yeah. Everything's good." Better than fine, really, now that he'd made the toughest decision of his life. "I just left Simon and—"

"Speaking of Simon, his birthday party is going to be fabulous. I got this local band to play—they special-ize in big-band music from the forties. I think Simon and his friends will love it."

"I'm sure they will," he said, smiling as she went on about the party. This was the right move to make, he told himself. The two of them were good together. She loved his grandfather. She was already a part of this town.

And while his mind was racing, he thought about Gretchen briefly and wondered why in the hell he'd ever even broached the subject of marriage to her. She would never have fit in here, never have wanted to. Springville was too small, too ordinary, too off-the-beaten-track. Gretchen would have hated this place, while Margie clearly thrived in it.

Yeah. He was doing the right thing.

"And the caterer is going to work with Simon's cook, so everything will be perfect," she said.

"Good."

"Are you okay?" she asked, and the washcloth slowed a bit as she asked the question.

"I am."

He walked into the bathroom, sat down on the edge of the tub and stared down at her. The scent of jasmine was so thick in the air that he drew it into his lungs with every breath, as if she were surrounding him. Her skin was rosy-pink from the hot water, and her lush, dark red curls were wet at the ends. Her lips were full and parted as though she were inviting a kiss, and he was too damn tempted to lean in and give her just what she wanted. But first he had to tell her about the decision he'd made.

Silently, he congratulated himself on finding the perfect solution for all of them and wondered why it had taken so long for him to consider it. Stubborn, like Simon said, he guessed. Didn't matter, though. He saw things clearly now, and he was sure Margie would agree. Why wouldn't she? It was a win-win for both of them.

"Who's Gretchen?" she asked.

"What?" That question threw everything else out of his head.

"I heard you and your friends talking about her when they were here," she said with a shrug that dissipated a few more strategically placed bubbles. "One of them mentioned you and Gretchen."

"Yeah." *Thanks, Hula.* "She's an old girlfriend."

"Ah," she said, dipping the washcloth into the water, then sliding it up her other arm slowly. "And she's a goddess?"

Hunter scowled and watched as the wet cloth slid along her wet skin. Yes, Gretchen was beautiful, but he'd never fantasized about being her washcloth. Besides, he hadn't come up here to talk about Gretchen. "Hula's got a big mouth."

Margie gave him a sad smile. "Which answers my question."

Frowning, he asked, "Why'd you wait until now to ask about her?"

"Maybe because I didn't want to know."

"So why'd you ask at all—" He stopped. "Never mind. This is female logic, right?"

"I was just curious, that's all," she said.

"Fine, but I don't want to talk about my ex or any of your exes, either."

"I don't have any," she told him, sliding her body down into the water until her knees poked through the water's surface and her nipples made tiny pink islands. "Exes, I mean. You'll be my first."

"What?" He stared at her and shook his head, not sure whether to believe that or not. Yes, she'd been a virgin, but she'd had no ex-boyfriends at all? "How is that possible? Do you only meet blind men?"

Margie laughed shortly. "I think that's a compliment, so thanks."

"Of course it's a compliment." Hadn't he complimented her before this? Apparently not. He should have. Hell, she'd stepped up and taken care of Simon when he wasn't around. She'd been there for this town, for his grandfather, for *him*, he thought, remembering the night she'd held him and eased him through a nightmare. The same night they'd had sex for the first time. He'd been so intent on shutting her out, he hadn't told her how much he appreciated everything she did.

But he'd make up for it. He could compliment her plenty over the coming years. He'd make a mental note to do just that. He stood up, not really trusting himself to stay so close to a wet, naked Margie without reaching out a hand to touch, to stroke, to…

"Look, Margie," he said, scraping one hand across his face as if he could wipe away the erotic images filling his mind, "I thought we should talk about the divorce."

"Oh." Her eyes looked suddenly cooler, more distant, as if she were deliberately closing herself off to him. Self-preservation? Probably.

Well, Hunter figured he had the answer to their problems.

"The month's almost up," he said as he walked back to the edge of the tub to look down at her.

"I know."

"Yeah, but you don't know things have changed."

Her gaze lifted to his. "What do you mean?"

"I mean," he said, "that I've decided to leave the Navy when my enlistment's up. I'm coming back home. To stay." Wasn't as hard to say it this time, he thought, and considered that a good sign.

She stilled, then slowly a small smile curved her mouth. "That's wonderful, Hunter. I'm sure Simon's happy."

"Yeah, he is. But I want to talk to you about us."

"I don't understand," she said, using her arms to sweep the remaining bubbles over her, covering her skin in a gleaming, nearly see-through cape.

"I know." He sat down again on the edge of the tub and wished she didn't look so uneasy. "But you will in a minute. I did a little thinking, and I realized there was an easy solution to our situation."

"Yes," she said, huffing out a breath that made the bubbles shudder. "The divorce."

"No," he told her. "The marriage."

She tipped her head up to meet his gaze. "What are you saying?"

"It's simple, really," he said and smiled at her. "I'm staying, so I think you should, too."

"What? Why?" She straightened a little in the water, and the bubbles slid down her skin.

"I'm suggesting that we stay married instead of getting divorced," he told her and waited for her smile.

It didn't come.

"You can't be serious."

"Okay," he admitted, wondering why she wasn't seeing the brilliance of this plan, "not the answer I was expecting."

"Well, you're not making sense," she said, and her voice sounded breathless. "Why would you want to stay married to me? You'll be here, so you won't need me to watch over Simon. You can do it yourself."

"This isn't about Simon," Hunter told her, then corrected himself, "well, it is partly, I suppose. But the main thing is, you love it here, right?"

"Yes…"

"You love Simon."

"Yes, but—"

Hunter was warming to his theme now and gave her a smile designed to convince her to agree. "We've already proven we get along fine. And the sex is good. So why shouldn't we stay married?"

"This is crazy," Margie said softly and stood up in the tub.

Faced with his naked wife, Hunter had a hard time keeping his mind on the subject at hand, but he managed. "What's crazy about it? Hell, I thought you'd be pleased."

She laughed and looked at him as if he were certifiably insane. Stepping out of the tub, she moved past him, grabbed a navy-blue towel off the closest rack and wrapped it around herself. "Oh yeah. Why wouldn't I be pleased?"

"Exactly." He stood up too and glowered at her. Damn it, he'd come up with the perfect solution. Couldn't she see that?

"Hunter," she said, taking a deep breath and holding it, "you've told me over and over that you don't want a wife."

"I changed my mind."

"Oh!" Margie threw both hands up. "Well, that's different, then. You changed your mind."

"What're you pissed about?" He sounded incredulous, as if he didn't understand why she wasn't jumping up and down for joy at his businesslike offer. Couldn't the damn woman see that this was good for both of them? "I thought you'd be happy to stay."

Barefoot, soaking wet and suddenly furious, Margie fisted her hands at her hips. "Why would I be happy to stay with a man who doesn't want me?"

"I just told you I *do* want you."

"Sure, in bed."

"Well, I'm a guy. Why wouldn't I want you in bed?"

"Marriage isn't about sex, Hunter." Shaking her head in disbelief, she turned away from him and started walking. She marched across the bedroom directly into the oversize closet. "My God, don't you get it?"

"Clearly not," he said from right behind her.

She whipped around fast to glare at him. "If I stayed married to you like this, I wouldn't be your wife—I'd be your legal mistress."

"What the hell—"

"You don't love me. I'm just convenient."

Why talk about love now? She'd married him by proxy, and he hadn't even *known* about it. She'd been willing to be *paid* to be his wife. Now she wanted love? What kind of sense did that make?

"Well, yeah, since you are my wife, that makes you pretty damn convenient," he argued. "What's wrong with that?"

"Is it all men?" Margie wondered aloud, shaking her head in exasperation. "Or is it just you?"

"Look, I didn't come up here to fight."

"No, you came to tell me how lucky I was to have been *allowed* to stay in this house and join you in bed." She blew out a breath, fluttered her eyelashes and said, "I'm *such* a lucky woman."

Hunter was lost. First, he was a bastard because he hadn't wanted her. Now, he's the bad guy because he *did?* None of this made sense to him. Why was she making this so hard?

"You know," he said as his features darkened like a thunder cloud, "I—"

"Oh, *and,* I'm even luckier that the great Hunter Cabot is willing to accept plain old Margie Donohue. She's no goddess, but he's willing to put up with his disappointment in that area because she's good with dogs and old people and—"

"Are you insane?" He looked at her as though she were, which only made Margie more furious.

"I should have known this was coming," she muttered to herself as she grabbed the closest pair of jeans and tugged them on. "You're an idiot, Margie. Just an idiot."

"For God's sake, you're taking this all the wrong way," he said tightly.

Inside the closet, Margie fumbled with her bra. "Some fantasy you turned out to be," she mumbled, then shouted, "you are *not* the man I married."

"You *are* crazy!" His shout was louder than hers. "And I never asked to be anyone's fantasy. Just like I never claimed to be a damn hero!" He threw the closet door open and glared at her. "Why bother hiding to dress? Not like I haven't seen you naked often enough."

"And that gives you the right to see me whenever you want to? I don't think so." Margie yanked a dark green T-shirt over her head and yelped when her long, wet hair got caught briefly. "I can't believe you want to keep me around for sex."

Her chest hurt, her eyes stung, but she would *not* cry. For heaven's sake, the first man she'd ever slept with wanted her as a mistress? What did that say about her? His "offer" ran through her mind again. *Stay married. Sex is good.* God, she felt so stupid, so…furious. She'd done this to herself, too. Set herself up for misery. She might as well have walked into his open arms and begged, *Please, Hunter. Break my heart.* And he'd done it.

Worse, he didn't even realize it.

"How could you think I'd agree to that?" she shouted.

"It's not like I asked you to service the fleet," he snarled. "I just thought that we could keep our arrangement going."

"For how long?" she snapped. "Will there be a contract? Severance pay? Oh, will you set up a 401k for me?"

"Margie—"

"And what happens when you 'change your mind' again? Do I get thirty days to find a new place to live, or do I just get tossed out?"

"I'm not going to change my mind again. If you'll just calm down…" His patient tone made her want to kick him.

All of her little dreams and fantasies were popping, just like the bubbles in her bath. They disappeared with hardly a sound, but Margie felt each one go like a crash of thunder. She'd allowed this to happen. She'd built him up in her mind over the last year, and in the last few weeks she'd done even more. She'd fallen in love with a man who didn't exist. The Hunter she wanted, the Hunter she loved would never have made such a suggestion.

So, that let her know exactly what he thought of her. Which only meant that once again, Margie hadn't been good enough.

He stepped up close, cupped her face in his palms and said quietly, "At least think about it, Margie. If you do, you'll see I'm right. You love this place. You love Simon—"

"And I love *you,* Hunter." The minute she said the words, she wanted to call them back. But it was far too late for that.

Instead of dropping his hands and leaping away from her, though, which is totally what she'd expected, Hunter only grinned, and the damn dimple in his cheek taunted her.

"But that makes it even better," he said, sounding like a kid who'd just found exactly what he'd wanted under the Christmas tree. "You love me, so you should want to stay married to me."

She pulled his hands down from her face, and her skin felt cold without his touch. But she'd better get used to that chilly sensation, she told herself, because she could never stay with him now.

"I can't stay with you, Hunter," she said, looking directly into his eyes so he would understand.

"But you love me."

"Which is exactly why I want a divorce."

# Ten

The ballroom in the Cabot mansion was beginning to look like a party extravaganza. Decorations were already starting to go up, from banners to colorful ribbons draped along the edges of the ceiling to the linen-draped tables staggered around the room. Tomorrow, there would be multicolored balloons and fresh flowers from the Cabot gardens decorating the tables. The caterers would be in place in the kitchen, and the musicians would be tuning up in the far corner.

Everything was perfect.

So why did Margie feel like crying?

Could it be because of the gaping hole in her chest, where her heart used to be?

Three days since Hunter had made his half-assed proposal and she'd confessed to being in love. Three long days and even longer nights. Right after their little chat, she'd moved her things to a guest room because, frankly, Margie was beyond caring what the household staff thought of the marriage that would soon be ending.

And better she start getting used to sleeping alone than torturing herself by snuggling up beside Hunter every night. But God, she missed him. Missed his touch, his kiss, the way he turned to her in his sleep and wrapped his strong arms around her. How was she supposed to live the rest of her life without him?

Oh, she never should have started this in the first place. If she hadn't agreed to Simon's plan a year ago, she wouldn't be in this fix. By tomorrow night, she'd be leaving. She still didn't know where she'd go. It didn't matter to her, either. Because wherever she ended up, she'd be alone. Again. With no one to love.

"What am I supposed to do now?" she whispered to the empty room.

"Well," a voice said from directly behind her, "you could stop being a damn fool."

"Simon!" Margie whirled around, embarrassed to be caught not only talking to herself but also throwing quite the self-pity party. "I didn't know you were there."

"Not surprising. You've been walking through the house like a ghost these last few days."

What could she say to that? He was absolutely right.

Simon's gaze was kind, but determined. Strange, she'd never noticed just how much he and his grandson had in common.

"Stay, Margie. Stop this foolishness and stay."

"I can't," she said, shaking her head as she looked into Simon's eyes. "I can't stay knowing he doesn't love me."

"Who says he doesn't?"

Margie laughed ruefully. "*He* does."

Simon frowned and brushed that information aside. "He wouldn't be the first man who needed a woman to tell him what he was feeling."

"If only it were that easy."

He shook his head, sending his wispy white hair flying. "You're every bit as stubborn as he is."

"I have to be," she told him. "I can't settle for half a life." Then she gave him a hug. As his arms came around her, she whispered, "I'm really going to miss you."

He patted her back and offered, "I'll beat him up for you if you want."

Margie smiled through her tears. "Thanks, Simon."

As she pulled away, he said, "Still doesn't seem like much of a birthday present for me. You leaving, I mean."

"I wish I could stay. I really do." She let her gaze slide around the room and out to the hall, as if looking all over the mansion she'd come to think of as home. It would be so hard to leave this place. But what choice did she have?

She couldn't stay, loving Hunter and knowing he didn't feel the same. That would be like a slow death. No. Better to go. To move on. Find a new place and try to forget what she'd had so briefly, here.

"It's a shame you don't love him enough to fight for him," Simon mused.

Surprised, Margie only said, "I do love him enough. But Simon, you can't fight a battle you can't win."

"Ah," he said solemnly, "sometimes those are the only battles worth fighting."

An hour later, there was a knock at the door, and when Margie opened it, a tall, elegantly dressed, absolutely breathtaking woman swept inside.

"Isn't this lovely." The blonde's cool blue eyes swept the interior of the mansion as if she were taking an inventory. Then she glanced at Margie, giving her a quick, dismissive glance as if finding her less than interesting.

Margie's spine stiffened a little in response. For the moment, this was her house and this blonde was the intruder, gorgeous though she might be.

"Can I help you?"

"Yes." The blonde looked down from her towering height and gave a smile that barely creased her lean cheeks. "You can tell Hunter that Gretchen is here to see him."

"Gretchen?" Margie could have sworn she felt a cold, hard piece of ice settle in the pit of her stomach. *This* was Hunter's ex-girlfriend? Oh dear God. No wonder his friend Hula had called her a goddess and had been so surprised to find out that Margie was Hunter's wife. In comparison with this—okay, *goddess* really was the only appropriately descriptive word—Margie felt like Cinderella. *Before* the big night with her fairy godmother.

"Yes. Is Hunter here?" The blonde walked farther down the hall, peeked into the living room, then turned back. "I was going to call him, but then I thought what fun it would be to surprise him."

"You have," Hunter said from the staircase.

Margie looked over her shoulder at him and tried to read his expression. His features were tight, his eyes shuttered and his jawline grim. Well, at least he didn't look delighted to see the fabulous Gretchen.

"Hunter, honey!" The tall blond actually squealed as she raced to his side on incredibly long legs.

Margie stood open-mouthed and watched as Gretchen flung herself at Hunter's chest. He caught her automatically, and for one brief moment the two of them were locked together. Margie's stomach lurched again. *This* was the kind of woman Hunter belonged with, she told herself. No wonder he wasn't interested in a ten-pound-overweight, curly-haired redhead with freckles in all the wrong places.

Hunter's gaze locked with hers over Gretchen's shoulder, and he looked frustrated. He tried to mouth something at her, but then the blonde pulled back, looked up at him and said, "I came to tell you I've decided I *will* marry you, after all!"

Margie's jaw dropped and her eyes narrowed as the rest of her world dissolved out from under her.

"Damn it." Hunter saw the look in Margie's eyes as he pried Gretchen's long fingers off his shoulders and set her onto her feet. His ex was babbling, but he wasn't listening. Instead, he was focused on the short redhead glaring at him. There was fury and pain mingling in Margie's green eyes, and Hunter wished Gretchen to the other side of the planet.

"Margie, I can explain," he said, and did some mental sprints trying to figure out just *what* he could say. And in the next instant, he reminded himself that she hadn't listened to him for the last few days, so why would she start now?

"Oh, there's nothing *to* explain, Hunter," she said from her position by the front door. "Really. Everything's very clear."

"Hunter, who is this person?" Gretchen's voice had a spike in it as if she were less than amused.

"Don't you worry about me," Margie told her with a way-too-sweet smile. "I'm just his wife."

"His *wife?*" she cried, with a gaping look at Margie. "Seriously?"

Hunter almost clapped one hand over Gretchen's mouth, but it wouldn't have helped anyway. Instead, he glared at her. "How the hell did you find me?"

"Well, you told me the name of your little town. Wasn't hard to find the only Cabots here."

"Right." So this was his own damn fault. He looked past the blonde. "Margie—"

"Hunter," Margie said as the toe of her tennis shoe tapped noisily against the floor, "don't you want to invite your fiancée in for a drink?"

"No," he shouted and tried to get past Gretchen, but the blonde latched onto his upper arm with strong fingers and deadly nails. "And she's not my fiancée."

"Yes, I am," Gretchen argued. "That's what I came here to tell you. And then I find you're already married."

"I never asked you to marry me," Hunter countered with a triumphant look at Margie.

"You said you were thinking about getting married

and asked me what I thought about the idea," she reminded him.

"How very romantic," Margie mused.

"It was an abstract idea," Hunter shouted.

"Is there a problem?" the housekeeper asked as she came running down the long hallway.

"Yes, Sophie," Margie told her, "would you bring Hunter and his fiancée some tea in the front parlor?"

"His what?" Sophie's big eyes slitted and focused on the tall blonde.

"She's not my fiancée," Hunter argued.

"Yes, I am," Gretchen said.

"Oh, how nice. Must be true love," Margie said and clasped both hands under her chin. "Isn't that special?"

"Damn it, Margie, you know this is all a mistake."

"Mistake?" Gretchen echoed, giving him a glare that could have fried bacon.

"Yes, a mistake. I can't be engaged, I'm already married," Hunter said and felt like he was talking to an empty room. Not one of the three women glaring at him was listening to him. They were all talking to one another and around him, but it was as if he weren't there.

"Not for long," Margie told him flatly.

"There," Gretchen said, looking very pleased, "problem solved."

When he gave Gretchen an impatient look, she blinked at him and worked up a pout. He'd seen her do it before and knew she could manage to squeeze out a theatrical tear or two if she had to, just as easily. And he really didn't have time for Gretchen's drama.

"Hunter, make that woman go away so we can talk."

"She's not going anywhere, and we have nothing to talk about," he ground out.

"But surely you want to make some wedding plans," Margie taunted and folded her arms across her chest. "After all, the divorce will be final soon—no sense wasting time."

"Divorce?" Gretchen smiled again.

"There's not going to be a divorce," Hunter said.

"Don't count on it," Margie muttered, then turned to Sophie. "Would you mind helping me out in the ballroom? I want to do another check on the party things."

"Yes, ma'am," Sophie said and gave Hunter a hard glare he hadn't seen since he was thirteen years old.

Could this day go to hell any faster?

"Margie, wait." Damn it. She'd hardly spoken to him in the last few days, and now with Gretchen showing up out of the blue things just got even more difficult. But Margie left, without so much as a glance over her shoulder, and he was faced with a tall blonde from his past giving him a cool, calculating stare.

"Just what is going on here, Hunter?" Gretchen smoothed her hair unnecessarily, then tapped the tip of her index finger against her chin. "I don't appreciate being made to look like a fool."

"I didn't invite you here, Gretchen," he reminded her, flicking a glance down the hall where Margie had gone.

She ignored that remark. "Strange that you never mentioned the fact that you were already married when we were together."

"It's a long story." And he wouldn't come out sounding too good in it, either. After all, he had been legally married while he was dating Gretchen. The fact that he hadn't known about the marriage would really be a hard sell.

But he knew it for a fact, so why did he feel like a cheating husband caught sneaking out of a motel?

"I'm sure," Gretchen said tightly. "Oddly enough, I'm not interested enough to hear it. I don't date married men, Hunter."

"Good for you," he said, easing her down the stairs with a tight grip on her elbow. "Then you should be going, right?"

He just wanted her the hell out of the house so he could talk to Margie. Make her understand. Make her see that he didn't want Gretchen. He wanted *her*.

Gretchen wouldn't be hurried, though. She glanced around the great hall, noting the stained glass, the polished wood and the obvious signs of a great deal of money. "But if you're in the process of a divorce, that changes things considerably. You know I'm happy to wait for you."

"No," he snapped, meeting her gaze with a hard look. "Don't bother waiting, Gretchen. I told you, there's not going to be a divorce." At least, not if he could find a way around it.

"Well then, it seems I've made a mistake," she said, her voice dropping to a low purr as she dragged the tips of her fingers down his chest. "Unless, of course, I can change your mind…."

Though Gretchen was planning a seduction, all Hunter felt was irritation. "You should go, Gretchen. Sorry you wasted the trip."

Instantly, she straightened up, dropped the sultry, heavy-lidded gaze and snapped, "Fine. Go to your fat little redhead. May you be cursed with a dozen fat babies who look just like her."

Babies? Instantly, an image of Margie carrying his child filled his mind, and Hunter realized he *wanted* that reality. He wanted Margie in his life more completely than he'd ever wanted anything. And he wanted kids. With her. Damned if he'd let her walk away from what they could have together.

Gretchen, meanwhile, huffed out a breath and swept out of the house as majestically as only a six-foot-tall, skinny model with delusions of grandeur could muster. Hunter shut the door behind her and took a long, deep breath. She never had taken rejection well.

How in the hell could he even briefly have considered a life with her? The drama. The pouting. The grasping nature. The viciousness. Margie wasn't fat. She was curvy, deliciously curvy. And kind. And good-hearted. And she loved him.

So why the hell didn't she want to stay married to him?

# Eleven

The party was everything Margie had hoped it would be. As her big farewell to the town of Springville and Simon, it was perfect. The fact that the smile she'd plastered on her face was almost painful to maintain was no one else's business.

Dance music soared through the air, and candles in glass bowls flickered on every table. Clusters of spring flowers made for bright splashes of color, and their scents mingled with the delicious aromas coming from the kitchen as the catering crew ran up and down the long hallway to the ballroom.

Balloons festooned every corner of the massive room, and there was a cheerful fire in the hearth at the far end of the room to combat the cool, nighttime breeze drifting in through the open French doors. The floors gleamed under the light thrown from the chandeliers, and in the backyard, fairy lights were strung in the trees ringing the garden. Everything was fabulous, and Simon's guests were all clearly having a good time.

"Yay me," Margie whispered as she rubbed her hands up and down her arms against the tiny chill snaking along her skin. But it didn't help, because this cold went bone-deep. This was the cold she was far too familiar with.

The cold of alone. The cold of unwanted. Unchosen. Not really even a word, she told herself, but it was so true. No one in her whole damn life had ever chosen her. She'd never been first. She'd never been important enough to matter.

And God, she'd so wanted to matter to Hunter.

Against her will, her gaze scanned the crowd for one man in particular. He wasn't hard to find. Wearing his dress whites uniform, Hunter Cabot looked impossibly handsome. Simply watching him made her heartbeat quicken and curls of heat spiral in the pit of her stomach. He was standing with his grandfather in a circle of friends, and Margie felt like the outsider she'd always been.

She had no place here. Not anymore. She shouldn't have even stayed for the party, but she'd felt that she owed it to Simon. Now, she wished she were anywhere but here.

"This is great, Margie," someone said from nearby, and she turned to foist her phony smile on Terry Gates. Terry was yet another friend she'd made here in Springville. Another person she'd miss. Another link lost in her own personal chain.

"Thanks, Terry," she managed to say past the hard lump in her throat. "I'm so glad you could come."

"Are you kidding? Wouldn't have missed it." Terry's green eyes danced as she leaned in. "The whole town's here."

"Seems like," she mused, her gaze once again going unerringly toward the man who was and *wasn't* her husband.

"Hmm…" Terry gave her a little nudge. "Why are you standing here alone when you should be dancing with that gorgeous man of yours?"

Because to dance with him to this music would mean being in Hunter's arms, and how could Margie ever force herself to leave that warm circle once she'd willingly gone into it? Better to keep her distance. Better to save whatever pride she had left and remember what Hunter had looked like with Gretchen. They'd actually made a gorgeous couple.

Blast it.

But Terry was watching her, waiting for an answer. "Oh, too busy to dance. Have to keep track of the caterers and—"

"Not a chance," Terry said with a laugh and grabbed hold of Margie's elbow. "You arranged it all, did all the work, and now you're going to take a minute to dance with your husband."

"No, really, I um—" Margie tried to pull away, but she couldn't get any traction out of the needle-thin high heels she was wearing with the strapless black dress Hunter had picked out for her what seemed like a lifetime ago. "I really need to—"

"Dance," Terry told her firmly and kept walking, threading their way through the crowd.

"Oh, for—" Margie stopped trying to argue, stopped

trying to fight her way free of her friend's good intentions. The more she struggled, the more attention she garnered from the watching crowd, and she was determined that no one here would know that her heart was breaking—or that her marriage was over as of tonight.

"Atta girl," Terry said, sensing the difference in her friend's attitude. Then she smiled and shrugged. "Look, I shouldn't say anything, but I know."

"Know?" Margie asked as they slowed down to get through a knot of people.

"About your argument with Hunter," Terry said with a shrug.

Oh, God. How could she know? Who would have said anything? Not Simon or Sophie. Surely not Hunter.

"He told me," Terry was saying. "Hunter said you were mad at him because he was going back to base before he was completely healed."

"Oh." Confused, Margie shifted her gaze from Terry to Hunter, who was watching their approach with a half smile on his face. "He told you that, did he?"

"Yeah, and between us, I so agree. But I feel bad for him that you're not speaking to him, so that's why I agreed to go and get you to dance with him."

"*Hunter* put you up to this?"

"Who else, silly?"

Who else indeed, Margie thought as she came to a stop right in front of the very man she'd been ignoring for days. The very man who held every corner of her heart. The man she'd never forget and would miss every day of her life.

His blue eyes locked with her green ones and he gave her a small, intimate smile that just barely nudged his dimple into existence. Without looking at the other woman, he said quietly, "Thanks, Terry."

"No problem," the brunette said, then turned her head to look out over the crowd. "Now, think I'll go find my own husband and force him to dance with me."

Hunter stepped up close to Margie and her heart did a quick, hard *thump*. His eyes were so deep, so clear and so intent on her that she couldn't have looked away if her life had depended on it.

"Dance with me, Margie," he said and held out one hand to her.

The people around them were watching—she could feel it. To one side of Hunter, Simon stood looking like a benevolent elf with his flyaway white hair and smiling blue eyes. Could she really turn away? Did she want to make everyone talk about them, wonder what was wrong between them? Wouldn't it be easier if no one knew a thing until she'd gone?

Besides all that, could she really pass up the chance to be held by him one last time?

Finally nodding, Margie slipped her hand into Hunter's, and instant warmth slid through her bloodstream, temporarily easing the cold inside her. He led her onto the dance floor just as the band ended one song and started another.

Margie recognized the tune, since Simon was a huge Frank Sinatra fan. And though the band's singer was no Ol' Blue Eyes, the melody and words of the song about a summer wind wrapped themselves around her and Hunter and drew them into the magic of the moment.

"You look beautiful tonight," he said, his voice a low rush of sensuality that seemed to slide right inside Margie.

"Thanks." She looked up into his eyes, felt her heart break a little and then shifted her gaze to one side. She couldn't look into his blue eyes. Couldn't read the regrets and goodbyes written there.

"You've been avoiding me," he said and moved her into a slow turn that made the lights at the edges of her vision swim.

"Yes." God, would this dance never end? Margie tried to pull back from Hunter's embrace, to put a little space between them, but he wouldn't allow that. Instead, he pulled her closer, held her more tightly, pressed her body into the length of his until she felt his heartbeat pounding in tandem with her own.

"I don't want you to go, Margie. Don't leave."

"Don't do this," she whispered brokenly. "Don't make it harder."

"It should be hard. You said you loved me."

She looked up at him, and it seemed as though every light in the room was reflected in his gaze. Those blue depths sparkled and shone down at her, and it took all of her courage to not look away. "I do," she said, forcing the words out. "I do love you, and that's why I won't stay."

His arm tightened around her even further until it felt as though she could hardly draw a breath. "I wasn't engaged to Gretchen."

Margie closed her eyes briefly, gathered up her strength and made herself ask, "Did you propose to her?"

The music pumped around them, other dancers drifted past and Hunter looked only at her. "In a way I guess I did," he said. "But—"

"No. You *wanted* Gretchen," she said as the song

slowly wound its way to the end. "You never wanted me. I wasn't your choice for a wife. She was."

"But she's not my wife. You are."

She shook her head. "It doesn't matter, Hunter. Don't you get it? It just doesn't matter."

The music ended, but Hunter wouldn't let her go. He stood there, on the dance floor, his arms still holding her tight, his gaze locked with hers, refusing to say goodbye. To let her walk away. From him.

"Of course it matters," he said, his voice low and dark, filled with a banked anger that nibbled at the edges of his self-control. Hell, he'd given her days to get past this hang-up of hers. Days to think about his offer. To reconsider. To stay the hell married to him. And this is what it was going to come down to? A quick goodbye on a dance floor, surrounded by too many damn people?

He didn't think so.

As if she could read his mind, she whispered, "Please don't do this, Hunter. Don't make it harder."

"It damn well *should* be hard," he told her, his voice low and hot with a temper crouched inside him.

She was bound and determined to walk away from him, and Hunter simply wasn't going to let that happen. Never once in his SEAL career had he given up on reaching his objective. He'd had guns misfire, plans go askew, ambushes fail, but he'd *always* won the day. Damned if he was going to ruin his record now.

His chest felt tight and his insides snapped to attention. Releasing her briefly, he then took her upper arm in a firm grip and turned her toward the French doors and the gardens beyond.

"Okay, that's it. You're coming with me."

"Oh no, I'm not," Margie countered and pulled free of his hold. Then she took two long steps in the opposite direction, obviously headed for the foyer.

"Like hell," Hunter muttered and caught up to her in a flat second. Spinning her around to face him, he held on to her shoulders, met her now furious, embarrassed gaze and said, "You're going to listen to me, Margie, even if I have to tie you to a chair."

From somewhere to his right, he absentmindedly heard his grandfather's chuckle. Well, Hunter was glad somebody was enjoying this.

*"Hunter…"* Her gaze shot from side to side, then up to him, as if to point out to him that they weren't exactly alone.

Hunter couldn't have cared less. Glaring at her, he said, "You think I give a good damn who's watching?"

"Well, I do."

"I don't. I've got some things to say to you, and I'm going to say 'em. Here or somewhere else. Your choice."

Margie glanced around again and apparently noticed the eager attention on the faces surrounding them. She finally looked up at him and said, "Fine. We can talk in the study."

"Nope, too far away," he told her and bent down. Tucking his shoulder into her abdomen, he straightened up with her head and shoulders now hanging down over his back.

*"What are you doing?"* she shrieked it, pushing herself up from his back and trying to shove herself free.

"What I should have done three days ago," Hunter

told her and threw one arm across her legs, pinning her to him.

"Simon!" Margie yelled as Hunter headed for the French doors, "help me!"

"Not a chance, honey," the old man shouted on a laugh.

The whole room was laughing, Hunter realized as the crowd parted before him and let him pass through the ballroom and into the gardens. And he didn't care. Didn't care what they thought, what they had to say or the fact that they'd be talking about this night for the next twenty years.

Nothing mattered but the stubborn redhead in his arms. And no way was he going to lose her.

Jaw tight, body rigid, he marched across the patio, muttering, "Excuse me," to those he passed.

"Let me down!" Margie shouted, then in a much lower voice adding, "You're showing the whole world my behind, you know!"

Hunter grinned, gave that sweet rear end of hers a friendly smack and told her, "It's a great behind. You've got nothing to be ashamed of."

"For heaven's sake, Hunter, put me down!"

"Soon." He kept walking. Hell, he knew these paths better than Calvin. This was home, and he felt as though the fairy lights in the trees and the garden itself were welcoming him back.

"Where are we going?" she demanded.

"To the fountain." It was the most secluded spot on the grounds. Surrounded by trees and flowering bushes, the old fountain was so far back, so near the edge of the cliff overlooking the ocean that almost no one went out there anymore. Much of the cliff's edge had been eroded over the years, so it wasn't the safest place on the estate. Therefore, Hunter told himself, none of the guests would be wandering out there.

He and Margie could be alone, and for what he wanted to say, he needed them to be alone.

When he set her onto her feet, she staggered a little, tossed her hair back out of her face and took a wild swing at him. He caught her fist in one hand, then bent and kissed her knuckles.

"Don't do that." She pulled her hand free and looked around wildly.

Hunter did too, just to check the area. There was no one there, and the only sound besides the wind in the trees was the soft hush of the ocean below and the cheerful splash of the fountain.

"Margie, Gretchen doesn't mean a thing to me," he started.

She blew out a breath, shook her head and said, "If you think that makes me feel better, you're wrong."

"I'm not finished," he snapped, watching as moonlight shimmered in her eyes. "There's something I need to say to you, and you're going to listen."

"There's nothing you can say, Hunter." Her voice broke, and something inside him twisted in response. She looked so lost, so lovely there in the moonlight. The ocean breeze twisted itself in her curls, and her eyes were wide, glimmering with the reflection of the moonlight. "Nothing's going to change my mind. I'm leaving."

He looked at her fiercely brave expression and felt an explosion of knowledge open up inside him. Couldn't figure out why he hadn't seen it before, because right now the truth was so crystal clear it was as if he'd been born knowing it. He didn't just want her. Didn't just need her. It was so much more than that.

"I love you," he said and smiled at the wonder of saying those words and meaning them with everything he had.

She gasped and looked up at him. Then she shook her head. "No, no, you don't. You only want me to stay because I'm already your wife. I'm easy."

Hunter laughed shortly, loudly. "Margie, you are many things, but you haven't been *easy* since the day we met."

She frowned at him.

"And I love you."

"Stop saying that."

"No," he told her, coming closer. "I like saying it. I like *feeling* it."

"No," she argued, her voice hardly more than a murmur, "you don't."

"Yeah, I do. And I'm going to say it until you believe me. I'll say it every damn day for the rest of our lives and find a way to say it after I'm dead, if that's what it takes to convince you."

"Hunter…" She bit down on her bottom lip, brushed a single tear from her cheek and turned away from him to stare out at the ocean and the moonlight striping its surface like a pathway to heaven.

"Why is that so hard to believe?"

She huffed out a breath, wrapped her arms around herself and whispered, "Because no one's ever loved me."

Her pain whipped through him with a hell of a lot

more force than that bullet had. He felt her broken heart and wanted to kick his own ass for ever bringing her to tears. "What do you mean?"

She shook her head, and her hair moved with the wind sighing past them. "I didn't grow up like you did, Hunter. I grew up in a series of foster homes that were never really mine."

Moving softly, quietly, Hunter laid his hands on her shoulders and stroked his palms down her arms. "I'm sorry for that, Margie. I am. But you have to believe, I do love you."

She sniffed, breathed fast and shook her head. "You have to stop saying it, Hunter. Please. Stop."

He turned her in his arms, never taking his hands from her, needing to feel her, needing her to feel his touch. To somehow understand just what she was to him.

"Margie, why can't you believe me? Why can't you see that I want you to be with me? Forever."

Crying now, in big gulping sobs, she turned her gaze up to his and said, "Because no one ever has. Never once, Hunter. In my whole life I've never been chosen. I've never been important to somebody. Until I came here. And Simon loved me. And I loved this place and convinced myself that I loved *you*."

He took a harsh breath and held it, wanting to hear her out, wanting her to get it all said so they could start again. Start fresh.

"But Hunter, you didn't *choose* me to be your wife." She sniffed again and waved one hand at the mansion behind them. "You picked a Swedish goddess. You didn't want me. You just got stuck with *me*. And now you're trying to do the right thing. But you're only making it harder—can't you see that?"

Shaken to his soul, Hunter wondered how he'd ever gotten lucky enough to have this woman tossed into his life. What had he done that had merited this warm, loving, gentle heart? And how could he keep her?

"You're wrong," he said and smiled in spite of the fresh bout of tears his words started. "I'm choosing you now, Margie. I know you. I love you. And I'm choosing you."

She still didn't believe him, and her tears were falling fast and furiously. Cupping her face in his palms, Hunter tipped her face up to his. Then he bent, kissed her cheeks and tasted the salt of her tears.

"Listen to me, *babe*," he said, using that word deliberately to make her roll her eyes and smile.

It worked, though that fragile curve of her lips was tremulous.

"You said no one ever wanted you to stay, Margie. Well, I do. I *need* you to stay here with me."

"Oh, God…" She shook her head as if she were tempted to believe but still too afraid of losing everything to take the chance.

Hunter looked deeply into her eyes, willing her to see all that he was feeling. "Margie, I've been in combat. I've been in situations so dark and terrifying I never thought I'd survive. I've faced gunfire, bombs and explosions with more ease than I can face the thought of living a life without you."

She blew out a breath that ruffled the curls on her forehead. Then her mouth worked as she tried to stem the tears that continued to rain down her face. "Hunter…"

"I've got seven more months in the Navy, Margie. Then I'm coming home. To a place that *you* made me see I belonged. I'm coming home to you, Margie. And if you're not here, it won't be *home.*"

"Hunter, you're not being fair," she murmured, shaking her head again and taking a shuddering breath. "I was going to leave and let you have your life back."

He laughed because he finally sensed that he was convincing her, and, God, he felt better than he had in years.

"My life? What kind of life would it be without you ordering me around? Without you organizing everything? Without you to hold in the night? Without you to wake up to? If you leave me, Margie," he added, and waited until she was looking into his eyes, so she could read just how serious he really was. "If you leave me, I'll follow you. I'll turn into some weirdo stalker, and then Simon'll be alone and the town will fall apart because you're not here to be the heart of it…." He paused and smiled gently. "Do you really want to be responsible for all of that?"

She sniffed again and smiled a little. "Well, if you put it like that…"

He gathered her in close, folding his arms around her, resting his chin on top of her head, and when she wrapped her arms around his middle, Hunter took his first easy breath in days. "You're right where you belong, Margie. With me."

"Oh, God," she said, leaning back and brushing at the front of his uniform, "I'm getting mascara all over your whites!"

Hunter laughed, delighted. "You can cry on me anytime you want to," he said, "but I swear, I'll try to make sure none of your tears are because of me."

"I do love you," she said.

"I love you, Margie." Then to make sure she heard his next words, he held her face in his hands again and looked directly into her eyes. "*You* are the most important thing in my life. I choose *you* to love forever. I choose *you* to make me complete and to make a family with. Please choose me back."

"Oh God, I'm gonna cry again," she said with a half laugh.

"Well, then, let's make sure it's worth it," he said, giving her a fast, hard kiss. "Here's something else for you to organize."

"What?"

"When I come home, you and I are going to have a real wedding. Right here in town," he told her, bending down to lift her into the curve of his arms.

"We are?" Margie grinned up at him and wrapped her arms around his neck.

"We damn sure are," he told her with a wink. "And *then,* we're going to Bali. I think we can improve on that 'honeymoon' we already had, don't you?"

"I don't know," Margie teased, "in my fantasies, you were pretty good…"

"Babe," he said, grinning down at her with a wink, "I'm a SEAL. I love a challenge."

Laughing, her heart lighter than it had ever been, Margie laid her cheek against her own personal hero's shoulder and let him carry her back into the light.

Back to the house where love waited.

* * * * *

# MARRYING
# THE MANHATTAN
# MILLIONAIRE

## BY
## JACKIE BRAUN

**Jackie Braun** is a three-time RITA® finalist, three-time National Readers Choice Award finalist, and past winner of the Rising Star Award. She worked as a copy-editor and editorial writer for a daily newspaper before quitting her day job in 2004 to write fiction full-time. She lives in Michigan with her family. She loves to hear from readers and can be reached through her website at www.jackiebraun.com.

For my nieces and nephews:
Jason, Michelle, Steve, Stacey, Joanne, Jackie, Abby,
Amy, Mary, Renee, Alex, Yui, Stephanie, Eric, Nicole,
Allison, Meredith, Garrett, Roman, Payton, Sammy,
Connor, Ben, Natalie, Todd and Elizabeth.
Remarkable young people, all.

# CHAPTER ONE

"AND the winner is…"

During the infinitesimal pause before the presenter read the Addy Award recipient's name, Samantha Bradford was sure her heart stopped beating.

*This is it,* she thought. *This is my moment.*

"Michael Lewis of the Grafton Surry Agency."

*Or not.*

Sam straightened in her seat, pasted a smile on her face and joined in the applause. As her palms slapped together with stinging force, her gaze narrowed on the man who was striding across the stage of the Atlanta Herriman Hotel's grand ballroom, buttoning the jacket of his superbly tailored suit as he went. She knew him well. He was admittedly handsome, sexy, smart, insightful and charismatic. He also sang off-key in the shower, preferred boxers to briefs, enjoyed watching old war movies, had the annoying habit of leaving the seat up and possessed an untouched trust fund whose worth was on par with the gross national product of some small countries.

Yes, she knew him *that* well.

Seven years earlier Samantha had been in love with him and blissfully counting down the days until she became his wife. They'd found advertising jobs in Los Angeles, put down a deposit on a town house and made all manner of grand plans for their new life together. Those plans never materialized. The reason no longer mattered as far as she was concerned, though at the time Michael had accused her of choosing her family over him. Sam saw things differently. Everything could have worked out if only the man had been capable of compromise.

They'd gone their separate ways, bitterness burning any bridge that might have remained. She'd been fine with that. Really. She'd patched up her heart, put her life back in order. Michael had moved to Los Angeles without her. Sam had stayed in Manhattan, but she too had moved on.

Then fifteen months ago he'd returned to the city and the advertising scene where she was now at the top of her game. Ever since then, all of the memories, both good and bad, that Sam had safely stored away kept threatening to tumble out. She found that damned irritating. She found the man to be even more so. Michael had taken a job with one of the city's largest ad agencies and a key rival to the one where Sam worked, which was owned by her father. She and Michael had been in competition ever since, angling for each other's clients and going head-to-head for the industry's highest accolades.

Such as the Addy.

The hands that a moment ago had engaged in polite applause balled into fists in her lap. What made tonight's loss all the more galling was the fact that just the previous month Michael had snatched up the honors she'd been nominated for in the print campaign category of the Clio Awards.

For anyone keeping score, and she knew damned well Michael was, tonight made it two and zip in his favor.

Sure enough, when he reached the podium and took the trophy in his hands, his gaze seemed to search the audience. She swore he was looking straight at her when he brought the Addy to his lips and gave it a lingering kiss. Afterward, he offered a sexy grin that had half the women in the room issuing a sigh and the other half wanting to. Sam's stomach did a familiar little flip and roll, but she reminded herself that she'd long ago conquered the weakness that would have had her falling into either category.

"Some people might say it's an honor just to be nominated for this award," Michael began. "But I'll let you in on a little secret. I really wanted to *win* this one. And victory is all the sweeter for having been chosen from a group of such talented people."

He winked in her direction.

*Why you arrogant son of a...*

She let the thought go unfinished. Instead, she instructed herself to take a deep breath and hold it before releasing it slowly between her teeth. She knew from past experience that the relaxation technique worked, so she tuned out the rest of Michael's short acceptance speech and continued, feeling some of her tension ebb away.

*Look forward, not back.*

That was her motto. The awards would be over soon. The American Advertising Federation's annual conference had wrapped up that afternoon. Tomorrow she would return to New York, and though it was a Sunday, she would be back at work. Nothing new in that. Sam spent a lot of weekends at the office. But while staying at the Atlanta Herriman she'd heard talk that the luxury chain of hotels might be looking for a new firm to handle its national campaigns. She intended for the Bradford Agency to be first in line should the rumor turn out to be true.

Thundering applause pulled her from her thoughts. Michael was leaving the stage. He held the trophy aloft in one hand as he made a fist of the other and pumped it in the air. It took an effort not to let her lip curl. She hadn't thought it possible for him to look cockier than he had on his way to receive the award. It just went to show that the man's potential in that area was limitless.

Three tables over, the people from Grafton Surry were on their feet, giving their golden boy a standing ovation. No doubt they would be toasting him with champagne late into the night. Perhaps one of the pretty, young account executives sitting at his table would offer to celebrate with him in private. Who knew? Who cared? Not Sam. Nope. She planned to go to bed early, rise before the sun and be at her desk in New York by noon. By the time Michael roused from sleep with what she hoped would be one very major hangover, she would have worked up a strategy for landing that big account.

Michael paid tribute to his win with a glass of the hotel's finest bourbon as he sat by himself in the upscale lounge that overlooked the lobby's impressive fountain. The trophy was in the center of the table, sharing space with a bowl of mixed nuts. He was pleased to have won it, especially since his success had come at Samantha's expense. Again. But victory didn't taste as sweet as he'd hoped it would. Something was missing. *Again.*

Several of his colleagues had gone to a nightclub outside the Herriman. They'd urged Michael to come along since he was the one they wanted to honor with raised glasses. He'd declined, claiming fatigue, even though he was 180 degrees the opposite of tired, which was why he was in the lounge rather than sitting alone in his room sampling something from the minibar. Wired, that's how he felt. Primed. Though for what he couldn't have said.

Until he saw her.

Sam stood framed in the lounge's arched entrance, looking like something straight out of his fantasies. But it wasn't fantasies that kept Michael awake at night. No. Memories were the culprit. Some were bitter, others sweet. All of them still beckoned him, remaining far too fresh and distracting, given the passage of time. The woman had hurt him. Now she haunted him, which, aside from the excellent job opportunity at Grafton Surry, was why he'd returned to New York. He wanted her exorcised once and for all.

Unfortunately, as he stared at her now, all he really wanted was *her*.

Sam had always had that effect on him. It wasn't until she'd essentially put her father's needs before Michael's, making her priorities painfully clear, that he'd resented her for it. He swallowed now and swore under his breath. Why did she have to be so beautiful?

Seven years hadn't changed that fact. If anything, she was lovelier now than she'd been at twenty-five. Her face had lost some of its fullness but none of its impact, dominated as it was by nearly black eyes that were topped off with a lush fringe of lashes and elegantly arched brows. Her hair was a couple of shades lighter than her eyes but just as rich, with a natural wave and sheen. She wore it shorter now. It hung to just below her shoulders, additional layers softening the appearance of her blunt chin and prominent cheekbones.

And then there was that body. Michael shifted uncomfortably in his seat as his gaze slipped south, pulled in that direction despite his best intentions. Soft curves made him want to moan. Sam had never been voluptuous, but nothing about her figure could be considered boyish. The cinnamon-colored halter-style gown she wore made it abundantly clear that every last inch of her was female. The gown dipped low enough in the front to offer a tantalizing peek of cleavage, under which a wide band of fabric highlighted the narrowness of her waist. From there, it flared out subtly at her hips. A slit up from the hem gave him a glimpse of one shapely calf. He remembered how those bare legs felt to his touch. He remembered how they felt wrapped around him.

Michael reached for his drink, finishing off the bourbon in a single gulp. Need began trickling back even before he returned the glass to the table. To counteract it, he reminded himself how ruthless she could be. Once upon a time he'd admired Sam's go-for-the-jugular approach in business. Now that they were competitors, he found it damned annoying. Last month she'd tried to sweet-talk away one of Grafton Surry's biggest clients. One of *his* biggest accounts. Only a sizable cut in his commission and long hours spent on a new campaign had kept the high-end watchmaker from jumping ship. He would be paying her back for that. Soon.

Right now he intended to call it a night. Michael raised his hand to signal the waiter for his check. Unfortunately, it was Samantha's attention he snagged. He knew the exact moment she spotted him. Her expression tightened, and for just a second he swore she looked…vulnerable. Trick of the lounge's dim lighting, he decided, and sent her a smile as he gave his Addy award a caressing stroke.

Samantha's dark gaze followed the motion and she scowled. She turned and took a step toward the exit, but then she was pivoting back and marching to his table on a pair of heels that made her legs look as if they belonged in a chorus line.

"Hello, Michael."

Her voice was as husky and provocative as he remembered. He ignored the tug of lust and in his most casual tone replied, "Hey, Sam. It's been a while."

They had seen each other a few times across crowded rooms at advertising functions, but this marked their first actual conversation since his return to town.

"Yes. It has."

"How have you been?" he asked.

"Good. Great, in fact. You?"

"The same. How's your family?"

Michael thought he'd managed to keep the sneer from his tone, but realized he wasn't successful when she replied, "I might tell you if I thought you really cared. In fact, as I recall, the last time I tried to tell you, you wouldn't even listen."

"Ancient history." He shrugged. But then couldn't resist adding, "I see you're still working for Daddy."

She crossed her arms, leaving the little beaded handbag she carried to swing from one elbow in her agitation. That wasn't what held his attention, though. The pose did sinful things to her cleavage, which in turn did sinful things to his line of thinking.

"Why wouldn't I be? The Bradford Agency is the best in town."

"*One* of the best," he corrected. "I guess I thought maybe after all these years you would have finally broken free of him."

"I don't need to break free," she objected. "I'm an account executive and a good one. I'm being primed, I might add, to take over the agency when my father retires in eight years. That means that by the time I'm forty, I'll be the one calling all the shots at Bradford. I could very well wind up in charge of my own agency before you do. I'm hardly the prisoner you assume me to be."

"Right." He nodded solemnly and ignored her jab about his foot-dragging on going into business for himself. "I forgot. You had a choice, Sam. And you made it."

They stared at each other for a long moment. He barely heard her voice above the din of conversations when she replied, "You made a choice, too."

He closed his eyes, shook his head. "Back to that already, are we?"

"What did you expect?"

"More originality on your part, I guess, given some of the advertising campaigns you've put together."

Her eyes narrowed. "I'm trying to figure out if that was intended as a compliment."

"Let me know when you decide." His smile was intentionally ambivalent.

Sam unfolded her arms. "Well, I just came over to offer my congratulations."

"That's big of you under the circumstances."

"Just say 'you're welcome,'" she said tightly.

"You're welcome." Michael angled sideways in his seat and settled one elbow over the back of the chair. Testing himself, he allowed his gaze to meander to the vee of her décolletage again. Even without her arms crossed, enough gently mounded skin was exposed to ignite his imagination and send his hormones into overdrive. "That dress looks good on you. And I do mean that as a compliment, in case you're wondering."

She shrugged dismissively. "It was just something I had hanging in my closet."

"Ah. I see you still have expensive taste." When she said nothing, Michael added, "That particular designer's fashions are very high end. I know because he's one of my clients."

"Yes. For now." She smiled sweetly and he felt a muscle begin to tick in his jaw.

"You work too hard, Sam. It makes me wonder if you're ever off the clock or if you're always scheming up ways to grab my accounts."

"I don't have to scheme for that, Michael. I just have to do my job well. As for my personal life, it's none of your business."

He shrugged. "Still, I'm surprised to see you in here.

I figured you'd be tucked in your bed by now, alarm set, bags packed and ready to head to the airport to catch the first flight to LaGuardia."

This time the muscle that ticked was in *her* jaw, making him wonder how close he'd come to the truth.

"If you must know, I was supposed to meet someone for drinks."

Michael glanced around. His amused expression belied his words when he said, "I hate to be the one to break it to you, but it looks as if you've been stood up."

"As amusing as you would find that to be, the truth is I'm the one who's late. Our meeting time was nearly an hour ago. Unfortunately, it completely slipped my mind."

"Better things to do, such as go to bed alone?"

Her eyes narrowed, making him wonder if he'd scored another hit. Then he pictured her in that bed, alone…and waiting. And he was the one who took the hit. "Sorry." Michael waved a hand. "It's none of my business."

"Right you are."

"Forget I said it."

"I've tried to forget everything you've ever said to me," she replied airily.

"Yeah?" He cocked his head to one side. "Had any success?"

"Plenty." She smiled.

"So, you're saying the past—our past—is water under the bridge?"

She nodded, looking pleased when she informed him, "That's *exactly* what I'm saying."

"Good. Glad to hear it." He reached for the chair next to his and pulled it away from the table. "Then it shouldn't be a problem for you to join me in a drink. You can drown your sorrows."

He told himself he'd only tendered the invitation to wipe that smug grin off her face. He half hoped she would refuse. His masochistic half, though, knew she would accept. Sam wasn't one to back down from a challenge or a dare. Essentially, his invitation was both. A chorus of *Halleluiah*—sung by that masochistic half—broke out in his head as she lowered herself slowly into the chair. He sought to silence it with a sip of bourbon, only to realize a little too late that his glass was empty.

Of course she noticed.

"What are *you* looking to drown, Michael?" One dark eyebrow arched as she asked the question. Before he could answer she signaled the waiter. "I tell you what. This round is on me."

Michael tapped the side of the empty glass with his index finger. He meant it when he said, "You'll get no objection. I'm only too happy to see you pay."

Sam gritted her teeth. Foolishness, that's what this was. She couldn't believe she'd let Michael trick her into having a drink with him, much less buying. She stared at the Addy award that was in the middle of the table and recalled his acceptance speech. She felt her blood pressure rise along with her anger. She should get up and leave. But that would be playing right into his hands. She'd stay. Let him be the first to call it a night. He was stuck with her company now.

When the waiter arrived, she asked for a glass of Chardonnay. Michael ordered bourbon. According to her watch, it took the server eleven minutes and forty-eight seconds to return with their beverages. She and Michael spent the time selecting nuts from the bowl and making inane comments about the conference, which was only marginally better than chatting about the weather.

"A Chardonnay for the lady and your bourbon, sir," the waiter said as he removed the glasses from his tray and set them on the table.

When he was gone, Sam asked, "What happened to Scotch?"

That had always been his drink of choice. He'd preferred it neat as opposed to on the rocks.

He shrugged. "Tastes change."

"Yes, they do." Samantha picked up her drink. "Here's to change."

"Are we drinking to any change in particular?"

She watched his fingers curl around his glass. They were long and, she recalled, exceptionally skilled. Sam chased away the memory with a sip of wine and lifted her shoulders in a negligent shrug. "I'll leave that to you to decide."

His eyebrows shot up. "I don't remember you being

so accommodating in the past, Sam. I like it. A lot." He winked then and raised his own glass. "To change."

She intended to let his remark pass without comment, even though Michael was dead wrong: he'd been the one with issues when it came to accommodation, to compromise, not her. Sam took another sip of her wine before setting the glass back on the table. Then she took a deep calming breath and offered him a bland smile. It promptly turned into a sneer. So much for biting her tongue, she thought as she launched into her attack.

"God, that's so like you to manipulate the truth. I'm not the one who issued the damned ultimatum that killed our relationship."

"No? Are you sure about that?"

"What's that supposed to mean?"

"You're the one who took a stand, Sam."

"Me? 'Come to California now or it's over.' Do those words ring a bell? If not, maybe you should go see a doctor. It appears your memory is failing." She reached over and tapped his temple where a few fine threads of silver shot through his otherwise sandy-brown hair. When had he acquired those? And why did they have to look so damned good on him?

Michael captured her fingers in his. "I postponed our wedding, moved to California without you and waited for you to come, only to have you call to say you were staying in Manhattan. So, it's your memory that could use a little improvement. Mine is just fine, sweetheart."

The endearment, issued as it was in such an insulting manner, rubbed roughly across her nerves. It didn't help that he was still holding her hand. She tugged free of his grasp. "Don't call me that. You lost the right a long time ago."

He made a scoffing sound. "I didn't lose it. I gave it up gladly when you sent back my ring. Daddy—you know, the same guy who spent your entire adolescence kicking your self-esteem to the curb—*needed* you."

"You still don't get it." Sam shook her head in frustration and even as she called herself a fool all these years later, she wanted him to understand. "After Sonya's accident—"

Just as he had seven years ago, though, he blocked her attempt to explain. "Don't. Let's not talk about your sister or your father or anything else to do with the past." Before she could object—and, boy, did she plan to give him an earful—he abruptly changed the subject. "How about another toast?"

"I can't imagine what else we have to drink to." She meant it. After all, almost everything between them was past tense.

Michael, of course, found the one thing that wasn't. "How about my win tonight. You know, just to show that you harbor no hard feelings."

He offered the same grin that he had from the podium. It was a challenge, a dare, and as such she found herself helpless to say no.

"Why not?" she replied.

"Ah. There's a good sport."

She doubted he would think so when she'd culled half of his accounts. That was her goal. Maybe then he'd leave New York again. In the interim, she could be magnanimous and humor him. "To your win tonight."

As Sam reached for her wine, Michael had the nerve to tack on, "And the one last month. You haven't forgotten the Clio, have you?"

"No. It's fresh in my mind," she assured him, twirling the thin stem of her glass between her thumb and fingers. Half of his accounts at Grafton Surry? Why stop there? She wanted them all. "To your win, both tonight and last month." Just before taking a sip of her wine she added, "May they be your last."

His laughter came as a surprise, erupting as it did just after he managed to choke down a swallow of bourbon. She remembered that laugh. There'd been a time when she'd loved hearing it.

"I thought there were no hard feelings," he sputtered.

"None whatsoever." She nodded toward the award. "But that doesn't mean I don't plan to be the one holding that thing next year."

"It sounds as if you've got a serious case of trophy envy, Sam." He picked up the Addy and held it out to her. His tone bordered on seductive when he leaned close and whispered, "Want to touch it?"

His words awakened needs that had nothing to do with advertising or awards, and stirred up memories of quiet mornings, lazy afternoons and late nights when temptation had turned into passion and obliterated all else.

"It's heavier than it looks," he went on. "But, damn, it feels so good."

*So good.*

The scent of his cologne wrapped around Sam, pulling her in. Sex. She remembered what it had been like with him, how glorious it had felt. She exhaled sharply and pushed both Michael and the award away.

"Thanks, but I'll wait until I'm alone." She cleared her throat, felt her face heat at what could only be called a Freudian slip. "I mean, I'll wait until I have my own."

He studied her a moment longer than was comfortable for her. Then he shrugged and returned the trophy to the table. "Suit yourself. Of course, that might be a while. The competition in your category has gotten pretty stiff these days."

"Is that your ego talking?"

He snagged a handful of nuts. "Call it what you will. Results are what matter. And we both know what those have been lately."

"Awards aren't everything," she reminded him.

"No. They're the icing on the cake. In the end, accounts are what matter."

"The bigger, the better," she agreed, her thoughts turning to the hotel chain. If the rumor was true and she could land the account, what a feather in her cap that would be. Even her father would be impressed, and

God knew earning Randolph Bradford's approval had never been easy. If not for her sister's accident and then... Sam refused to allow the thought to be finished.

"Like Sentinel Timepieces?" Michael asked, referring to the watchmaker she'd tried to entice away.

That hadn't been what she'd had in mind, but she shrugged. "Perhaps. I go after what I want and I usually get it. Sentinel was an anomaly."

He looked slightly amused. "Is that your polite way of telling me to watch my back?" He wagged his eyebrows and added, "I'd rather watch yours."

She rolled her eyes, even as his juvenile comeback had heat curling through her belly. "Suit yourself, but don't cry foul when your preoccupation with my posterior results in a mass exodus of clients from Grafton Surry."

"Preoccupied goes a little too far. Your butt, as fondly as I remember it, isn't going to stop me from spending a little one-on-one time with the folks who are signed with Bradford."

The gloves were off, which was fine with Sam. She liked this better. Work, rivalry—they were straightforward.

"Unlike your clientele, mine is loyal, which I think you've already found out."

"I've only called a couple so far."

"Then I'll save you some time. I offer them what they want and I deliver the market. None of them is looking to switch."

"Sure about that? I can deliver the market, too." His lips curved. "And I can do an even better job of it than you."

Sam snorted. "God, you've never been short on confidence."

"Neither have you." He'd been smiling, but now he sobered. "You know, even more than your butt, I always found *that* to be an incredible turn-on."

Sam tucked some hair behind her ears and moistened her lips. Laugh in his face, she ordered herself. At the very least deliver an emasculating comeback. All she came up with was, "Me, too."

As soon as the words were out, Sam wanted to throttle herself. Why did she have to go and admit something so potentially volatile? It was bad enough to think it. After all, she'd been trying to sift out all of the softer emotions she had when it came to Michael. Here was a doozy and it was threatening to whisk her back in time.

She blamed the wine, even though more than half a glass remained. Most of all, she blamed Michael. He'd been the one to bring it up. Glancing at him now, she found a modicum of comfort in the fact that he looked as out of sorts as she felt, as if he too were wishing he could snatch back his words.

"I think I should call it a night," Sam said, reversing her earlier decision to have him leave first. "I have an early flight."

"Yeah. Same here."

With her luck they would be on the same plane, seated next to each other and then stuck on the runway during an extended delay.

After the waiter came with their check, Sam paid the bill. Michael insisted on leaving the tip, though she'd told him she had that covered, too. They argued back and forth, neither one backing down. Just like old times. In the end, the waiter wound up with one whopper of a gratuity.

They walked out of the lounge together yet not to-gether. Sam groped for something to say as they stepped into the elevator, and the awkward silence stretched. Even when the bell dinged and the doors slid open on the tenth floor, nothing came to mind.

She chanced a glance in Michael's direction as he got out. There'd been a time when she could read every one of his expressions. She didn't recognize this one. His smile was tight as he reached for the doors to prevent them from closing.

"See you back in New York," he said, which was unlikely. They'd managed to avoid each other for more than a year.

"Sure," she nodded. "Maybe I'll bump into you at the office of one of your clients."

"Now, Sam." He tipped his head to one side and made a tsking noise. "Be good."

"Oh, I'm better than good and…" She blinked. The words were a joke, an old and very private one between the pair of them. Her rejoinder usually ended with the sensual promise: "I'll prove it to you later."

Michael's smoky gaze told her he remembered the joke, too. He leaned forward and for one brief moment she thought he was considering kissing her. A bell chimed then and the doors jolted his elbow in their effort to shut. He released them and stepped back. But the last thing Sam saw before they closed completely was Michael reaching out as if to stop them.

# CHAPTER TWO

SAMANTHA overslept.

The alarm went off at the appointed time, right after which she received a wakeup call from the hotel's front desk. She ignored both and burrowed deeper under the covers, eager to go back to sleep. She could catch a later flight.

Now, as she sat in the first-class section of a 747, awaiting the departure of her noon flight, she flipped through a magazine and admitted that missing the red-eye had been no accident. She had not wanted to chance facing Michael again so soon.

She'd dreamed about him. Her face felt warm now as she recalled that in her dream, before the elevator doors closed, he'd kissed her, deeply, passionately. And he hadn't stopped there. No, he'd stepped back inside, let the doors slide closed behind him and as the lift traveled to the hotel's highest floor, he'd helped Sam off with her clothes. She'd returned the favor, every bit as eager as he. What would have happened next was obvious. But before their bodies touched, her alarm had gone off.

Sam had woken up panting and so aroused that she'd actually tried to go back to sleep and let Michael finish what he'd started. Of course, that hadn't happened. But the mere fact that she'd wanted it to, even in a dream, had her reeling. She'd been keyed up ever since, a feeling she attributed to confusion and irritation rather than sexual frustration or a flaring of old feelings. No, no. It wasn't either of those things. Closing her eyes she exhaled shakily.

"Nervous flyer?" a deep male voice inquired, jolting Sam's eyes open.

She glanced up to find Michael standing in the narrow aisle, a laptop computer slung over one shoulder and a smile turning up the corners of the mouth that had once trailed its way down her neck.

Glancing away, Sam accused, "I thought you were taking the red-eye back to the city."

"Looks like we both missed it." He dumped the laptop onto the roomy leather chair directly across the aisle from hers and shrugged out of his sports coat.

"Looks like," she managed as he arranged his belongings and took his seat.

"Actually, I turned off my alarm. When it went off, I was in the middle of a really good dream. I wanted to see how it ended."

Because she knew exactly what he meant, Sam said nothing. But as Michael fastened his seat belt, she clearly recalled helping him undo the belt on his trousers in her dream. He was a tall man, surpassing the six-foot mark by at least a couple inches. In first class, however, he was able to stretch out his legs, which he did now, looking the picture of relaxation. In contrast, Sam tensed, as if waiting for a trap to spring.

It did a moment later when he asked, "So, what did you dream about last night?"

"I have no idea. I never remember anything after I wake up," she claimed, even though that highly sensual encounter was burned into her memory.

He tipped his head sideways. "Really? Nothing? That must be a recent development. We used to lie in bed sharing our fantasies all the time."

He was dead on, but she wasn't going to go there. "Fantasies aren't the same as dreams," Sam told him matter-of-factly.

"I guess you're right, even though you can act out both." He smiled wolfishly.

She heaved an exaggerated sigh and reached for the magazine that was open on her lap. The flight to New York would be a very long one if Michael was determined to chat. Maybe if she pretended to read he would take the hint and stop talking to her.

Of course he didn't. "So, you really don't remember your dreams?" He didn't wait for her to answer, not that she planned to. He went on. "That's a shame. I *always* remember mine."

"How nice for you," she muttered with a definite lack of sincerity.

He wasn't put off. No. A sideways glance in his direction revealed he was grinning. Then rich laughter rumbled. "And I have a feeling the one from last night is going to stay with me for a long, long time."

He winked at her, once again leaving Sam with the uncomfortable yet highly erotic impression that she'd played a starring role in his dreams, too.

Thankfully, the flight attendants came through then to ready the cabin for take-off. Once the plane was in the air, Sam reclined her seat and closed her eyes, determined to nap or at least feign sleep to deter further conversation with Michael. The man was getting under her skin. It was just her bad luck that part of her wanted him there.

The captain had just announced their cruising altitude and turned off the seat belt sign when she felt Michael nudge her elbow. "Hey, Sam."

"I'm trying to sleep here," she replied, eyes still closed.

"No you're not. You're trying to ignore me."

She turned her head and allowed one eyelid to open. "Yes, but I was being polite about it."

"Right." The magazine in his hand was turned to an inside page, which he held out for her inspection. "What do you think of this?"

She opened both eyes. "The perfume?"

"No, the ad for it."

She straightened in her seat, reaching for the periodical before she could think better of it.

"The client certainly spared no expense," she said of the full-page, full-color advertisement that featured a top-name model standing in the middle of a field of flowers and holding out an ornate bottle of perfume as if making a sacrificial offering. "Is this one of yours?"

"Does this *look* like my work?" He sounded insulted.

In truth, it didn't. The composition was too stiff and staged, and the accompanying text about letting love bloom sounded sophomoric. But Sam merely shrugged. No need to feed Michael's massive ego.

"All that money to spend and this is what they came up with. Amazing." His voice dripped with such disgust that Sam had to chuckle.

"Are you jealous?"

"Hell yes, I'm jealous," he surprised her by admitting. "In addition to spreads in several national publications, this same ad is appearing on billboards and the sides of buses all over the country. And there's a corresponding television campaign under way."

She saw the dollar signs and whistled. "Someone's dining on steak."

"Want to know who?"

Curiosity piqued, she nodded.

"Stuart Baker."

The name rang a bell. "Wiseman Multimedia, right?"

"That's him. That guy can't spell innovation, much less employ it." Michael snorted.

"Yes, but look at it this way. Unlike me, Stuart Baker

will never be a threat to you in the Clio or Addy competitions. And the client obviously likes Baker's work."

"Right. Want to know what I think?" Michael asked.

"I'm waiting with bated breath," she replied dryly.

"He's got something on the person holding the purse strings at the fragrance company. You know, compromising photos or a lurid videotape."

"You have a vivid imagination. More likely, the client has more money than marketing sense."

He shrugged. "Maybe, but you have to admit, my theory is more interesting than yours."

She shrugged and put her head back and closed her eyes, figuring the conversation was over. But a moment later Michael nudged her arm again.

"If this were your client, what would you do differently?"

Sam kept her eyes closed. "I'm either trying to sleep right now or politely ignoring you. Take your pick."

"Come on, Sam. We've got some time to kill before we land in New York. Let's make the most of it. What would your ad look like?"

It was an old game, one they'd played often when they were fresh out of college and eager to tear up the advertising scene. They would analyze various campaigns, print or television, and decide what they would do to improve them. Sam had no intention of playing along now. But she made the mistake of opening her eyes and glancing at the glossy page Michael held out to her. A statuesque blonde pouted up at her. She couldn't help herself. Besides, she rationalized, talking shop with Michael was far safer than discussing dreams…or fantasies.

"Well, for one thing, I would have gone with a lesser-known model," she said.

"Why?"

"Sasha Herman has pitched everything from cow's milk to men's undershirts."

"So she resonates with the public," he countered, playing devil's advocate.

"That might be, but she also causes waves. Her increasingly radical political views aren't winning many fans among women in middle America."

"Everyone is entitled to an opinion," Michael retorted. "So Sasha is a little more vocal than most people, so what? Should she be punished for exercising her constitutional right?"

"I'm all for the First Amendment, but the fact remains that she's used her celebrity as a platform for some pretty extreme views, and it's costing her. She's fallen out of favor with a lot of Americans, including the very women who make up the client's target market." She sent him a quelling look. "No one ever said free speech was free."

"Okay. Point taken. So you'd change models and go with a less recognizable face," he said.

"Actually, I'd go with a complete unknown," Sam decided as a new ad took shape in her mind. It was black-and-white and far more sensual, fitting with the perfume's name: Beguile.

"To play up the mystery?" he asked.

"That's right." Sam nibbled her lower lip and allowed the vision to expand. "It should be a man wearing a white dress shirt, left unbuttoned to show off his incredible abs. After all, perfume is really just sex in a bottle. Women want to buy it from a good-looking man. It's part of the fantasy. If I wear this scent I'm desirable. I can entice anyone. I can *have* anyone. Even this drop-dead gorgeous stud whose eyes are saying, 'Beguile me.'"

"God, it's scary how the female mind works," Michael replied dryly.

"Oh, please," she huffed. "The female mind is no different from the male mind. We think about sex, too."

Think about it and dream about it in vivid detail, a small voice whispered.

"Go on," Michael encouraged with an engaging smile. "I'm all ears."

Uh-oh. She had wandered into boggy territory. As quickly as she could, Sam retreated. Conjuring up her most-patient and instructive voice, she replied, "Even though we're rivals, here's a key trade secret that I'm willing to share with you." She leaned toward him and whispered, "Sex sells."

"Gee. It seems to me I've heard that somewhere." He rubbed his chin thoughtfully. "Like maybe in the first advertising class I took back in college."

She lifted her shoulders. "It doesn't sound like you paid close attention."

"I did when the curvy blond junior who sat in front of me was absent. Otherwise I found her a bit too distracting, if you know what I mean."

Sam cast her gaze skyward and settled back in her seat.

"Come on. That was before we met, Sam. There's no need for you to be jealous."

"Jealous? I'm not—"

"What about the rest of the ad?" he said with a smile.

She frowned. "What do you mean?"

"What other changes would you make? I'm assuming you'd do more than switch the gender of the model."

Though she wanted to ignore him, Sam straightened in her seat and studied the ad again. It really was hideous. She tapped the bottom of the page. "Well, for sure I'd eighty-six the field of flowers."

"What's wrong with flowers? I thought women liked flowers? I send my mother a bouquet for her birthday every year. Daisies. They're her favorite. And you always liked roses. Long-stemmed red ones."

He'd surprised her with them often, she recalled now. No special occasion necessary. She'd loved getting them, loved reading the sweet notes on the cards. She still had those cards, wrapped in a ribbon and tucked away in a dresser drawer beneath her unmentionables. Somehow, they'd survived the big purge she'd done of all things Michael after their final blowup. She would burn them when she got home, she decided and concentrated on the ad.

"Women do like flowers, but that's not the point. The name of the perfume is Beguile. A patch of posies isn't a fitting image, especially since the perfume isn't even a floral scent."

"You've smelled it?"

She wrinkled her nose. "Not on purpose, believe me. One of those paper samples was tucked into last month's *Cosmopolitan*. It fell out while I was taking a quiz on…never mind."

He chuckled softly and raised gooseflesh on her arms when he said, "I remember the quizzes in that magazine. They were very eye-opening and, um, educational."

And she and Michael had a lot of fun putting into practice what they had learned from them.

Sam cleared her throat. "In case you're wondering, the perfume smells very musky and heavy."

"The kind that lingers in elevators long after the wearer is gone?" he asked.

She nearly groaned. He had to go and mention elevators and lingering. The dream was back, popping up in her mind like one of those annoying Internet ads. It chased away all thought of redesigning a perfume ad.

"Sam? You look a little flushed," he said, bringing her back to the present and making her aware that she'd been staring at him. "Are you okay?"

No, she wasn't. At the moment, she was the exact opposite of okay, and it was his fault. She handed him the magazine and settled back in her seat. "Will you be going after the account?"

His brow furrowed. "What?"

She nodded toward the magazine. "Beguile perfume. Feel free to use my ideas. I'm sure they're better than anything you can come up with on your own."

He shook his head slowly, his gaze disapproving. "That was low, Sam. Even for you."

She hated that he was right. He might try to steal another advertising executive's client, but he would never poach an idea. But at least Michael was glaring at her now rather than setting off her pulse with his sexy smile.

They passed the rest of the flight in stony silence, and when the aircraft touched down in New York they each gathered up their belongings and deplaned without exchanging so much as a word.

"So, did you win?" her mother asked.

Joy called as Sam was unpacking her suitcase that evening.

"No. I'm an also-ran once again. And you know how Dad feels about also-rans. No one remembers them," she said doing a fair impersonation of her father's resonating alto.

Joy snorted. "No one remembers them except for him. There's no pleasing that man." Which was why her mother had called it quits on her marriage the summer Sam turned thirteen.

Sam's sister Sonya, who was older than Sam by a couple of years, had chosen to live with Randolph. Sam had stayed with Joy. Even before then Randolph had been obvious in his preference for his eldest daughter, who was so like him in both coloring and temperament. Sam, as Randolph had told her often enough, was the spitting image of her mother. Even before her parents' bitter split, she'd known he hadn't meant it as a compliment.

"I hope your father was at least supportive at the awards ceremony."

"Actually, Dad left before then."

She heard her mother curse. "Figures. I'm sorry, sweetie. I know the Addy was important to you."

"Thanks, Mom." She sat on the bed next to the open suitcase and sighed. "Michael won it."

"Again? I mean—"

"It's okay. That was my reaction, too, when his name was announced. I ran into him afterward. The man is every bit as arrogant and self-righteous as he was seven years ago," she muttered.

"And as good-looking?"

"That, too," Sam admitted sourly.

"You said you saw him. Did you talk?"

"We have nothing to talk about," Sam said, before adding, "But, yes, we did have a conversation. I bought him a drink, even, to celebrate his win."

"Big of you," Joy murmured.

"I thought so. Of course, I also plan to put it on my expense report."

"Good for you." Her mother chuckled, but when she

spoke again, her tone had turned serious. "But was it all business, Sam?"

"There's nothing between us but business, unless you count bad blood." And way too much sexual attraction, she added silently.

"You know, I always liked Michael."

"Liked him? You were practically the president of his fan club, Mom. It was embarrassing."

Joy was unfazed. "He was the only young man you ever dated who wasn't scared witless of your father."

Okay, she had Sam there. "Well, he was far from perfect." The toilet seat offenses and off-key singing weren't the only things that came to mind. "Yet you thought I was making a mistake when I sent him back his ring rather than calling him again or flying out to California to work things out."

"I still think you made a mistake."

"How can you say that?" Sam all but shouted into the telephone. "You know why I did that. He wanted me to leave Sonya."

"Be fair, Sam. What he really wanted was to be sure you left your father. Michael didn't know that your sister had taken a serious turn for the worse."

"Yes, but only because he wouldn't listen when I tried to tell him. He jumped to the conclusion that I was staying in Manhattan and taking the job at Bradford to please Dad and gain his favor. Is it my fault that he got it wrong?"

"Did he?" Joy asked.

They talked about other things then, the dress Sam had worn to the awards dinner and the style she'd gone with for her hair. Hours after they hung up, though, Joy's words had memories churning.

*I need you, Samantha.*

Both Michael and Randolph had said so. In her father's case, though, it was the first time he'd used that exact combination of words. As Sam stalked about the quiet apartment that should have been Sonya's, she remembered the occasion quite clearly.

One month prior to her wedding to Michael and three months to the day after Sonya's car accident, he'd called Sam at the apartment she shared with Michael to ask her to meet him for lunch at Tavern on the Green. The invitation itself was unusual and should have given her an inkling that something unprecedented was about to take place. Still, the conversation that occurred in the time between their salads and their entrees had her wishing she'd followed her father's lead and ordered a vodka martini.

Randolph wanted her to stay in Manhattan and join him at the Bradford Agency. It was the first time he'd voiced any sort of objection to her moving to California. Indeed, it was the first time he'd voiced his desire to have her work with him, though she'd majored in advertising with just that intention. After earning her degree, Sonya had become an account executive at Bradford. As for Sam, even two years after graduating from New York University, her father had claimed that no account executive positions were available. He suggested she continue as an office assistant until something opened up. Michael had been the one to mop up Sam's tears and suggest not only a clean break from her father but a cross-country move.

"He doesn't appreciate you, Sam. He doesn't deserve you." Michael's words had been a balm to her wounded spirit.

So when Randolph had made his offer, Sam wanted to refuse it as too little too late. Her lips had even begun to form the words when he'd trumped every last one of her objections with his wild card.

*I need you, Samantha.*

There had been more to his argument than those four words, of course, as potent and ultimately persuasive as Sam found them to be. Actually, he'd laid out his case with surprising emotion for a man who rarely displayed much. He feared it would be months before Sonya was capable of returning to Bradford in any capacity. At that point she wasn't capable of independent living much less being groomed to take over the agency as he'd long intended.

Absent the heir, he'd turned to the spare.

That had been Michael's unflattering assessment when she discussed it with him later in the day. Randolph had asked Sam to take Sonya's place. Temporarily. She'd agreed. She'd already asked Michael to postpone their wedding. She wanted Sonya to be her maid of honor. Despite their father's obvious favoritism, the two had always been close.

The argument that ensued hadn't been pleasant. Recalling it now made Sam ache all over again:

Michael had been incredulous at first.

"I've given my word to my new employer that I'll start in six weeks. So have you."

They'd both landed positions at the same agency, one of the biggest and most respected in Los Angeles.

"I know. You can go ahead without me. I'll just have to hope that when I make the move, the opening will still be there."

He had run his hands through his hair. In Michael's expression she'd seen frustration, anger and, worst of all, hurt. "He's using you, just like he's used you as a glorified gopher for the past couple of years. Can't you see that?"

"He needs me," she told him.

"*I* need you, too. Don't stay, Sam."

She closed her eyes, holding back tears. Torn. That's how she felt. She still wanted, *needed* to believe that her father would someday love her as unconditionally as he did Sonya. "I can't leave right now. I'm sorry."

"You can," Michael insisted. For him, this issue had always been black-and-white. "Randolph doesn't deserve your loyalty, Sam. He won't return it."

She ignored the comment, ignored the little voice that told her Michael was right. "It's only for a little while, at most six months. The doctors say Sonya is making terrific progress."

He snorted in disgust. "And once she's as good as

new, then what? He'll have no need for you and you'll be broken up into pieces again."

"It's not like that."

Michael's voice rose. "It's *exactly* like that, and you know it."

"Sonya needs me, too."

"I like Sonya and I know it's not her fault that she's your father's favorite, but when are you going to step out of her shadow and start living your own life?" he asked. When Sam said nothing, he reminded her unnecessarily, "You're being naive if you think the job in California is going to wait six months while you work at another firm in New York."

"I know." The bigger question was, "Will you wait, Michael?"

He swallowed, looking pained. "That's unfair."

"Just answer me, please."

"Your father has made you jump through hoops your entire life for the scraps of his affection. I thought you were finally finished with that."

"This is different." It was. It had to be.

But Michael shook his head. "No, it isn't, Sam. It's just a bigger hoop with better scraps. I love you and I want to marry you more than anything in the world. But if you stay here now, I have a bad feeling that isn't going to happen."

She hurried to Michael, wrapped her arms around him and held on tightly, maybe because part of her already knew she was losing him. "Don't say that!"

He sighed and rested his forehead against hers. "Believe me. I don't want to say it. But I need to be honest."

She appreciated his honesty, but she also wanted his support. "It's just till Sonya is on her feet again and able to return to work, I promise."

She broke that promise, though not intentionally. After Sonya suffered a major setback, she called Michael in tears.

"I have bad news," she began and started to cry.

"You're staying in Manhattan, aren't you?"

"Yes. I have to. Sonya—"

"I knew it, Sam," Michael said before she could tell him about the unexpected aneurism that had burst in Sonya's brain and the doctors' subsequent grim prognosis.

"Please, listen," she cried. "You don't understand."

"I don't understand what? That you've decided our wedding isn't going to happen after all. I think I figured that out on my own."

"No. I love you, Michael. I was hoping you would come back to New York," she said. "You'll have no trouble finding a job here. We can still get married."

"Why would I move back, Sam? You've made it pretty clear where I fall on your list of priorities. You've picked trying to please your father over having a life with me."

She sank down on the bed they hadn't shared since his last trip to Manhattan more than a month earlier. Even then, things had been strained. "That isn't fair."

"Tell me about it." His tone had taken on an edge she'd never heard before. It scraped over her emotions, leaving them raw. "So, what scrap is Daddy offering you now?" he asked, alluding to their earlier conversation.

She wanted to weep, to lie back on the down comforter and cry out her heartache. She might have if pride had not come to her rescue. "I wouldn't exactly call it a scrap. He's made me an account executive at Bradford."

"Account executive, huh? It sounds like you got what you wanted."

No. What she wanted most was slipping from her grasp, but she wasn't about to grovel. Michael had made it clear where she ranked on *his* list of priorities. "Yes."

"Well, I guess there's nothing more to talk about."

"I guess not."

After she'd hung up, Sam had curled up on the bed and indulged herself in that long cry.

Now, lost in the memories from seven years earlier, she curled up on a different bed in a different apartment, surprised to discover that she still had tears to shed where Michael Lewis was concerned.

# CHAPTER THREE

MICHAEL had been back in New York for more than a week, and he couldn't get Sam out of his mind. She stayed there, as pesky as a damned burr.

It was probably just as well that her nasty accusation had ended what had been an otherwise pleasant conversation. Because before then, he'd wanted to kiss her. Hell, the night prior he'd wanted to do much more than that when he'd left her in the elevator. The fact that he hadn't so much as shaken her hand was of small comfort. Ever since that night he'd been preoccupied with memories of the two of them.

She'd haunted him before, but this was ridiculous. Not to mention counterproductive. That was probably her intent, he decided. She wanted him rattled and off his game.

Seated behind his desk at Grafton Surry, Michael gave up all pretense of proofreading the copy for a print ad and gazed out the window, which boasted a respectable view of midtown. It was spring in Manhattan.

Even in this gritty, urban setting, signs of life renewing itself were obvious and abundant. As were signs of the primal urge to mate, if the pair of pigeons cooing and strutting about on his window ledge were any indication.

Maybe it was the season that had kicked his libido into high gear. Maybe it had nothing to do with Samantha Bradford at all. Or only a little, he conceded, recalling the feminine sway of her hips as she walked and the habit she had of tucking her hair behind her ears. For no reason he could put a finger on, he'd always found that habit incredibly sexy. Not to mention the sinuous way she stretched in the morning or…

He closed his eyes and bit back a groan. Damn spring. Damn hormones and urges and chemistry. And damn Sam for still having the power to mess with his mind.

"Am I interrupting something?"

Michael opened his eyes to find Russell Zelnick standing in the open doorway. Russ was an account supervisor and as such had the coveted corner office. Russ didn't like Michael. Apparently, he assumed Michael was after his job. Michael did envy Russ his larger corner office, but he wasn't after the man's position at Grafton Surry. He had no ambition to climb the ladder here. Starting his own agency was Michael's ultimate goal. It had been his goal since the day he graduated from Princeton and tossed his mortar board in the air. He was getting closer to that goal by the day, soaking up experience and knowledge, getting his name known and saving for a proper office with money he'd earned rather than inherited.

"You're not interrupting anything." Michael straightened in his seat, cleared his throat. "Is there something you needed to see me about, Russ?"

"Yes."

The other man stepped fully into the office and closed the door behind him. That was never a good sign. Nor was the fact that Russ's face was florid, his expression grim. He was breathing heavily, as if he had jogged down the hall from his office, though Michael knew Russ eschewed any kind of exercise. The man was only forty-five, but thanks to high blood pressure and the few dozen extra pounds that padded his waistline, he was a heart attack waiting to happen. His next words had Michael fearing that the big one might be coming any minute.

"I got a call a few minutes ago from John Wells at Rawley Fitness Centers. He says he wants to take Rawley in a new direction, and he feels another agency can offer him that."

The account was Michael's, one of the first he'd landed for Grafton Surry when he'd moved back from California to join their operation more than a year ago.

Michael shook his head in disbelief. "There must be some mistake. He's been happy with the current campaign. He said it was one of the best he's ever seen and very effective in reaching a wide range of demographics. We have the numbers to back that up."

"Well, someone else is offering him something better," Russ snapped.

Michael's own chest felt tight hearing that. He had a pretty good idea who that someone else was.

Russ went on. "Just what in the hell is going on here, Lewis? This makes the second account of yours in the past eight months that has wanted to bail."

"Don't worry," Michael said. "I'll call him and get this straightened out."

Russ's eyes narrowed. "Like last time? Are you saying this is just *another* misunderstanding?"

"No. More likely it's a negotiating strategy," Michael said evenly. "The economy being what it is, everyone is looking to tighten their belts."

"Yeah, well if your accounts keep looking elsewhere, belts might have to be tightened around here."

With that ominous pronouncement, Russ left. Michael wasn't worried about losing his job. If worse came to worst, he'd move up his schedule for opening the Lewis Agency. It might require him to dip into the funds he'd inherited to afford the offices he was after. Though he preferred to earn his own way, that wouldn't be the end of the world. Losing the Rawley Fitness Centers account, however, wasn't an option. Especially losing it to Sam.

He was on the phone a moment later, making his case. But after a lengthy phone conversation, the only promise he managed to secure from John Wells was for a mere half-hour appointment later in the week.

He decided it was time to pay Sam a little visit. First, however, he placed a second call. He'd already begun to play her game. Now it was time to up the ante.

Randolph never knocked before entering Sam's office. He might be her boss as well as her father, but it still bugged her that he didn't feel the need to abide by the rules of common courtesy. He burst in now as she spoke to a client on the telephone. Rather than leave when he noticed she was otherwise occupied, he stalked around the room and waited for her to wrap up the call.

The moment she did, he said, "What's the status of the Herriman account?"

Even though Randolph and a handful of other Bradford account executives had gone to the advertising conference in Atlanta, Sam was the only one who'd heard the rumors. She considered that a coup, and it helped to make up for the fact that she'd lost the Addy to Michael. Her father hadn't been pleased to learn that. Monday morning at the office had been a tense affair until she'd told him about the hotel chain's advertising concerns.

"It doesn't appear to be a rumor, although I haven't been able to get it confirmed through Herriman's advertising manager."

"I have," he shocked her by announcing.

Sam rose from her seat, not incredulous but angry and, yes, wounded. This was her account, assuming it turned out to be an account at all. And he'd gone behind her back as if he didn't trust her to do her job. "You called Sidney Dumont?"

"No, but I ran into her assistant at the gym yesterday evening. I acted as if I knew it was a done deal that they wouldn't be re-signing with their current agency, and he didn't contradict me." Randolph offered a cunning grin. "I gave him my business card and told him we would be putting together something fantastic for them to consider, and to expect a call from us in the near future."

She blinked. "Us? You mean me, right?"

Randolph smoothed down his silk tie, fussing with the diamond tack that held it in place. He liked fine things and spared no expense when it came to his wardrobe. It was only with his affection or praise of Sam that he was stingy.

"This is a big account," he began. "Herriman's advertising budget is, well, astronomical."

"I know exactly how large their budget is, Dad. I've spent the past few days researching it and their market, remember?" She folded her arms. "Are you saying you don't think I can handle it on my own?"

His smile bordered on condescending. "I think you've made tremendous strides since you stepped in for Sonya, but—"

"No!" Sam stalked from behind the desk to stand in front of him. He was a tall man, and though she had to look up to him, she didn't respect him at that moment. "I won't allow it. This is my account."

His gaze narrowed. "What do you mean, *you* won't allow it? Might I remind you who owns this agency? Might I remind you who works for whom?"

"You're not being fair to me." *Again.* She had to bite her tongue to keep from adding that. Randolph had never treated her fairly, either as an employee or as a daughter. The fact that after all these years and all of Sam's hard work he still considered the job to be Sonya's proved that.

"This is business, Sam."

"Fine." She nodded vigorously. "Then let's look at my work record. I've been an exemplary employee and you know it. I've landed some pretty major accounts for Bradford. I put in longer hours around here than anyone but you. During this past year, two of my print campaigns have finaled in the Clio and Addy competitions."

"Neither of which you won," he pointed out.

Sam lifted her chin. "That may be, but no one else at Bradford had their work in the finals."

"Awards aren't everything."

"Right you are." She went back behind her desk and with a few clicks of the mouse brought up a spreadsheet on the computer screen. "So once again I'll defer to my sales record."

"You've done well," he conceded without looking at the numbers, which no doubt he'd already committed to memory.

"So, why are you treating me as if I'm a green account executive who still needs hand holding?"

Randolph tugged on his mustache. Finally he relented with a curt nod.

"Fine. The account is yours. But I'll be following your progress closely. I don't want this one to get away."

"I'm not going to let it." Then she grinned. "Oh, and speaking of landing new accounts."

Sam told Randolph about Rawley Fitness Center's all but guaranteed defection from Grafton Surry.

"Isn't that Michael's account?"

"It *was,*" she corrected.

"He's going to regret having you for an enemy." Randolph chuckled softly. "Hell hath no fury and all that."

Sam didn't care for the description. "It's not like that, Dad. Whatever was between us is long over. This is purely business."

But once she was alone she could admit that stealing her former fiancé's client offered the side benefit of being personally satisfying.

This was business but it was also a pleasure, Michael decided as the taxi cab pulled to the curb in front of the building that housed Bradford's offices in midtown. He was smiling when the receptionist took him to see Sam.

The grin slipped a notch when he stepped into her office. It was bigger than his, its view of Manhattan better since it had a higher vantage point and boasted an entire wall of windows. He found those details irksome, but since she was the boss's daughter, Michael decided not to get his ego in a knot. Nepotism had its perks.

"This is a surprise," Samantha said. She didn't rise behind her desk, which looked like a cement rectangle balanced on four metal pipes. Rather, she motioned for him to take a seat on the three-legged chair opposite it that looked about as comfortable as it did sturdy.

The decor surprised Michael. It was eclectic and far too modern for his taste. For that matter, he wouldn't have suspected it to be Sam's. They'd lived together for a time, after all. After moving into their small studio apartment in the Village, they'd picked out the furniture together, both of them gravitating toward clean lines that provided comfort.

"I'm sure it is. I thought about calling, but decided I wanted to have this conversation in person."

"Oh? Everything all right over at Grafton Surry?" She smiled sweetly after making the inquiry.

"Fine, although I had an interesting talk with the advertising manager at Rawley Fitness Centers a couple of hours ago. I believe you're familiar with John Wells."

"We've become fast friends, yes."

It took an effort not to grind his molars together when she offered a second beatific smile. "He mentioned wanting to take the advertising for Rawley in a different direction and doesn't want to renew the contract with Grafton Surry."

She made a tsking sound. "I know. Apparently he

wasn't completely satisfied with what you had to offer, though your campaign's reach is admittedly broad and well thought out. Still, when I dropped in the other day with a mock-up of my idea and some numbers I thought he might appreciate…" She shrugged. "As the saying goes, I had him at hello."

"John mentioned that he likes some of your ideas," he said slowly. That bugged Michael. Even more, it intrigued him. Just what in the hell had Sam come up with that could cost him the contract? Not to be egotistical, but he felt the Rawley campaign was one of his best.

"Stellar is what he called them when we last talked." She tucked a hunk of dark hair behind one ear and fiddled with the small silver hoop that was revealed.

Michael forced his gaze back to Sam's eyes. The amusement he saw reflected in their dark depths went a long way toward making his hormones behave. "I think I have something even better to offer him."

"Gee, Michael, isn't it a little late to bring out your A game?"

He ignored the insinuation that his other work had been below par. "John's agreed to meet with me later in the week."

He enjoyed watching her smile dissolve at the news, though he had to admit, she rallied fast. With a negligent shrug Sam replied, "A professional courtesy, I'm sure."

Michael didn't want to admit that she might be right. "I guess we'll see."

"Well, good luck." She almost sounded sincere until she added, "You're going to need it. I'm particularly proud of the new angle I came up with for the company's gyms."

She fiddled with her earring again and then tucked a handful of hair behind her other ear, leaving him with the feeling that she remembered his weakness and was doing it on purpose.

"Fitness centers," he ground out.

"Excuse me?"

"John says that calling them gyms tends to put off the female clientele. But you probably know that from all of your *research* into the company. I'm sure it was just a slip of the tongue."

It was small of him, but he enjoyed watching Sam's jaw clench.

"Is this what you rushed across town to tell me in person? That you're going to try to win back the account I snatched away with my superior campaign?"

Michael chose to ignore the superior barb. "I wouldn't say I *rushed* across town." He crossed his arms over his chest and leaned on the chair's boomerang-shaped back. "Actually, I stopped for a cup of coffee on the way. Have you tried that new place on Forty-Third Street near Fifth Avenue? They roast their own beans, you know."

"Potential client?"

"Given recent events I'm not sure I should tell you that," he said with a wry smile.

Samantha folded her hands on the desk blotter and chuckled. "Wow, Michael, you're taking this well. You're even making jokes. I thought you'd be furious to lose Rawley to me, especially given how large the account is." Her lips puckered and she whistled for effect before adding, "I probably shouldn't tell you this, but when the receptionist buzzed to say you were in the lobby, I figured you were going to be all threatening and irate."

"Would you have called security?"

"Oh, in a heartbeat." She offered a giddy smile. "And then I would have had you forcibly removed from the premises."

"Tasered, too?" he asked.

"Only if the use of a stun gun proved necessary."

"You must be disappointed, then."

The corners of her mouth turned up as she admitted, "Maybe just a little."

"Well, I prefer acting civilized…in a professional setting at least."

She sent him a quizzical look. "Is there a setting where you believe in acting like a savage?"

He hiked his eyebrows. "You don't remember?"

Sam said nothing, but the flush creeping up from her neck told him that she did remember. Vividly. Unfortunately, so did he, which was why heat of a different sort wound its way through Michael. Despite his best efforts, awareness sizzled.

"All's fair in…war and advertising," she managed after clearing her throat.

"Yes, it is."

"I'm glad that you understand that."

"Oh, I do, Sam. I do."

"It's nothing personal," she added.

But of course she was lying. *Everything* between them, past and present, was personal. His next words made that clear.

"I'm glad we agree on that, because I have an appointment with the folks at Aphrodite's Boudoir a week from Friday. I've been eyeing them for a while. After I gave them a little preview of what I have in mind for a new print campaign, they were very intrigued."

"I guess we'll see," she said blandly.

Beneath the slab of her desktop her legs were crossed. Michael nearly grinned as her foot began to swing in agitation. She wasn't as relaxed and unconcerned as she pretended to be.

"I guess we will." In a bid to turn the screws a little tighter, he added, "You must enjoy working with their advertising manager. Joanna Clarkson has been very nice to me the times we've met in person and then again today when we spoke on the phone to set up an appointment."

"She's a peach," Sam said. The foot swung faster.

"Yeah, a ripe one."

At that she planted both feet firmly on the carpet and grabbed the edge of her desk. Relaxed and unconcerned? Not in the least.

It took an effort for Sam not to shoot out of her seat.

Not only was Aphrodite's Boudoir her biggest account, the print campaign she'd put together for the high-end lingerie maker had been a finalist for the Clio. Michael knew that, of course. Just as he no doubt was hoping his references to the "very nice" and "ripe"—not to mention stunningly attractive—Joanna Clarkson would get a rise out of Sam. As if she cared. She wouldn't give him the satisfaction of losing her cool. Breathing deeply, she pried her fingers from the edge of the desk and crossed her legs.

"What? No comment?" he had the gall to ask around his smug smile.

"None. Why?" She blinked innocently. "I believe we just agreed that all's fair."

Michael nodded. "That we did."

"But you were hoping to get a rise out of me," she accused.

"I admit it. I was," he said.

"Then you must feel let down."

"As let down as you were not to have to call security," Michael agreed, but then he was shaking his head. "No, I'm more disappointed than that."

"Oh?"

"You always looked incredible when you were mad. The more ticked off you were, the lovelier and sexier you got." He appeared surprised he'd said that, but then he turned on his high-voltage smile.

Just what kind of game was he playing? Sam wondered, but found herself going along, sucked back in time. Whoever said makeup sex was the best knew what they were talking about. For a moment she was mired in memories that made her want to blush. Memories that made her burn. She plucked out a recollection that was more mundane than erotic.

"So that's why you used to leave the toilet seat up all the time? You wanted to see me turn into a raving beauty?"

He wasn't put off. "Seven years late, but you finally get it," he replied on an exaggerated wink.

"I thought you just did it to be annoying."

And, oh, how annoying she'd found it, though at weaker moments since Michael had exited her life she'd almost missed sitting on the cold ceramic of the toilet bowl. Sam drummed her fingernails on the desktop, a habit he'd once told her grated mightily on his nerves. If a blackboard had been handy, she would have scraped them down it just to cap off the experience.

Michael's expression turned brittle as he watched her hand, but then his gaze shot back to her face. "I see annoying you as a side benefit now, though not back then. I guess you could say I was blinded by love."

His tone was mocking. His flippant reference to the one-time depth of his emotions shouldn't have hurt Sam, but it did. It cut to the quick, and that left her feeling exposed as well as wounded. This time when she flattened her palms on the desktop, she pushed to her feet. It was time to show him the door while she still had a hold of her temper, not to mention her dignity.

"As entertaining as I find this short stroll down memory lane, Michael, you'll have to excuse me now. I have a lot of work to do."

He stood, as well, and with false politeness inquired, "More of my clients to woo away?"

"Oh, I've got one or two on the hook," she replied, though it wasn't quite the case…yet. The second he cleared Bradford's lobby, though, she planned to start laying the groundwork and doing the necessary research into products and markets.

"Well, don't work too hard or too late. You'll find it won't be worth it," he advised before he started for the door. Two steps from it, he stopped abruptly. Though he stood in profile to her she could tell his face had paled.

Sam followed his line of vision to the small gallery of pictures that topped the credenza on the far wall. Even before he walked over and picked up the silver-edged frame, she knew it was the one that had snagged his attention. In the photograph, Sonya was seated in a wheelchair, her head braced against its high back. Even though her blond hair was the same boyishly spiky mess it had been seven years earlier, she didn't much resemble the outgoing and energetic young woman she'd been.

It was a long moment before Michael said anything, though his throat seemed to work the entire time. Finally he asked in a quiet voice, "When…when was this taken?"

Sam walked around the desk and joined him. "This past Christmas."

"But I thought…" He glanced at her, shaking his head as if to clear it. "I thought she'd recovered."

If only that were the case. How different all of their lives and futures might be—Sonya's most of all. Sam took the photograph from his hand.

"No."

"But she was getting better. She was making excellent progress when I left for California."

He sounded baffled and no wonder, since he hadn't allowed Sam to tell him otherwise the day that she'd called. The day their relationship had suffered a fatal blow.

"She was." The head injury Sonya sustained in the car accident had affected her gross motor skills more than her cognitive abilities. With time and physical therapy she'd been expected to recover fully. "But then she suffered a brain aneurism, a residual effect of the accident, or so the doctors said. It did far worse damage than the crash."

Indeed, it had robbed Sonya of more than agility and grace. It had wiped away the last traces of her sparkling personality and keen intellect. What remained all these years later was a shell of a woman. Some things were worse than death. Every time Sam visited her beloved sister, that phrase came to mind.

"When did this happen?" he demanded.

"I think you know."

What little color had returned to Michael's face leached out again. "This is why you called to tell me you were staying in Manhattan."

"I couldn't leave, Michael. How could I pack up and go after that?"

He scrubbed a hand over his face, visibly shaken. "I didn't know, Sam. I didn't know."

"That's only because you wouldn't listen when I tried to tell you." Saying so now held none of the satisfaction she'd long thought it would, which explained why her tone was not angry but resigned.

His gaze connected with hers. Stricken, that's how he looked, along with sad, sorry and definitely shaken.

"Would it have changed anything?" she almost asked. But then she thought better of it. Maybe it was best not to know.

So instead, even though he hadn't asked, she told him. "Sonya's in a nursing facility in Bakerville. It's a little town on Long Island that's about an hour's train ride from the city."

The decision had been hard for her father to make. So hard, in fact, that Randolph had actually consulted Sam about it, one of the rare times he'd sought out her opinion on anything.

"Why not in the city?"

"Dad felt Rising Sun was the best around and that Sonya might find the small-town setting soothing. He wanted to hire a full-time nurse and keep her at home, but that was impossible since she's on a feeding tube and prone to respiratory infections."

"So, there's nothing more that can be done?" Michael asked.

A familiar sadness slipped over Sam as she considered his question. Gazing at the photograph, she used the pad of her thumb to stroke her sister's pale cheek. How Sam longed to see Sonya's face light up with her signature grin or to hear her booming laughter.

"They can keep her comfortable. They can work her muscles to ensure they don't atrophy any more than they already have."

"That's all?"

She set the photo back on the credenza. "She can't walk or talk and she doesn't appear to react voluntarily to voices or other stimuli. The doctors have been pretty clear that outside of a miracle, the way she is now is as good as it's going to get."

Michael laid a hand on her arm. "I'm sorry, Sam. *Really* sorry."

She swallowed, nodded. "I am, too." Maybe it was the sincerity in his tone that had her foolishly confessing, "Sometimes I feel very guilty for living her life. After all, the position at Bradford wouldn't be mine if this hadn't happened to Sonya."

The account executive job, as well as the uptown apartment that their father had deeded to her older sister, were both Sam's now. She'd earned them. She'd worked her fanny off for the past seven years and had the client list to prove it, even if she had yet to hear her father utter a compliment. But that didn't make the guilt ebb, especially when she looked at Sonya.

Michael's hand fell away. Sam felt it slip off her arm,

not realizing how much his touch had warmed her until it was gone. She told herself that was why she shivered when he said, "Then why don't you ask yourself why you're you still doing it?"

# CHAPTER FOUR

SAM hadn't intended to make the long commute to Rising Sun Long-Term Care that evening. After Michael's unexpected visit to her office, she'd planned to work late plotting ways to reel in every last one of his clients. Work, after all, had long been her refuge, as evidenced by her appalling lack of a social life, a fact her mother pointed out at every chance.

His question nagged at her, though.

*Then why don't you ask yourself why you're still doing it?*

She had answers for him. Loads of them. The same answers she'd had for the past seven years when her mother posed similar questions.

As the train clacked over the tracks to Bakerville, she admitted that part of her might still be trying to earn her father's approval. That's what Joy claimed. That's certainly what Michael thought. But what child, adolescent or adult, didn't seek a parent's praise?

Besides, hearing Randolph finally say he was proud

of Sam—every bit as proud as he'd been of Sonya—wasn't the main reason she stayed on at Bradford. She'd built a career there and she was helping to build the agency that someday would be hers to run. That was why Sam worked herself to near exhaustion each week. She had an investment in her father's agency that went well beyond fulfilling an emotional need. She saw no reason to walk away from that.

She fell asleep on the train, waking with a start when it pulled into Bakerville. The nursing facility was a little over a mile from the station. Generally, Sam didn't mind the walk. In fact, she almost looked forward to it. Once one got away from the depot and small downtown area, it was all tree-lined residential streets. But today she wasn't exactly prepared for the trek. Her snug-fitting black pencil skirt and three-inch high heels were perfect for the office, but they slowed her progress on the uneven pavement.

It didn't help that it was nearly dark outside or that halfway to her destination it began to rain. By the time she reached the unassuming two-story brick building at the end of Cloverdale Lane, the light sprinkling was well on its way to a torrential downpour.

The facility sat back from the street on impeccably groomed grounds that during the day teemed with spring flowers and budding shrubs. Sam raced up the lighted walkway toward the entrance, ignoring the protest of her feet and nearly oblivious to the scent of lilacs. Inside the lobby, she took a moment to dry the rain from her face and fuss with her hair. No doubt both were a mess. Not that Sonya would notice, much less care, she thought sadly.

Technically, visiting hours ended at eight and it was ten past that now, but all of the nurses knew her and tended to look the other way. Still, she felt the need to apologize as she passed the front desk.

"Sorry that I'm a little late getting here tonight. I hope it's all right, Mae."

The heavyset blonde smiled at Sam. "No problem. Sonya's awake. In fact, she still has company."

This news came as a surprise. Sam crinkled her brow. "Company?"

Randolph had been in a managerial meeting when she'd left for the day. As for her mother, Joy wasn't likely to make the trek to Long Island by herself, especially at this time of day.

"It's a gentleman," Mae said. She leaned across the laminate countertop and in a hushed tone added, "A very good-looking one, too. Sandy-brown hair and to-die-for eyes. He had all of the second-shift nurses flipping coins to see who got to deliver your sister's evening meds."

A good-looking man? Sandy brown hair? To-die-for-eyes? A face took shape in Sam's mind. No. It couldn't be Michael. Just the same, she hurried down the corridor past the nurses' station. Her sister's room was at the end of the hall. When she was halfway to it, the door opened and Michael stepped out. He was wearing the same suit he'd had on earlier in the day, though he'd loosened the tie and undone the top button of his shirt. They both stopped, eyeing each other across the distance like a pair of Old West gunslingers waiting for high noon.

"What are you doing here?" Samantha managed at last as she continued toward him on a pair of legs that had turned to rubber.

"I…I came to…" He hooked a thumb over his shoulder in the direction of the door, but then he shook his head and let whatever words he'd been about to say drift off.

He didn't look cocky now. Rather, he appeared pale. His mouth was pinched, his gaze hollow. Grief. As Sam drew even with him, she saw it reflected clearly in the deep blue of his eyes.

"It's a bit of a shock when people who haven't been by in a while first see her," she allowed.

He gave a jerky nod. "Yes. The picture—"

"In some ways it makes her look better than she actually does," Sam finished. Maybe that was the reason she'd framed it and put it on display in her office. Sonya's office. Other than changing out the pictures on the credenza, Sam had left it exactly as her sister had decorated it.

"I'd hoped it made her look worse. I'd hoped you were—" he swallowed hard before finishing "—exaggerating."

"So you came out here to see for yourself."

"Yeah. Sorry. God, Sam, I wanted you to be wrong."

His voice was emphatic, despite being soft. Hearing it did funny things to her heart.

"I wish that were the case."

"I always liked Sonya. She had so much energy, so much imagination."

Michael referred to her in the past tense, but Sam didn't correct him. That's how they all referred to her sister when they talked about the person Sonya had been.

"She liked you, too. In fact, before the aneurism, she was pretty annoyed with me for postponing our wedding, even though she was in no shape to walk down the aisle. She thought I should have married you before letting you leave for California."

"I thought so, too, remember?"

Sam had no comeback for that. She changed the subject. "It was really nice of you to come all the way out here to see her tonight. Sonya doesn't get many visitors these days other than family. Even her closest friends only make it out a couple times a year. This is a great facility. The staff and caliber of care are outstanding, the absolute best according to my father. But its location..." She lifted her shoulders. "It's not exactly convenient."

"But you're here, and often, too, if the nurses are to be believed."

"I try to make it out a few times a week. She's my sister."

"Yeah."

Because looking at him was too hard, she focused on a spot on the wall just past his shoulder. "You know, people always expected Sonya and me to be rivals. They figured that since we were only a couple of years apart and both in advertising that we were in competition. But that was never the case. We wanted the best for each other. Sonya loved me and I loved her. I still love her."

"This must be so difficult for you." He squeezed her arm just below the elbow.

"It's harder for her."

"You know what I mean."

Yes, she did. "Some days I don't want to come," Sam admitted. "After the doctors told us she'd never recover, I just wanted to pretend that she was away somewhere. Later, God forgive me, I just wished she had died."

She didn't realize she was crying until he brushed the tears from her cheeks.

"I think that's normal, Sam. Seeing her like this is hell."

"For my parents, too." She laughed roughly. "They may not agree on anything else, but they both have been devastated by this. For the first year, my mother was sure Sonya was going to just snap out of it, like something you see in a made-for-television movie. Dad was more skeptical, but I think he wanted to believe that, too."

"And you?"

"I still want to believe it," she murmured. "Even if I know it's all but impossible."

"She wasn't very responsive when I was in there," Michael said, hooking a thumb in the direction of Sonya's room.

"She's the same way with me. Still, I have to believe she knows I come and that she looks forward to my visits…in her own way."

"I'm sure she does." They stood in awkward silence for a moment before he added, "Well, I won't keep you."

Sam nodded and stepped around him, managing to paste a bright smile on her face before she stepped through the door to her sister's room.

Michael stayed. When Sam wrapped up her visit half an hour later, he was seated on one of the sofas in the lobby. He stood as she approached. She looked exhausted, he thought, noting the slight droop to her usually squared shoulders and the dark smudges under her eyes. Despite all that, she also managed to look lovely.

"You're still here?" She sounded surprised, but was she pleased? And why, exactly, did he hope that she was?

"I decided to wait for you."

Her brows pulled together. "Why?"

Good question. Michael tucked his hands into the front pockets of his trousers and rocked back on his heels. After exhaling, he admitted, "I'm not sure."

Sam let out a weary laugh. "Well, at least you're honest."

"I was always honest."

She nodded slowly. "Yes, you were."

"Do you want a ride?" he asked.

The question had her blinking. "You drove here?"

"No, I'm offering to carry you on my back all the way to Manhattan," he replied dryly. "Of course I drove. One thing I got used to in L.A. was having a car at my disposal. I decided not to give it up when I moved back, even if I still rely on cabs and the subway at times."

She tilted her head to one side and studied him. "What kind of car do you have?"

"Why? Is that going to sway your decision?" he asked.

"No, but I am curious. You always talked about owning a Porsche."

"You've got a good memory."

"Cherry red with a stick shift," she said.

"I stand corrected. You have a *great* memory." He smiled and in a conspiratorial voice added, "You wouldn't believe the way that baby hugs the road on turns, or how fast she can go from zero to sixty on a straightaway."

Sam looked to be on the verge of grinning back at him, but then she lectured, "It's not terribly practical to own a car in New York. You must pay a fortune in insurance premiums, not to mention parking fees."

He cast his gaze skyward. "I can afford it, Sam. Remember?"

"Ah, yes. Mr. Independently Wealthy." She was one of the few women who knew Michael's net worth and was unfazed by it. Maybe that's why he'd fallen for her all those years earlier. At the moment, though, her indifference was annoying, especially when she asked, "I can't believe you dipped into your trust fund for a phallic symbol on wheels."

"It's not a phallic symbol."

"Whatever. I thought you believed in earning your own way. Isn't that why we lived in that closet of an apartment in the Village with a view of an alley rather than something uptown that offered a view of the park?"

The mention of their apartment had nostalgia beckoning before he could stop it. "The place wasn't that bad. We had a lot of good times there." He cleared his throat, snapped his mind back to the present. "As for my trust fund, I haven't dipped into it. What I spend is what I've earned."

"Self-made," she murmured.

Was she impressed? God help him, Michael wanted her to be.

"That's my plan and despite some temptation over the years, I haven't deviated."

"Right." She nodded. "No rerouting for you. Once you're set on a destination, you don't believe in taking a detour, no matter what the reason. In fact, you won't even listen to the reason."

The color rose in her cheeks. She was talking about their relationship, and they both knew it.

Michael grimaced. "We've tap-danced around this ever since I learned about Sonya, but I still haven't offered a sincere apology for what happened. If I do that now, will you accept it? Will you forgive me, Sam?"

He watched her eyes widen and her lips part. "You've waited a long time to hear me say that, haven't you?" he said.

She nodded.

"You know, you once accused me of being unable to compromise."

Her voice returned along with a wisp of humor. "Actually, I've accused you of all sorts of unflattering things over the years. That was only one of them."

"Well, you were only partly right. I would have compromised if I'd known this had happened to Sonya." He held up a hand to stop her from interrupting. "And I take full responsibility for not listening when you called to explain. I was so angry."

"I know. I was angry, too."

Since they were clearing the air, he wanted it cleared all the way. "I think you should know I still feel I was right about your father. You can't please him, Sam. Has he ever told you that he appreciates the sacrifices you've made or the hard work you do at Bradford?"

"He might not say it, but—" She shook her head. "Let's not talk about my family anymore."

"Okay."

"I'd like that ride if you're still offering." She pushed

a hand through her unruly hair. "I got caught in the rain on my walk here from the train station."

"I noticed."

He'd always liked it when Sam left her hair natural and wavy, rather than turning it sleek with a blow dryer and round brush. He reached out and wrapped one of her wayward curls around his index finger. He released it quickly, a little embarrassed to have touched her in such a familiar manner despite their personal history. Or maybe because of it.

"I look a mess." She sounded oddly self-conscious as she straightened the lapels of the soggy blouse that peeked out from the collar of her equally soggy jacket.

"I wouldn't say that." He contradicted her only to say, "More like pleasantly disheveled."

She laughed, as he'd intended. "Isn't that the same thing?"

"Maybe, but pleasantly disheveled sounds better, kind of like the difference between *used* and *preowned*. In our business, it's all about word choice. Use the right ones and even a frozen dinner can sound like haute cuisine."

Sam didn't appear convinced. In fact, she frowned at him. "I have a low-calorie grilled chicken dinner waiting for me in the freezer at home. I'm sorry, but no amount of flattery is going to make that thing more appetizing, although I'm thinking a couple of glasses of Chardonnay might do the trick."

He chuckled. "Mine is Salisbury steak smothered in

clumpy brown gravy. I was going to pair it with the nice Merlot my boss gave me for winning the Addy."

"You just had to bring that up again," she said, but her tone held humor rather than irritation. The fragile truce they'd reached appeared to be holding.

"Yeah, I did."

"Figures."

"What do you say we have dinner together?" Michael ignored the part of his brain that warned he was playing with fire. Truce or no truce, too much between them remained unsettled…and unsettling. Still he asked, "Do you know of a place around here where we can stop without having reservations?"

Sam began to laugh, delicately at first and then with unbridled humor. "God, Michael, Bakerville isn't Manhattan. I doubt any of the restaurants here require reservations. Not that it matters. They roll up the sidewalks in this town about the same time the streetlights come on."

"Oh. Then we'll head back to the city and stop someplace suitable along the way. How does that sound to you?"

"I don't know," she hedged.

"Come on. You've got to eat, and so do I. We've both admitted that we have unappetizing prospects in that regard waiting for us back at our homes. Besides, you've already accepted my offer of a ride."

"You could always drop me off at the station. The

next train leaves in about forty minutes," she said, consulting her watch.

"Is that what you want, Sam?" It was a dangerous question to ask, Michael realized, when she looked up and he found himself submerged in her dark eyes.

Wants, needs—he thought he saw them there and they had nothing to do with his Porsche. But then she blinked and whatever spell she'd cast was broken.

"What I want—would love, in fact—is a change of clothes and the opportunity to take off these damned shoes. They're proving downright lethal."

Michael tapped his chin thoughtfully. "I can't do much about the first I'm afraid, but I won't object if you lose the shoes once you're seated in my car."

"I'd just have to put them back on to go inside a restaurant."

"True, but you can kick them off again under the table." He leaned toward her, lowered his voice. "It will be our little secret."

She took a moment to answer. "Fine," Sam said at last, waving a hand. "I'm too cold, tired and hungry to argue with you."

"I don't necessarily like to win by default, but I'll take it in this instance," he said.

As they walked to his car, Michael peeled off the jacket to his suit and settled it around her shoulders. When Sam snuggled inside of it rather than handing it back, he felt another small sense of victory.

## CHAPTER FIVE

THEY'D been traveling west on I-495 for half an hour, engaged in polite conversation, when Michael spied a billboard for a newly opened restaurant just off the interstate. Two exits and a few turns later, they were pulling into its parking lot in a strip mall that featured several other shops, all of which were closed for the day.

"Casablanca. Nice name for a restaurant," Sam mused as Michael nosed the Porsche into a spot under a light. "I caught part of the movie again the other night when I was flipping through channels. Humphrey Bogart and Ingrid Bergman. God, I love that movie."

Her sigh had him swallowing. "I remember."

She'd talked Michael into watching it with her once, claiming that it was, in a way, a war movie. Since he was partial to that genre, he'd agreed. It wasn't a war movie, a few Nazis notwithstanding, but he hadn't re-gretted snuggling under an afghan on their couch to watch it with Sam…especially given what had trans-

pired between the pair of them by the time the credits
rolled.

"Sex."

"Excuse me?" she said, and he realized he'd said the
word aloud.

"Sexy," he backpedaled, as he switched off the
ignition. Jingling the keys in one hand he added, "You
know, the movie, the era, the characters."

"Oh." She didn't look convinced.

Hoping to take the focus off his Freudian gaffe, he
pointed toward the restaurant. "I'm guessing the food
here won't be quite as sophisticated as the film that
inspired the place's name, but it's bound to have our
frozen dinners beat all to hell."

"True enough." Sam slipped her shoes back on and
then flipped down the passenger-side sun visor, exposing the lighted mirror on its back. As she pulled an as-
sortment of compacts and tubes from her handbag, she
said, "This will just take me a minute."

He shrugged. "No hurry."

Although Michael tried not to, he couldn't help
sneaking a peek as she applied lipstick, freshened up
her blush and eyeliner, and then attempted to tame her
wild hair with a little finger combing. Sam was a no-
frills sort of female in so many other ways. Maybe that
was why he'd always found watching her primp to be
such a damned turn-on.

Uh-oh. We're not going there, he warned his already
wayward libido. He got out of the car, taking refuge in

the cool evening air. When she joined him a moment later, he'd managed to shift his hormones back into neutral, but he had the sinking feeling they wouldn't be staying there.

Given the hour, the dinner crowd had thinned considerably, so he and Sam were seated immediately. The place was hardly on par with the restaurants back in the city where Michael regularly dined, but the atmosphere was pleasant, the staff friendly and efficient and, well, he couldn't fault the company.

Warm Italian bread and the wine they ordered arrived while they looked over the menu.

"Are you still crazy for pasta?" he asked. "The fettuccine with asparagus and roasted red peppers sounds pretty good."

"Ooh, it does. But I was thinking about something I could really sink my teeth into, like a nice medium-rare steak that's just dripping in juice." She made a moaning noise that had his interest shifting away from the menu's selections. "I haven't had something like that in a long, long time."

"I know exactly what you mean," he mumbled.

Though he'd hardly lived as a monk since their split, Michael hadn't enjoyed a truly satisfying sexual encounter with a woman since Sam. That was galling to admit even to himself. She glanced over at Michael now and smiled. Though it was clear from her open expression that she had no idea the direction his thoughts had taken, he felt the blood begin to drain away from his head. He stanched the flow by looking away and reaching for his wineglass. Asking the woman to dine with him was proving to be the kind of challenge that made Odysseus's trials look like a walk in the park.

He took a liberal sip of Chianti. "Why don't we order both entrees?"

Her gaze connected with his. "And share?"

"Sure."

She seemed surprised by his suggestion, though they'd always done that in the past. As a couple. Of course, they weren't a couple now. They were…

"I guess we could do that," she said slowly. "As long as I get to choose the dressing for the salad that comes with the steak."

Sam had always been good at bargaining.

"Can I put in a request for the house Italian?" he asked.

"You can." She'd always been good at getting her way, he recalled when she added with a smile, "That doesn't mean I'll order it."

No, they weren't a couple. At this time, Michael wouldn't consider them to be friends, although it was possible they were heading in that direction. He wasn't sure friendship was what he wanted or even in his best interests. What he did know was that they were rivals. They were a pair of driven and determined competitors. Adversaries, if John Wells's defection was any proof. Even so, Michael was smiling right back at her when he set his menu aside.

* * *

They had finished their meal and passed on dessert. Though the hour had grown late and only a couple other tables in the quaint eatery were occupied, they lingered, talking about everything but advertising accounts and steering clear of any mention of Sam's father.

After finishing his initial glass of wine, Michael had switched to coffee, not only because he was driving but because he'd decided it was best to keep a clear head around Sam. Without anger, misguided though it had turned out to be, to act as a stopper, old feelings and desires kept bubbling to the surface. He was now on his third cup. He blamed caffeine for the fact that his pulse was racing, though part of him suspected the woman across from him was partly to blame. He'd forgotten how alluring, how downright intoxicating, her company could be.

Sam also had switched from wine after a single glass. Now, she was sipping tea, some herbal variety that she claimed was rich in antioxidants. She smiled at him, further revving his pulse. "You know, Michael, I'd forgotten what a good conversationalist you are."

"Conversationalist," he repeated, slightly annoyed. It wasn't exactly what a man wanted to be known for.

"Do you still subscribe to three different newspapers and half a dozen magazines?" She laughed then, the sound taking him back in time right along with her words. "God, our recycling bin was always overflowing."

"I've cut back on traditional subscriptions," he

replied. "I read a lot of publications online these days. It's more convenient, given my schedule, and fewer trees have to die so I can remain informed."

She rested her chin on her linked hands, looking suitably impressed. "Are you an activist now, too?"

"I wouldn't go that far, but I try to do my part for the environment where I can." Since she'd been the one to insist on recycling, he added, "See, Sam, it turns out you were a good influence on me."

"Not good enough if you're driving a car in Manhattan where public transportation is not only abundant but relatively cheap and convenient."

He drained the last of his coffee and set the cup back on its white saucer. "Tell me you don't like my car," he challenged.

"I don't like your car." But she glanced down at her teacup after making the statement.

"You are such a liar. I saw you stroke the leather seat when you thought I wasn't looking. You all but purred." And he'd nearly moaned.

"I don't like your car," she stated a second time. This time she maintained eye contact, but a grin lurked around the corners of her mouth. Then her laughter, as rich and inviting as he remembered, erupted. "I love it, okay? I absolutely *love* your car." She leaned back in her chair, folded her arms. "There. Are you happy?"

"Ecstatic. I knew you did. I could always read you like a book, Sam. And you haven't changed a bit."

She straightened, mirth vanishing as quickly as it had

come and he was sorry to see it go. "I have, Michael. I've changed a lot."

"I didn't mean it as an insult. Honest. Why are you taking it as one?"

"Because I don't want you to think that I've been stuck in some sort of time warp since we parted ways seven years ago. I might still be working for my father, Michael, but I'm a different person these days."

He nodded slowly. He could see it for himself, though he still found her ties to Randolph troubling. After all, Sam may have changed, but he doubted her father had. The bigger worry for Michael, though, was that he found this new Sam to be just as interesting and, if possible, even more appealing than the old one. How did that fit into his present plans? How was he supposed to move on with his life and purge all remnants of her from his consciousness if he started falling under her spell once again?

As much for her benefit as for his, he said, "We're both different, Sam."

"I suppose so. Experience and maturity have a way of changing people."

Her words offered a way to lighten the mood, and Michael decided to take it. "Is that a polite way of saying that you think I was immature before?"

"I don't think I should answer that question while we're in the midst of an otherwise pleasant evening."

"It has been a pleasant evening," he said.

"Surprisingly so," she replied, sounding amazed.

He ran his tongue over his teeth. "There's no need to pull out the sledgehammer. The point has been made."

Sam laughed, as she was sure was his intention. He'd always been able to take a potentially volatile situation and add just enough humor to keep it from exploding. She opted to follow his lead.

"In advertising jargon, I guess we're what they call new and improved."

He chuckled. "Yeah."

Though they'd shied away from discussing work, she figured this was a safe topic, and so she added, "I've always wondered who coined that phrase and how it managed to catch on. I mean, how can something that's new also be improved? It's either one or the other. It can't be both."

"I don't know," he surprised her by saying. "I like to think of myself as both."

She sipped her tea to keep from asking the obvious questions his rejoinder raised. Of course, that didn't stop her from thinking them. How was Michael new? How had he improved? As Sam began considering possibilities to the latter question, a sound vibrated from the back of her throat.

All hope that Michael hadn't heard it evaporated when his brows rose. Even in the dim light of the restaurant, she saw speculation and something a little more potent infuse his gaze. "Is that a good *hmm?*" he asked.

"A sigh is just a sigh, as the song goes and sometimes a *hmm* is just a *hmm*," she told him.

"Ah." He nodded. "That's a clever reply given where we're eating."

"I thought so."

Their waiter arrived then. "Can I get either of you anything else?"

Michael glanced at Sam, who shook her head, and so he told the young man, "No, we're all set. You can bring the check any time."

After the waiter withdrew, Sam reached for her handbag. "Let me pick up the bill. It's the least I can do to thank you for the ride back to the city."

"Not this time, Sam. Besides, technically, it's my turn to buy." When she frowned, he added. "You paid in Atlanta. Remember?"

She nodded. She remembered. Indeed, her memory was in overdrive at the moment. She was recalling all sorts of things. "You were a pretty cheap date on that occasion."

He sent her a cocky grin. "I won't be the next time."

*The next time?*

I should correct him, Sam thought. They may have reached a fragile truce and settled a painful misunderstanding from their past, but they wouldn't be sitting down to dine or drink together again anytime soon. She *was* a different person than she'd been seven years ago. Despite that, she couldn't risk her heart again. She also had her career to think about, and at the moment it put her and Michael squarely at odds.

She opened her mouth to tell him this evening would be the end of it. There would be no next time. But the words that came out were, "Fair enough."

As they walked through the parking lot, Michael surprised Sam by handing her the keys.

"What are you doing?"

"Letting you drive." His smile was slow and knowing and all the sexier for it. "You know you want to."

She merely shrugged. But, oh, how she did. It had been years since she'd been behind the wheel of a car with an automatic transmission, let alone a finely honed sports coupe with a stick, but that didn't stop her from being eager to put the Porsche through its paces.

Sam gave him high marks for patience and restraint as gears ground and the clutch popped during her first few attempts to go from first to second.

Glancing sideways, she offered, "Sorry."

"Don't apologize. You're doing well," he told her. "You're almost a pro."

"Right." She snorted out a laugh. Now she knew for sure he was just being polite. "I'll understand if you want to rescind the offer to let me drive."

"No. Keep going. I'll help." He laid his hand over hers on the stick, applying subtle pressure when it was time to shift. Even after she'd merged the Porsche onto the highway and shifting was no longer necessary, Sam left her hand on the stick and Michael's fingers remained loosely threaded through hers.

They were back in Manhattan before she was ready to be. Once there Sam turned the driving back over to Michael. Though the hour was late, the traffic remained far too heavy for her comfort, and the lights required too much shifting.

Her apartment was on the Upper West Side. It wasn't large, but it did have an outdoor space, something rare in its price range. At one time the apartment had belonged to her paternal grandparents, who'd bequeathed it to Randolph. He'd deeded it to Sonya upon her graduation from college. When Sam matriculated from New York University a couple of years later, she'd received an all-expenses-paid trip to Hawaii. As gifts went, it was generous, but it paled in comparison to what her father had given his eldest daughter. Everyone knew it. Sonya, hoping to keep the peace at the time, had asked Sam to come live with her in the apartment rent free. Pride had forced Sam to decline. She'd swallowed that same pride, she realized now, when two years later she'd moved into it alone.

As Michael circled the block for the fourth time, looking for a parking space that was within reasonable distance of her building, Sam said, "You don't need to walk me to my door, you know."

"Right. I'll just drop you at the curb, or better yet, slow down and have you jump out." He made a scoffing sound. "Please. My mom would have my hide."

At the mention of his mother, Sam smiled. If there was one thing Sam envied Michael, it was the relationship he had with both of his parents. Drew and Carolyn Lewis were kind, generous to a fault and loving. She and Michael had spent lots of time in their company, not out of a sense of duty as she'd often felt when visiting with her father, but because they'd genuinely enjoyed being with them.

"How is Carolyn?" she asked.

"As active and outspoken as ever." He snorted out a laugh. "I think my dad's a little worried that a few of the women in her Friends of the Arts committee are going to pool their money and put out a hit on her."

Sam chuckled. Carolyn, much like her son, preferred things done a certain way. *Her* way. It helped to smooth most ruffled feathers that her way often made the most sense.

"She must be happy to have you back in New York."

"Yeah." Even in profile his smile was easy to read. "She is. Dad, too. He and I try to meet at his club once a week for a game of squash."

"Is he still beating you?"

"Only every single time," Michael admitted with a wry chuckle. "The guy may be in his late sixties and retired but he hasn't slowed down at all."

"Maybe you're the one who's slowing down," she teased. "All those caterers' spreads at photo and commercial shoots. They start to take their toll."

He grunted. "Please. I'm the same weight I was when I graduated college. Dad only beats me because he has more free time to polish his game."

"What a spin, Lewis. Maybe you should forget advertising and go into politics," she said.

"Well, that's my story and I'm sticking to it."

He sent her a wink that shouldn't have had her pulse revving, but it did. Sam concentrated on the purr of the Porsche's engine instead. On the fifth time around the block he finally spied an open space. Michael sped up to beat a more humble subcompact to the spot, wedging the sports coupe into place with a minimum of jockeying.

After coming around to open Sam's door, he warned, "No lecture on how impractical it is to drive an automobile in the city."

"You may not believe this, but I wasn't planning to offer one." She patted the dashboard before rising. "After getting behind the wheel of this bad boy, I understand perfectly your decision to keep a car."

He acted startled. "My God. That guy I passed in Times Square last week was right. It *is* the end times."

"Very funny. Let's just say I'm a little more forgiving of your participation in the destruction of the Earth's ozone layer. This car's like an addiction. You can't help yourself."

"Isn't that the truth?" he murmured.

Sam swore he leaned closer as he said it, his gaze turning molten before dipping to her mouth. But then he pressed a button on the key fob, causing the car to chirp. It was secured. She felt vulnerable as he placed his hand on the small of her back and nudged her in the direction of her building.

Sam didn't say a word until they arrived. After nodding a greeting to her doorman as they crossed to the elevator, she told Michael, "Thank you again for tonight."

"You're welcome." The elevator arrived and they got inside. As the doors closed, he added, "I can honestly say I didn't think I would be buying you dinner after learning about the Rawley Fitness Centers account this morning."

"We agreed that wasn't personal, just a hazard of our business." Sam knew it was more than that, though. For the first time, she had regrets, not about her attempt to win over one of his accounts, but about her motives for doing so.

"Business. Right." He waited for her to press her floor number. As the elevator began its ascent, he said, "It looks like we're going to keep getting in each other's way, Sam."

"I don't think so. Manhattan's a large enough city."

"That's not what I mean and you know it." He stepped closer and in a seductive whisper said, "We're both after the same thing."

"The Rawley Fitness Centers account?" she inquired.

He waved a hand in dismissal. "That's a symptom, not the actual condition."

"What are you saying? That we're sick?" She wanted to laugh, but it came out sounding more like a moan. She was feeling a bit peaked right now.

"Yeah. And it's incurable," he confirmed. "We both want to be the best."

The elevator reached her floor and the doors parted, which was a good thing since the space inside the car had gotten much too confining for her comfort. Her apartment was the third door down. Needing to have something to do with her hands, she pulled out the key as they walked.

"Well, thank you, Dr. Lewis, for that eye-opening diagnosis. I didn't realize being competitive was a disease."

"It is. A contagious one, too."

"I'm sorry," she said in her most sincere voice.

He appeared baffled. "For what?"

"For giving this disease to you. We both know it wasn't the other way around."

She figured he'd argue. In fact, she almost hoped that he would. But he merely shrugged. "Who gave it to whom doesn't matter now. We've both got it." He leaned close enough for his breath to tickle her ear when he whispered, "Bad."

"W-well, here we are," Sam stammered. "This is my door." Having said so, she still checked the number to be sure. Then she slipped the key into the lock and turned it. Conjuring up a polite smile, she told Michael, "I guess this is where I say good-night."

"I guess it is."

"Good night."

"Good night, Sam." But he didn't turn to leave. He

leaned against the wall just outside her apartment, looking entirely too sexy. And that was before he inquired, "So, what happens in the morning?"

"What do you mean?"

"Will you resume targeting my accounts?"

Oh. That. She hadn't decided.

"I can't very well back away from the ones I've already contacted," she admitted in all honesty. Although she would have to closely examine her motives. So she told him, "If I think I can offer any of your clients a superior campaign, I'll go after them."

"Fair enough." He nodded. "You can expect the same from me."

"All right." When he continued to regard her in that intense way of his, she opened the door and stepped inside her apartment. Facing him, she said, "Maybe it isn't such a good idea for you to fraternize with the enemy."

Far more than the threshold was between them and they both knew it. Yet, despite the day's revelations, an invitation hovered on Sam's lips. Though the hour was late, she didn't want the evening to end, which was why she decided to close the door.

Michael knocked almost immediately, a fact that had her grinning. So, she wasn't the only one who wasn't eager to part. Excitement bubbled, a good portion of it sexual. She reminded herself to play it cool. Pasting a bored expression on her face, she pulled open the door. Blinking at him, she said, "Yes?"

"I take issue with that fraternizing comment."

"What?" She cleared her throat. The bubbles of a moment ago popped unceremoniously, forcing her to quickly realign her thoughts. "It's just a figure of speech, for heaven's sake."

Michael shook his head. "It's inaccurate, Sam. And I want to be sure you're clear on this. *Nothing* that has occurred up until this point can be considered fraternizing with the enemy."

Well, that was blunt, not to mention humbling. It was her ego that popped this time. And to think she hadn't wanted the night to end. Now she couldn't wait to close the door and have it be over.

"Look, Michael, I—"

The rest of her reply never made it past her lips. He cut it off when he framed her face with his hands and leaned in to cover her mouth with his. Michael didn't step into her apartment, but he'd breached a boundary just the same. And Sam allowed it. Allowed it? Hell, she contributed to it, kissing him back every bit as enthusiastically. The encounter was infused with all of the passion and promise she remembered so vividly, though she'd done everything in her power during the past seven years to forget it. And it ended far too quickly for her liking. Even so, they were both breathing hard and heavily when he pulled away. They stared at each other in stunned silence.

"Wow." Sam murmured the only word that sprang to mind and, in truth, she felt lucky to be able to verbalize anything intelligible.

"Exactly." Though Michael appeared to be just as dazed as she was, he also looked pleased.

He touched her lips with the tip of one finger and then backed away. Just before turning to leave, he said, "Now *that's* what's called fraternizing with the enemy."

# CHAPTER SIX

IN THE days that followed, Michael considered calling Sam. For that matter, immediately after the kiss he'd wanted to finish what he'd started. Sam hadn't appeared eager for it to end, either. But he'd nixed that idea, and for the better part of a week, he'd managed to resist the urge to dial her office number.

What would he say to her? "Hey, Sam. I was wondering if you'd like to *fraternize* again."

That wasn't a good idea, for too many reasons to count. One of those reasons, however, ultimately prompted him to call her. She picked up after the first ring.

"This is Samantha Bradford," she offered in a no-nonsense tone that still somehow managed to turn him on.

He pictured her wearing something professional as she sat behind that ugly industrial-looking desk and tucked a handful of dark hair behind one of her ears. In the image that his mind conjured up, a flirty little gemstone winked at him from the exposed lobe. It was all he could do not to groan.

"Hi, Sam. It's Michael. I'm calling to offer my congratulations."

There was a pause, then, "Are you referring to the Rawley Fitness Centers account?"

"You haven't gotten any of my other clients to sign on the dotted line, have you?"

Her laughter trilled. "Not yet. These things take time, Michael. So, you spoke with John Wells?"

"A few minutes ago, yes. He said that while the work Grafton Surry has done for Rawley Fitness Centers has been top-notch—and that's a direct quote, by the way—they've decided to go in a different creative direction and won't be renewing their contract with us."

"For some reason I almost want to apologize," she surprised him by saying.

Where a week ago Michael had been angry enough to punch out a wall over the Rawley account, today he was feeling more philosophical.

"Don't. It's the nature of the business. Besides, it frees up some of my time to go after a new client or two, hopefully with even deeper pockets."

That was his plan. Just the day before, his father had shared some promising news with Michael—right after annihilating him in their weekly squash game.

After Michael had mopped the perspiration from his face and demanded a rematch, Drew had said, "Sorry. I don't have time to beat you again. Your mother and I are meeting friends for dinner. But I heard something that might make losing to me for the fourth straight week less painful. Our gardener has a cousin who works as concierge in the Manhattan Herriman. Apparently vacancies are up at Herriman hotels in several key American markets, including New York. Management is looking to change that, starting with an improved multimedia advertising campaign. Whatever agency they have now is out."

Michael wanted to ensure that Grafton Surry was in.

On the other end of the phone line, Sam said, "Clients with deeper pockets. Do these clients have names?"

He may have lost the Rawley account, but his competitive spirit hadn't died. "Like I'd tell you."

She laughed. "I had to try."

Yes, she did. Sam had always been relentless in pursuing what she was after. Some men might have been put off by that. Michael had considered it an attractive quality since it mirrored his own determination. Indeed, the only time he'd found it tedious was when she'd applied it to gaining her father's notice. In that case, he'd wished she would finally accept defeat and move on.

He brushed that counterproductive thought aside and asked, "What do you say I treat you to dinner to show you there are no hard feelings?"

"Dinner?"

"Yeah." When she still said nothing, he added, "It's the last meal of the day, generally eaten late in the afternoon or early in the evening."

"Funny. You want to treat me? I thought it was my turn to buy," she reminded him.

"Does that mean you'll have dinner with me, then?"

"I probably shouldn't, but I suppose now that you've clarified your definition of what constitutes fraternization it won't hurt."

Michael cleared his throat. "About that, Sam. I'm wondering if I should apologize."

"For what?"

"For the kiss," he replied.

"Gee, Michael, it wasn't *that* bad."

His laughter rumbled out even as his ego deflated. "Oh, I can do better. Much better. As you well know. So are we on for tonight?" Then, to clarify, he added, "For dinner, not the other."

"Oh, sorry. I'm not free tonight." She waited a beat. "For either, but especially not the other."

"I see." God help him, he did. In his mind Michael pictured Sam looking as lovely as ever and out on the town with someone else. Someone male. Someone male who had his hands on her hips and his lips cruising down her naked…

Thankfully the image popped when she said, "I'm going to see Sonya after work."

He expelled a breath but didn't think twice before asking, "Do you want some company?"

Sam was clearly surprised. "You're offering to come with me? You want to see her again?"

"I am and I do." Even though it hurt like hell to see

Sonya the way she was, he did want to see her. Like Sam, he wanted to believe that in some way she knew Michael was there, sitting by her bedside, filling in both sides of the conversation and stroking her hand. What's more, he didn't want Sam to have to go alone. "I can drive. Or if you'd prefer, you can get behind the wheel."

"Does that mean we'll be eating at Casablanca again?" she asked.

"Only if that's what you want."

She made a sexy humming noise that had his mouth going dry. "Not tonight. Why don't we grab a bite before we head out of the city? I'm in the mood for Thai food. Are you game?"

"Yeah, but what about visiting hours? Won't we be cutting it close if we have dinner first?"

"That's all right. The nurses are pretty flexible when it comes to family. As long as I leave by nine-thirty, they don't care what time I get there."

"Okay. So, Thai food it is. I know this great place," he began at the same time Sam said, "I've been wanting to try…"

"Sorry. You were saying?" Michael asked.

"There's a relatively new restaurant that I've wanted to try, but not many of my friends are fans of Thai food." And she'd remembered that Michael was. "But we can go to the place you were mentioning. Where is it?"

"A couple blocks from the Guggenheim Museum on Fifth Avenue."

Her laughter rippled. "That's the one I'm talking about. Sounds like we're on the same wavelength."

That had happened a lot back when they were a couple, he recalled. They'd finished each other's sentences. He'd sworn sometimes she'd been privy to his thoughts and he to hers, which made it all the more ironic and painful that a lack of communication had contributed to their breakup.

"What time should I pick you up and where? Your office? Or do you need to swing by your apartment first?" he asked.

"How about we meet at the restaurant at five-thirty? I'll call and make reservations."

"Afraid to let Randolph to see you…fraternizing?" Michael decided to let her decide in what way he meant the word this time.

Sam bypassed his innuendo completely. "Actually, I'm doing this for the benefit of the environment. You'll be driving out of your way to come pick me up here."

Michael didn't buy her excuse, but he let it go. He was in no hurry to see the man who at one time was to become his father-in-law.

"See you at five-thirty."

Sam had switched off her computer and was pulling on her jacket, happy to call it a day, when Randolph walked into her office.

Without so much as a greeting he said, "Catch me up on the status of the Herriman account."

Sam glanced at her watch. She would be pushing it to make it to the restaurant on time, especially if she couldn't get a taxi right away. "Can this wait until tomorrow, Dad? I've got someplace to be."

"Are you going to see Sonya?"

"Yes," she answered. Then, because she wasn't one to lie, even by omission, Sam added, "And before that I'm having dinner. With Michael."

"Michael Lewis." Randolph spat out the name as if it were poison. "When did this happen?"

She tucked some files into her attaché case and feigned confusion. "When did what happen?"

"You know exactly what I'm referring to. Good God, Sam!" he exploded. "I can't believe you're seeing him again."

"I'm not *seeing* Michael. Exactly. We're just…" The kiss made it impossible to finish the sentence with friends. Friends didn't kiss the way she and Michael had the other night. Nor did they respond to such kisses with feverish abandon.

"Can't you see what he's up to here? You've taken away one of his clients, nearly two when you think about the deal that fell through with the watchmaker. Mark my words. He's after something."

"Like what, my accounts?" She laughed. "Sure he is. There's nothing unethical about competition."

This didn't sit well with Randolph. "Tell me you haven't shared news about Herriman with him."

"Please. I'm not stupid. Of course, neither is Michael.

I wouldn't doubt he's heard the news. For that matter, I wouldn't doubt that half a dozen other Manhattan ad executives are angling for it as we speak." She sent her father a flinty stare. "But I have no intention of letting that account go to anyone but Bradford."

Her father nodded, but he didn't look reassured. "Heed my advice and watch your back, Sam. Don't trust him."

She exhaled in annoyance. She and Michael weren't back together, but she still felt pitted between the two men. "You make it sound as if he's out for revenge or something."

"Maybe he is. You didn't part on the best of terms."

"That was seven years ago." Yet it felt like yesterday. But for her father's benefit Sam asked, "What's he going to do to get revenge, Dad? Try to break my heart?"

Randolph folded his arms over his chest. "He did that once, as I recall."

"Only because I let him."

"Sam—"

He was winding up for a lecture, she could tell. Even if she'd had the time, Sam didn't want to hear it. "We're not back together." That much was true. Whatever they were, she and Michael weren't a couple. "He's taking me out to dinner as a goodwill gesture, more or less. He wants to show me there are no hard feelings over the Rawley account."

Randolph's harsh laughter echoed in the room. "Sure

he is. And you buy that? If so, maybe you're not the right person to run Bradford when I retire after all."

Sam blinked. She wanted to believe that her father had only said that to make a point. She needed to know with certainty that after the seven years she'd all but slaved at his knee that he couldn't possibly consider leaving her out in the cold. But a lifetime of falling short in his eyes made it impossible to muster the conviction required to chase away all doubt.

On the cab ride to the restaurant, she mulled over Randolph's words. She arrived fifteen minutes late thanks to an accident that had further snarled rush-hour traffic.

As soon as she saw Michael, the conversation with her father was forgotten. Everything was forgotten except the lovely, albeit dangerous, effect the man had on her pulse.

"Sorry I'm late," she said as he rose to his feet to greet her.

"No problem." Then he smiled and asked, "Mind if I satisfy my curiosity?"

The unexpected question threw her, but only for a moment. "I guess not, as long as it doesn't involve lewd and lascivious conduct. I hear that the law frowns on that."

"Spoilsports." He reached out to tuck some hair behind her ear and frowned. "Hmm. Little silver hoops. I was picturing gemstones."

She blinked at him. "You were? When?"

"When I talked to you on the telephone earlier."

His response had heat zipping through her. Before Sam could think better of it she asked, "What else were you picturing?"

Michael shook his head. "I'd better not say. I think that might fall under the heading of lewd and lascivious."

She laughed even as she fought the urge to fan herself. "You know, I always found your obsession with my earrings to be a little weird."

"It wasn't just your earrings. It was your ears, too. And, as I recall, you liked it when I did this." He leaned over and expelled a soft breath that caused her to shiver.

Given her reaction, Sam figured there was no point in denying his claim. Instead, she said, "Why don't we take our seats?"

Once again it was late when they returned to the city from visiting Sonya. Once again Michael insisted on walking Sam to the door of her apartment. And once again he kissed her until they were both breathless and feeling needy.

"This is quickly becoming a habit." He shoved the hair back from his forehead.

"I was thinking the same thing."

"Yeah?" One brow shot up. "Have you determined whether it's a good habit or the kind that needs to be kicked and quick?"

"Not yet."

"Me neither." He exhaled sharply. "I'd better go."

Sam wanted him to stay. In fact, an invitation hovered on her lips. They could uncork the bottle of wine that was chilling in her refrigerator and…talk. Clamping her mouth shut, she nodded in agreement with him.

Michael had been sure she'd been about to ask him to come in. He wasn't sure whether he felt relieved or disappointed that she decided against that. Nor was he sure why he told her, "I'll be out of town for the next few days on a commercial shoot in Big Sur, but I'll have my cell if you need to reach me."

"Big Sur, hmm?" she said. He pictured her there, wearing a skimpy bikini and frolicking in the surf. The image popped like an overinflated balloon when she added, "Remind me to go after that account next."

"Very funny."

She grinned. "Have a safe trip. I'll see you when you get back."

Even though she offered the words casually, Michael's heart gave a curious thump.

Michael was happy to return to New York even though the weather in California had been gorgeous and the trip productive in more ways than one. After wrapping up the photo shoot, he'd spent a night in the Beverley Hills Herriman. He'd toured some of the newly renovated rooms and then sat poolside with other guests, subtly gathering their thoughts on the services and amenities that were available either for an extra fee or gratis.

Afterward, ideas began bubbling, percolating intensely for a flashy multimedia campaign that he felt certain would deliver the numbers Herriman's people were seeking. He'd spent the nonstop flight home working on it and then headed straight to his office to go over his ideas with the art department and run some more numbers. He didn't arrive home until after eleven, too late to call Sam, even though with her equally crazy schedule, there was a good chance she was up. He just wanted to hear her voice.

Not sure how he felt about that, he decided against calling her the following day, too.

In the end it didn't matter. They literally bumped into each other late that morning in the lobby of a midtown office building.

"Of all the lobbies in all the buildings in Manhattan, you had to walk into this one," Michael said, borrowing and doctoring a line from *Casablanca*.

Sam couldn't believe her eyes. She'd just been thinking about Michael and here he was. His hair was slightly windblown and, of course, all the sexier for it. He wore a charcoal suit that fit his broad shoulders perfectly. The handkerchief peeking from the coat's breast pocket caught her attention. She'd given it to him, surprised him with it actually when he'd gone for the job interview in Los Angeles. He'd kept it? She'd figured he would have burned every last reminder of their life together.

She dragged her gaze back to his face. A pair of blue eyes smiled along with his mouth. She nearly sighed.

As much as he liked her earlobes, she loved his mouth. He had the best pair of lips she'd ever seen on a man. Wide and decidedly masculine despite being somewhat full. And she was staring at them, she realized.

"What are you doing here?" she asked.

"I'm meeting with a client. What about you?"

"The same."

His gaze narrowed. "That makes me nervous and I think you know why."

"I could say the same thing. A little birdie at Aphrodite's Boudoir mentioned that you were in to see Joanna Clarkson again. You've been busy since losing Rawley."

"I was busy before then." He winked, looking both smug and sexy. Sam wasn't sure whether she wanted to sigh or slap him.

"What floor is your client on?"

"The fifteenth."

"Ah. I'm heading up to the twenty-eighth. Care to share an elevator?" she asked.

"I'll go one better. I'll buy you lunch."

"Picking up the tab again?"

"Yes." His brows arched in challenge. "Are you going to argue about it again?"

She took a moment. "I guess not." And then, because she couldn't resist goading him, Sam added, "If your generosity keeps up I won't feel the least bit guilty about spending such an outrageous sum on the designer heels I bought last week."

"Women and shoes," Michael muttered as they walked toward the bank of elevators with a crowd of other suit-clad professionals. While they waited to board a car, he asked, "How long do you think your appointment will last?"

"I don't know." She shrugged. "Not that long, forty minutes tops."

"Mine shouldn't take more than an hour. We're just going over a couple of proposed changes."

"I'll wait for you in the lobby," Sam told him. "It's such a nice day out, maybe we can dine al fresco."

"This isn't what I had in mind when I said al fresco," Sam said. "And I don't consider this to be a real meal."

They were seated on a bench in Central Park. Michael was two bites away from finishing the hot dog he'd purchased from a vendor. Sam had yet to start hers. Despite her complaints, he was enjoying himself and he was pretty sure she was, too.

It was a gorgeous day despite the breeze, with a cloudless sky and temperatures approaching the seventies. It was far too nice to be cooped up inside a crowded restaurant when Michael would be spending the rest of the afternoon and a good portion of the evening holed up in his office fine-tuning the national print campaign for a client.

"You used to get a craving for a good dog at least once a week. Tony said you helped keep him in business," Michael said of the street vendor they'd frequented.

Sam fussed with the straw sticking out of her can of diet soda. "No one made a dog like Tony. His buns were always so soft." She glanced sideways. "You know what I mean."

"God, I hope so," Michael replied on a chuckle.

She sipped her soda and went on. "I haven't had a hot dog since I moved out of our apartment."

*Our.* He chased away the nostalgia and regrets the word conjured up by asking, "Why'd you give them up?"

"I prefer to live a long and healthy life. Do you have any idea the kind of stuff they put in these things?"

"No and please don't share it with me now. I'm eating." He popped the last bite into his mouth and chewed contentedly.

"Here you go." She handed over her hot dog, which was still wrapped in foil and warm to the touch. "Help yourself to mine."

"Are you sure you don't want it? A bag of pretzels isn't much of a lunch."

"No, it's not," she replied pointedly. "I plan to order something when I get back to my office. I'm thinking a nice grilled chicken breast on a bed of organic greens. *Mmm.*"

It hadn't sounded all that appetizing until that noise vibrated from the back of her throat. Now, Michael swore his mouth was watering. He swallowed. Yep. Definitely watering.

"Let me guess. Low-fat dressing."

"No dressing at all. A slight drizzle of lemon juice will do."

"You're living large these days, Sam. What will you have for dinner? Bean sprouts and tofu?"

She shook her head. "That's not on the takeout menu."

"When did you turn into such a health nut?"

"I'm not a health nut. I still like a big bowl of triple-fudge ice cream now and then and I'll never give up red meat, even if I do try to eat it less often. I've just been trying to eat healthy, take care of myself."

"That's probably a good idea," he conceded. "You're not getting any younger."

Her lip curled. "Gee, thanks for pointing that out."

"No problem." He grinned.

"As if I could forget with my mother's constant reminders that my biological clock is ticking like a time bomb." Sam's cheeks grew pink after saying so. She popped a pretzel in her mouth and chewed.

"You're not *that* old," he assured her, though the topic of biological clocks made Michael decidedly uncomfortable. "There's still plenty of time for…well, you know."

"They're called children," she said dryly.

"Right." And he and Sam had wanted a couple of them, though they'd planned to wait a few years after marriage before starting their family. If things had worked out between them, would they be parents by now? Something soft and unfamiliar tugged at him, a yearning he didn't quite understand and had never felt before. He cleared his throat and changed the subject.

"Well, if you're eating takeout at your office again tonight it sounds like you've got a long afternoon and evening ahead of you." He reached over to filch one of her pretzels.

She swatted his hand away. "I do. *Very* long. I should have brought a change of clothes for the little time I'll have to sleep tonight before heading back to the office in the morning."

He snorted out a laugh. "I know the feeling. I've been living at Grafton Surry lately."

"Your social life must be as exciting as mine." Her expression sobered, giving him the impression she regretted making such an admission. He, on the other hand, was ridiculously pleased. Not caring to examine why, he decided to goad her.

"Is that a polite way of trying to find out if I have a significant other?"

He expected Sam to take the bait and blow up. She didn't. After taking a lengthy sip of cola, she instead turned toward him and boldly asked, "Well, do you? After the way you've kissed me twice now, I find myself wanting to know."

"No." He shifted so he could place an elbow on the back of the park bench. The breeze caught her hair, tugging it this way and that. Before he could think better of it, he again reached over and tucked some of it behind one ear. The pad of his thumb lingered on her cheek. Her skin was so soft. He pulled his hand back. But it was too late. Now he had to know. "What about you? Any significant others?"

She brushed some pretzel crumbs from her lap. "I think I just made it pretty clear that I'm not seriously involved with anyone."

Yes, she had. And, God help him, Michael liked knowing that. But now her use of the word seriously had him wondering. "Does that mean you're *casually* involved with someone?"

"At the moment, no."

*At the moment.* Another disturbing caveat that served up another helping of curiosity. Michael opened his mouth to seek further clarification only to have Sam shove a pretzel into it.

Her dark eyes glittered with amusement and challenge when she said, "Unless you're willing to go into detail about your romantic pursuits for the past seven years, I don't think you want to ask me about mine."

"I suppose that's fair," Michael muttered. Though it didn't make him any less curious.

Sam rose to her feet and reached for the jacket she'd removed earlier. "Well, I should get back. The only thing I'm working on here is my tan."

He stood as well. "I got a chance to work on mine during the photo shoot in California."

"I noticed." Sam's smile twisted up his hormones. "See you later, Michael."

# CHAPTER SEVEN

WHETHER it was the result of winning the Addy, the loss of the Rawley account or spending time with Sam, during the past several weeks Michael had felt more energized and creative than he had in months, maybe even in years.

He had an appointment with Sidney Dumont set for the following week to pitch his campaign. And it was a good thing, too, since the Herriman rumors had been confirmed in the current issue of *Advertising Age*.

Around the corner from Michael's apartment was a little market that offered a decent selection of meats, produce and freshly baked breads. He wasn't much of a cook, but whenever he grew tired of takeout food and microwavable fare he stopped there on his way home from the office. That was the case on this Thursday evening. But after looking at a neatly trimmed porterhouse steak, he changed his mind.

It was after eight o'clock and the idea of a heavy meal wasn't all that appealing, especially if he not only had to cook it, but eat it alone.

Of course, he didn't have to eat alone. He didn't have to *be* alone. He knew a couple of women who'd made it plain they'd welcome his advances. The one he wanted, though, was Sam, who was eager and reckless one minute and then every bit as cautious and restrained as he was the next.

A habit, he'd called it after they'd kissed. He still hadn't decided if it was the kind he would come to regret. Maybe it was time to find out.

Sam did a double take after glancing through the security hole on her door. What was Michael doing outside? And why did he have to visit when she looked a mess? She'd worked late, as usual. Afterward, she'd felt too keyed up to go home, so she'd gone to the health club to work off excess energy, which she refused to believe might be sexual frustration. She'd overdone it a bit on the weight machines. Her quad muscles felt as if they'd just scaled Everest. So, for the past fifteen minutes, she'd been soaking in a hot bath complete with lavender-scented salts and lighted candles. She considered ignoring his knock and getting back to it, but in the end she pulled the lapels of her terry cloth robe together, sucked in a breath and opened the door.

"I'm catching you at a bad time," Michael said, sounding appropriately apologetic, even as his gaze slipped and his lips curved in male appreciation.

"I was taking a bath," she admitted.

"With bubbles?"

Memories of the things the pair of them used to do in the tub flooded back, but Sam maintained her poise and asked, "Is there any other kind?"

His grin spread. "At last, something we agree on."

She shifted her weight to one foot. "What are you doing here at this time of night, Michael?"

"Would you believe me if I said I was just passing by and decided to drop in?"

"No."

"Okay, how about this. I wanted to see you."

The words had her flesh tingling, but she ignored the sensation. It was late, she was barely clothed, he looked like sin in a suit, and a bottle of wine was peeking from the top of the grocery bag he held. Sam could do the math. Even so, she asked, "Why?"

Instead of answering her question, he coaxed, "Come on, Sam. Invite me in."

No. Sam definitely was not going to invite Michael into her apartment, especially while she was wearing nothing more than terry cloth and he was wearing that grin.

But she heard herself say, "It depends on what you've got in the bag."

"You sure know how to put pressure on a guy," he grumbled good-naturedly.

"You're in advertising, Michael. You're used to pressure."

"I also know the value of presentation and doing

research." He reached into the bag and slowly extracted a loaf of bread. "Italian. Hard crust and made just this morning." His tone was a seductive whisper that stroked each syllable. She found herself swallowing as he added, with a comical bob of his eyebrows, "Best of all, no additives or preservatives."

Sam folded her arms. "All right. Go on. You've got my attention."

He tucked the bread back inside and pulled out a package of herb-coated goat cheese. "This is not exactly low calorie, but you did say the other day that you indulge yourself now and again with ice cream. I figure this is worth a little indulgence, too."

"I've got nothing against treating myself on occasion," she said with a careless shrug.

"Good." His gaze lingered on her lips for a moment. Then, with a flourish of his hand, he extracted the wine from the bag. "And the coup de grace, an award-winning Cabernet Franc that offers a succulent display of berries and silky tannins."

"Did you write the ad copy for that?"

"Nope. I'm just a huge fan of the product."

"Medallion," she said, glancing at the label. "I've heard of them. They're in Michigan, right?"

"Yes, and they took the gold at an international competition with this particular vintage."

"I can't wait to try it."

"Does that mean you're inviting me in?"

Sam stepped back from the doorway and heaved a

sigh, though she was feeling anything but resigned. "Why not? My bath is probably cold by now, anyway."

"Don't be so gracious," she heard him mutter.

After handing Michael a corkscrew and acquainting him with her galley kitchen, Sam went to let the water out of the tub and blow out the candles. Then she changed into blue jeans and a fleece pullover. She resisted the urge to reapply her makeup or fuss with her hair, which had turned curly from the humidity. This was Michael. For six months before their wedding that wasn't they'd lived together. Sam's lease had been up and she'd spent most of her time at Michael's anyway. He'd seen her without makeup or perfectly groomed hair on plenty of occasions.

Sam slid her feet into the fuzzy slippers at the side of her bed and ignored the taunting inner voice that whispered, "He always claimed you were the most beautiful woman on the planet."

When she returned to her living room he was stalking around it. Energy. Michael had always had an endless supply. She'd appreciated that, too. At certain times more than others, she recalled now, as heat spiraled through her body. Fanning her face, she decided the fleece pullover was a bad idea. She felt too warm.

And he looked positively hot. He'd shed his jacket along with his tie. The sleeves of his shirt were rolled up, as if he was eager to get down to some sort of business. Hmm.

Sam cleared her throat. "Are you going to take a seat or would you rather wear a path in my Oriental rug?"

Michael turned around quickly, looking a little startled. Then he went perfectly still.

"Wh-what?"

"You are the only woman I've ever known who looks as good dressed down as she does done up for a night out on the town."

His compliment warmed her far more than she wanted it to. Her heart thumped and then it began to ache as memories shifted to the forefront. To counteract her reaction she forced a note of flippancy into her tone and pointed to the food he'd laid out on a cutting board and placed in the center of her coffee table.

"Flattery won't get you as far as a little bit of goat cheese spread on a thin slice of that bread."

With a half smile, he got to work. When he handed her the bread he asked in a frightfully serious voice, "How far exactly do you want to go, Sam?"

"The balcony," Sam remarked, striving to keep her tone light. "It's a nice night." And she was feeling overheated once again.

After collecting her glass of wine, she exited the room through the pair of French doors on the far end. They opened to a tiny outdoor space lined with planter boxes that were empty at the moment, though she had plans to fill them with annuals soon. In the center stood a bistro table and chairs. She sat on one of the chairs, expecting Michael to take the other one and join her in the light that shone through the doors. He leaned against the railing instead, leaving his face in shadow.

"That's not what I meant, and you know it," he said after taking a sip of his wine.

Sam moistened her lips. "Can we talk about something else?"

"Coward," he said, but he changed the subject. "I like your apartment, by the way. The decor suits you far more than the furniture at your office does." He tilted his head to one side. "Please tell me you didn't pick out that desk."

"No. It was Sonya's. The office was Sonya's. She decorated it."

"And you've kept it exactly as it was. Why?"

She shrugged. "It felt wrong to change things."

"Why?" he persisted.

"You *know* why."

"I know you love your sister and that at one point the job you have was hers and so was the office. Both of them are yours now. They have been for seven years."

"I know exactly how long it's been," she snapped.

"Sorry. Of course you do."

"Just so you know, I'm not rooted in the past. This apartment was hers before the accident, too. After I moved in I changed the window treatments and carpets, repainted the walls and furnished it to my taste."

Our taste, she thought, recalling their studio. She wondered if Michael had noticed that the couch was of the same sleek European styling as the one they'd picked out together.

"But not your office, where, arguably you spend more time," he said. "Are you afraid of what your father would say?"

"No!" But the denial sounded forced, even to her own ears. Could that be the reason? She didn't care to mull it over now. "Can we talk about something else, please?"

"Fine. How about the Herriman account," he asked as he stepped from the shadows.

She blinked in surprise but kept her voice bland. "The Herriman account?"

He chuckled and took the seat across from her. "Come on, Sam. It's in *Advertising Age*. Are you telling me you don't know they're looking for new blood?"

She allowed one side of her mouth to slide upward. "I might have heard something to that effect."

"Are you going for it?"

She sniffed, vaguely insulted. "You have to ask?"

Michael's hearty laughter rang out into the night. "No. I figured as much. Of course, now that the news has been confirmed publicly, every advertising agency in Manhattan and beyond will be gunning for the account, too."

"I'm not afraid of a little competition. So, did you know about it beforehand?" she inquired.

"I've been working on a campaign for weeks."

He looked awfully pleased with himself, which is why Sam said, "I have, too. Ever since Atlanta."

"Atlanta?" That brought him up short as she'd hoped it would.

Sam said nothing. She ran the tip of one index finger around the rim of her wineglass and shrugged.

"You've got a bit of a jump on me, then." Michael let out a whistle.

Straining to keep her smile in check, she inquired, "Are you worried?"

"Maybe just a little. After all, I know what you're capable of, Sam." Though he said it in an offhanded manner, the compliment still warmed her. "But the race doesn't always go to the swiftest."

"True. But I have no problem standing at the finish line waiting for the rest of the pack to catch up with me."

"Does that mean you've already met with Sidney Dumont?" he asked.

She didn't like having to say, "Not yet. I'm waiting to hear back from her."

Sam wished she hadn't put it that way when he grinned. "She can be a bit eccentric when it comes to returning calls, but she did return mine. I've got an appointment on Monday, first thing. I'd offer to put in a good word for you, but that would be counterproductive."

"I don't need a good word," she said stiffly.

"Of course you don't. So, may the best ad exec win?" His brows lifted.

"Yes, and I will."

His laughter was low. "Who knew that arrogance could be such a damned turn-on?"

I did, Sam thought. Even at his cockiest, Michael had managed to get under her skin in a way no other man had ever managed to do. In fact, Michael was doing it now. She sipped her wine.

"Why did you come here tonight, Michael? Surely it wasn't to compare notes on the Herriman account?"

"Do you *want* to compare notes?"

"You know what I mean. So?"

His cockiness vanished. For just a moment he appeared almost vulnerable, but then he stood and walked to the railing. Once again his face was obscured, making it hard for her to gauge his emotions, especially when he said in a conversational tone, "The other night I said kissing you had become a habit. Remember?"

"Yes."

"Nothing about being with you is as mundane as a habit."

"Oh?" It came out a whisper. How she wished she could see his face since she didn't have a clue where he was going with this conversation.

"Uh-uh. It's more lethal than that." He huffed out a breath. "You're like a damned addiction." Finally he stepped into the light. The intensity of his gaze stole her breath, and that was before he said, "I want you."

Even as her heart thumped unsteadily and her pulse began to rev, Sam planned to be casual about his startling confession. But she botched the attempt by dropping her wineglass when she went to set it on the table. The wine splattered. The glass shattered. Michael's expression never wavered.

"I see we're both on the same page," he remarked dryly and lowered himself into the chair.

Were they? She needed to be sure. "Define *want*."

His gaze turned molten. "I'd rather offer a demonstration."

"Michael, I'm being serious."

"So am I. I want you, Sam." He snorted. "Do I really need to define the word for you?"

She shook her head. "I guess not."

He waited a beat. "Got anything else to add?"

She wanted him, too, though she couldn't quite bring herself to say so. She still recalled the old hurt too vividly. Instead she said, "We had our chance."

"I know, Sam. I keep telling myself that. We came this close to forever." He measured out an inch between his index finger and thumb. "Then we blew it."

*We.* Though Sam had preferred to blame him fully over the years, she nodded now. We. Yes, it had been a joint effort. She could have called Michael back or gone to see him. She could have tried harder to make him understand.

The fact that she hadn't had her whispering, "Maybe some things just aren't meant to be."

"I've told myself that, too." He scrubbed his hands down his face, looking weary suddenly, where a moment earlier he'd had the energy of a caged tiger. "Maybe that's why I came back to New York, to prove it to myself."

His admission came as a newsflash. So, his uncertainty and lingering feelings for her weren't recent.

"Any luck in that regard?" she asked.

"Yeah," he said with wounding honesty. But then he added, "Until I talked to you after the Addy Awards in Atlanta."

That brought her back to a most salient point. "So much time has passed. So much between us has changed. We're rivals, Michael. We work at competing agencies."

"And you work for your father." It came out not as an accusation, but almost as a regret.

"I have no plans to quit," she told him. They needed to be clear on that.

"I know. You're next in line for the throne," he murmured.

"I've worked hard, Michael. I've earned it." She said it emphatically to quell the worries that her father still might not view it that way.

Michael seemed to read her mind. "I know that you have, Sam. But has Randolph noticed? Has he given you the pat on the back you've been hungering for your entire life? Has he finally looked at you not as a fill-in for Sonya, but as being competent and talented in your own right?"

Anger bubbled to the surface, hot and lethal. God, she wished she hadn't dropped her wine. She'd be throwing it in his face right now.

"It's always been so damned easy for you to judge

me!" she shouted, slashing a hand through the air. "After all these years, how is it possible that you still haven't got a clue? You were born not only with a silver spoon in your mouth, but with a set of doting parents who've tripped over themselves in their praise of your accomplishments and helped you get back up on the occasions when you failed."

He folded his hands on the tabletop and leaned forward. "That's the way it's supposed to work. Parents are supposed to be there for you. They aren't supposed to make you earn their affection. And they're sure as hell not supposed to play favorites."

Her eyes began to sting. "As an only child you know this how?"

"Don't try to cloud the issue with an argument over family size. I was the one who wiped your tears when Randolph kept insisting there were no openings at Bradford for an account executive even though he created a position for Sonya after she graduated. I was the one who suggested a fresh start in Los Angeles where we could both work at the same agency and you wouldn't feel so funny about working for someone other than your dad. You know I'm right."

Yes, she did. So she changed tactics. "You don't have to work."

"Why not? My parents and grandparents worked hard for what they have. I've never felt my inheritance should make me lazy. I knew too many people like that growing up. Besides, my wealth isn't the issue!"

"Maybe not, but since you're having a field day analyzing my motivations and missteps, I'd say a little quid pro quo is in order. Why haven't you started your own agency yet? What's stopping you?

His gaze narrowed and he shifted back in his seat. "You know my reasons, Sam. They haven't changed."

"Yes, yes." She nodded and waved a hand. "But you know what I think? I think all your talk about gaining experience and using only money you've earned on your own is a convenient excuse."

"So what's the real reason?"

"I don't know." She hunched her shoulders, and though it was low, she asked, "Could the mighty Michael Lewis be afraid of failure?"

Her comment didn't get the reaction she expected. He didn't shoot out of his chair and then stomp out of the apartment. No. He regarded her quietly, his brow crinkling as if something had just occurred to him.

"I'm not afraid of failing, Sam. But maybe you're right. Maybe I do have other reasons for dragging my feet."

"Look, it's late. I'm tired and this is old ground. There's really no point in plowing through it a second time." Sam stood and took a step toward the French doors. She had forgotten all about the busted wineglass until a pointy shard of it pierced the thin sole of her slipper and wedged itself in her heel.

"Ow!"

She crumpled back onto the chair, sucking a deep breath in through clenched teeth as she pulled the injured foot onto the opposite knee to inspect the damage. Michael was at her side before she'd removed the slipper. He did the honors for her, taking the glass with it. Blood had already pooled at the wound site. He pulled a handkerchief from his rear pocket and wiped it away.

"I don't think you'll require stitches, but let's get you inside where the light is better and take care of it."

Before Sam could protest, he'd swung her up into his arms. Holding her firmly to his chest, he strode into the apartment.

"It's just a little cut," she objected, though admittedly it hurt like the dickens. "I can take care of it myself."

Michael lowered her onto the couch without saying a word and disappeared down the hall. He returned a moment later with a hand towel, bandages, some cotton balls and a bottle of rubbing alcohol.

"Wh-what do you think you're going to do with that?" Sam asked, pointing at the rubbing alcohol.

"I'm going to disinfect the wound."

"My glass was filled with wine." She picked up the bottle of Cabernet Franc that sat on the coffee table and tapped its label. "Twelve percent alcohol by volume. It says so right here. Under the circumstances, I'd say the use of rubbing alcohol is overkill."

"Germs won't think so." He offered his most charming smile. "And I'd hate to have you lose your foot to some nasty infection because I was remiss."

"I promise not to sue."

"Even a little infection would make it difficult for you to walk." He stopped, shrugged. "Maybe that's not such a bad thing. If you're out of commission you won't be able to go after my clients."

Sam stuck out her foot. "Have at it."

Michael uncapped the bottle and soaked the cotton ball before kneeling in front of her. Cradling her heel in one hand, he said, "This won't hurt…much."

Of course it did. So much so she nearly kicked him in the chin. "God! Are you trying to kill me?"

"You always were such a wimp when it came to pain," he remarked.

"Please. I wear three-inch heels to work every day. I can tolerate…pain…very well." Her thoughts fractured when he began to blow on her foot.

He glanced up, eyes gleaming. "Better?"

"Somewhat." Actually, it was other parts of her that had begun to ache now.

He applied a bandage and she figured that was the end of it. But he kept hold of her foot. "Maybe I should rub your arch so it doesn't feel neglected."

"Knock yourself out." She shrugged though she wanted to purr. How embarrassing would that be? But the man had a great set of hands and he knew how to use them.

Michael didn't just rub her arch. He massaged it,

pressing firmly with his thumbs. She was teetering on the edge of insanity when he leaned over and kissed the spot where his thumbs had been, and she was sent into a freefall. On the way down, Sam was pretty sure she purred.

Chagrinned, she stole a glance at him. He didn't look triumphant or smug. He looked every bit as tortured and turned on as she felt. Heaven help them both.

"Sam." He whispered her name as he set her foot aside, giving him the opportunity to move into the space between her legs. Still kneeling on the floor, he settled his hands on her hips.

"We can't…"

He pulled her forward, to the edge of the couch cushion. Nuzzling her neck, he asked, "Why not?"

"Michael, we're different people now," she began.

"I think so, too. Which, in a way, means we have no history." His mouth was on her shoulder and he was tugging aside the pullover so he could have better access to it. "When you think about it that way, it makes sense."

"No, it doesn't." Of course, nothing was making sense at the moment. "We're going after each other's clients."

"So?" His teeth nipped at her heated skin.

"S-s-so?" she managed to gasp out. "Even without our history, I'd say that makes us rivals."

"In business," he agreed. He gave up on the neckline of her pullover and reached for the hem. His gaze shot to hers. The look in his eyes was challenging, hungry and damned persuasive. "This is pure—"

"Pleasure." She sighed out the word and helped him pull the top over her head.

# CHAPTER EIGHT

MICHAEL woke up a few hours before dawn. He considered staying the night. He wanted to and he doubted Sam would object if he did, but he climbed out of bed, dressed quietly in her dark bedroom and, after leaving a note next to the coffeemaker, let himself out of the apartment.

He needed to think and he couldn't do that with Sam's heated body pressed up against his.

The sex had been phenomenal, of course. Better even than he remembered, and that was saying a lot. Despite their mutual hunger and eagerness, they'd taken their time getting reacquainted with one another's bodies. They'd definitely been rewarded for their restraint. But as he made his way back to his apartment in the wee hours of the morning, he thought about Sam's comment about opening an agency.

He wasn't afraid of failing. He had the know-how and he certainly could muster enough clients to kick his business venture off in high gear. Nor was it purely a matter of using his own funds to finance start-up costs, which had been his most handy excuse during the past seven years. No, the fact was, Michael had put it off because he didn't want to do it alone. He wanted a partner.

Back when they'd been engaged, he'd known Sam would be that partner. Though they'd never really talked about it, it had been assumed they'd go into business together. She had such a fine eye for detail. He could always see the big picture. Together they made an excellent team.

After their breakup, Michael still had harbored dreams of becoming his own boss. He'd told himself that just as he didn't need Sam as his wife, he didn't need her professionally. Still he'd found reasons to tread slowly. Now he thought he knew why, and it scared the hell out of him.

Maybe rekindling their relationship wasn't such a good idea. Of course, it wasn't as if he'd proposed marriage again or anything else so serious. But where else was this heading? Casual and Sam were two things he knew didn't mix. They might be able to keep business and pleasure separate and distinct, but could they pick up where they'd left off seven years ago without risking falling in love again? Or hurting each other for the second time? And if the latter occurred, could he survive it?

Sam was woven into every facet of his life, which was why their first breakup still haunted him. How ironic, he thought, that he'd come back to New York with the hope of exorcising the woman from his heart, only to wind up welcoming her back into it.

Of course, certain things were clearer to him now than they were then. Given Sonya's worsened condition, he understood why Sam had stayed in Manhattan. But it also was clear that Sam was still eager for her father's affection and approval.

What if that never changed?

A few hours later, Michael was still struggling to find the answers to his many questions when his cell phone trilled. He'd already showered, shaved and dressed and was on his way to the office after having stopped at the coffee shop on the corner for a bagel and cup of French roast. It was a nice morning, still cool since the sun hadn't made it over the tops of the buildings. Though the distance between his apartment and his office was anything but short, he'd opted to walk.

After juggling his briefcase, the coffee and the bag that held the bagel so that he could answer the phone, he said, "Good morning."

"Is it?" Sam's tone was dubious. "I wouldn't know since I woke up alone."

He pictured her in the big four-poster bed, a cream-colored duvet hiding satiny skin. After swallowing hard, he said, "Sorry about that. I didn't want to disturb you. You were sleeping so peacefully when I got up."

He should have known Sam would see right through his embellishment of the truth.

"You're a liar as well as a coward, Michael." Her tone was curiously conversational, though, leaving him to wonder if she was truly angry with him. "You ducked out on me because you wanted to deal with your morning-after regrets in private."

The silence stretched as he tried to come up with a suitable reply.

"Well?" she nudged.

"I wouldn't call them regrets," he said slowly. "Although I do have some…concerns."

She let out an indelicate snort. "You might have mentioned those *concerns* to me last night before you helped me off with my shirt."

Don't forget the lacy bra, he thought. He certainly hadn't, which was why he stammered, "I…I got caught up in the moment." He sucked in a breath. "It was one hell of a moment."

Her husky laughter came as a relief. "Yes, it was. I guess I got caught up in it, too."

"Twice," he reminded her.

More laughter followed, even huskier than before. "Yeah, well, I was hoping for a third bout with insanity this morning, but your side of the bed was empty."

Michael had reached a corner just as she offered the suggestive comment. Failing to heed the Don't Walk sign, he stepped out into traffic and nearly got run over by a speeding taxi. Its blaring horn and the driver's shouted curse brought him back to his senses.

"It sounds like you're in your car," Sam noted.

At the moment, he wished he was. "Actually, I'm walking down Columbus Avenue. And thanks to your very distracting comment I nearly became a taxi cab's hood ornament."

"Why are you walking and where are you going?"

"You're just full of questions this morning," he said.

"You know me. I always feel chatty after sex."

"Yeah." They used to lie awake for hours, wrapped in each others arms as they shared their dreams and secrets. He diluted that dangerous memory with teasing humor. "Maybe it's a good thing then that we stopped after two rounds between the sheets or you'd never shut up."

"I'm going to forget you said that." But then her tone turned serious. "Instead of telling me where you're going, why don't you tell me where we're headed?"

"I've been trying to figure that out ever since I left your place, Sam."

"And?"

"Just for the record, I'm sorry for leaving this morning without saying goodbye, even if I did kiss you while you were sleeping and leave a note by the coffeepot."

"Thanks for that."

He sighed. "If you were anyone else, this would be simple. We'd spend some time together, get to know each other better. You know, go on dates, talk, fool around a lot."

"Last night you said that since we'd changed so much in the past seven years it meant we didn't really have a history," Sam reminded him.

Michael stopped walking. "I know I said that. But we do, Sam. And it's been front and center in my mind ever since I woke up."

"I see."

"No," he protested. "I don't think you do. After things ended between us, it took me a long time to feel whole again and start living my life solo." Thinking of his stalled agency plans, he finished with, "In fact, I don't know if I really ever have."

It was a hell of an admission, one he'd never thought he'd make, especially to her. It left him feeling exposed, but he needed to be totally honest.

"A piece of me has been missing, too," she replied.

At her words, Michael closed his eyes. God, they were a pair. They couldn't go back, undo the mistakes they'd made in the past. It remained to be seen if they could move forward.

"I'd say we both have a lot at stake."

"Yes," she agreed.

"Why don't we take a few days, do some hard thinking about what we want?" he suggested.

"You mean, look at the situation without the haze of hormones obscuring our vision?"

"Yeah." He chuckled softly.

"That's probably a good idea," she conceded. "In the meantime I have plenty to keep me busy at work, if you know what I mean."

He did indeed. The Herriman account.

* * *

Research. Landing an account as large as Herriman Luxury Hotels required a lot of it. Sam had spent the better part of the past couple of weeks establishing a target market. It had been no easy task since she was doing so without input from anyone at Herriman, but she was comfortable with her conclusions. The chain was known for its high-end amenities and services for wealthy guests, but that didn't mean it couldn't also appeal to business travelers and vacationing families.

The chain had hotels in every major metropolitan area in the United States as well as select cities abroad. Accommodations in several of them were currently being renovated, which, as she sat at her desk late one night, Sam concluded could be the jumping-off point for a new campaign.

She rubbed her weary eyes and tried to envision a television commercial, but thoughts of Michael distracted her. It had been nearly a week since she'd woken up alone after that incredible night of sex. Oddly enough, when she'd glanced over to find the opposite side of the bed empty, she hadn't been angry or hurt as much as curious. What was Michael feeling? So, she'd called him, hoping to ferret out a clue.

*After things ended between us, it took me a long time to feel whole again and start living my life solo. In fact, I don't know if I really ever have.*

She could still hear him saying the words. They played through her mind at regular intervals. How she wished she could have seen his face when he said them.

Not to determine his sincerity, that had come through loud and clear, but to revel in it.

His honesty had staggered her, which was why she'd agreed to his suggestion that they step back and take time to evaluate the situation before seeing each other again. The idea had seemed so sensible at the time. It was turning out to be pure torture, especially since her body and her mind kept reaching conflicting conclusions.

Her head said take care. This was one flame that might be best left to flicker out completely lest Sam find herself burned beyond any hope of recovery.

Her body said stoke the embers. It will be worth turning to ash to enjoy that hot blast of passion again for however long it lasts.

Was a compromise between those two schools of thought possible? If so, were she and Michael capable of such compromise? Sam didn't know.

She refocused on the computer screen, where her cursor blinked impatiently. She couldn't think of Michael now. Tucking her hair behind her ears, she straightened in her seat and reminded herself that the question she needed to concentrate on was how to get Sidney Dumont to return her calls.

It had been nearly a month since Sam had first contacted Herriman's advertising manager, but she had yet to secure an appointment. In fact, she got the odd feeling Sidney Dumont was purposely snubbing her, which made no sense. The two women had never even met.

Randolph, of course, was breathing down Sam's neck now that news of the hotel chain's quest for a fresh advertising campaign had become common knowledge in industry circles.

Sam remained confident that she had what it took to compete, no matter how many contenders entered the field. She'd spent the lead time she'd had since Atlanta well. She'd pulled together a number of ideas for a first-class multimedia campaign that she felt would meet Herriman's needs, but it would all be for naught if she didn't get the chance to present it.

She was feeling desperate. And desperate times called for desperate measures. So, when she saw the article about the Tempest Herriman-McKinnon Children's Charity Ball on the front of the *New York Times* feature section, she not only read it, she clipped it out.

The ball, which was that Friday, was only in its fifth year, but already had become one of the highlights of the Manhattan social scene. Attendance was limited to five hundred people, making the tickets hard to come by and much sought after, even though they went for a thousand dollars each.

Tempest herself had no direct involvement in her family's hotel business, but she had grown close to her parents now that she was happily married to a U.S. senator and the mother of twins. Surely they—and perhaps key members of the hotel staff—would be there. If Sam got really lucky, perhaps even Sidney

Dumont would be in attendance. It was a long shot, Sam knew. But at this time she was willing to take it.

She shelled out the money for a ticket to the ball without any regrets. She would write it off as a business expense. Not only did the ball attract the mayor and other New York dignitaries, in the past the guest list had included a good number of the city's elite entrepreneurs, who also tended to have the deepest pockets when it came to their business's advertising budgets. One way or another, she planned to get her money's worth.

The first person Michael considered calling when he left Sidney's office was Sam. Not to gloat that the meeting had gone well, but to share his excitement. He'd dialed his parents instead. His father answered.

"Congratulations, son," Drew said, his voice thick with warmth and pride. "I knew you could do it."

"I haven't done anything yet," Michael reminded him. "It was only a preliminary meeting and I'm sure the advertising manager has meetings with at least a couple of other firms scheduled." Bizarrely, he hoped Bradford was one of them. "She said she'll get back with me if they decide they want to go with Grafton Surry. Then we'll really start playing ball."

"Well, I have every confidence in your talent, even if it turns out that the people at Herriman fail to recognize it."

It was Drew's polite way of saying that, win or lose, he would remain proud of Michael. That knowledge warmed him.

"Thanks, Dad."

Michael hung up, smiling until Sam's words of the other evening came back to him. He'd never had reason to question whether his parents were proud of him or wonder if they truly accepted him. She was right about how fortunate he was to have their unwavering love and support. What might Michael do if, like Sam's father, they'd withheld both?

Michael mulled that question over for the next few days, even as he was supposed to be sorting out the current status of their relationship. He still believed Sam should have made a clean break from Randolph when she'd had the chance seven years earlier, Sonya's accident and subsequent health crisis notwithstanding. But had he been fair in demanding it?

The conclusion he reached was humbling. Randolph wasn't the only one to attach strings to his love. Michael had had conditions, too. He'd made their future together contingent on Sam severing ties with her father.

He still wasn't sure where they were heading, but he knew with certainty he wouldn't make that mistake a second time.

# CHAPTER NINE

THE week before his meeting with Sidney, Michael had received a personalized note from Tempest Herriman-McKinnon inviting him to her annual Children's Charity Ball at the Manhattan Herriman. That was no surprise. While living in California, Michael had been a generous supporter of Tempest's husband's Senate campaign. He'd also contributed to the many worthwhile causes the hotel-chain-heiress-turned-actress championed. He didn't let the personalized invitation go to his head. She was trying to raise funds, and going to the event meant shelling out a thousand dollars. Still, he considered attending.

Unfortunately, the only woman he wanted to ask to accompany him was Sam. And that was a problem. In addition to the fact that the ball was linked, however loosely, to the account for which they were both vying, he and Sam were supposed to be taking a step back and thinking carefully before seeing each other again.

For that reason Michael decided he would send Tempest a generous donation in lieu of attending. But while he was in Sidney's office for their meeting, he'd noticed a similar personalized note from Tempest in the woman's in-box. Though he generally wasn't one for name-dropping, in this instance it seemed appropriate.

"Are you going, too?" he'd asked and with a smile added, "Tempest can be pretty persuasive."

"You know Tempest?"

"Not well, no. But since I supported her husband's Senate bid as well as some of her pet projects when I lived in California, I'm still on her mailing list." He'd grinned engagingly, turning on what Sam long ago had dubbed the Lewis charm.

"Well, perhaps I'll see you there," Sidney had replied. Then, even though the woman was downright stingy with her smiles, one had lit up her face. "You can buy me a drink."

So now Michael was committed. At the very least he had to put in an appearance. Between now and the time an agency was named, he needed to keep Grafton Surry front and center in Sidney's mind. He just wished he could do so while also enjoying Sam's company.

"Will you be going to see Sonya tonight?" Randolph asked from the doorway to Samantha's office midafternoon the following Friday. "I have some new clothes I want to send."

Sam glanced up from her computer screen a little surprised. Her father always went to see Sonya on Fridays and so she asked, "Why can't you go?"

Randolph tugged at the corners of his mustache, looking uncharacteristically nervous. "Something's come up—a late meeting with a potential client."

"Must be someone important," she mused.

"Oh, it is."

"Well, sorry. But I already have plans for this evening," Sam told him.

"Plans?" Randolph frowned as if the word were foreign to him.

"Yes." When she'd purchased the ticket, she'd debated telling him about going to the ball, but ultimately she'd decided against it. Until she had an actual appointment with Ms. Dumont, she wasn't going to say a thing.

"Can't they be changed?" he demanded irritably. "Sonya will be expecting company tonight. I don't want her to be disappointed."

Despite the guilt that bubbled up and the anger that threatened, Sam remained polite, but firm. "No, Dad. Sorry. I was out to see Sonya twice already this week. I'll visit her tomorrow. If the weather's nice, I'll take her out on the grounds in her wheelchair. She seems to like that."

He grunted, but apparently was mollified. "I'll go Sunday, then."

"Um, Mom will be there."

"God." Divorced nearly two decades and he still could barely tolerate hearing her mentioned. "Did she say when?"

"I think she and Chad are shooting for early afternoon." Chad was the man—the much younger man—Joy had married a few years after leaving Sam's father.

Randolph's upper lip curled beneath his mustache. "I'll visit in the evening." He pointed a finger at Sam. "And I'll see you bright and early on Monday. Don't forget that the staff meeting was moved up two hours. Try to be more prepared this time."

She'd had to run back to her office at last month's meeting for the sales numbers he wanted on one of her clients. He still hadn't let her forget it. "Of course, Dad. Have a good weekend."

Randolph left without bidding her the same.

Michael suppressed the urge to unknot his bow tie. His tuxedo was Armani, but that didn't make it or the sleek black tie he'd paired it with any more comfortable, especially since he felt conspicuous. Not that his attire was inappropriate. The ball was definitely a black-tie affair. But he hated that he was here alone.

His plan for the evening was to locate Sidney, maybe share a drink and some polite conversation, and then discreetly head for the exits immediately after dinner was served. Though he'd heard a big-name band and a couple of Grammy-Award-winning singers were on tap for the entertainment, he wanted to be home in time to catch the last couple of innings of the ball game. The Yankees were playing their arch rivals, the Red Sox, in Boston and it promised to be one hell of a game.

Rivalries always were, he thought, as he turned and caught a glimpse of dark hair and pale skin.

*Sam.*

Awareness charged up his spine like a stampeding elephant. Sipping his champagne, Michael decided that catching the end of the baseball game wasn't such a big deal, nor was he in a hurry to find Sidney. Grabbing a second flute of bubbly from a passing waiter's tray, he started off in Sam's direction.

"How's your foot?" he asked when he reached her.

She turned and her eyes opened wide. "Michael! What are you—"

"Doing here?" he finished for her. He held out the champagne. "Having a drink with you and inquiring about your sole. The one that ends in *e*."

She accepted the glass with a smile. "Thank you. As for my foot it's as good as new." She pulled aside the hem of her gown, showing off a strappy sandal the same color as the dress. She'd painted her toenails blood red for the occasion.

After clearing his throat, Michael said, "I'm glad to see that you suffered no lasting effects from your injury."

"None whatsoever. I'm sure it was your careful ministrations that made all the difference in my full recovery. So, thank you."

"Are you referring to the first aid I administered, or what came afterward?" He arched his brows meaning-fully.

She ignored the question. "So what are you doing here?"

"I was invited. In the past I've supported Tempest's husband's political ambitions as well as her philanthropic endeavors. Apparently she remembered that and decided to send me a personalized note urging me to attend." He shrugged and came completely clean. "Of course, it's more likely she figured I wouldn't blink at the donation and hoped I might be willing to pony up a bit more."

Sam grinned now. "And have you?"

"Well, it is for a good cause."

"Yes, it is," she agreed. "The after-school program Tempest wants to see expanded throughout New York's boroughs is a proven winner at keeping 'tweens and teens from getting involved in drugs, gangs and sex."

"I see you read the brochure," he said to keep from groaning aloud. Sam looked like sin in a low-plunging sapphire gown and she'd had to go and mention sex.

He took a slow, bracing sip of his champagne, reminding himself of the business at hand. After swallowing, he asked, "So, that's the only reason you shelled out big money to be here tonight? You wanted to support a worthy cause?"

"What other reason would I have?" She smiled sweetly, apparently choosing to keep her cards close to her vest in the high-stakes game they were playing.

Michael opted to up the ante, but only enough to keep things interesting. "Oh, I don't know. I thought maybe you wanted to get an up-close-and-personal view of the Manhattan Herriman and its banquet facilities. They are top of the line and a major selling feature when it comes to conventions."

Sam's lips were painted a ripe shade of red, making her crafty smile a complete turn-on. "Do you really think I haven't already done that, Michael?"

"No. I've done it myself." He decided to toss in all of his chips. "So, maybe the real reason you're here is that you're hoping to catch Sidney Dumont alone, give her a little preview of what the Bradford Agency has to offer and then slip her your business card."

Sam's eyelids flickered in surprise and he figured he'd nailed it. Nonetheless, he gave her high marks for maintaining a bored tone when she replied, "Please, Michael. I wouldn't be as blatant as that."

He glanced over her shoulder and couldn't believe his luck. "That's good to know, because she's coming this way."

Sam barely had time to compose herself before she was face-to-face with the woman she'd been trying to snag a meeting with for more than a month.

"Michael," Sidney said, extending a hand. Though the woman was fifty if she was a day, Sam swore she batted her stubby eyelashes at him. And no wonder. The man did things for a tuxedo that should have been outlawed. "It's good to see you again."

*Again.* Sam had known they'd already met, but for some reason she seethed at the reminder.

As for Michael, he was oozing charm when he replied, "I was going to say the same." He turned toward Sam then, offering a wink that shouldn't have set off her pulse the way it did, especially given their surroundings. "This is Samantha Bradford. I'm sure you recognize the name. She works for the Bradford Agency. Sam, Sidney Dumont, the advertising manager at Herriman," he added unnecessarily.

"Ms. Dumont, I'm pleased to finally meet you." Sam offered her hand, which the other woman shook less than enthusiastically.

The three of them chatted politely about Tempest's charity for a few minutes, then Sidney made her excuses and left.

"I get the feeling she doesn't like me," Sam murmured as she watched the other woman disappear through the crowd. Turning to Michael, she added, "Which makes absolutely no sense. While I've called her office and left messages, I've never met her before tonight. You don't think she's put off by my persistence, do you?"

Michael was frowning. "I was pretty persistent myself. I had her office number on my speed dial at one point. I can't see where that would be an issue for someone in her position." Then, in a low, seductive voice, he said, "Maybe she's jealous of your beauty."

"And maybe you're full of—"

"Flattery?"

"Other words come to mind, but I guess that will do."

She smiled then, letting her puzzlement over Sidney's demeanor slip to the background. "Speaking of flattery, I suppose it's only fair I tell you how handsome you look this evening."

"Thanks. That's a great dress, by the way. I like what it does for your…waist." His gaze, however, was lingering a little higher than that. "It's by the same designer as the one you wore to the Addy's, I believe."

"You've got a good eye."

"Women's fashion isn't exactly my forte, but I try to pay attention when it's my client's work. So, are you still trying to lure him over to Bradford?" Michael inquired.

Sam shook her head. "I've got bigger fish to fry these days."

That wasn't the only reason, though. It felt wrong to go after Michael's clients if she was only doing so because they were his clients.

He seemed to understand. "I know what you mean." Then he leaned over to whisper in her ear, "You do look lovely."

"Thanks."

"I didn't realize you were going to be here."

"Does the fact that I am complicate matters for you?" she inquired.

"Only a lot." But he smiled after saying so. "The evening promises to be far more interesting now, so that's a plus. I like your hair like that, by the way."

She'd worn it up, sleekly twisted in the back.

Michael had always preferred it off her neck when they went out to formal events, she recalled now. He'd enjoyed the easy access to her nape and, when they were alone, he'd liked taking it down, pin by pin, and then running his fingers through it. Sam swallowed.

"Have you been doing a lot of thinking since we last saw each other?" she asked.

"Probably too much," he admitted. "I made a list of pros and cons the other night when I couldn't sleep. And not sleeping, by the way, has become a regular occurrence."

She knew exactly what he meant. All she seemed to do lately was toss and turn…and yearn. But she merely shrugged. "So, which column had more, the pros or the cons?"

"It was pretty much a tie."

"That's interesting." She sipped her champagne. And though it was a bold-faced lie, she told him, "I did the same thing myself."

"Really?"

"Yeah."

"And?"

She laughed softly. "Same outcome, I'm afraid."

"Should we go for a tie-breaker?" Michael stepped closer, close enough that she could smell his cologne. That masculine scent still lingered on her pillow.

"I don't know." She shrugged. "What will it prove? It shouldn't take a list of pros and cons to determine compatibility."

"No. There are other, more interactive ways to do that," he whispered suggestively into her ear, causing her to shiver.

Even though Sam wanted to move forward, she took a step back. "I believe we've already determined that we're more than compatible in that regard. That's one of the reasons we decided not to see each other for a while. It's hard to think when all you want to do is get naked."

"Did you have to put it like that? The mental image is…" He closed his eyes and groaned.

"Sorry." And she was. Michael wasn't the only one getting wound up. "Maybe we should talk about other things."

"Yes. Please. Although, let me say, we were good together, Sam. And I'm not just talking about in the bedroom."

She smiled and, as promised, changed the subject.

"I probably shouldn't ask this, but I've been dying to know. How did your meeting with Sidney go?"

"Well, I probably shouldn't tell you this, but it went well." It wasn't arrogance that lit up his eyes. It was excitement as he offered the highlights. "I wanted to call you afterward, just because I knew you'd understand how pumped up I was." He sobered then. "Hell, Sam, I've wanted to call more than just then. I've picked up the phone at least a dozen times with the intention of dialing your number."

"But you haven't."

"No." He unbuttoned his tuxedo jacket and tucked his free hand into the front pocket of his trousers. "What about you? Have you been tempted to call me?"

"Not in the least. I've wanted to *see* you," she admitted to him. To herself she added, and touch you, make love to you.

"And here I am." The carnal edge to his smile made her wonder if he'd been reading her mind.

"Did you come alone?"

"There was no one else I wanted to bring." Something behind Sam snagged Michael's attention then and his expression changed from turned on to ticked off. "I see you didn't have that problem."

Sam followed the direction of Michael's gaze. Just inside the entrance to the Grand Ballroom stood her father.

"What's he doing here?" she hissed.

Michael's attention snapped back to her. "You didn't know he was coming?"

"No. He said he had a late meeting with…a potential client," she finished as the edges of her vision turned red.

Her father was decked out in formal wear and already working the room like the professional he was, shaking hands, slapping backs and making introductions with Roger Louten, one of Bradford's newest account executives, at his side. When he spied Sam, Randolph's thousand-watt smile dimmed. Did he feel guilty at being caught or was he merely annoyed? At the moment Sam didn't really care.

She saw him lean over to say something to Roger, apparently excusing himself. A moment later he joined her and Michael.

"Hello, Samantha."

Randolph pointedly ignored Michael, who took a step back and said, "I'll go find us a couple of seats."

When they were alone, her father demanded in a hushed tone, "What are you doing here?"

"I guess you could say I have a late meeting with a potential client," she replied, parroting his earlier words. "I think we both know who that potential client is. How could you go behind my back this way, Dad?"

"I haven't gone behind your back. I'm just offering a little assistance. We work on the same team, remember. Michael Lewis is the one you have to watch out for."

She didn't see it that way. Michael might be her rival, but he respected her talents far more than her father did. Indeed, if they were talking adversaries, Sam considered Roger a bigger one than Michael ever was. "Why is Roger here, Dad? You think I need help landing this account so you bring in someone who's been with our agency all of a year?"

"It's not like that." But he glanced away, tugged on his mustache, leaving Sam with the sinking certainty that it was exactly like that. "He's a smart young man, if a little green. I thought you both might benefit from working together on this account."

"When were you going to mention this to me?"

But then she shook her head. "No, what I really want to know is, how long ago did you make this decision?"

"I've had Roger working on it for a couple of weeks now. You weren't getting anywhere, Sam."

It took an effort to maintain her composure. Her voice rose only a little as she replied, "I beg to differ! I've spent hours researching the market and spent late nights working up a creative strategy."

"That's your strength," Randolph agreed, throwing her a bone. "Roger, however, is more aggressive than you are. He's made several contacts with Sidney's people."

She expelled a breath and in a dry tone said, "And yet we're both here tonight trying to get a few minutes of her time. It doesn't appear that wonder boy is all that wonderful, and I'm not sharing my account with him. I don't care if we're on the same team or not."

"This isn't your call."

She crossed her arms. "It should be and you know it." In the hope that he would see reason, she pointed out for a second time, "I'm the one who first heard the rumors and followed up on them. I've done the research, spent hours on it as a matter of fact. You know that, since you've dogged me every step of the way."

"I'm sorry, Sam. We can't afford to let an account of this size slip to a competitor."

"And you have so little faith in my ability after my seven years at Bradford that you think I'd allow that to happen?"

"It's not personal," he said.

Would he offer that same excuse if in the end he handed over the reins of the agency to someone else? "It is, Dad. It's completely personal. You've never believed in me. Not when I was twelve or twenty or even now that I'm in my thirties. Sonya could do no wrong as far as you were concerned and I still can't get anything right."

"Sam, please." He rolled his eyes. "Now is not the time for female histrionics or family squabbles."

She chose to ignore the female histrionics comment, but not the other. "When is the time for family disagreements? We rarely socialize outside of work, Dad. When you get right down to it, our relationship is far more professional than it is personal."

"You've been listening to Lewis again," he accused. "He's always been eager to turn you against me."

"Do you really think he's had to try? You've managed that all on your own."

"Don't push it, Sam."

"Or what? You'll disown me? You'll *fire* me?" She expelled a liberating breath. "Aren't they one and the same thing where our relationship is concerned?"

Randolph's jaw clenched. She expected an explosion. Instead he said, "Let's mind the matter at hand and leave this for another time. I see that Roger has already managed to engage Ms. Dumont in conversation."

He sounded so triumphant that Sam had to say, "I've talked to Sidney tonight, too. I was introduced to her just before you arrived."

Randolph's eyes narrowed, but at least she had his full attention. "And?"

Although it was an utter embellishment of the truth, Sam said, "She promised me a moment of her time later this evening." She gestured toward Roger, who apparently was receiving the same cool reception and quick dismissal Sam had earlier. "It doesn't appear she appreciates having another Bradford representative stalking her between now and then."

Randolph nodded begrudgingly. "Roger and I will leave after dinner. But you'd better have something concrete to show for tonight or changes may be in order."

She resented the warning. Even more, she hated that it had her stomach knotting with the same dread she'd always experienced as a child. "Of course," she said just as Michael returned.

Turning to her father, she said a little awkwardly, "You remember Michael."

"Only too well," Randolph muttered as his gaze slid to the side. Not surprisingly, he failed to offer a hand.

Michael took his rudeness in stride. "Hello, Randolph. It's been a while."

"Not long enough. And I prefer that you call me Mr. Bradford," came her father's stony reply.

"Gee, and to think that at one time I was all set to call you Dad."

Sam felt her lips twitch as her father's face turned an unbecoming shade of purple. Michael and her father had never gotten along, and it had irked Randolph to no end that he'd been unable to intimidate the younger man.

He turned to Sam. "If you're really serious about the matter we just discussed, Samantha, you'd better think twice about the company you keep."

Her mirth of a moment ago evaporated. "I have."

"Good." Randolph flashed a smile at Michael. "Roger and I will save you a place at our table."

"That won't be necessary." She pushed her arm through Michael's. "I have other plans. I'll see you Monday morning."

## CHAPTER TEN

MICHAEL didn't say anything as he escorted Sam to the seats he'd found for them at a table near the stage. Even though he was pleased and a little surprised by the way she'd just stood up to her father, he didn't think she'd appreciate hearing him say so at the moment. She looked wound tight enough to explode.

A couple of other people were already seated at their table. They introduced themselves, chatted briefly, as was only polite. Once they were settled in their seats, he told her, "I took the liberty of getting you another glass of champagne."

"I could use something a little stronger than that," she muttered.

"What would you like?" When he started to rise, she stopped him by laying a hand on his arm.

"That's okay, Michael. I need to keep a clear head." She huffed out a breath, looking both angry and perplexed when she added, "Suddenly everything seems to be riding on tonight."

"What do you mean?"

"Never mind."

"So you didn't know Randolph was coming," he remarked casually.

"No. Of course, I kept him in the dark about my plans, too."

"Why?"

She shook her head, as if to signal an end to the questioning, but then she admitted, "Dad's been fly-specking my every move ever since I told him about Herriman. He's always badgering me for an update and when I don't have anything new to report, which lately I haven't, he's…" Sam sighed.

She didn't have to finish. Michael knew just how un-reasonable and demanding her father could be, especially when it came to his younger daughter.

"So, who's the guy he brought with him?"

"Apparently, competition," she grumbled.

"What?"

She shook her head. "Forget it."

When she remained silent, Michael coaxed, "Come on. You can talk to me, Sam. Friend to friend."

Sam turned sideways in her chair and faced him fully. "Is that what we are, Michael? Friends?"

A pair of dark eyes brimmed with other, more spe-cific questions regarding their relationship. He had answers for her. Suddenly, he had answers for himself, but now was neither the right time nor place. So he offered a trimmed-down version of the truth.

"We're also a lot more than friends, and I'm not re-ferring to anything to do with our careers."

She closed her eyes and sighed. "It doesn't matter anyway. Here I've been worried about you and it turns out that my biggest adversary is in the office three doors down the hall."

"The guy with your father," he surmised.

"Roger Louten," she spat out the name. "He's a young and very hungry account executive. Dad hired him fresh from college barely a year ago, and I just found out that he's been working on the Herriman account behind my back. Dad tried to pass it off as wanting me to act as a mentor. You know, help season the new kid. But that doesn't change the fact that my father is treating me like an inexperienced rookie."

Michael seethed for her at the insult. Sam was so damned talented and creative. Her campaigns were nothing shy of brilliant. If her peers in the industry recognized that, why couldn't her father?

"What an ass," he mumbled.

"Who? Roger, Randolph or me?" Her laughter was laced with disgust. "And I had to go and inflate the truth, make it sound like Sidney has agreed to talk to me this evening."

"The night's young. You can make that happen." He didn't stop to question why he hoped that Sam got her chance. Suddenly calling the Herriman account his wasn't as important as seeing Sam happy and confident again.

"God, I hope so."

Because she sounded so glum, he said, "Even if it doesn't, it's not the end of the world. Call her office first thing Monday and go from there."

"Monday will be too late. You're right about my father, Michael. You've always been right."

He knew that, of course, but it pained him to see her so miserable, so damned defeated. "I'm sorry, Sam. For what it's worth, I don't want to be right." When her eyes grew bright and he saw her swallow, his own throat ached. "Don't, Sam," he whispered hoarsely and reached for her hand. "Don't cry."

She blinked rapidly and worked up a smile, rallying in a way that made Michael proud of her and eager to go a few rounds in a boxing ring, gloves optional, with Randolph.

"Thanks." She squeezed his hand, laced her fingers through his. "If nothing else good comes of tonight, at least I got to dance with you."

Michael blinked in confusion. "Did I miss something? The music hasn't started yet."

"No, but when it does I know you'll ask me."

"I will," he promised. Not only because Samantha Bradford was a hard woman to resist, but because Michael no longer wanted to.

They dined on mixed baby greens drizzled in a light vinaigrette, grilled salmon served on a bed of asparagus risotto and tender green beans topped with sliced almonds. Though the food was first class, Sam merely picked at it. Michael understood completely her lack of appetite. But when dessert arrived, she perked up considerably. It was a rich chocolate layer cake topped with a fresh raspberry sauce and chocolate shavings.

"Appetite coming back?" he asked, as she nipped off a corner with her fork.

"It's chocolate, Michael. I'd have to be dead not to eat chocolate." She eyed his cake. "Are you going to eat that?"

"Yeah. But I could be persuaded to share."

"How so?"

"I'll tell you later."

And he did, while they danced, holding Sam close and whispering a suggestion in her ear that made them both eager to call it an evening. First, though, Sam needed to speak to Sidney.

Michael walked the perimeter of the room while Sam went to the ladies' room to freshen up. Sidney actually found him.

"I couldn't help but notice how cozy you were with Samantha Bradford on the dance floor," she remarked. "I find that rather interesting considering that you're both after the same thing."

Yes, they were. And it had nothing to do with advertising, he thought. But he said, "Business is business."

"Yes."

"You don't seem to like her," he commented. "Or maybe I'm reading you wrong."

"You're not reading me wrong. I don't like pushy advertising execs who step over boundaries. The Bradford Agency seems to be full of them. Her father accosted my assistant at the gym, got him to confirm that we were looking for new blood before I was ready to do so publicly. Now tonight, both she and another young man from their agency have approached me."

"Sam didn't approach you," he felt compelled to point out. "Actually, you approached the two of us and I introduced you. Work was never mentioned."

Sidney let out an indelicate snort. "Yes, but it's a good bet it would have been, given the number of times she's called my office in the past few weeks."

"Can I ask why you haven't returned her calls?"

"Call it an idiosyncrasy of mine," Sidney said with a wave of her hand. "I spend nearly seventy hours in my office each week. When I leave for the day, I prefer not to discuss work unless it's with my employer. I certainly don't appreciate having my assistant ambushed after hours."

"So you've blackballed the Bradford Agency," he said.

"Yes."

"That's a shame."

"A shame?" Sidney eyed him in surprise. "I should think that news would make you happy. I plan to make my decision soon and there are already enough hats in the ring. Don't you want to come out on top?"

"I like to be the best," Michael said slowly. "To that end I prefer to compete against the best."

Her eyes narrowed. "You're saying Samantha Bradford is so good you wouldn't mind losing to her."

"Oh, I'd mind," he corrected. "But I'd know the best campaign won."

"With all of the other advertising executives out there, you assume that one or the other of you is the best?"

"That's right," he agreed with a nod.

"You're cocky, Michael." But Sidney chuckled.

"I've been told that before. I like to think of myself as confident."

"Yes, well, for all that I still like you." Sidney tilted her head to one side. "Does Samantha Bradford know how much you love her?"

Michael swallowed. That obvious, he thought? He didn't care. Shaking his head, he said, "I don't think so, but I'm planning to remedy that soon."

Sidney laughed. "You do realize that yours is going to be a complicated relationship given your jobs?"

"Yes." But life without Sam had its own set of complications. He'd prefer her in it, and they could work out whatever problems arose, even if she forgave Randolph again and decided to stay at his agency.

Over Sidney's shoulder, he spied Sam. She was heading their way, no doubt preparing to offer a subtle pitch. Given what he'd just learned, he had to stop her. Otherwise she would blow what little chance she had of getting her foot in the door.

"Will you excuse me?"

"Of course." Glancing in Sam's direction, Sidney said, "Tell her to call my office on Monday. First thing after lunch."

He blinked in surprise. "Really?"

"I'm not promising anything," the woman warned. "But I'll talk to her. After all, while she's been tenacious, she's also been the least offensive one from her agency to approach me. Perhaps I've been unfair."

"Thanks."

Sidney waved her hand in dismissal. "Fools," he thought he heard her mutter as he walked away.

"Sam." Michael reached for her arm, stopping her in her tracks a dozen feet from where Sidney stood. "I have to talk to you."

"In a minute."

"Now."

She glanced up at him. "Can't it wait, Michael? Sidney is right there. And she's alone."

"I know. That's what I need to talk to you about. Please."

"But—"

"Trust me," he said.

He experienced relief and something far deeper when Sam nodded and let him lead her to a quiet corner of the room.

"I was talking to Sidney and she mentioned how much she hates being approached in public about work. Apparently, she's especially irritated with your father for 'accosting' her assistant, and that's a quote."

"That would explain the cold shoulder she's been giving me."

"Yes."

"So talking to her now would be the kiss of death." Sam closed her eyes and let out a sigh. "Great. She won't return my calls and the one time I see her I can't talk to her about business."

He squeezed her arm. "Call her Monday."

"Why? What difference will it make?" Sam asked.

"Call her." He smiled and for a second time said, "Trust me, okay?"

"What did you do, Michael?"

He shrugged. "I just told her the truth. That you're one of the best in the business."

Sam swallowed. "You did that? For me? Why?"

A number of reasons came to mind. The one he offered was, "When I beat you, I want it to be fair and square."

The phone rang first thing the following morning. Sam had to wriggle from beneath Michael's heavy arm to reach for it.

Into the receiver she offered a sleepy, "Hello."

"What happened after Roger and I left last night?"

It was her father. Apparently, he'd decided he couldn't wait until Monday morning to get a report.

"What time is it?" she mumbled, pushing the hair out of her eyes so she could squint at the clock. It was barely 8:00 a.m.

"Never mind the time," he said impatiently. "Did you talk to Sidney last night? What did she say?"

"I…I'm to call her Monday."

"And?" Randolph pressed.

"There is no and. I imagine she'll let me know then if she wants to set up an appointment."

"That's all?" His disappointment came through loud and clear.

"That's more than Roger has managed while working behind my back," she snapped. "And by the way, Dad, it turns out that Sidney is a little peeved with you for approaching her assistant at the gym and tricking him into confirming the rumors. That's why she hasn't returned any of my calls. I'm lucky she's agreed to speak to me at all."

She glanced at Michael, who had begun to stir. Lucky, she thought again, when his eyes opened and his lips curved in irresistible invitation.

"Well, all that is water under the bridge now," Randolph was saying. "We'll get together first thing Monday and you, Roger and I can—"

Whatever else her father was about to say was lost as Sam hung up the phone.

"Good morning," she told Michael.

"Yeah." Pulling her close, he murmured against her neck, "I know a way to make it even better."

# CHAPTER ELEVEN

SAM was smiling when she arrived at the Bradford Agency bright and early Monday. She and Michael had spent the entire weekend together, visiting with Sonya on Saturday, after which they'd enjoyed a quiet dinner in her apartment. As for Sunday, they'd spent most of it in bed talking, reading, watching old movies and making love.

In addition to showing Sam how much he loved her, Michael had said the words, quietly, passionately and with the hint of a promise.

This morning, before they'd each headed off to their respective places of work, he'd kissed her soundly before hailing her a cab.

"Good luck."

"Same to you," she'd said.

"Dinner tonight?"

"Yes. And let's eat in again." She'd grinned, he'd groaned and all had been right with the world…until she walked into her office half an hour later.

Randolph was in the chair behind her desk, peering at the screen of her computer, which had been booted up. Roger was sifting through some mock-ups that Sam had had the art department prepare the previous week.

"What's going on? What are you doing in here?" she demanded, setting her attaché case aside.

"We're just doing some prep work for your meeting with Sidney. I expected you to be in earlier," Randolph said, his tone censorious.

"It's only eight o'clock. And I don't have a meeting with Sidney." Yet, she added silently. "She said to call her after lunch."

"Have a seat. Between now and then I want you to become acquainted with some of the ideas Roger has and work them into your campaign."

"Work them into—" Sam was seething. She was furious and ready to blow. She inhaled deeply, trying to employ the breathing technique she'd relied on in the past to help her relax. Instead of expelling the breath slowly, she let it whoosh out along with a couple of choice expletives. She didn't want to relax.

"Absolutely not! I have a clear vision for Herriman Hotels. If I get the account and once I've met with the Herriman people, if *they* decide they want something different than what I have to offer, then *and only then*," she stressed, "will I make changes."

"There's no *i* in teamwork, Sam," Roger intoned at the same time her father said, "Be reasonable."

"Being reasonable hasn't gotten me very far with

you, Dad." She crossed her arms. A couple of ultimatums came to mind. She opted to keep the more permanent one in reserve. "I do this my way or I don't make the call. Since she won't take one from either of you, think carefully before making your decision."

For the rest of the morning, Sam remained closeted in her office, going over the data from the market research department, Herriman's current advertising strategy and paring down her pitch enough to pique Sidney's curiosity.

It was five minutes past one o'clock when she reached for the phone and with a shaking finger dialed the advertising manager's number. When the receptionist put her right through Sam nearly sighed, but then Sidney was on the other end of the line.

"Samantha, hello."

"Hello and thank you for taking my call."

"You've been pretty persistent," Sidney said coolly.

It wasn't exactly what Sam wanted to hear. She cleared her throat and fingered the sheaf of papers before her on the desk blotter. "Yes. Well, I know you're a busy woman so I'll try to make this as brief as possible, while also keeping it irresistible. Quite obviously, the Bradford Agency wants your account. And I think we can offer you an effective multimedia campaign unlike anything you'll get elsewhere."

It was as far as she got before Sidney stopped her. "I'm sorry. I don't want to waste any more of your time or mine. We've already made a decision."

"A decision," Sam repeated dully.

"Yes. Goodbye."

Sam hung up the phone in a daze. What had just happened here? She was still trying to figure that out when Randolph barged into her office a little later.

"I don't get it. Why would she agree to talk to you and then make a decision before even taking your call? Instead of acting as if you were on a date with Lewis, you should have given her something to whet her appetite on Friday. God!" he thundered. "I can't believe you let an account this large just slip away." He shook his head in disgust as he stalked about the room, muttering other comments under his breath. Finally, his anger spent, he asked, "What agency did they go with?"

"I don't know."

"Most likely Grafton Surry," Randolph sneered. "Michael is probably out celebrating even as we speak. Hell, he probably had the account all sewn up on Friday and let Sidney string you along."

"No. Michael would have no reason to do that."

"Revenge," Randolph replied. "I told you that once, and you wouldn't listen."

Revenge. That wasn't what Michael was after.

"He wouldn't do that," she said. But might he have told Sam to call Monday rather than risk having her pique Sidney's interest at the ball, especially if he knew the Herriman people would be making a decision soon?

No, she told herself. Absolutely not. But doubts niggled, growing more insistent when she hadn't heard from him by late afternoon. Sam considered calling him, but in the end decided this was a conversation that needed to occur face to face.

She'd never been to the offices of Grafton Surry. She barely noticed the tasteful furnishings and artwork now as she followed the receptionist to the one where Michael sat behind a desk.

"Hey, Sam. I take it you heard the news about Herriman?" he said when they were alone. His phone began to ring, but he ignored it.

"Yes, I did. I got it from the horse's mouth, so to speak, when I called Sidney."

"Oh. That stinks."

"Yeah." She tilted her head to one side and studied him. "I'm surprised you didn't call after you got word."

"I wanted to, but I've been tied up in a meeting. This is the first break I've had all afternoon."

I bet, she thought. But then she reminded herself not to jump to conclusions. The pledge lasted only until the receptionist poked her head around the door a moment later to inform him, "I have Sidney Dumont on the line, Mr. Lewis. She said she needs to speak to you again."

Michael blinked and Sam gave him high marks for managing to act so surprised. Where her father's betrayals hurt, this one cut to the bone.

"My God, Michael. I can't believe you did this."

"What are you talking about?"

She shoved the hair back from her face. "Offering that tripe about Sidney not liking to be approached outside of work and then getting me to wait to talk to her until today when you knew damned well it would be too late."

"I knew no such thing. I was just as surprised as you when she called to say they'd made a decision."

She shook her head in disgust. "What was it you said that night when I asked you why you would encourage Sidney to hear me out? That you wanted to beat me fair and square. And to think I believed you."

"I didn't lie, Sam." He reached for arm, but she tugged it away. "Why would I lie?"

"I think I've already spelled it out."

"You're not making sense."

"No, Michael. I'm finally done letting my emotions run my life and rule my career."

Michael wasn't sure what had just happened. All he knew was that he didn't understand any of it. He hadn't lied about anything and he sure as hell hadn't set Sam up for failure.

Glancing up, he realized the receptionist and Russ were standing in the same doorway through which Sam had just exited. The receptionist looked embarrassed to have overheard the private exchange. Russ looked livid.

"Miss Dumont on line one," the young woman reminded him before turning to leave.

"I want to see you immediately after you hang up," Russ barked ominously.

"Sidney, hello. Calling back to tell me you made a mistake and want to go with Grafton Surry?"

She chuckled. "Sorry. Actually, it occurred to me that when we spoke earlier I should have apologized about Samantha Bradford. I told you to have her call, but then we wound up moving more quickly than I anticipated."

"I figured that out."

"Anyway, I'm sorry. For what it's worth, I think it's probably a good thing that neither of you got the account, given how hungry you both were for it."

Michael thanked her and hung up. He doubted Sam would agree, especially since at the moment she thought Michael had bested her. She'd know better, of course, if she had allowed him a chance to tell his side of things. But no, she'd jumped to the wrong and unflattering conclusion that he'd cheated. Michael's anger spiked, but then, just as quickly, it ebbed. He had a choice to make. He could simmer in his own self-righteousness and let her walk out of his life as he had done seven years ago or he could go after her and try to put things right.

Back then they'd both been too hard-headed to compromise. He didn't intend to let miscommunication stand between them a second time.

Michael was on his way to the elevator when he remembered Russ and made what he hoped would be a quick detour to his supervisor's office. When he left Grafton Surry two hours later, it was with the boxed-up belongings from his desk and a supreme sense of satisfaction.

\* \* \*

Sam glanced through the peep hole and clenched her teeth. She'd have to have a word with the doorman about letting just anyone up.

"Come on, Sam," Michael hollered. "I know you're in there. I've already been to your office."

It was only out of deference to her neighbors that she opened the door the width of the security chain and, glaring, informed him, "Then you know that I no longer work there."

"I heard that, yes. Was it because of what happened with the Herriman account?"

"The Herriman account was the last straw of many," she replied.

"I'm sorry, Sam." Michael shook his head. "I can't believe he fired you."

"You think I was fired?" Her laughter was brittle. "I quit."

She enjoyed watching Michael's mouth fall open. When he recovered from his surprise, he asked slowly, "How do you feel about that?"

"Good." She nodded for emphasis when she added, "Great, in fact, even though he threatened to disown me. You know, that's when it struck me. To disown somebody you have to own them first. And when you own somebody they're a possession, not a person."

Michael's expression turned soft. "Come on, Sam. Let me in so we can talk."

"What more is there to say? Congratulations?"

He shrugged. "If you really want to offer those, you'll have to call William Daniels at Quest Advertising."

"What?" she asked, sure she'd heard him wrong.

"He got the account." Michael shook his head, looking chagrined. "I'd sure as hell like to know what he offered that was better than what I did."

Sam slammed the door in his face, but only to undo the chain and fling it back open. "I thought you got it."

"Yes." He rubbed his chin. "I realized that when you were standing in my office making all sorts of wild accusations and refusing to listen to my side of the story."

"I…but you…and then Sidney…oh." Sam decided it was best to stop talking.

"You're kind of cute when you're in the wrong." He tipped up her chin with his index finger and dropped a kiss on her lips. "And I have to say, I never thought I'd see the day you were rendered all but speechless."

"You're enjoying this?" Her bafflement was real. She'd accused him of horrible things, yet here he was at her door making light of it.

"I wouldn't say I'm enjoying it, exactly. Do you know why I came here, Sam?"

She wasn't sure of anything at the moment, except that she owed him one huge apology, so she shook her head.

"I came here because seven years ago I was the one jumping to all the wrong conclusions and failing to let you explain. That bit of stupidity cost me dearly."

"Michael—"

He laid his fingers over her lips. "Let me finish, Sam. This needs to be said. I don't know how I got through the past seven years of my life without you. I did, but only because I was too proud and too pig-headed to call you back and try to work things out."

"I could have done that, too," she said. "We're both at fault."

"I know that. Don't think I'm letting you off the hook completely, sweetheart, either then or now," he said with a grin, but then his expression sobered. "It's just that this time, I decided that no matter who was the one jumping to conclusions, I wasn't going to risk losing you again. So here I am, on your door-step." She watched him swallow. "Are you going to let me in?"

Tears spilled down Sam's cheeks as she reached for him and pulled him inside. With her cheek pressed against his, she whispered, "I love you, Michael."

"I love you, too."

Though they'd made love just that morning, when they did so now much had changed. *They* had changed, Sam realized, both of them breaking free of the past.

She sighed contentedly as she lay next to Michael and the shadows grew long in her bedroom.

"So, what are you going to do now?" Michael asked.

"I was thinking about ordering takeout. I'm starving and I want to keep up my strength."

His laughter shook the bed. "I second that idea, but I was talking about your job."

"Ah. Do you know if Grafton Surry is hiring?" she asked.

He levered up on one elbow. "As a matter of fact, they are."

"Great. Maybe you can put in a good word for me. It might be nice for us both to work at the same agency for a change."

"I was thinking the same thing." He grinned, but left her confused when he said, "But that won't happen at Grafton Surry."

"Why not?"

"I don't work there any longer."

"What?" She sat up, causing the covers to fall away from her breasts. When Michael's gaze lowered, Sam poked his bare chest. "Focus, Lewis."

"I am."

"On the conversation," she said dryly. "You were saying?"

"I quit today, too."

"You quit?"

"Resigned. It sounds nicer and you know how I am about phrasing."

"But why? What happened?"

"Russ was irritated as hell when he overheard you mention that I talked to Sidney on your behalf. Before he could launch into a lecture that I truly didn't want to hear, I explained a few pertinent facts to him."

"Such as?"

"One, I didn't like working under his supervision. Two, I didn't like working under anyone's supervision. I've talked about starting my own agency for a long time now."

"You mentioned that you shared a few pertinent facts. What was the third?"

"That I love you."

"You told Russ you loved him?"

He laughed, pulled her toward him. "You know what I mean."

"Yeah."

"And I told him that you and I were going into business together."

Sam pulled back. "You…that's what you want?"

"I do. You're too good. I can't let you work for someone else."

The sincerity in his voice touched her deeply. "Oh, Michael."

"So, how does Lewis and Bradford sound to you?"

"It sounds wonderful, and almost as good as Bradford and Lewis."

"It was my idea."

"Bradford comes before Lewis in the alphabet."

"True." He nuzzled her neck just below her ear and began to work his way down.

When she caught her breath, Sam asked, "So, it's settled?"

His head lifted and he smiled. "I've got a better idea. How about Lewis and Lewis?"

Her heart did a crazy roll. "As in Samantha Lewis and Michael Lewis?"

"You just have to have top billing, don't you?" But he chuckled. "So, is that yes?"

"It's better than yes."

In the dwindling light, he squinted at her. "What's better than yes?"

Pushing him down on the mattress, Sam said, "Let me show you."

# MYSTERIOUS MILLIONAIRE

BY
CASSIE MILES

For **Cassie Miles**, the best part about writing a story set in Eagle County near the Vail ski area is the ready-made excuse to head into the mountains for research. Though the winter snows are great for skiing, her favourite season is autumn, when the aspens turn gold.

The rest of the time Cassie lives in Denver, where she takes urban hikes around Cheesman Park, reads a ton and critiques often. Her current plans include a Vespa and a road trip, despite eye-rolling objections from her adult children.

To those who love guitars and wooden boats.
As always, to Rick.

# Chapter One

Being a part-time private eye put a serious crimp in Liz Norton's social life. At half-past eleven on a Friday night in May, she ought to be wearing lip gloss, dancing, flirting and licking the suds off a beer that somebody else had paid for. Instead, she'd spent the past two hours and seventeen minutes on stakeout with Harry Schooner, her sixty-something boss.

She slouched behind the steering wheel of Harry's beat-up Chevy. Even with the windows cracked for ventilation, she still smelled stale hamburger buns from the crumpled bags littering the backseat. On the plus side, the cruddy, old car blended with the rundown Denver neighborhood where they were parked at the curb away from the streetlight, watching and waiting.

In the passenger seat, Harry pressed his fist against his chest and grunted.

"Are you okay?" she asked.

"Heartburn."

His digestive system provided a source of constant complaint. Long ago, she'd given up lecturing him on the evils of a strictly fast-food diet. "Did you take your pill?"

"What are you? My mother?"

"A concerned employee," she said. "If you keel over from a heart attack, where am I going to find another job as glamorous as this one?"

He peeled off the silver wrapping on a roll of antacid tablets, popped the last one in his mouth and tossed the wrapper over his shoulder into the trashed-out backseat. "That reminds me. You're done with your semester. Right?"

"Took my last exam two days ago."

At age twenty-six, she'd put herself halfway through law school. The accomplishment made her proud, even though she still heard echoes of her mother's refrain: *"Why bother with an education? The only way a girl like you can make it is to find a man to support you."* This bit of advice came right before the grooming tips: *"Lighten your hair, shorten your skirts and stand up straight so your boobs stick out."*

Of course, Liz did the exact opposite. Her thick, multi-colored blond hair remained undyed and unstyled—except for her own occasional hacking to keep the jagged ends near chin-length. Her wardrobe included exactly one skirt—knee-length and khaki—that she'd picked up at a thrift store for a buck. Mostly, she wore jeans and T-shirts. Tonight, a faded brown one under a black wind-breaker. As for Mom's advice to show off her chest, Liz had given up on that plan long ago. Even if she arched her back like a pretzel, nobody would ever confuse her with a beauty queen.

Her twice-married mom had actually done her a favor when she'd shoved her only daughter out the door on her eighteenth birthday and told her that she was on her own.

Liz had done okay. Without a man.

Harry groaned again and shifted in the passenger seat.

"You'll come to work for me full-time during your summer break. I could use the help. I'm getting too damn old for this job."

"Thanks, Harry." She'd been counting on this summer job. "But I still need Monday and Wednesday nights free to teach the under-twelve kids at the karate school."

"I got no problem with that." He made a wheezy noise through his nostrils and shrugged his heavy shoulders. His formerly athletic physique had settled into a doughy lump. Only his close-cropped white hair suggested the discipline of long-ago military service and twenty years as a cop. "How's my grandson doing at karate?"

"Not exactly a black belt, but he's hanging in there." She'd met Harry at Dragon Lou's Karate School when he'd come to watch his six-year-old grandson and ended up offering Liz a couple of part-time assignments.

Some aspects of being a P.I. were just plain nasty, like serving subpoenas or confirming the suspicions of a heartbroken wife about her cheating husband. But Liz enjoyed the occasional undercover disguise. Most of all, she liked grumpy old Harry and his two grown daughters. The Schooners represented the family she'd never had.

She peered through the scummy windshield at a ramshackle bungalow, landscaped with weeds and two rusty vehicles up on blocks. Gangsta music blared through the open windows. In the past hour, a half-dozen visitors had come and gone. She'd caught glimpses of three or four skinny children playing, even though it was way past normal bedtime, and she hoped the drug dealers inside the house weren't selling in front of the kids. Or to them.

"Are you sure we have the right address?"

"My source gave me the place, but not the time. He'll be here tonight." Harry rubbed his palms together. "Once we have photos of Mr. Crawford making a drug buy, we're in for a real big payday."

Liz found it hard to believe that Ben Crawford—millionaire adventurer and playboy—would show up in person. Didn't rich people hire underlings to do their dirty work?

But she hoped Harry was right. The Schooner Detective Agency could use the cash. They'd been retained by Ben's estranged wife, Victoria, who wanted enough dirt on her husband to void the prenup and gain sole custody of their five-year-old daughter. Photos of Ben making a drug buy would insure that Victoria got what she wanted, and she'd promised a huge bonus for the results.

Though Liz felt a twinge of regret about separating a father from his child, Ben Crawford deserved to be exposed. He'd been born with every advantage and was throwing his life away on drugs. In her book, that made him a lousy human being and definitely an unfit father.

A shiny, black Mustang glided to the curb in front of the house. This had to be their millionaire.

Harry shoved the camera into her hands. "You take the pictures. Don't worry. I'll back you up."

"Stay in the car, Harry."

"Get close to the front window," he said as he flipped open the glove compartment and took out an ancient Remington automatic.

A jolt of adrenaline turned her stakeout lethargy to tension. If Harry started waving his gun, this situation could get ugly. "Put that thing away."

"Don't you worry, Missy. I don't plan to shoot anybody." With another grunt, he opened his car door. "Go for the money shot. Crawford with the drugs in his hand."

The camera was foolproof—geared to automatically focus and adjust to minimal lighting. But she doubted she'd get a chance to use it. Most of the visitors to the house went inside, did their business and came out with hands shoved deeply into their pockets.

She darted across the street toward the dealer's house and ducked behind one of the junker cars in the driveway. Ben Crawford stood at the front door beside a bare bulb porch light. His shaggy brown hair fell over the collar of his worn denim shirt, only a few shades lighter than his jeans. He looked like a tall, rangy cowboy who had somehow gotten lost in the big city.

Holding the camera to her eye, Liz zoomed in on his face. *Wow.* Not only rich but incredibly good-looking, he had a firm jaw, high cheekbones and deep-set eyes. What was he doing here?

She pulled back on the zoom to include the dealer in his black mesh T-shirt and striped track pants. He pushed open the torn screen door and stepped onto the concrete slab porch under a rusted metal awning.

The pounding beat of rap music covered any noise Liz made as she clicked off several photos to make sure she caught them together.

Instead of going inside, Ben remained on the porch. For a moment, she hoped he wasn't here to make a buy, that there was a legitimate reason. Then he pulled a roll of bills from his pocket. The dealer handed over three brown, plastic vials.

*Click. Click. Click.* She had the money shot. A big payday for the Schooner Detective Agency.

The two men shook hands. Ben pivoted and returned to his Mustang while the dealer stood on the porch and watched Ben's taillights as he drove away.

Another man with a scraggly beard staggered outside and pointed.

Liz glanced over her shoulder to see what they were looking at. Harry crouched between two cars at the curb, his white hair gleaming in the moonlight.

"Hey, old man." The dealer came off the porch. "What the hell you doing?"

Harry straightened his stiff joints. "Guess I got lost."

"You watching us?" The two men stepped into the yard. From down the street, she heard ferocious barking, the prelude to a fight, and she knew Harry wasn't up to it.

She stashed the camera in the pocket of her windbreaker and rushed toward her partner. "There you are, Gramps. I've been looking all over for you." To the two men in the yard, she said, "Sorry if he bothered you. He wanders sometimes."

Their cold sneers told her that they weren't buying her story. The dealer snapped, "Stop right there, bitch."

"I'll just take Gramps home and—"

The crack of a gunshot brought her to a halt. She froze at the edge of the yard, praying that Harry wouldn't return fire. A shootout wouldn't be good for anybody.

Liz turned and faced the two men, who swaggered toward her. Her pulse raced, not so much from fear as uncertainty. She didn't know what to expect. Forcing an innocent smile, she said, "There's no need for guns."

"What's in your pocket? You carrying heat?"

As long as they didn't immobilize her, she ought to be able to take these two guys. Her five years studying martial arts at Dragon Lou's gave her an edge. Liz was capable of shattering a cinderblock with her bare hand.

From across the street, Harry yelled, "Leave her alone."

*Please, Harry. Please don't use your gun.* She had to act fast. No time to wait and see.

Liz aimed a flying kick at the bearded guy, neatly disarming him. Before his buddy could react, she whirled, chopped at his arm and kicked again. Though her hand missed, the heavy sole of her boot connected with his knee, and he stumbled.

The bearded man grabbed her forearm. Worst possible scenario. Both men had more brute strength than she did. Her advantage was speed and agility. She twisted and flipped, wrenching her arm free. He still clung to the sleeve of her windbreaker. She escaped by slipping out of her jacket.

Before they could brace themselves for another assault, she unleashed a series of kicks and straight-hand chops. Not a pretty, precise display. She wouldn't win any tournament points for style, but she got the job done with several swift blows to vulnerable parts of their anatomy. Throat. Gut. Groin.

Both were on their knees.

Another man rushed out the door. And another.

Behind her back, she heard Harry fire his automatic. Five shots.

She ran for the car.

Harry collapsed into the passenger side as she dived behind the wheel and cranked the ignition. Without turning on the headlights, she burned rubber and tore down the street.

Gunfire exploded behind them.

Liz didn't cut her speed until they reached a major intersection, where she turned on the headlights and merged into traffic. Her heart hammered inside her rib cage. They could have been killed. The aftermath of intense danger exploded behind her eyelids like belated fireworks.

Thank God for Dragon Lou and his martial arts training.

Beside her in the passenger seat, Harry was breathing heavily. With the back of his hand, he wiped sweat from his forehead. "Did you get the pictures?"

She cringed. "The camera was in my windbreaker. The bearded guy pulled it off me."

"It's okay."

"But you're not." She took note of his pasty complexion and heaving chest. "I'm taking you to the emergency room."

"You'd like that, wouldn't you? Kick the old man out of the way and take over his business."

"Yeah, that's my evil plan. Adding your debt to my student loans." Sarcasm covered her concern for him. "That's every girl's dream."

"Seriously, Liz. I don't need a doc." He exhaled in a long *whoosh* that dissolved into a hacking cough. "This was a little too much excitement for the old ticker."

"Is this your way of telling me that you have heart problems?"

"Forget it. Just drive back to the office."

Checking her rearview mirrors, she continued along Colfax Avenue. She didn't see anyone following them; they'd made a clean getaway. Just in case, she turned south at the next intersection and drove toward the highway. "We need to call the police."

"Nope."

"Harry, those guys shot at us. They assaulted us."

"But I returned fire." He cleared his throat, breathing more easily. His clenched fist lifted from his chest. "And you kicked ass. You might look like a Pop-Tart, but you were a fire-breathing dragon."

"My form wasn't terrific."

"You did good." He reached over and patted her shoulder. Always stingy with his compliments, Harry followed up with a complaint. "Too bad you messed up and lost the camera."

"Don't even think about taking the cost out of my wages." At a stoplight, she studied him again. He seemed to have recovered. "We need to fill out a police report. Those people are dealing drugs."

"And I guarantee that the narcs are well aware. Leave the drug dealers to the cops, we've got problems of our own. Like how to get that juicy bonus from Victoria."

Tomorrow, she'd put in a call to a friend at the Denver PD. At the very least, she wanted to see those children removed from a dangerous environment.

Harry sat up straighter. "Time to switch to Plan B."

"I don't like the sound of this."

"My source is the housekeeper who works at the Crawford estate near Evergreen. She can—"

"Wait a sec. How did you get to know a housekeeper?" She glanced toward the backseat. "You've never tidied up anything in your whole life."

"I served with her dad in Vietnam, and we stay in touch. Her name is Rachel Frakes. She's actually the one who recommended me to Victoria."

That connection explained a lot. The Schooner Detective Agency wasn't usually the first choice of the rich and famous. "What's Plan B?"

"Rachel gets you inside the estate. While you're there, you dig up the dirt on Ben."

"An undercover assignment."

That didn't sound too shabby. Maybe she'd impersonate a fancy-pants interior decorator. Or a horse wrangler. An upscale estate near Evergreen had to have several acres and a stable. Or she could be a guest—maybe an eccentric jet-setting heiress. A descendant of the Romanov czars. "Who am I supposed to be?"

He almost smiled. "You'll see."

# *Chapter Two*

The next afternoon, Liz tromped down the back staircase from her brand-new undercover home—a third-floor garret at the Crawford mansion. Her starched gray uniform with the white apron reminded her of a Pilgrim costume she'd worn in fourth grade. The hem drooped below her knees, which was probably a good thing because she belatedly realized that she hadn't shaved her legs since before she started studying for final exams. Entering the kitchen, she adjusted the starched white cap that clung with four bobby pins to her unruly blond hair.

A maid. She was supposed to be a maid. The thrills just kept coming.

At the bottom of the staircase, Rachel the housekeeper stood with fists planted on her hips. She was a tall, solidly built woman who would have fit right in with the Russian women's weightlifting team. Her short blond hair was neatly slicked back away from her face. "Liz, may I remind you that a maid is supposed to be as unobtrusive as a piece of furniture."

"Okay." *Call me Chippendale.*

"While descending the staircase, you sounded like a herd of bison. We walk softly on the pads of our feet."

"If I walk softly, can I carry a big stick?"

Rachel's eyebrows shot up to her hairline. "Surely, you don't intend to hit anything."

"I'm joking." If this had been a real job, Liz would have already quit. "Any other advice?"

"The proper answer to a question is yes or no. Not 'okay.' And certainly not a joke. Is that clear?"

Liz poked at her silly white cap. "Yes, ma'am."

"Do something with your hair. It's all over the place."

She bit the inside of her mouth. "Yes, ma'am."

"No perfume. No nail polish. No makeup."

"No problem." That part of the assignment suited her normal procedure. "You know, Rachel, Harry and I really appreciate this—"

"Say nothing more." She pulled the door to the stairwell closed, making sure they were alone. "If anyone finds out what you're doing here, I'll deny any knowledge of your true profession."

"Yes, ma'am." In a low voice, she asked, "What can you tell me about Ben?"

"A fine-looking man but brooding. When Victoria told me about his drug problem, I had to act. I can't stand the thought of his daughter being raised by an addict."

"He doesn't usually live here, does he?"

"His home is in Seattle where he runs Crawford Aero-Equipment. They supply parts to the big airplane manufacturers and also build small custom jets."

Seemed like an extremely responsible job for a drug addict. "Why is he in Colorado?"

"This is his grandfather's house. Jerod Crawford." Her forehead pinched. "Jerod is a generous, brave man. He's dying from a brain tumor."

"And his grandson came home to take care of him."

Again, Ben's behavior wasn't what she'd expect from a druggie degenerate. Maybe he was here to make sure he inherited big bucks when grandpa died.

"For right now, you're needed in the kitchen," Rachel said. "We have a dinner party for sixteen scheduled for this evening."

Maybe some of these guests would provide negative evidence she could use against Ben. "Anybody I should watch for?"

"In what sense?"

"Other drug users. He must have gotten the name of his dealer from somebody."

"That's for you to investigate," Rachel said. "In the meantime, report to the kitchen."

"I'll be there in a flash. Right after I comb my hair."

Liz tiptoed up the stairs to the second floor. No matter what Rachel thought, her first order of business was to locate Ben's bedroom and search for his drug stash. She opened the door and stepped into the center of a long hallway decorated with oil paintings of landscapes hung above a natural cedar wainscoting. She peeked into an open door and saw an attractive bedroom with rustic furnishings—nothing opulent but a hundred times better than the tiny garret on the third floor where she'd dropped off her backpack and changed into the starchy maid outfit.

A tall brunette in a black pantsuit emerged from one of the rooms and stalked down the hallway.

Though Liz beamed a friendly smile, the brunette went past her without acknowledging her presence. Apparently, this was what it felt like to be furniture.

"Excuse me," Liz piped up.

The woman paused. "What?"

"I'm new here. And I'm looking for Ben's bedroom."

"My brother's room is right down there. Close to Grandpa."

The double doors to Jerod's room were open, and she heard other people inside. "Thank you."

There were too many people milling around to make a thorough search of Ben's room. Later, she'd come back. And right now? Liz wasn't anxious to report for maid duty in the kitchen. She'd use this time to explore, to get a sense of this sprawling house and the acreage that surrounded it.

On the drive here, she hadn't seen much. After the turnoff in Evergreen, she'd gone three-point-four miles on a narrow road that twisted through a thick forest of ponderosa pine, spruce and conifer. A wrought-iron gate between two stone pillars protected the entrance, and a chain-link fence enclosed the grounds. She'd had to identify herself over an intercom before the gates opened electronically.

The stone-and-cedar mansion nestled against a granite ridge. The main section rose three stories. Several different levels—landscaped terraces and cantilevered decks—made the house seem as though it had grown organically from the surrounding rocks and trees.

Liz went down a short hallway beside the staircase. A beveled glass door opened onto the second-story outdoor walkway made of wood planks. At the far end, the walkway opened onto a huge, sunlit deck.

Towering pines edged up to the railing. Hummingbird feeders and birdhouses hung from the branches. Several padded, redwood chairs and chaises faced outward to enjoy the view, but no one was outside. Floor-to-ceiling windows lined this side of the house, which was very likely Jerod Crawford's bedroom. Lucky for her, the drapes were closed.

As Liz walked to the railing, a fresh mountain breeze caressed her cheeks. Twitters from chipmunks and birds serenaded her. Multicolored petunias in attached wooden flower boxes bobbed cheerfully.

People like her didn't live in places like this. A grassy field dotted with scarlet Indian paintbrush and daisies rolled downhill, past a barn and another outbuilding, to a shimmering blue lake, surrounded by pines. In the distance, snow-covered peaks formed a majestic skyline.

At the edge of the lake, a wood dock stretched into the water. Though she was over a hundred yards away, she thought she recognized Ben. He faced a woman with platinum-blond hair and a bright red sweater.

Though Liz couldn't hear their words, they were obviously arguing. The woman gestured angrily. Ben pulled back as though he couldn't stand being close to her.

She stamped her foot.

And then, she slapped him.

BEN RESTRAINED AN URGE to strike back at Charlene. Much as she had earned the right to have her ass thrown off his grandpa's property, that wasn't Ben's call.

Through tight lips, he said, "You're not always going to have things your way."

"No matter what you think, I'm the one in charge around here. Me. I'm Jerod's wife."

A ridiculous but undeniably true statement. At age thirty-six, she was only two years older than Ben himself. He hated having to consult with her on his grandpa's medical care and would never understand why the old man listened to her.

"Be reasonable, Charlene. I've been talking to specialists and neurosurgeons. They think Jerod's tumor could be removed."

"I don't want your doctors." She screeched like a harpy. "Jerod is happy with Dr. Mancini. And so am I."

Dr. Al Mancini had been the Crawford family doctor for years, and he was competent to treat sniffles and scraped knees. But a brain tumor? "Mancini isn't even practicing anymore. He's retired."

"And Jerod is his only patient. Dr. Mancini comes here every single day. Your specialist would put Jerod in the hospital. And he refuses."

Unfortunately, Charlene was correct. His stubborn, Texas-born grandpa had planted himself here and wouldn't budge. Every day, the tumor inside his head continued to grow. His vision was seriously impaired, and he barely had the strength to get out of his wheelchair. "If not an operation, he needs access to other treatments. Radiation. Cutting-edge medications."

"He won't go. And I'm not going to force him."

For the moment, he abandoned this topic. There were other bones to pick. "At least, cancel your damn dinner party. Jerod needs peace and quiet."

"You want to pretend like he's already dead. Well, he's not. He needs activity and excitement. That's why he married me."

"Really? I thought it had more to do with your thirty-six double-D chest."

She slapped him again. This time, he'd earned it.

With a swish of her hips, Charlene flounced up the hill toward the house.

Five years ago, when his grandpa had announced that he wanted to marry a Las Vegas showgirl, Ben had been almost proud of the old guy. After a lifetime of hard work that had started in the Texas oil fields, Jerod had the right to amuse himself. Even if it meant the rest of the family had to put up with a gold digger.

Charlene had readily agreed to a very generous pre-nuptial agreement. Whether their marriage was ended by divorce or death, she walked away with a cool half million in cash. Not a bad deal.

Ben had expected Charlene to divorce his grandpa after a year and grab the cash, but she'd stayed…and stayed…and stayed. In her shallow way, she might even love Jerod. And he had to admit that their May–December marriage had turned out better than his. Nothing good had come from that union, except for his daughter.

He walked to the end of the small dock. A spring wind rippled the waters. Trout were jumping. In the rolling foothills of Colorado, he saw the swells of the ocean. He missed his home in Seattle that overlooked the sea, but he cherished every moment here with his grandpa as the old man prepared for his final voyage.

Behind his back, Ben heard someone step onto the dock. Had Charlene come back? He turned and saw a gray maid's uniform. "What is it?"

"You must be Ben." She marched toward him with her hand outthrust. "I'm Liz Norton. The new maid."

He accepted her handshake. Though she was a slender little thing, her grip was strong. He took a second look at her. The expression in her luminous green eyes showed a surprising challenge. Not the usual demeanor for house-hold staff. "Is this your first job as a servant?"

"Servant?" Her nose wrinkled in disgust. "I can't say that I like that job description. Sounds like I ought to curtsey."

"I suppose you have a more politically correct job title in mind."

She pulled her hand away from his grasp and thought for half a second. "Housekeeping engineer."

In spite of her droopy gray uniform, she radiated electricity, which might explain why her hair looked like she'd stuck her finger in a wall socket. He would have dismissed her as being too cute. Except for the sharp intelligence in her green eyes.

"Nice place you've got here." She stepped up beside him. "Are there horses?"

"Not anymore. Horses were my grandmother's passion. Arabians. God, they were beautiful." He had fond memories of grooming the horses with his grandmother. "After she passed away, ten years ago, Jerod sold them to someone who would love them as much as she had."

"Wise decision. Every living creature needs to be with someone who loves them."

A hell of a profound statement. "Are you? With someone who loves you?"

"I do okay." She cocked her head and looked up at him. "How about you, Ben? Who loves you?"

"My daughter," he responded quickly. "Natalie."

Her expression went blank as if she had something to hide. All of a sudden, her adorable freckled face seemed less innocent. He wondered why she'd approached him, why she spoke of love.

There had been incidents in the past when female employees had tried to seduce him, but Liz's body language wasn't flirtatious. Her arms hung loosely at her sides. Her feet were planted solidly. Something else motivated her.

"You have a reputation as an adventurer," she said.

"What kind of stuff do you do? Something with the airplanes you manufacture?"

"I test-pilot our planes. Not for adventure. It's work."

She arched an eyebrow. "Cool job."

"I'm not complaining." He glanced up the hill toward the house. It was time to get his grandpa outside in the sun. Maybe he could talk some sense into the old man. "Please excuse me, Liz."

Instead of stepping politely aside, she stayed beside him, matching her gait to his stride. "I think I met your sister at the house. Real slim. Dressed in black."

"That's Patrice." And *not* good news. He'd known that his sister and her husband, Monte, were coming to dinner, but he hadn't expected her until later. As a rule, he tried to keep his sister and Charlene separate. The two women hated each other.

"Is your sister married?" Liz asked.

"Yes."

"Any kids?"

Patrice was far too selfish to spoil her rail-thin figure by getting pregnant. "None."

From the house, he heard a high-pitched scream.

Ben took off running.

When he looked over, he saw Liz with her uniform hiked up, racing along beside him. She had to be the most unusual maid he'd ever met.

# Chapter Three

Liz charged up the incline from the lake toward the house. Though her legs churned at top speed, she couldn't keep pace with Ben's stride.

She heard a second scream…and a third that trailed off into an incoherent, staccato wail that reminded her of a kid throwing a tantrum in the grocery store aisle. The cries seemed to be coming from the front entrance.

Trailing behind Ben, she couldn't help but admire his running form. His long legs pumped. His forest-green shirt stretched tightly across his muscular shoulders. For a supposed drug addict, he appeared to be in amazing physical condition. As he approached the shiny, black Escalade parked at the front door, he muttered, "Son of a bitch."

Two bitches, actually. Beside the SUV, two women grappled. Patrice shrieked again. Still clad in her sleek black pantsuit, she had both arms clutched possessively around a large metal object. Charlene tugged at her arms and delivered a couple of ineffectual swats on Patrice's skinny bottom.

Liz stopped and stared at the spectacle of two grown women scuffling like brats on a playground. She didn't envy Ben as he waded into the middle of the wrestling match and pulled them apart. "What the hell is going on?"

Without loosening her grip on what appeared to be a two-foot-tall bronze statue of a rearing bronco, Patrice tossed her head. Her smooth, chin-length mahogany hair fell magically into place. "Grandma Crawford gave this original Remington to me. It once belonged to Zane Grey, you know."

"You're a thief." Charlene jabbed in her direction with a red manicured fingernail that matched her sweater. "How dare you come to *my house* and steal from me."

"*Your* house?"

"That's right." Charlene's blue eyes flashed like butane flames. "I'm Jerod's wife. All this is mine."

Patrice's nostrils flared as she inhaled and exhaled loudly. She spat her words. "You. Are. Sadly. Mistaken."

"I'll show you who's wrong." Charlene lunged.

Ben caught the small woman by her waist, lifted her off her feet, carried her a few paces and dropped her. "Stop it," he growled. "Both of you."

Other residents of the house had responded to the shrieks. The gardener and chauffeur peeked around a hedge. On the landing, a man in a chef hat hovered behind another maid with eyes round as silver dollars. Rachel Frakes glared disapprovingly. When her gaze hit Liz, she remembered the lecture on decorum and reached up to adjust the starched white maid's cap that hung precariously from one bobby pin.

Ben strode toward his sister. "Give me the damn horse."

"It's mine." She stuck out her chin. "Besides, you're supposed to be on *my* side."

"Give it to me. Now." His eyes—which were an incredible shade of teal—narrowed. An aura of command and determination emanated from him, and Liz recognized the strong charisma of a born leader. It would take a stronger woman than Patrice to stand up to Ben.

His right hand closed around the neck of the rearing bronco, and he gave a tug. Reluctantly, his sister released her grip.

Quickly, he passed the sculpture to Liz. "Would you take this inside, please."

"Sure." She remembered her earlier conversation with Rachel about proper responses and amended, "I mean, yes."

The burnished bronze was still warm from being cradled against Patrice's body. Liz held it gingerly. She wasn't a big fan of Western art, even if it had belonged to the legendary Western writer Zane Grey, but this lump of metal must be worth a lot.

Ben turned back to Patrice and Charlene. "Shake hands and make up, ladies."

"No way," Charlene responded. "I'm not going to touch that skinny witch."

"This feud has gone far enough." His baritone took on an ominous rumble. "Like it or not, we're family. We stick together."

Liz edged around the three of them on her way toward the front door. This squabble—though plenty juicy and perversely entertaining—really wasn't her concern. Her job as a private investigator meant finding evidence proving that Ben was an unfit father—a task that had taken on a layer of complication. She'd expected him to be an addict or a crazed playboy or an irresponsible adventurer. None of those identities fit. He seemed family oriented and rational…even admirable.

Before Liz could step inside, a well-tanned man—dressed in the male version of Patrice's black suit—appeared in the doorway and struck a pose as if waiting for a *GQ* photographer. Though his blond hair was thinning on top, he'd compensated with a long ponytail. He squinted at Liz's face, then his gaze caught on the sculpture. "What do you think you're doing with that horse?"

"I was planning to saddle up and ride in the Kentucky Derby."

"It's mine." He gestured toward Patrice. "Ours."

"And who are you?" Liz inquired. "The great-grandson of Zane Grey? A Rider of the Purple Sage?"

"Monte. Monte Welles." *Like Bond. James Bond.* "Patrice's husband."

When he made the mistake of reaching for the statue that had been entrusted to her care by Ben, her reaction came from pure instinct. With both arms busy holding the bronze horse, Liz relied on her feet. Two quick, light kicks tapped on his ankle, then the toe of his left foot.

He gave a yelp and backed off. "You're fired."

"The hell she is," Ben said. "Monte, get your butt over here and talk some sense into your wife. She and Charlene need to kiss and make up."

"Hah!" Patrice tossed her head again. "I'd rather kiss a toad."

"I'll bet," Charlene countered. "That's why you married Monte."

Liz stifled a chuckle. Though she wasn't taking sides, she gave a point to Charlene for her nifty insult.

Patrice planted her fists on her nonexistent hips. "Leave my husband out of this."

"Gladly."

"And I want an apology. I wasn't stealing. Just reclaiming something that belongs to me."

"Wrong," Charlene said. "This is my house. Everything in it belongs to me."

"Not for long—prenup. Remember the prenup," Patrice said smugly. "When Jerod dies, you get a payoff and nothing more. Not a stick of furniture. Not one square foot of property. And certainly not my Remington sculpture."

A sly grin curved Charlene's glossy lips. "What would you say if I told you that Jerod has decided to change his will?"

Patrice looked like she might faint. Her complexion went ghostly pale. Her arms fell limply to her sides. "How could you say such a thing?"

"Maybe because it's true." Charlene preened. "You can check with the family attorney. He'll be at dinner."

"Grandpa wouldn't do that," she mumbled. "He couldn't. Not on his deathbed."

"He's not going to die," Charlene said with vehement conviction. "He's going to get better."

"Damn straight, honey. You tell 'em."

Those few words, spoken in a Texan drawl, riveted everyone's attention to the doorway. A white-haired man in a wheelchair was pushed onto the landing by a nurse in scrubs. Dark sunglasses perched on his beaklike nose. A plaid wool bathrobe hung from the frame of his shoulders. Though debilitated by illness, he was clearly the patriarch. Jerod Crawford, age seventy-six, took immediate, unquestioned control of the situation. "You girls quit your squabbling. And I mean now."

A laugh bubbled from Charlene's lips as she bounced toward her husband, leaned down and planted a quick kiss on his forehead. "You look good today. Excited about our party?"

"I'm waiting to see what you'll wear. I like you all gussied up and smelling like roses."

"I know you do." She checked her wristwatch. "I need to run into town and pick up my dress from the seamstress. Don't get yourself too tired before our guests arrive."

"Ain't much strain sitting in this here chair."

She held both of his gnarled hands and squeezed. "Take care, lover boy. You're my bumblebee."

"And you're my honey."

Even though Charlene was probably a gold digger, Liz thought her fondness for Jerod rang true. Likewise for Ben, who stepped behind his grandpa's wheelchair and pushed him along the driveway toward a narrow asphalt path leading toward the lake.

Rachel tapped Liz's shoulder. "Put the sculpture on the table in the den and report to the kitchen."

"Yes, ma'am."

As she entered the house, Liz reflected. She'd learned a lot about the dynamics of the Crawford family. Their greed. Their hostility. The seething undercurrent of hate and anger masked by these luxurious surroundings. Unfortunately, she'd gained zero evidence that Ben was an unfit father.

LIZ ALWAYS HAD TROUBLE following orders, but she tried to do as Rachel asked. Now she was baffled. Her assign-

ment was to put together the place settings with half a
dozen utensils, four plates, three different glasses and
cup and saucer. She stood at the head of the table, shuffled
the forks, switched the positions of the wineglass and
water glass. Was that how it went?

When she looked up and saw Ben watching her with
an amused smile, she felt a hot flush creeping up her
throat. Blushing? She hadn't blushed since sophomore
year of high school when the captain of the baseball team
had kissed her in the hallway, and she'd let him get to
second base.

Ben came closer. "Could you use some help?"

Embarrassed about blushing, she thought of icebergs
and snowstorms—anything to cool her off. Though she
hated to admit that she didn't have a clue about the third
fork, Liz feared that Rachel would have a coronary if the
place settings weren't perfect. "I could use some expert
advice."

His shoulder brushed her arm as he reached across the
plate setting to rearrange the knives. She was aware of his
bodily warmth and a natural masculine scent that was far
more enticing than aftershave. Not that she should be
noticing the way he smelled. Her focus should be on
gathering evidence to prove that he was an unfit father.

When she finished with the formal setting and stepped
back, she nodded. "I knew that."

He gave her a sidelong glance. "Did you?"

"Not really, but it's not something that bothers me. In
the grand scheme of things, why should I waste brain cells
on knowing where to put the forks?"

"You're not really a maid. Sorry, housekeeping
engineer. Why are you really here?"

His intense blue-eyed gaze rested suspiciously upon

her face. He wanted the truth, which wasn't something she could give.

From her other undercover experiences, she'd learned that successful lies were based on truth, so she stuck to reality. "I'm a law student, paying my own way. I need a summer job, and I heard about this maid gig through a friend of a friend."

His scrutiny continued; he wasn't totally satisfied with her answer. "I liked the way you handled Monte. You know karate."

Now the truth got more complicated. If she mentioned Dragon Lou, Ben might check her out with a phone call, which might lead to someone mentioning her part-time work as a private eye. "I learned the basics of self-defense. Seemed like a smart thing for a woman living alone."

Having offered a rational explanation, she should have stopped talking but really wanted him to believe her. She continued, "You probably won't find it hard to believe that I've gotten myself into a few scrapes. About six years ago, I went out with this guy…" A warning voice inside her head told her to shut up. *Shut up, now.* "Maybe I had too much to drink. Maybe he did. I don't know."

Ben's attention never wavered. "Go on."

"Somehow," she said, "I ended up at his apartment. He got aggressive. When I told him no, he didn't stop."

She had never told anyone—not her mother, not her friends, not Harry Schooner—about that night. She'd been date raped. Remembering her weakness made her sad and angry at the same time. "That's when I started taking karate lessons. And I'm good. No one can force me to do something I don't want to do. Never again. No means no."

He took a step toward her, and she feared he would offer sympathy. A shoulder to cry on. Or a gentle platitude that could never make things better.

Instead he shook her hand. "Smart decision, Liz."

"Thank you, Ben."

She was beginning to really like this guy.

# Chapter Four

To Liz, the flurry of anticipation and activity surrounding the arrival of the dinner guests seemed out of proportion. It wasn't as if the Queen of England would be popping by for a state dinner. Her attitude was in direct contrast to the other maid, Annette Peltier, who twittered excitedly as she rearranged the centerpiece on the dining room table.

"Isn't it beautiful?" Annette gushed. Her maid's cap nestled perfectly above a neat chignon at the back of her head. "I just love these dinner parties."

"Who's coming, anyway?"

"Patrice and her husband. He's a famous athlete, you know."

"Monte? What sport?"

"He was in the winter Olympics. In the biathalon. The one where they ski and shoot. He's a marksman."

"Who else?"

"Dr. Mancini and Tony Lansing, the family lawyer." She fussed over the elegant china and crystal, adjusting the place settings one centimeter left, then right. "And Charlene's friends from Denver. They're so beautiful, especially Ramon Stephens. He's dreamy."

Rachel came into the dining room and gave a snort. "Watch out for Ramon when he has a couple of martinis in him. That young man thinks he's God's gift to women."

Though there were wineglasses on the table, Liz hadn't noticed a liquor setup. "Where's the bar?"

"In the downstairs lounge. Which is, undoubtedly, where they'll go after dinner."

"I used to be a bartender. Maybe I could—"

"Why didn't you mention this before?" For the first time, Rachel regarded her as though she were more than a waste of space. "Bartending will be your primary assignment. Run downstairs and make sure everything is in order."

"I'm on it."

"Liz, please," Rachel chided. "Proper response."

"Yes, ma'am."

Liz skipped down the staircase into a long, low room with a beamed ceiling and a fireplace. Classic leather furniture arrayed around a red-felt pool table and giant flat-screen television. The carved cherrywood bar was stocked with an inventory of mixes for a very upscale selection of liquor. Nothing but the best for the Crawfords.

In the fridge, Liz found garnishes—lemons, limes, cherries and olives—everything she'd need for cocktails. An impressive bit of organization.

From upstairs, she heard the chatter of the first guests arriving. She ought to trot up there and see if she could be helpful, but Liz wasn't planning on winning any prizes for Maid of the Year. Instead, she went to the far end of the room where sliding glass doors opened onto the forest. Outside, the sun dipped toward the mountains and colored the underbellies of clouds with a golden glow. From this vantage point, she could see down to the lake.

To the south, there were two outbuildings. The big one was probably where the Arabian stallions of the first Mrs. Jerod Crawford had been kept. The other, constructed of rough logs, had only one story with garage-sized double doors across the front.

As she watched, she saw Ben emerge from a side door of the log barn. Though she was too far away to clearly see what he was doing, it looked like he was fastening a lock on the door. That kind of secrecy suggested nefarious purposes. The barn might be where he hid his drug stash.

How could he be an addict? The guy reeked of integrity. But she'd seen him making a buy from the dealer in Denver. Seen him with her own eyes.

She went back into the lounge in time to greet two men coming down the stairs. The white-haired man, neatly packaged in a three-piece gray suit with a red bow tie, was Dr. Al Mancini, the family doctor, who had been pointed out to her when he'd arrived at the house. Though the other man wore a casual sweater and jeans, he had the arrogance of a well-paid professional. From his precisely trimmed brown hair to his buffed fingernails, he was polished. In law school, she'd learned to recognize these guys on sight: lawyers. This had to be Tony Lansing, family attorney.

"Gentlemen," she said. "May I get you something to drink?"

Barely noticing her, the doc ordered a whiskey on the rocks. The attorney wanted vodka with a twist.

"About Jerod's new will," the doctor said.

"I can't discuss it, except to say that the amended document has just been signed, witnessed and filed away in my briefcase."

"I can guess what it says." The doctor leaned his elbow on the bar with the attitude of someone accustomed to drinking. In spite of his white hair, he didn't look all that ancient. He was probably only in his fifties. "Jerod intends to cut the family and leave the bulk of his estate to Charlene. Is that about right, Tony?"

"I can't say."

But he gave a nearly imperceptible nod. Liz hadn't come to the Crawford estate to investigate family matters, but the intrigue surrounding Jerod's will was too juicy to ignore. She placed the whiskey on the bar in front of the doctor. With a deft flick of a paring knife, she peeled off a lemon twist for the vodka.

Picking up his whiskey, the doctor said, "I've known Jerod for nearly twenty years. He's no fool. Charlene hasn't tricked him into leaving her the millions. I think he truly loves that little blond cupcake."

"Can't blame him for that."

"But here's the kicker. I think she loves him back. If Charlene wasn't here to enforce what Jerod wants, Ben would have put the old man in a hospital with a troop of specialists poking and prodding."

Which didn't sound like such a bad idea to Liz. Jerod had a brain tumor and gazillions of bucks to spend on medical treatment. Why not get the very best care?

Both men drank in silence.

The doctor licked his lips and grinned. "There's one big problem with the new will."

"What's that?" Tony asked.

"Patrice is going to kill Charlene."

When the two men had finished their drinks, Liz cleaned up the glasses. Straightening the starched white maid cap on her unruly blond hair, she ascended the staircase into a maelstrom of activity. Guests had been greeted at the door with flutes of champagne and were mostly in the living room, where a wall of windows displayed a magenta sunset. Patrice wore her trademark black, but the other women were a couture rainbow. The men were equally chic but in more subdued tones.

Her gaze went immediately to Ben. Though he still wore jeans, he'd thrown on a white fisherman's knit sweater that made his shoulders look impossibly broad. She was surprised to find him looking back at her. With a subtle grin and a lift of his eyebrow, he communicated volumes. He'd been here before, heard all the chitchat before. And he'd rather be standing by the lake counting the ripples. Or soaring through the sunset in a sleek jet.

Or maybe she was reading too much into a glance.

Purposely turning away, Liz reported to the kitchen, where she did her best to follow the orders of the very nervous chef and Rachel.

Throughout the dinner, her assigned task would be serving each course and unobtrusively whisking away the dirty dishes. Her *real* agenda? Listening for clues. One of these guests might be Ben's drug connection. He took a seat at the foot of the table. To his right sat an impassive blond woman with a plunging neckline and arms as skinny as pipe cleaners. Though she was as gaunt as a heroin addict, Liz guessed that her vacant expression came from hunger rather than drugs. On Ben's left was Tony Lansing, who held up his empty cocktail glass, signaling to Liz that he wanted a refill.

She darted downstairs, whipped up another vodka with a twist and returned to the dining room in time to see Jerod make his entrance. Rising from his wheelchair, he leaned on Charlene's arm as he made his way to the head of the table.

Illness had not diminished the charisma of this former Texas oil baron's personality. As he greeted his guests, he showed dignity rather than weakness. Nor did Charlene treat him like an invalid. Standing close at his side, she effortlessly outshone every other woman in the room. Though small and slim, her hot-pink dress emphasized her curves. Her blond hair caught the light from the chandelier and shimmered as she gave her husband a peck on the cheek and took a seat beside him.

"I'm hungry as a bear," Jerod announced. "Let's eat."

Liz and the rest of the staff leaped into action. Serving a formal dinner wasn't as simple as when she'd worked as a waitress in a pancake house. Though she tried to follow the moves of Annette and Rachel, she bumped against chairs and the shoulders of the guests. The appetizer plates made loud clinks when she placed them into the formal setting. When she cleared those plates and stacked them one on top of the other, Rachel was waiting for her in the kitchen.

"You're doing it all wrong," she snapped. "Take the plates two at a time. One in each hand and return them to the kitchen."

"Seems like a waste of time," Liz said.

"This china is antique and worth a small fortune. Handle it carefully. We don't want chips."

Serving the clear consommé soup was a choreographed ritual with Liz holding the tureen while Annette ladled. Should have been easy. But Liz had never before moved with a glide. Her steps bounced. The soup sloshed. Hot droplets hit her hands, clinging tightly to the handles.

*Don't drop it. Whatever you do, don't drop this slippery, heavy piece of heirloom china.*

When they got to Ben, he looked up at her. "Are we having fun yet?"

*How would you like this whole tureen dumped onto your lap, Mister?* She muttered, "Yes, sir."

When the main course—filet mignon so tender that it could be cut with a fork—hit the table, Liz realized that she hadn't eaten. Hunger pangs roiled in her belly as she stood at attention with a pitcher of ice water to replenish the glasses. She tensed her abs. *Don't growl. Please, stomach. Don't growl.*

Dinner conversation twittered around the table. Though the basic topics involved golf scores and vacation plans for the summer, Liz recognized an undercurrent of tension in the too-shrill laughter and hostile grimaces. Patrice fired hate-filled stares at Charlene. One of the couples were former lovers who sniped mercilessly at each other. The dark, handsome man who sat to Charlene's left eyeballed her cleavage with undisguised longing and spewed compliments as if Charlene herself had cooked this fabulous dinner. That had to be the infamous Ramon.

As she leaned close to Ben to fill his water glass, her stomach let loose with a roar loud enough to stop conversation at that end of the table.

Patrice glared at her.

Rachel gaped.

Gallantly, Ben patted his own belly. "Excuse me," he said. "I must be enjoying the meal."

Instead of being grateful, Liz felt a surge of annoyance. She didn't need for him to rescue her from embarrassment; she had nothing to be ashamed of. But her cheeks burned. Another blush?

At that moment, she hated all these people with their expensive clothes, hidden agendas and cost-a-fortune dishes. She remembered every time she'd been hungry— not from a self-imposed diet but because she couldn't afford a loaf of bread. In the real world, stomachs growled, and she wanted to stand up and take credit. Demure, silent serving definitely wasn't her thing.

Tony Lansing waggled his cocktail glass at her. "I'd like another."

"Yes, sir."

Though he was the only person drinking hard liquor, the others had gone through more than a dozen bottles of wine. The pipe-cleaner woman next to Ben had barely touched her food but managed to polish off several glasses of Chablis. She leaned to the left like the Tower of Pisa.

Downstairs at the bar, Liz attacked the garnishes in the fridge, devouring a blood orange in two seconds flat. Of course, she drooled the juice onto the front of her uniform. *Of course.*

Her choices were to go through the rest of the meal with a big, fat stain on her chest or to wash it out and be soggy. Another idea popped into her head. She could go up to her maid's garret bedroom and change—maybe using the time to make a quick search in Ben's bedroom.

After she delivered the vodka to Tony Lansing, she pointed out the stain to Rachel. "I should change."

"No time," she said. "Clear the dinner plates. Serve the dessert. Then you can change."

She whipped through her duties, noting that a couple

of guests had already left the table to take bathroom breaks or "freshen up."

As soon as the last dessert plate was delivered, she headed for the back staircase, ducking into a darkened hallway off the kitchen. There was just enough light for her to see a couple locked in a passionate kiss.

Consumed by desire, they didn't notice her. But Liz soaked in every detail. The bouncy blond hair belonged to Charlene. The man was the very polished lawyer, Tony Lansing. Their embrace put a whole different light on Jerod's changed will. They might be working together to siphon all the money away from the Crawford estate. Should she tell Ben? Was it any of her business?

The overhead hallway light flashed on. Ramon charged past her.

"Bastard," he shouted as he stalked toward the couple.

Charlene and Tony broke apart. In the sudden burst of light, she blinked wildly. Her bruised lips parted in a breathless gasp. Tony seemed disoriented, which wasn't a surprise to Liz. The lawyer had tossed back a gallon of wine and three vodkas during dinner.

Ramon's arm raised over his head.

Liz saw the glint of light on a kitchen knife. Her reaction was pure reflex. She kicked hard at the back of Ramon's knee, sending him sprawling against the wall.

He whirled, facing her. "Stay out of this," he warned.

"Drop your weapon."

He lowered the blade, threatening her.

There wasn't much room to maneuver in the narrow corridor, and the skirt on her uniform restricted her ability to kick high. Aiming carefully, she delivered a quick chop to his wrist. The knife clattered to the floor.

Ramon blocked her next blow. He flung his entire

body at her, pinning her to the wall. His breath smelled like the inside of a garbage disposal. "Not so tough now, are you?"

The only way out of this hold was a knee to the groin as soon as he gave her the space to strike. And she was looking forward to that ultimately disabling attack.

Before she could act, Ramon was yanked away from her and thrown facedown on the floor.

Ben stood over his prone body with the heel of his boot planted firmly between Ramon's shoulder blades. He turned toward Liz. "Are you all right?"

"I could have taken him down," she said as she adjusted her stained uniform. "I don't need you to rescue me."

"I'll keep that in mind." He looked down at the knife on the floor, then confronted Tony and Charlene. "I want an explanation."

"A misunderstanding," Tony said smoothly. "Nothing to worry about."

"He lies," Ramon wailed from the floor. "He has insulted me. And my beautiful Charlene."

Ben lifted him off the floor as if the muscular young man weighed no more than a sack of feathers. Ben's large hand clamped around Ramon's throat.

"Charlene is Jerod's wife," Ben reminded him. "She doesn't belong to you."

Charlene rushed forward. "Let him go, Ben."

"I want this son of a bitch out of here."

"Too damned bad." Charlene tossed her head. "This is my house. I say who stays and who goes. Ramon amuses me."

A vein in Ben's forehead throbbed, and Liz sympathized with his anger. Some women enjoyed having men fight over them; the danger acted as an aphrodisiac. Indeed, Charlene appeared to be turned on. Her lips drew back from her whitened teeth. "I want Ramon to stay. And Tony, too."

The lawyer found his voice. "Actually, I should be going. Thought I could catch a ride with Doctor Al."

"If you must," Charlene said.

"Thank you," he said in a formal tone that was comical, given the threatening situation. "For a lovely evening."

When the lawyer sidled out of the hallway, Ben released his hold on Ramon who slouched forward, rubbing his throat.

"One more thing," Ben said to him. "Apologize to the lady."

Ramon turned toward Charlene. "You know I would never hurt you. From the bottom of my heart, I am—"

"Not her," Ben interrupted by physically turning him toward Liz. "Apologize to this lady."

Ramon's dark eyebrows pulled down in an angry scowl. His full lips pursed as he forced the words. "I am sorry."

"Accepted," Liz said quickly. She definitely wanted this episode to be over.

"There," Charlene said. "Everything's fine. And the night is young. I want to have some real fun tonight."

In a low, dangerous voice, Ben warned, "Be careful what you ask for, Charlene."

# Chapter Five

Less than an hour later, Ben accompanied his grandpa upstairs to his bedroom suite, where the nurse would help him into bed.

"Wish I could stay awake," Jerod said. "Charlene's friends remind me of the days when I used to party all night long. Then I'd go home with the prettiest little gal in the whole damn place."

"Good times," Ben muttered with thinly disguised insincerity. He'd never been as social as his grandpa.

"Listen up, boy. It's high time you find yourself a girl-friend."

"Technically, I'm still married to Victoria." They'd been living apart for over a year—far apart. Victoria had taken up residence in the Denver house while Ben stayed in Seattle, where his business was based.

The final court date for their divorce was in a couple of weeks, and he'd gotten to the point where he would gladly relinquish all the cash and property she wanted. But not custody. He'd never give up one precious moment with his beautiful five-year-old daughter. Natalie was the one bright spot in his life.

"Ain't telling you to get married," Jerod said. "But it

wouldn't hurt to start dating. Weren't you sitting next to some cute thing at dinner?"

"Not my type."

The only woman at dinner who had appealed to him was Liz. When he'd stepped into that hallway and had seen Ramon crushing her against the wall, he'd wanted to kill that sleazy jerk for laying his hands on her. If she'd given the word, he would have happily dragged Ramon out the door and thrown him in the lake. But those weren't Liz's wishes. Instead of fawning, she'd coolly informed him that she could take care of herself.

He had no doubt that she could have handled the situation. If he hadn't intruded, she probably would have broken both Ramon's kneecaps and knocked out his front teeth. He grinned at his mental image of a karate queen with tangled hair and a prickly attitude. Definitely a woman who could kick ass.

"What you need," his grandpa said, "is to get back on the horse. Sure, you got bucked off once. That don't mean it's time to hang up your spurs."

"We're still talking about women, right?"

"Women. Horses. Same basic rules apply."

Ben chuckled. If he compared Liz to the old gray mare, she'd likely buck him through a plate-glass window. "Sleep well, Grandpa."

The hallway on the upper floor was calm and quiet. This multi-level house had been well built and sound-proofed with plenty of room for noisy family or guests. Ben was tempted to retire to his bedroom and forget about the party that was ongoing in the lounge, but Charlene and her friends were as irresponsible as two-year-olds. He needed to keep an eye on things. To quell fights if they got physical and make sure nobody ripped off their clothes and dived into the lake. For the rest of the night, Ben would be the self-appointed sheriff.

He descended to the main floor, where Rachel and the staff bustled around, cleaning up the dining room and kitchen. He paused to compliment her and the chef on a job well done.

Then he went downstairs into the noise. With the fully stocked bar, carefully placed lighting and a state-of-the-art sound system, the lounge easily duplicated the atmosphere of a small, private club for eight or nine of Charlene's friends. He wasn't sure how many, couldn't be bothered to remember their names. The guys seemed to be varying shades of Ramon. Big talkers. Some with trust funds. One of them—Andy?—Arty?—wanted to sell him a used Mercedes. As for the women—these were high-maintenance babes—much like his estranged wife. Been there, done them.

He was glad to see Liz stationed behind the bar. She'd discarded her maid cap and rolled up the sleeves on her uniform. For an apron, she wore a black sweatshirt with the arms tied tightly around her tiny waist. It was a goofy outfit that she somehow made look sexy as she juggled a silver martini shaker, poured a drink and garnished it with two olives speared on a toothpick. She slid the glass across the bar to a young man with a shaved head, who sipped, gave her an approving nod and strolled back to the pool table.

Ben rested an elbow on the bar. "You've done this before."

"I'm a lot better at mixing drinks than serving a formal dinner."

"You did fine."

"Tell that to my growling belly. So, what'll you have?"

Her nose crinkled when she grinned. "No, wait. Let me guess."

"Another of your hidden talents? You're psychic?"

"No, but I'm a pretty decent bartender. That means remembering what people drink."

He gestured to the guy who was walking away. "How will you remember him?"

"Baldy likes olives. That's easy." She lowered her voice to a conspiratorial level. "See the woman with black hair and a hateful attitude? She's a Bloody Mary."

And a potential problem. Bloody Mary looked like she might go ballistic. "What about Charlene?"

"Top-of-the-line champagne. Lots of fizz and bubbles. And I wouldn't try to pull a substitute because she'd know the difference."

"How about Ramon?"

"Vodka and orange juice, the typical screwdriver. But with 7-UP. I call it a screwup."

"Appropriate," he said. "If I hadn't shown up when I did, what would have been your next move?"

"Groin." She illustrated with an emphatic jab of her knee.

He winced in sympathetic pain. "I'm glad you're here. If things start getting out of hand—"

"I've got your back." Her green eyes studied him. "Now, let me figure out your drink. Something basic and manly. No frills. Outdoorsy."

He liked that description. "Go on."

"Something strong. Maybe tequila. Are you the kind of guy who likes to get blitzed?"

An odd question. Even more strange was the way her attitude shifted from playful to serious, as if probing for a deeper answer. "I'm not a drunk."

She held out both her fists. "Suppose in my right hand, I had a magic pill that would give you energy. In my left is one that makes you sleep. Which would you choose?"

"An upper or a downer." He closed his hands over both her fists and pulled them together. "Neither. I like to be in control at all times."

Charlene bounced up beside them. "What's going on here? Ben, are you propositioning the help?"

"Go away, Charlene."

"You're such a grump." She made eye contact with Liz. "You'd be doing everybody a favor if you got this guy to lighten up. He really needs a woman."

Liz pulled her hands away from him. "That's not part of my job description."

"Speaking of uptight jerks," Charlene said, "Where are Patrice and Monte?"

"You don't want to see my sister," he advised.

"Oh, but I do. I want my chance to gloat."

The background music got louder and a couple of the women started dancing. Charlene shimmied toward them. When Ben turned back toward the bar, he saw an opened bottle of dark beer. The logo showed a sailboat scudding in the wind. "Good choice, Liz. It's my favorite drink."

"I knew somebody liked it." She poured the beer into a tall, frosted glass. "There were two six-packs in the fridge."

He settled onto a bar stool and spent the rest of the evening talking to Liz. Usually Ben kept to himself, but she was a good listener. He opened up. Spoke of his dreams, his love of the ocean and the purity of sailing in a hand-crafted wooden boat with a streamlined hull and perfectly designed sail—not unlike the wing of an aircraft—to catch the wind and soar.

Her green eyes shone with a steady light, encouraging him to wax poetic about the lure of open sea. "In a different era, I could have been a captain on a tallship."

"Or a pirate," she said. "A renegade."

"Aye, matey."

Though he probed, she avoided saying much about herself, claiming that her dreams generally revolved around mundane issues like paying her rent and having groceries. "What about your family?" he asked.

"Raised by a single mother." She shrugged. "Her only dream for me was that I'd find a man to marry me and take care of me. And her."

"You don't share that dream."

"Nightmare," she corrected. "I don't like people telling me what to do."

"Nobody does."

"Your family is a lot more interesting." She refilled his beer glass. "From what I hear, you're in the midst of the divorce from hell."

He wasn't surprised that she knew about Victoria. The staff overheard everything. Talk about his miserable marriage evolved into memories of better times. With his beloved daughter. With his grandpa.

Though their conversation was frequently interrupted by Charlene's friends, he and Liz seemed to be afloat on an island of calm. When he looked at his wristwatch, he could hardly believe that it was after one.

The party had begun to wind down. In a dark corner, Bloody Mary and Baldy carried on a breathy conversation with a lot of groping. Others played pool. Charlene swayed and danced by herself while Ramon watched with eager eyes.

Ben was surprised when Patrice and Monte joined him

at the bar. His sister was visibly upset, with makeup askew and eyes glowing like hot embers. She snarled at Liz. "Vodka and pomegranate juice in a tall glass. Make it a double."

"Same for me," Monte said.

"I didn't expect to see you down here," Ben said.

"Couldn't sleep," Patrice complained. "I can't believe Jerod intends to leave everything to that witch."

"We're family," Monte whined. "We deserve that inheritance. We need it."

Ben filled his mouth with beer to keep from commenting. His sister had a healthy annual income from trust funds, owned houses and cars and anything else her greedy heart desired. Not exactly living in the gutter.

"Maybe I should get pregnant." Patrice patted her concave belly. "Then Jerod would leave my child big bucks. The way he's done with your kid."

Anger clenched Ben's throat. "What about Natalie?"

Charlene sidled up to them. "She's the other big winner in the new will. A third for me. A third for your darling daughter. And the rest to be divided with dozens and dozens of others."

Beside him, Patrice scraped her fingernails on the bar. "The new will won't stand up in court. You tricked my grandpa."

"I love him," Charlene said. "That's something you wouldn't understand. Love. True love."

Ramon had appeared behind her shoulder. It didn't take a behavioral scientist to see that this conversation was about to turn nasty.

"Love?" Patrice spat the word. "Is that why you were humping Tony Lansing in the back hallway?"

Charlene tossed her head. "Just a congratulations kiss. No big deal."

Liz placed the drinks for Patrice and Monte on the bar. "Here you go, folks. Drink up. And settle down."

"Shut up," Patrice snapped. "When I need advice from a maid, I'll ask for it."

His sister closed her talons around her glass, and Ben guessed her intention. Patrice was about to throw her drink, just like a soap-opera diva. Before he could stop her, she let fly.

Charlene ducked.

Ramon got drenched.

Ben waded in to stop the scuffle. Fortunately, Liz had come around the bar and helped. Between them, they subdued the women and their partners.

Patrice and Monte flounced back up the stairs.

Charlene stood at the bar beside him. Her chest heaved as she breathed heavily. "Go to bed, Ben. I'm not going to do anything naughty."

He had absolutely no reason to believe her.

THOUGH LIZ HAD BEEN DRINKING nothing but ginger ale all night, she felt unsteady on her feet. It had been a long day; she was pooped.

The momentary adrenaline rush from the catfight between Patrice and Charlene faded in about two seconds. All she could think about was bed.

"Thanks for your help," Ben said.

"I've been in bar fights before." It almost pleased her to see these upper-crust snobs get down and dirty. "But this is the first time with people wearing Manolos and diamonds."

"You look tired. Time to close down the bar."

"I promised Rachel I'd stay until all these people went to bed."

"They're all spending the night. Could be here until dawn." He came around the bar to stand beside her and took the white towel she'd been using to wipe down the bar surface from her hand. "Allow me to escort you upstairs to your bedroom."

When she gazed up into his dreamy blue eyes, she had trouble focusing. For a second, she saw him in double vision. Two Bens. Twice as sexy.

Tired. She was so very tired. At the same time, a thread of arousal wove through her consciousness, making her aware of her own sensuality and awakening her guarded passions.

Allowing Ben to take her to bed seemed like a risky plan. Her defenses were down. She didn't want to take a chance on succumbing to her natural urges and dragging him into the bed with her. "I can make it on my own."

"I'm sure you can." A lazy grin lifted the corner of his mouth. "I was being polite."

Polite was the furthest thing from her mind. After seeing him in action, she wanted to feel those strong arms wrapped around her, to snuggle against his chest and drown herself in his masculine scent.

*Enough.* She lurched into action, dodging around him and heading for the staircase. "Good night, Ben."

By the time she reached her third-floor bedroom, her legs weighed a thousand pounds apiece. The inside of her head whirled like a mad carousel.

Collapsed across the narrow bed in her maid's garret, her last conscious thought was, Had she been drugged?

## Chapter Six

The next morning, Liz eased from her bed. She moved slowly, very slowly. Her muscles creaked. She'd picked up a couple of bruises in her scuffle with Ramon—minor injuries that were nothing compared to the morning-after agony following a karate competition.

After a visit to the bathroom down the hall, she returned to her room, stripped off her stinky maid uniform and stretched. Knots of tension released with audible crackles. This stiffness and her groggy head reminded her of a hangover. But she hadn't been drinking.

Sucking the cottony insides of her cheeks, she *knew* that she'd been drugged last night. During the skirmish with Charlene and Patrice, Liz had been distracted. Someone could have slipped a narcotic into her ginger ale. Had it been Ben?

During the hours they'd spent talking across the bar, he hadn't seemed suspicious of her. The opposite, in fact. He'd shared his familial concerns and his memories. When he'd talked about sailing and being on the crew at the America's Cup, his voice had turned wistfully poetic, warm and so charming that she'd wanted to share his dreams, to sail away with him.

She had to stop thinking of Ben with all those pastel, romantic sensations. *He's not innocent. I saw him make a drug buy.*

But had he drugged her? It didn't make sense.

If someone had slipped a Mickey Finn into Liz's ginger ale, the more likely suspect was Charlene. That woman was up to something, and Liz wanted to know what. Before she started her second day as an undercover maid, she'd pay a quick visit to Charlene's bedroom. Though the blond bombshell wasn't the target of her investigation, she didn't like being manipulated…or drugged.

Dressed in a sleeveless maroon T-shirt and jeans, she crept barefoot down the staircase to the second floor. The smell of bacon and coffee wafted from the kitchen downstairs. Longingly, Liz gazed toward the staircase. She'd love a mug of dark French roast. At the dinner last night, her growling stomach had taught her an important lesson. Before she started serving everybody else, she needed to take care of her own needs.

Charlene's bedroom stood directly opposite Ben's. Their bedrooms flanked the end suite that belonged to Jerod. His door was ajar, and she heard Ben's voice coming from inside. Quickly, Liz turned the knob on Charlene's door and stepped inside—prepared to confront the blond diva.

Charlene wasn't there.

The curtains were drawn, and the queen-sized bed looked like it hadn't slept in. Discarded clothing scattered haphazardly on the antique desk, makeup table, dresser and pink-upholstered lounging chair. This large room was cluttered with too much furniture. Like Charlene herself, the bedroom seemed greedy.

Liz's detective instincts told her that something was wrong. The general messiness felt different than the usual clutter left behind by a woman getting dressed for a party.

For one thing, the smell of perfume was overpowering. The open jewelry box on the dresser glittered in a flashy display. Diamonds? Was Charlene dumb enough to leave valuables lying around?

The stool in front of the makeup table had been overturned. The huge mirror surrounded by lights tilted at an angle, and the makeup containers were shoved back as though someone had leaned against the surface.

Liz imagined a struggle. Someone—like the hotheaded Ramon—might have forced Charlene backward against the makeup table.

Being careful not to touch anything and leave fingerprints, Liz tiptoed barefoot across the hardwood floor toward the dressing table. She stepped in a puddle, reached down to touch the wetness and held her fingers to her nose. The heavy floral scent made her eyes water.

The pink bottle of cologne lay on the floor where it had spilled. No way had Charlene left this mess. Not when she had a staff of servants to clean up after her.

Even if Charlene had gotten up early, she wouldn't have left her room this way. Liz suspected foul play; she needed to inform Ben immediately.

She stepped back into the hallway and entered Jerod's suite through the opened door. The sliding glass doors were open. Outside on the deck, she saw Jerod in his wheelchair with Ben and the nurse standing on either side of him. Ben wore a gray suit with a white shirt. His necktie was loosely knotted.

The moment she stepped outside, Jerod brightened. He

held out a hand toward her. "Get your butt over here, sweetheart."

Liz obeyed. When she took his hand, he pulled her closer with surprising strength. As she leaned down, she saw him take a couple of sniffs of the perfume. He closed his eyes and grinned. "Honey, you smell like a whole damn bouquet of roses."

"I guess I do." Obviously, he thought she was Charlene. His vision must be worse than anyone knew.

"Give me a peck on the cheek and run along. My nurse has got to take my blood pressure before Doctor Al gets here."

Liz didn't want to embarrass him by pointing out his mistake. Instead, she lightly kissed his cheek.

He beamed. "Thank you, honey."

BEN HADN'T REALIZED that Jerod's eyesight was so bad. Confusing Liz with Charlene? He must be nearly blind.

As Liz dragged him out of his grandpa's room and into the hall, he said quietly, "Thanks for playing along. Jerod won't start his day until he sees Charlene."

"Or smells her," she said as she looked him up and down. "You're all dressed up."

"I have a meeting with my divorce lawyers this morning. Not something I'm looking forward to." He looked down at Liz. Her jeans and T-shirt showed off her fine little body. "I like what you're wearing."

"Great," she said dismissively. "What time did you leave the party last night?"

"About fifteen minutes after you. I was bored into a stupor."

"Was Charlene still there? Did you notice anything strange about her?"

"She's always strange. What's this about?"

She pulled him into Charlene's room and closed the door. "Charlene might be missing. The bed doesn't look slept in. There are signs of a struggle."

He waved his hand in front of his face, trying to dispel the stink. "I've got to open a window."

"Don't touch anything. This could be a crime scene."

She illustrated her theory of a struggle by pointing out the position of the mirror, the messed-up bottles on the makeup table and the broken perfume bottle.

"Or," he said, "Charlene might be sacked out in someone else's bed."

"Does she sleep around?"

Ben thought for a moment. Though Charlene was an equal opportunity tease, he had no proof that she'd ever gone beyond a couple of kisses. "I don't think she's adulterous. But we both saw her playing Ramon against Tony last night."

"And her situation has changed."

He wasn't sure what she meant. "How so?"

"Jerod's will has changed. Charlene might behave differently."

Anger shot through him. If that gold digger planned to betray Jerod after conning him into leaving her his fortune, Ben would make sure she never saw a penny. He'd burn the damn house down before he let her inherit.

Liz said, "We should call the police."

"Not yet." His first concern was his grandpa. If Jerod found out that his beloved was messing around, it would break his heart. "First, we'll try to find her. I'll lock her bedroom door until we figure out where the hell she is."

Her eyebrows pinched in a scowl. "If we don't have an explanation in half an hour, we need to notify the sheriff. He'll want to talk to the witnesses before they leave."

"Witnesses?"

"I don't see traces of blood in here, but the CSI's can use luminol and—"

"Luminol? You sound like a TV detective show."

Suddenly defensive, she took a step backwards. "I've taken criminal law courses at school. I know about chain of evidence."

"Well, let's not hang out the yellow crime-scene tape just yet. There could be a simple explanation."

"I hope so."

Though she had obviously just crawled out of bed with her blond hair sticking out in wild tufts, she radiated intensity. Her bare feet, snug jeans and sleeveless shirt were cuter than hell, but the muscles in her well-toned arms flexed as her fingers drew into fists. She was a time bomb set to explode. "What's going on with you?"

"It's nothing." Her smile was forced. "You're probably right. There's a simple explanation."

Liz hoped her suspicions were groundless, but her instincts told her otherwise. This classy, beautiful mountain estate seethed with an undercurrent of hostility, jealousy and greed. At the center of every skirmish was Charlene. She'd argued with Ben about Jerod's care, battled Patrice about the will and whipped Ramon into a frenzy of sexual possessiveness. Liz feared the trophy wife might have pushed someone too far.

Downstairs, she snagged a cup of coffee and explained to Rachel that she had a few things to take care of before she put on her maid uniform and got to work. After her late-night stint at bartending, it only seemed fair.

A quick survey of the houseguests showed that Ramon

was missing. When she and Ben went to the parking area near the garage, they discovered that his car was gone. The most likely scenario: Charlene and Ramon had run off together.

Ben drained his coffee mug. "I guess that's it. The simple explanation."

"What about the struggle in her bedroom?"

"Passion." His jaw clenched. "Ramon and Charlene tussled in her bedroom before they headed out to find somewhere more private."

A plausible theory. But Liz wasn't completely convinced. Charlene might be a bimbo, but she wasn't a fool. She wouldn't do anything that might cause Jerod to change his mind about the will. "You have surveillance cameras at the front gate. Would the tape show Charlene and Ramon driving off together?"

"The cameras are on a twenty-four-hour loop. Not the most high-tech security available, but sufficient. We'll check."

As he marched up the asphalt driveway toward the gate, she had to jog to keep up. In contrast to his openness last night, anger had turned him cold. He'd do anything to protect his grandfather.

Inside the closet-sized security house beside the locked wrought-iron gates, Ben flipped open a metal locker door. Inside were an array of control switches and four small screens. He juggled a couple of switches.

"Pretty casual security system," she remarked. "Nothing is locked up."

"Mostly we use the cameras to monitor vehicles at the front gate. The visual image is transmitted to a couple of receivers in the house so we can see who we're buzzing inside."

"Not worried about burglary?"

"The only truly effective way to protect this much acreage requires dozens of cameras, sensors and monitors. Not to mention full-time security personnel. Never seemed worth the effort."

*Typical.* People seldom bothered with deadbolts, cameras and coded locks until *after* they'd experienced a break-in.

Ben pointed to the lower screen. "Here's the taping from last night." The time code on the lower right corner showed that at 9:32 p.m. Dr. Mancini drove to the gate, pressed the button to open it and left. In the passenger seat, she saw Tony Lansing, the lawyer.

The feed from two rotating cameras showed several hours of pastoral nighttime scenery. They fast-forwarded through sights of elk crossing the road and pine boughs tossing in the night winds. The view that encompassed the house showed a couple who had stepped outside for a smoke. Patrice and Monte came out to their vehicle and got something from the glove compartment. No one else entered or left.

In the tight space of the security shed, Liz leaned close to Ben's shoulder so she could see the screens. His suit coat still felt warm from the morning sun. Her hand lingered near the small of his back, but she hesitated to actually make physical contact. One touch might lead to another.

On the tapes, nothing happened until 11:47 p.m. when the screen went black.

Liz drew back. "A malfunction?"

He checked the controls. "It appears that the cameras were turned off."

"Can the controls be turned off from inside the house?"

"No," he said. "Only from here."

Her suspicions about foul play returned. Why else would the surveillance be deliberately manipulated? "If someone walked to the gates from the house or from the road outside, their approach would be seen on the surveillance cameras. Right?"

"There are blind spots," he said. "Especially along the fence line. And Charlene knew about them. She could have slipped away from the party and come out here."

The surveillance tape resumed at 2:37 a.m. Once again, the scene was peaceful.

"There." Liz pointed to the screen that showed the view of the house and the vehicles parked by the garage. "Ramon's car is already gone. If he left with Charlene, it wasn't caught on camera."

Ben shrugged. "Maybe we're making too much of this. Possibly, the cameras were down. Maybe some sort of electronic glitch."

"A very convenient lapse," she said. "We need to call the sheriff."

He turned and faced her. The walls of the tiny surveillance shed wrapped tightly around them. As she looked up into his eyes, her heartbeat accelerated. Too close. They were too close for her to ignore the attraction that sang through her veins.

He held her bare arms in a gentle grasp. "I need a favor, Liz. Don't say no until you've heard me out."

Unable to speak, she nodded.

"Jerod's health is my only concern. He loves Charlene. If she's run off with Ramon, my grandpa is the one who'll suffer."

"If he dies, she inherits." The words popped out before

she had a chance to censor her thoughts. She hadn't meant to speak lightly of Jerod's death.

Ben winced. His grip on her arms tightened. "Until I have a chance to check out Ramon and see if Charlene is with him, I don't want to involve the police. Maybe I can find her. Talk sense into her."

"I can't—"

"Please, Liz. Until I have this figured out, I need for you to remain silent."

She pulled free from his grasp. In this tiny space, she had nowhere to go. Even with her back against the opposite wall, his nearness confounded her.

He was asking her to betray her ethics, possibly to cover up a crime. As a private eye, she was duty-bound to report suspicions of wrongdoing to the authorities. As a law student, she knew her actions amounted to aiding and abetting.

Only two days ago, Harry Schooner had stuck her in a similar situation when he had refused to report the drug dealers. She'd waited until the next morning to contact a friend at the Denver PD and give him the location of the drug house.

Some decisions had to be based on the greater good. Protecting Jerod from unnecessary frustration and complication was important. She met Ben's intent gaze. "I'm not doing this for you. It's for Jerod."

The warmth of his smile was far more pleasing than it should have been. She hated herself for being so vulnerable.

"One more thing," he said. "Jerod needs to see Charlene again this morning. You could play that role. Tell him you're going into town and won't be back until later. Put his mind at ease."

"You want me to dress up like Charlene and deliberately deceive your grandfather?"

"To save him pain."

When he put it like that, how could she refuse?

# Chapter Seven

Finally, she'd gotten into Ben's bedroom.

Ever since Liz had arrived at the Crawford estate, she'd been trying to sneak into his room and search for the illegal drugs she had seen him buy in Denver. She really hadn't expected him to be holding the door open and welcoming her across the threshold.

Together, they'd grabbed clothes and a wig from Charlene's room across the hall, but Liz had insisted on preserving the possible crime scene and had refused to change in Charlene's room.

Ben stood in the doorway. "Make sure you douse yourself in her perfume. That seems to be how Jerod recognizes her."

"Don't worry about me," she said. "Just keep Dr. Mancini and the nurse out of the room."

"No problem." He closed the door behind him.

She didn't have much time for a search. Not with Ben standing right outside. Every minute had to count. Tossing the platinum wig on the bed, she scanned the room. The style of the natural wood furniture was sleek, modern and somewhat bland—more like a hotel than a personal space. Apart from a few issues of *Wooden Boat* magazine on the bedside table, there was nothing of Ben. She reminded herself that this wasn't his primary residence; his real home was in Seattle.

Hiding drugs in the attached bathroom was too obvious so she concentrated on the bedroom, reaching into the backs of drawers and feeling behind furniture. Though she hated to mess up the bed, she slid her hand between the mattress and crawled underneath to check the box springs. So many hiding places, so little time.

As she dug through his closet, she threw on Charlene's tiny mini skirt and short-sleeved, pink cashmere sweater. Her instincts told her that this room was only the place where Ben slept. His drug stash was elsewhere.

After she settled the wig on her head, she stepped into the hallway where he waited. His eyebrows lifted at the sight of her, but he was smart enough not to tease. In a low voice, he said, "Charlene usually spends about fifteen minutes with Jerod."

"And what do they talk about?"

He shrugged. "The conversation is light. They laugh. He usually pats her bottom."

She looked over her shoulder. "I'm not built like Charlene. My butt might be okay, but if he reaches for my boobs, he'll know I'm a fake."

"You'll manage."

She didn't share his confidence. Undercover work usually involved being inconspicuous, but she would be trying to convince a man that she was his wife—someone he knew intimately. Her only advantage was that Jerod apparently saw her only as a vague outline.

With Ben keeping watch at the door so she wouldn't be disturbed, she entered Jerod's bedroom suite. He sat outside in his wheelchair on the deck. As she approached, she straightened her shoulders and put a bounce in her step. Since Charlene's shoes were a size too small, Liz remained barefoot.

She searched her auditory memory for the pitch of Charlene's voice, remembering a hint of Texas twang. Sidling up beside Jerod's chair, she used the pet name Charlene had spoken last night. "Howdy, bumblebee."

"Howdy yourself, honey." He turned his head toward her—his manner confident though unseeing. "Y'all have a good time last night?"

"Would have been better if you were there." Though Liz felt creepy about deceiving Jerod, she lightly laced her fingers with his and gave a squeeze. "What were we talking about yesterday?"

"Same as always. Family history. After I'm gone, you're fixing to be the head of the family. There's things you need to know." He frowned. "I sure as heck don't want you getting into more catfights with Patrice."

"But she's such a…" Liz searched for the right word. What would Charlene say? "Such a skinny witch."

"Go easy on her. She had a hard time after she lost her mama and papa in that damn car accident. That's when she told us not to call her Patty Sue any more. She was Patrice. Only fourteen years old and an orphan."

"That means Ben was…how old?"

"Sixteen. Sophomore in high school." Jerod leaned back in his wheelchair, giving up any pretense of looking at her. "He was as tall as he is right now. But scrawny as a wet barn cat. In the summers, the boy worked in the company oil business, and I'm proud to say he held his own with roughnecks who were twice his size."

"I'm confused." She fluttered her free hand in a gesture

she'd seen Charlene use. "The oil business was in Texas, but Ben settled in Seattle."

"I explained this before, honey. Ain't you been paying attention?"

"You know me." She fluttered again. "Gosh, I get ever so distracted."

His gnarled and weathered hand, still holding hers, tightened. "Don't you go playing the dumb blonde with me. We both know better."

*Interesting.* Apparently, there was more to Charlene than met the eye. "I never could fool you."

"Pay attention now. You hear me?"

"No need to be a grouch." The words slipped out before Liz could censor herself. She was accustomed to dealing with grumpy old Harold, who would ride rough-shod over her if she didn't stand up for herself.

"Huh? You think I'm grouchy?"

"Like a grizzly bear."

He chuckled. "That's my honey."

His posture relaxed as he bought into her performance. Apparently, Liz had more in common with Charlene than she'd thought. After they talked a bit more about the family and Charlene's new responsibilities as the matri-arch, Liz wrapped up their conversation. "I should get moving, bumblebee. After our guests clear out, I'm going shopping."

"Whatever you want." When he patted her butt, he frowned. "You been working out?"

"A bit." Liz stepped out of reach.

"Don't go getting too skinny," he said. "Take care of yourself. Your voice sounds like you might be coming down with a cold."

She darted forward and gave him a peck on the cheek. "See you later."

As she stepped through the bedroom and met Ben, she pulled off the blond wig. Looking at his solid, muscular body, it was difficult to imagine him as a scrawny teenager working the oil fields. "I like your grandpa."

"He's a good man, but too damned stubborn for his own good." In his left hand, he held a cell phone. "I called Ramon but got no answer. I'll drive into town and pay him a visit."

And she would go back to her maid duties. The disappearance of Charlene put a new wrinkle in her investigation, but her focus needed to stay clear: find Ben's drug stash.

The warmth of his smile made that search seem utterly repugnant. From all she'd seen of Ben, he was a good man. How could she ruin his chances for joint custody of his child?

"Thanks," he said, "for talking to grandpa. He doesn't need any more heartache."

He leaned closer. If she'd wanted to shove him away, she had ample opportunity. In no way was he forcing himself on her or taking advantage.

She should have objected. Instead, she tilted her chin up, welcoming his kiss. When his lips brushed hers, a brilliant flash of white heat exploded behind her eyes and blinded her to common sense. A burst of passion surged, forceful and challenging. She wanted the kiss to deepen and continue for long, intense moments. She wanted to know his body in every sense of the word. Her ferocious need for him felt unlike anything she'd experienced, as though they were destined to be together.

She had to be mistaken. Her instincts were dead wrong.

The maid and the millionaire? *No way.*

Reality was even worse. A detective and the subject of her investigation could not, should not, must not ever be involved on a personal level.

But as he moved away from her, she grabbed the lapels of his suit jacket and yanked him close, kissing him with all the wildfire passion that burned inside. His arms encircled her. The flames leapt higher.

She deepened the kiss, plunging her tongue into his mouth, and he responded with a fierce passion. His body pressed tightly against hers. She felt his hard arousal, and reveled in this evidence that she turned him on.

He felt the magnetism, too. They were a match. In spite of all their differences, they connected.

*Oh, damn. This was all wrong.*

WHEN BEN FINALLY LOCATED Ramon Stephens in the weight room at his posh Denver apartment building, Ramon was quick to point out the bruising on his shoulder and throat. "You did this to me, man."

He was lucky Ben hadn't torn his head off. "Where's Charlene?"

"I ought to sue." Ramon pouted. "I can't get any modeling jobs with bruises."

After canceling his lawyer's appointment and spending far too much time tracking this jerk down, Ben didn't have the patience to play games. He flipped the lock on the door handle of the weight room. No one else occupied the exercise equipment. "Where is she?"

"Damned if I know." Pumped from his workout, he checked out his reflection in the mirrors.

"What time did you and Charlene leave the party last night?"

"I left at around two in the morning. Alone."

He shrugged, sending a ripple across his pecs. All those muscles were impressive but served little purpose other than being decorative. This pretty boy looked like he'd never done an honest day's work in his whole life.

A long time ago in his grandpa's oil fields, Ben had learned what it meant to be a man, how to get what he wanted and how to fight for it. He also knew how to spot a liar. "There's something you're not telling me."

"Hey, man. I don't have to talk to you."

"Yeah. You do."

In a couple of simple moves, Ben had Ramon in a choke hold with his arm twisted up behind his back. "Did you leave with Charlene? Yes or no?"

"Let go of me."

When he wriggled, Ben hiked his arm higher. "Don't make me break your arm, Ramon. Answer my question."

"No. I didn't leave with her."

"Who did?"

"I don't know." His face in the mirror was an ugly grimace of pain.

"What are you hiding?"

"She dumped me. Okay? Is that what you want to hear? She told me to stay away from her. And I left."

Ben released his grasp and stepped out of range in case the pretty boy decided to retaliate. But there was no fight in Ramon. Cradling his arm against his chest, he sank to his knees and groaned.

Remembering the mess in Charlene's room and Liz's theory that there had been a struggle, Ben wondered if

Ramon had pushed Charlene around. "Did you go up to her room?"

"I tried. But no. I don't care about her anymore." He whimpered like a two-year-old. "I've got plenty of other dates."

No doubt, he was Mister Popularity. But that wasn't Ben's concern. "Who's Charlene's new boy toy?"

"The lawyer."

Tony Lansing, the attorney. His father had handled the Crawford family business for decades before passing the mantle. When Tony had taken over five years ago, Ben hadn't been impressed but hadn't expected any major problems. Jerod had sold his oil fields. No lawsuits were pending. Tony should have been able to handle the personal business.

As he walked out the door, Ben reached down and patted Ramon's shoulder. "Might want to ice that elbow."

DRIVING BACK INTO THE MOUNTAINS, Ben's frustration level grew. As he crested the last hill on I-70 before his turnoff, the panoramic view of the Rocky Mountains failed to lighten his mood. He wished himself back in Seattle where Crawford Aero-Equipment ran like clockwork. During his long physical absence in Colorado, his trusted vice presidents and supervisors kept production and sales on target. No need for worry.

It was his personal life that confounded him. His failed marriage. Jerod's illness. And now…Charlene's disappearance.

At the front gate to the estate, he punched the security code into the keypad. Why had the cameras been turned off from 11:47 until 2:37? The missing three hours indicated a premeditated plan. But not by Ramon.

There was no choice other than notifying the sheriff, but Ben needed to control the situation. He had strings he could pull, highly placed people who owed him favors. If possible, he intended to keep Jerod in the dark until they had everything figured out. Therefore, his first order of business was to talk privately to Liz and convince her to keep pretending to be Charlene.

The thought of Liz sent his mind racing off on a wild and not unpleasant tangent. Her kiss had surprised him. When he'd lightly tasted her sweet lips, he'd wanted more. But she'd turned out to be the aggressor. Of her own passionate accord, she had taken their connection deeper.

He needed to know more about Liz. In spite of her straightforward manner, he saw something mysterious about her. Just as he'd known that Ramon didn't want to talk about how he'd been dumped, he knew that Liz had a secret.

She was the first person he saw when he entered the house. Dressed in a maid uniform that fit marginally better than the one she wore yesterday, she flicked a feather duster across the back of a carved antique chair.

When she turned toward him, he placed a finger across his lips, indicating silence. Immediately, she dropped the duster and followed him outside.

"Did you find Charlene?" she asked.

He set off across the asphalt circle drive toward the log barn. They needed privacy for this conversation. "Ramon says he left by himself last night. I'm inclined to believe him."

"You didn't beat him up, did you?"

"Of course not." Just a little arm twisting.

"Where are we going?"

He pointed toward the one-story log barn. "I need to

make plans for how to handle Charlene's absence, and I want you to—"

"Call the sheriff," she said firmly. "The longer you wait, the more suspicious it looks."

"Suspicious?"

She jogged around in front of him, blocking his path and causing him to halt. "If something bad happened to Charlene, you're a suspect. You hated her."

"*Hate* is a strong word."

"Jerod's will was changed yesterday, and you were disinherited."

He scoffed. "I don't care about Jerod's money."

"That's not how it's going to look to the police."

He circumvented her and proceeded to the barn—the one place on this mountain property where he could go to calm his nerves. He plugged his key into the side door of the barn and shoved it open. Sunlight from high windows poured down on his woodworking shop and the partially completed hull of a twelve-foot-long sailboat he was building himself. Nothing in the world was more relaxing than sanding and smoothing the white oak planking.

Liz stepped past him into the barn as he hit the light switch. "A boat," she said.

"I plan to have it finished in a couple of weeks so I can take my daughter out on the lake and show her the basics of sailing."

When she looked up at him, her green eyes softened. "Every time I start thinking that you're nothing but a millionaire jerk, you pull something like this."

"Like what?"

"Something sweet and sensitive," she said as she

glided her hand along the satiny white oak surface. "Almost artistic."

At the stern of the boat, she came to a sudden stop. Her gaze aimed at the floor on the opposite side of the hull— a place he couldn't see.

"It's Charlene." Liz's voice trembled. "She's dead."

# *Chapter Eight*

Liz had seen corpses before, at funerals and wakes, where the dead were displayed with carefully groomed hairdos, rouge and lipstick. Once in the city morgue, she and Harry had had to identify the remains of a client who had committed suicide. None of those prior experiences prepared her for seeing Charlene's body on the concrete floor beside Ben's boat.

In death, she seemed smaller and somehow flattened as if the air had deflated from her body, leaving a two-dimensional shell. Her eyes were half-closed. Her mouth gaped, and the rosy-pink lipstick contrasted with her waxen cheeks. The shiny blond hair that she loved to toss was matted with blood.

A piece of metal tackle, bloodied, rested beside her. It had to be the murder weapon.

*Murder?* Her knees wobbled. Her nerves clenched in a knot. For a moment, she forgot how to breathe. When Ben stepped up close behind her, she leaned against his chest, grateful for his support.

"Are you okay?" he asked.

"Fine," she replied automatically, not wanting her weakness to show. "Who would do this? Why?"

"I don't know."

She turned in the circle of his arms and clung to him. Inside his rib cage, she heard the steady thump of his heartbeat—an affirmation of life. His self-control and strength should have reassured her. Instead, she felt even more unnerved. "Finding her here. In your little hideout. It doesn't look good for you."

"I'm aware of that." His chest rose and fell as he drew in a deep breath and exhaled. "Other people have keys to this workshop."

"Who?" She choked out the word. "Who has a key?"

"The entire household has access. Rachel has duplicate keys to everything hanging on a labeled rack in the pantry."

"Then why bother to lock up?"

"A deterrent. I don't want my workshop turning into a place where the staff can come to grab a smoke and a beer. Or a place where guests can wander freely."

As he gently stroked her shoulder, she felt a trembling in his hand. From shock? From anger? She really didn't know a thing about him. They were barely acquainted. "This is a crime scene," she said. "We should get out of here."

Keeping his arm wrapped protectively around her waist, he escorted her to the door into the daylight. The perfect spring weather seemed like a travesty. She sucked down a lungful of the clean mountain air. Thankfully, her head began to clear.

Looking up at Ben, she studied the angles of his handsome face. His jaw was set firmly. The fine lines on his forehead deepened. Though she'd felt that tremor, the only evidence that he might be disturbed showed in his blue eyes. His gaze flickered. His lids blinked. *Wasn't that a sign of lying? Rapidly blinking eyelids?* Did he know more about the murder than he was saying?

"It's time," she said. "Call the sheriff."

"I don't think so." His brow furrowed as he took the cell phone from his suit coat pocket. "I'm going to start a bit higher up on the food chain."

"You can't orchestrate a murder investigation."

"Watch me," he said.

She stopped his hand before he could punch in a number. "I don't care if you have the governor on speed dial, you need to let the police do their job."

"I have no intention of standing in the way of an investigation, but I'll start with the Colorado Bureau of Investigation. I don't want a bunch of deputies running around here causing trouble."

"Heaven forbid they should make a mess," she said coldly.

"I'll handle this my way." His decision was made, and his voice took on the unmistakable ring of authority. Before her eyes, he transformed into a high-powered CEO—the sort of individual she'd spent most of her life resenting. He said, "I don't want Jerod to know what happened."

"There's no way you can keep Charlene's murder a secret."

"Everyone else will know. But not Jerod. God damn it." His voice cracked. "Not Jerod."

His arrogant facade slipped as the corners of his mouth tightened. "He's dying, Liz. Until this morning when he thought you were Charlene, I had no idea how bad his vision had become. He may have only a few weeks left."

Though she empathized with his feelings, she couldn't agree with his plan. "Jerod is weak, but his mental abilities are sharp. Even if you organize the most subtle murder investigation of all time, he'll know."

"You're right." He gazed skyward as if to search for answers in the wisps of clouds.

"You can't control this," she said. "All we can do right now is tell the truth."

"Jerod doesn't have to know…." She could almost see his mind working, analyzing the situation and coming to a solution. "He won't know if he's in the hospital."

"What?"

"With Charlene out of the way, I can convince Jerod to see my specialists."

*With Charlene out of the way?* In one callous phrase, he had dismissed the brutal murder of a young, vibrant woman. As if she were nothing more than an obstacle. "I can't believe you said that."

"About the specialists?"

"About Charlene. Her death counts, Ben." He couldn't just sweep her under the rug. Her murder needed to be taken seriously. "Yesterday, she was a living, breathing human being with dreams and schemes and hopes."

"And there were times when I liked her, when I believed that she loved my grandpa. She brightened his life, and I'm sorry that she's dead."

"A touching eulogy. I almost believe you."

"Now isn't the time for mourning. I need to handle the situation, and I need your help." He concentrated on her with a compelling intensity. "Will you help me, Liz?"

"To do what?"

"You'll impersonate Charlene one more time. Together, we'll see Jerod. Don't worry. I'll do most of the talking. I'll convince him to listen to reason and go into the hospital."

"Not a chance." She wanted no part of him or his plan. "I'll talk to the police, and then I'm out of here."

"What would it take to convince you? Money?"

Disgusted, she turned away from him. He was a different person. Gone was the wistful dreamer who talked of sailboats and sunsets. She saw no trace of the craftsman who had worked on the beautiful hull inside the workshop—the crime scene.

He continued. "I'd pay you enough to cover your law school tuition."

"This isn't about money," she said. "I won't lie to a dying man."

"Not even if your lie might save his life?"

Though she hated to admit it, he had a point. Jerod deserved the very best neurological care, and daily visits from Dr. Mancini, a retired general practitioner, didn't fall into that category. "I thought the main reason Jerod was here was because it was his preference, because he wanted to die at home?"

"It's been six weeks of slow deterioration—enough time that he might now change his mind if Charlene asks him to reconsider. You could give him this chance."

Ben wasn't someone she could trust; he trafficked with drug dealers. The staff thought he was a brooding loner. His estranged wife wanted to withhold custody of their child. But her instincts told her otherwise. She'd trusted Ben enough to kiss him. In his tone of voice, she heard nothing but sincerity; he truly cared for his grandpa. As did she. Jerod Crawford was a good person, and she wanted to help him.

She couldn't ignore the possibility that advanced medical care might save his life. "I'll do it."

PUTTING HER CONCERNS AND reservations on hold, Liz allowed herself to be swept into Ben's whirlwind plans. Cell phone in hand, he made rapid-fire calls as he tore through the house, pulling her in his wake. Through the door. Up the staircase.

Liz changed into the platinum wig. *God forgive me.* This was so wrong.

In his grandpa's bedroom, she played her role as Charlene, holding Jerod's hand and gazing into his nearly sightless eyes as Ben directed the conversation toward a new phase in Jerod's treatment.

When she spoke, her words stuttered. She was blatantly working a deception on a dying man, withholding the tragedy of his wife's murder. *He ought to know. He ought to be told.*

The only way she could get through this performance was to think of Harry Schooner and his unwavering refusal to take care of himself in spite of her concerns. If Jerod had been Harry, which really wasn't a far stretch of the imagination, she might be inclined to do the same thing Ben was doing with his grandpa.

Surprisingly, Jerod acquiesced to Ben's plan with hardly an objection, which made her think that he'd already been considering a similar action.

After she switched back into her maid uniform and stepped out of Ben's bedroom into the hall, she had only three words for him. "Nine. One. One."

"Not yet," he said. "The ambulance will be here in half an hour. Then I'll call in the police."

"Half an hour?" The last time she'd consulted a medical specialist about a knee injury, it had taken three weeks to make an appointment. "How did you make these arrangements so quickly?"

"I've had this plan in place for weeks, hoping Jerod would change his mind. The neurosurgeon will be waiting for the ambulance."

And how much would that cost? A new wing for the hospital? It certainly helped to have money, lots of money. Every procedure moved more smoothly when the road was paved with hundred-dollar bills.

AFTER JEROD WAS WHISKED AWAY in the ambulance, Liz watched as Ben made the calls to the authorities, to several people who owed him favors and to his attorneys. A complicated procedure.

Normal people rang up 9-1-1 and took whatever and whomever responded. Normal people had the common sense to step back and allow the lawmen to do their jobs. The rich, she realized, were different. And Ben was in a league of his own.

She couldn't fault his performance as he gathered the staff together with Patrice and Monte. He informed them all that Charlene had been murdered. "Liz and I found her body in the log barn."

"Are you sure?" Patrice asked. "She was murdered?"

"Yes," he said briskly.

Rachel seemed to be at a loss. Her large hands gestured clumsily. "What are we supposed to do? What are we supposed to say?"

Liz bit her lower lip to keep from snapping at her. *You're supposed to tell the truth. That's how murder investigations work.*

Ben said, "The police will be here shortly, and you're to cooperate with them."

Annette adjusted her maid cap and edged closer to the chauffeur. "Was it a serial killer? Are we in danger?"

*Yeah, sure.* A psycho killer just happened to show up at this remote estate and kill the most hated person on the premises. Liz glanced toward Patrice and Monte, who both seemed to be holding back whoops of joy. *Ding, dong, the witch is dead.*

"Oh, this is terrible," Monte said as he stifled his grin. "A real scandal."

"Does Jerod know?" Patrice asked.

"No," Ben responded. "And you're not to tell him. He's finally consented to seeing my specialists and needs to concentrate on getting better. He'll be told when the time is right."

Liz was dying to ask a few questions, maybe to do a quick interrogation before the police got here. Not that she had any authority to do so.

The chef wiped his hands on his white apron and stepped forward. "You mentioned that the police were on their way. Should I prepare something for them to eat?"

Liz couldn't help blurting, "Doughnuts."

All eyes turned toward her.

"A joke," she said. "You know, cops and doughnuts?" Silence.

But now she had their attention. Might as well jump in. "When was the last time any of you saw Charlene?"

Everyone talked at once, recalling haphazardly their last encounter with the victim. Victim? Inwardly, Liz cringed. It was hard to think of the brazen, demanding Charlene that way.

The only person who remained silent was Annette. Her mousy, little face puckered, and her cheeks flushed a bright red.

Ben had also noticed her reticence. In a low, calm voice, he said. "Annette."

"Yes, sir." She jumped.

"Did you see something?"

"Yes, sir," she responded properly.

"Tell us about it."

"Well, it was very late." Her voice was thin and tiny. "When Liz came to bed, she made quite a lot of noise and woke me up."

"Sorry," Liz mumbled. Last night, she'd been reeling.

"Anyway," Annette said. "I couldn't get back to sleep. I thought maybe a beverage would help, so I went down to the kitchen." She drew a ragged breath. "While I was making my herbal tea, all the guests were going upstairs to the bedrooms. How very embarrassing. I didn't want to be seen in my bathrobe."

"Very proper," Rachel said approvingly. "The help should always be unobtrusive."

Ben shot a silencing glare in her direction and turned back to Annette. "Then what?"

"I went outside on the second floor deck where Mr. Jerod usually sits. There was a nice, thick wool blanket. So I curled up in a chair and drank my tea. I must have dozed off. Then I woke up. And I saw…" She covered her face with her hands and took a step back, away from Ben.

Liz went to her side and wrapped her arm around Annette's shoulders. The poor, meek, little thing was trembling. Had she witnessed the murder? "It's okay," she cooed. "Everything is going to be okay."

"I thought I was having a nightmare." Her eyes flooded with tears. "I saw a man carrying a woman down the hill and through the shadows. It was dark, and they were really far away. I couldn't see very well. It scared me. Like a monster movie."

"Nobody is going to hurt you." Liz pulled a crumpled

but unused tissue from her pocket and dabbed at Annette's tears. "You're safe now."

"The monster was carrying her toward the log barn."

"Can you describe him?" Liz asked.

With a loud sob, Annette collapsed against her. The tears gushed. "Can't say anything else. I can't."

For a few long moments while the traumatized girl sobbed uncontrollably, Liz simply held her. Her gaze linked with Ben's. In spite of his overbearing CEO demeanor, he seemed troubled and far more sympathetic to Annette's outburst than Liz. Patience had never been one of her finer qualities, and she was ready to shake Annette until the rest of her story fell out.

"Dry those tears," Liz said. "Concentrate, Annette. I need for you to tell us the rest of your story. What was the man wearing?"

"Excuse me," Patrice said coldly. "Why is the maid asking these questions? She has no authority to—"

"Leave her alone," Ben said. "Continue, Liz."

She nodded her thanks to him and repeated her question. "What was he wearing?"

"All black. Or dark blue." Gasping, she continued, "I think he had on a knit cap. In the moonlight, he looked huge."

"Like a monster," Liz said.

"It was awful. I was scared."

"Did you recognize him?"

"I'm not sure." She shook her head. "I can't be sure. Please don't make me say anything else."

"Here's the thing." She held Annette by the upper arms and confronted her. "The police will need to hear about this. You'll have to talk to them."

"No," she moaned. "It was only a nightmare."

"Start by telling us," Liz said firmly. "Who did you see? Who was the monster?"

Annette's arm thrust straight out, and she pointed. "It was Ben."

# Chapter Nine

Two hours and thirty-seven minutes later, Ben sat behind the L-shaped teak desk in the downstairs study. The spacious, book-lined room—decorated in cool earth tones and equipped with computer, fax and file cabinets—was usually a quiet place. Not today.

Two attorneys from the firm that had been handling his divorce sat side-by-side on the cinnamon-colored sofa and argued with Tony Lansing, who perched on the edge of his chair and gestured emphatically. Patrice and Monte paced at the edge of the Navajo rug, occasionally tossing in commentary of their own.

The main topic at the moment was the handling of what promised to be a high-profile murder investigation. Surely, the press would be involved, and the family needed to be ready with a statement.

Ben wasn't listening. His fingers toyed with the mouse that rested on a Kermit the Frog mousepad that his daughter had given him for Christmas. One thought remained foremost in his mind: he wanted Liz to trust him again.

When Annette had made her semi-hysterical accusation that he had carried the limp and lifeless body of

Charlene into the night like a monster from a horror film, he'd almost laughed out loud. Then he had looked into Liz's face. While the others had gasped in shock, her gaze had remained steady, and he had seen disappointment in her eyes. He had known what she was thinking— that he had purposely avoided calling the police. She thought he was a cold-blooded killer.

The two plainclothes detectives from the Colorado Bureau of Investigation seemed to have reached the same conclusion. They'd arrived a few minutes after the local sheriff. The argument over jurisdiction was brief; the CBI had taken charge.

While their forensic team had gathered evidence and removed the body, Agent Lattimer had questioned the staff and gathered names and phone numbers for all the guests from last night who had already gone home.

In his interview, Ben had accepted full responsibility for allowing the guests to leave, for tampering with the potential crime scene in Charlene's bedroom and for not informing the police when he first suspected she might be missing. He had told the truth. Sure, he'd played fast and loose with proper procedure. But he wasn't a murderer.

The door to the study opened, and Rachel stepped inside. Her broad body eclipsed Liz, who followed behind her carrying a silver serving tray piled high with plates of little sandwiches and bowls of fresh fruit.

In her maid uniform, Liz seemed uncomfortable as usual. She'd given up on fastening the starched white cap into her sandy-colored hair. Though he stared at her, she didn't return his gaze.

After she placed the food on the coffee table, she approached Ben behind the desk. Reaching into her pocket, she took out a folded scrap of paper, which she slid across the desk toward him.

He flipped the note open. The slanted handwriting seemed to have been penned in haste. Likewise, her thoughts were in shorthand.

I quit. Heading back to Denver. My best to Jerod.
Liz.

He didn't want her to go. He needed her. She was his touchstone, his connection with reality in an increasingly unreal world. Her snippy attitude provided exactly the right antidote to the poisonous spewing of verbiage from the lawyers.

"Wait," he said as he rose from his chair.

The discussion fell silent. Rachel and Liz paused near the door.

Ben paced around the desk. The time had come to put an end to this legalese yammering. "Patrice will be our media spokesperson."

"Me?" Her eyelashes fluttered. "I couldn't."

"You'll do fine." And she already had the appropriate clothing for a mourner. Most of her wardrobe was black. "We'll need a written statement expressing our sorrow and our willingness to cooperate with the authorities."

Tony stood. "I'll get right on it."

"Not you." Ben hadn't forgotten last night when the family lawyer had been kissing Charlene in the hallway behind the kitchen. "Matter of fact, I want you out of here."

Tony stuck out his closely shaven chin and frowned in an attempt to show grave concern. "May I remind you," he said, "that my firm has represented the Crawford family for decades."

"Not anymore."

"Before you fire me, keep in mind that I know about all the skeletons in the family closet. I know the terms of Jerod's latest will."

"Big deal," Patrice said. "We all know that Grandpa was going to leave the bulk of his estate to Charlene. Obviously, that no longer applies."

"You don't know all the terms of the will," he said with a smug little grin. "There's a section about what happens if Charlene predeceases Jerod. And the terms don't look good for Ben."

Patrice darted across the room and stood before him. "With Charlene dead, everything ought to go back to the way it was before. An even split between me and Ben."

"Not at all." He preened. "Charlene's death means that her share of the estate will go to…Natalie."

"Ben's daughter?" Patrice trembled at the verge of tears. "That can't be. She's only a child."

One of Ben's divorce lawyers, a slender brunette with her hair pulled back in a bun, spoke up. "That information raises a number of concerns. The custody and guardianship of Natalie will be worth millions."

"For the last time," Ben said, "I don't care about the money."

His brunette lawyer made a clucking noise in the back of her throat. "In the midst of a divorce, many people make decisions that they later regret. That's why you hired us. We're here to protect your interests."

Her partner added, "And Tony's right. This looks bad for you."

"Why?"

"Motive," said the brunette. "Charlene's death means millions for your daughter. And for her legal guardians."

"Let's make one thing clear." Ben's gaze rested on Liz, who frowned and stared at her shoes. "I didn't kill Charlene. I didn't harm one single hair on her platinum-blond head."

"So," Tony said. "Am I fired?"

"Certainly not," Patrice said as she glared at Ben. "Let's get working on that statement. I need to be prepared."

Ben stalked toward the door, hooked his arm through Liz's and headed across the front room to the deck. As they went through the sliding doors to the outside, he kept a firm grasp.

She balked. "Take your hand off me."

"I want to make sure you won't run away."

"Let go," she growled. "Now."

Remembering her energetic demonstration of the knee-to-groin move, he released her. "I don't want you to quit."

Bristling, she strode to the railing at the edge of the deck into the mid-afternoon sunlight. This large cedar deck formed the center tier. Above them was Jerod's bedroom, with the best view of the lake and surrounding trees. Below was the stone terrace outside the party room with the bar.

He stepped up beside her and leaned his elbows on the railing. A soft wind brushed the buffalo grass and wild-flowers on the slope leading to the lake, but the serenity of the mountain valley was disrupted by a van that had driven down to the log barn. A couple of men in dark jackets with the letters *CBI* stenciled on the back slowly paced up the hill, staring at the ground.

"What did you tell the detectives?" she asked.

"The truth. I mentioned that you were in favor of notifying the authorities from the minute you noticed Charlene hadn't slept in her bed."

She nodded. "They weren't real happy with me for not using my own little fingers to dial 9-1-1."

"I put you in a difficult position," he said. "And I apologize for that."

"Don't worry about protecting me."

"Somebody needs to worry about you, Liz. Might as well be me."

"I can take care of myself, thank you." Her mouth puckered in a tight bow. "How's Jerod?"

"The doctors are still running tests. They won't know until tomorrow if he's a good candidate for surgery." He pointed to the two CBI investigators who were walking up the hill, occasionally pausing to take photographs. "What do you think they're doing?"

"Looking for the path that Annette's monster took when he was carrying Charlene. They might find evidence. A fiber or a footprint."

Another clue that would point to him as the primary suspect. He walked from the house to the log barn at least once every day.

He caught her gaze and held it. "Do you think I killed her?"

"I ought to believe it. Every bit of evidence, every action, every motive points to you." Her hand clenched into a fist, and she hammered on the railing. "You manipulated me. You kept me from calling the police, convinced me to lie to a dying man. I have absolutely no reason to believe in your innocence."

"But do you?"

He waited. Her opinion mattered more to him than the CBI and the lawyers.

"I don't believe you killed her."

"Good." For the first time in hours, his tension eased. But when he reached toward her, she batted his hand away.

"I'm not staying, Ben. I quit. I'm gone."

She darted across the deck and through the sliding glass doors. As he watched her disappear into the house, he promised himself that this would not be the last time he saw Liz Norton. For reasons he couldn't explain, she'd become important to him. He wouldn't let her go. Not without a fight.

A FULL DAY HAD PASSED, twenty-four long hours. Liz had slept for most of that time. Actually, she'd tossed and turned on her bed, torn by conflicting emotions.

Now, she parked her beat-up Toyota on the street outside the two-story stucco house that belonged to Victoria Crawford, Ben's estranged wife. She scowled at Harry, who sprawled in the passenger seat. For the past half hour, she'd been talking nonstop, giving a full report on what had happened at the Crawford estate.

Harry had said nothing. Behind his sunglasses, his eyes were probably closed. At least he wasn't snoring.

"This is the address," she said.

"Nice place, don't you think?"

In a glance, she took in the carpet of green lawn and tidy shrubbery. The red tile roof and elaborate iron lat-ticework gave the impression of an urban villa. Before spending time at the palatial Crawford mountain estate, she would have been impressed. Now she had a new standard of opulence.

"Cute house," she said. "I still don't understand why we're here."

As far as she was concerned, her P.I. assignment had been a total bust. She hadn't found evidence that Ben was a drug user, had been a disaster as an undercover maid and had ended up knee-deep in a murder investigation.

Though she hadn't lied to the CBI detectives, she had most certainly withheld the fact that she worked for Schooner Detective Agency. Rachel had begged her not to say anything unless directly confronted, and Liz had complied with her wishes.

She hadn't told Ben, and she regretted her deception. While she'd been accusing him of lying and manipulating her, she'd been equally guilty. Probably more so.

The CBI Investigators hadn't pressed her for background information. Apparently, she wasn't a suspect. Only a maid. Putting on that uniform had made her invisible—even to the cops.

"We're here," Harry said, "because Mrs. Crawford paid us a good-sized retainer, and we want another big payday."

"But I didn't get what she wanted. I wasn't—"

"Let me do the talking." He pushed open the car door. "And try not to let her see that you've got the hots for her almost ex-husband."

"I do not."

He lowered his dark glasses and peeked over the rim. "Every time you say his name, you start drooling. Lovesick. That's what you are."

"Wrong, wrong, wrong. I can't stand guys like him. Arrogant, rich people who think they run the world. Ben lawyered up before the cops got there. I hate that."

With a groan, he hauled his bulk out of her car. "It

figures that when you finally get yourself hooked with a new boyfriend, he's a murder suspect."

"Ben is not my boyfriend," she said as she chased him up the sidewalk to the front door.

The woman who opened the door and graciously introduced herself to Liz as Victoria Crawford looked like a supermodel. Tall—nearly six feet—and skinny with shiny, shoulder-length black hair. Her casual summer walking shorts and tasteful jewelry looked like she'd stepped out of a *Vogue* photo shoot.

She swept Liz with a glance and said, "Rachel tells me you're not much of a maid."

"No, ma'am," she said, following Rachel's instructions for proper response.

"She did, however, say that you were handy to have around. You broke up a knife fight with Ramon and Tony?"

"Yes, ma'am."

"And spent the night bartending?"

Liz nodded. The repetition of *ma'am* was wearing on her nerves.

"And you seem to have done the impossible. You got Ben interested in you."

"Not really." Well, this was uncomfortable. What was the correct response to the estranged wife? Liz had never played the role of the "other woman" before.

"Don't bother to deny it." Victoria led them into a charming, antique-furnished living room. "I've moved on. My only interest in Ben is the size of his…wallet."

"Speaking of wallets," Harry said as he settled his bulk in a brocade chair. "How would you like for us to proceed with our investigation?"

"I want Liz to go back to the house and resume her undercover role as a maid."

Victoria's request was the last thing she had expected. "Why?"

"You're a detective, aren't you? And now there's a murder to investigate." She lifted her chin and looked down her nose. "I'm quite sure Ben is responsible for Charlene's death. He despised her. And he was seen carrying Charlene's body to his workshop. He's building a wooden boat, isn't he?"

"Yes."

"God, how I hate those woodworking projects of his! Always tinkering around, redesigning the hull, sanding the frame. He can afford a massive yacht with all the amenities. Why waste countless hours on something no bigger than a dinghy?"

Liz knew the answer. Ben enjoyed working with his hands, dreaming of the endless sea while he created his own craft. His woodworking project endeared him to her, made him less like a CEO and more like a regular guy.

Victoria turned toward Harry. "I will pay the balance of our contract after Ben is arrested for murder."

"Wait." Liz couldn't agree to those terms. "What if he didn't do it?"

"Liz brings up a good point," Harry said. "It might turn out that someone else is the killer."

"In that very unlikely case, I will honor our contract."

"So we get paid," Harry said. "Either way."

"Exactly so." Victoria rose to her feet and checked her wristwatch. "I hate to rush you off, but Dr. Mancini will be here at any moment. Natalie has the sniffles, and he agreed to stop by for a visit."

"Mancini?" Harry frowned. "Isn't that the same doc who was treating Jerod Crawford?"

"Family doctor. Natalie likes him." She glanced between them. "Are we agreed?"

Liz hated this plan. "Why should I pretend to be a maid? Since you want me to be a detective, I should go there as a private investigator."

"In an undercover position, you'll find out a lot more. Ben won't trust you for a moment if he knows you're working for me."

"At least, it would be the truth."

Anger glittered in Victoria's eyes. "I'm not paying for the truth. I want Ben charged with murder so I get sole custody of our daughter."

And complete control of the inheritance?

A bitter taste prickled on Liz's tongue. She didn't want to work against Ben. She liked him, and she didn't believe he was a killer. The only way this could turn out right was for her to prove her conviction.

# *Chapter Ten*

Later that evening, alone in her one-bedroom apartment, Liz stared out her third-floor window at the Dumpsters in the alley and street lamps shining on the asphalt parking lot. When she'd stood on the cedar deck beside Ben, she'd seen snow-covered peaks, forests and a shimmering lake—a million-dollar panorama. The view from her apartment was worth about a buck twenty-five.

She contemplated the three withered houseplants lined up in a row across her windowsill while she pondered the ethical problem of returning to the Crawford estate. Harry wanted her to do it, wanted the big payoff from Victoria and didn't see anything wrong with her going there.

According to him, all she had to do was play her role as a maid—set the table and flick a feather duster until the CBI did their job and arrested someone for Charlene's murder.

Though she hated the idea of merely hanging around and watching, Harry probably had it right. All she needed was patience. The real issue—the problem that tied her gut in a knot—was that she'd be lying to Ben. Again.

She turned her glare on the deceased plants in their

plastic containers. This feeble attempt at beautifying her home had come during the dead of winter when the days had been short and everything had felt gloomy. During finals, she'd forgotten to water them.

At the well-run Crawford estate, the petunias in the flower box on Jerod's deck would never be allowed to shrivel. After experiencing firsthand how the upper one percent lived, her hand-to-mouth lifestyle seemed shabby—and yet, blissfully simple. She didn't need a chef, chauffeur, housekeeper and maids to keep her household running. No attorneys. No family doctors.

She was on her own and liked it that way.

Grabbing a black plastic garbage bag, she dumped the dead foliage. Simple. Problem solved.

She flung herself into the big, comfy reading chair—the only real piece of furniture in her front room, which was set up as an office with a huge desk for her computer and research papers, lots of bookshelves and a beat-up entertainment center. Maybe if she made a list of pluses and minuses, she could decide.

Resting a legal pad on the knees of her black yoga pants, she scribbled reasons why she shouldn't go back.

Number one: incompetence. She was a lousy maid.

Number two: pride. She'd stormed out the door earlier. How could she return without looking like a jerk?

Number three: danger. No matter how lovely the estate, there was a murderer on the loose.

Number four: Ben. She wrote his name twice, underlined and put a row of exclamation points at the end.

When he wasn't acting like a pushy CEO, he intrigued her with his stories about flying solo and crewing for the America's Cup. His selfless concern for his grandfather was admirable. In capital letters, she wrote the word *sexy*.

She groaned. It was crazy to think that there could ever be anything between them. Men like Ben hooked up with statuesque supermodels like his estranged wife.

She scratched through his twice-written name, then cross-hatched and scribbled over the letters again.

A knock at the door startled her. Leaping from her chair, she peeked through the fisheye and saw him. Ben.

He hadn't buzzed from downstairs, but that wasn't unusual. People were always walking in and out of this three-story building, and nobody bothered to ask for I.D.

He knocked again. She could pretend not to be home, avoid the problem for as long as possible. But she wasn't a coward.

Flipping the door lock, she opened wide.

"Thanks for seeing me," he said.

"Do I have a choice?"

"May I come in?"

She glanced over her shoulder at her drab little apartment and squashed the impulse to apologize. She didn't need his approval. "You've got five minutes."

When he walked through the door, he filled up her apartment with his masculine energy. During the two years she'd lived there, she'd probably had only three male guests. None of them compared to Ben. Surprisingly, he didn't look out of place. Though his suit probably cost more than her semester's tuition at law school, he'd been under stress and looked as rumpled as the Dumpster divers who patrolled her alley.

She perched on the swivel chair beside her computer and pointed to the big, comfy armchair. Ben filled the space nicely. Too nicely.

Abruptly, she said, "What do you want?"

"You always jump right in. Ask the hard questions."

When he grinned, the whole apartment lit up. Her seventy-five-watt bulbs blazed like spotlights. "When we met, you asked, Who loves you?"

*Me*, she wanted to shout. *Wrong*. She was too smart to fall for a guy she could never have. "Got an answer?"

"To which question?"

"Why are you here?"

"I want you to come back to work for me," he said. "I have two reasons. The first is Jerod. I want you to play the role of Charlene."

"He still doesn't know that she's dead? The murder has been all over the news. Patrice almost looks like she's really in mourning with that black dress."

"The pearls are a nice touch," he agreed.

"Why hasn't Jerod seen it?"

"Since he's been in the hospital, they've kept him busy with tests. Mostly, he's been sleeping." He leaned forward, and his hair fell across his forehead. Absently, he pushed it back. "It's likely the doctors will operate tomorrow. I don't want Jerod to be jolted by this tragedy when he's going into surgery. He needs a reason to live."

Though she didn't approve, she understood. "And the second reason you want me back?"

"The murder investigation. It's possible that you're the only person who believes I'm innocent." His blue eyes shone with a sincerity she really wanted to believe. "The only way I'm going to get out of this in one piece is to solve the crime myself. And I want you to help me."

Solving a real crime? A tickle of excitement raised goose bumps on her forearms. In all the time she'd been working for Schooner Private Investigations, the closest she'd gotten to sleuthing was tracking down an unfaithful husband who wore a fake mustache when he met his mistress. Being involved in a real investigation? She liked the idea, liked it a lot.

"I'd pay you," he said.

"Not necessary." She was already getting paid by Victoria who, ironically, wanted exactly the same thing as her estranged husband: to find Charlene's murderer.

He reached down and picked up the legal pad she'd discarded on the floor. "Interesting list," he said. "Incompetence. Pride. Danger. And sexy? Sounds like the plot for a soap opera."

She yanked the pad from his hands. "That's mine."

"What's the word you scratched out?"

"None of your business." She felt herself blushing again. Whenever she was around him, she got flushed and her cheeks turned scarlet. *Way too sexy.* Flipping the page on her legal pad, she picked up her pen. "We need a list. First issue. Who turned off the surveillance at the gate? And why?"

"I assume this marks the start of the investigation," he said. "*Our* investigation."

"Guess so."

He came toward her. Resting his hands on the arms of her swivel chair, he leaned down and lightly kissed her forehead.

Now she was blushing all over, which wasn't something she wanted to share with him. She shoved at his chest. "Don't get all mushy. I could still change my mind."

His smile communicated a warmth and appreciation that could never be expressed in words. "You're right, Liz. We should get down to business. Bring your legal pad, and let's go."

She lurched into her bedroom to throw some clothes

and a couple of changes of underwear into a gym bag. Ethically, everything had fallen into place. Except for the tiny problem that she was being paid by his estranged wife.

WHEN LIZ HAD DONE HER IMPERSONATION of Charlene in Jerod's private room at the hospital, Ben had almost been jealous of the way she'd lavished attention on his grandpa. With whispers and giggles, she'd teased Jerod. Willingly, she'd given him a good-night kiss.

That sure as hell wasn't the way she treated Ben. With him, her shields were up.

As he drove west toward the mountains, she still wore the low-cut red silk shirt that she'd used for her Charlene persona, but she'd covered up with a denim jacket. Scowling, she complained, "I still think I should have taken my own car."

"We'll be in and out of Denver every day to see Jerod. Tomorrow, you can get your car. I want to use this drive time to create a strategy for our investigation."

"Multitasking. I'll bet you're a good CEO."

"It's what I do."

"Okay, let's not waste any more time." She wriggled around in the passenger seat, turned on the roof light and dug around in the back of his Mustang. When she returned to her seat, she had the legal pad in hand. "We need a list of suspects."

An obvious first step. Finally, he was with someone who was ready for action. After all the suspicion, innuendo and hand-wringing, he welcomed a task he could sink his teeth into. "Since the surveillance at the front gate was turned off, we can assume that Charlene's murder was premeditated."

"Which rules out a crime of passion," she said.

"Therefore, Ramon's story must be true. He wanted to get Charlene into bed, but she dumped him. And he left."

"With his tail tucked between his legs." She gave a sardonic chuckle. "I'm writing Ramon's name down, anyway. He's suspicious. And what about the third member of that love triangle?"

"Tony Lansing." Ben's intuitive distrust of the lawyer had grown deeper when Tony had threatened him about exposing the skeletons in the Crawford family closet.

"Is he an alcoholic?" she asked as she scribbled Tony's name onto her list.

"Not as far as I know."

"Two days ago, during dinner, he tossed back three straight vodkas and a bottle of wine. That's the kind of thing you notice when you're tending bar."

"Being drunk might explain why he was dumb enough to grope Charlene in a house full of people."

"Or he might have been drinking for liquid courage. Knowing that he'd come back later, turn off the surveillance camera and commit murder."

Accelerating with a satisfying roar from the Mustang engine, Ben exited the highway onto the access road. Though only a little after nine o'clock, it felt like midnight. Today had been hell.

"Tony had no motive," he said. "With Jerod's will leaving the bulk of his estate to Charlene, Tony had reason to romance her in the hope that she'd soon be a wealthy widow. He wouldn't want her dead."

"Good point." She made a note on her legal pad. "Still, it might be good to talk to him. Find out where he was on the night of the murder."

"No problem."

Tony had been adamant about his role as the Crawford family lawyer; now it was time for him to live up to that responsibility. Ben flipped open his cell phone, called Tony Lansing on speed dial and left a message on the answering machine about wanting to see him as soon as possible.

He disconnected the call. "I hope that ruins his evening."

"Ben, there's something I didn't tell you about the night of the murder. After I left the bar and went to bed, I was hammered. Dizzy and wobbling all over the place even though I hadn't had a drop of alcohol. I'm pretty sure I was drugged."

*What the hell?* He turned his head and looked at her.

Immediately, he was distracted from crime solving. Even in the shadowy light from the dashboard, she was cute. No matter how high she piled the chips on her shoulder, she still had a sweetness about her. Maybe it was the way her mouth turned up at the corners. Or her hair, that wild hair.

"Ben? Are you with me?"

"Right." He needed to stay focused. "Why would somebody drug you?"

"Don't know *why*." Her shoulders rose and fell in a shrug. "But I do know *how*. During the catfight between Charlene and Patrice, somebody could have slipped a powder into the ginger ale I was drinking."

"If you were drugged, it could mean—"

"If?" Her voice rose. "I *was* drugged. It's a fact. I know what it feels like."

"Do you take drugs?"

"Do you?"

"That's the second time you've asked that question.

And it's absurd. Are my eyes dilated? My speech slurred? Do I strike you as being out of control?"

"I wouldn't blame you," she said. "You might need a little something to take the edge off. Every now and then."

"My edge is an asset."

He needed to stay sharp to make business decisions. Running a multi-million-dollar company required acuity and the innate sense of responsibility he'd been born with. Even before his parents had died, he'd liked being in charge—learning from the ground up, analyzing, then taking control.

In that sense, he was much like his grandpa. More than wealth and privilege, Jerod's legacy to Ben was an ability to see what was needed, plan a course of action and succeed. "Let's get back to the suspects. *When* you were drugged, who was nearby?"

"Charlene. Ramon. Patrice and Monte."

"My sister and her husband need to go on the suspect list." He hated that undeniable fact. "Their motive is the changed will."

She made a note on her legal pad. "The timing of the new will can't be a coincidence. Within hours of its being signed and witnessed, Charlene was dead."

"Following that logic, the person who most benefits from Charlene's death is me. My daughter inherits the bulk of the estate."

As he turned onto the winding two-lane road that led to the house, the night closed more tightly around them. The facts weighed against him.

"Someone else benefits," she pointed out. "Your estranged wife."

"Victoria? She wasn't anywhere near the estate last night."

"We don't know that. The surveillance camera was off." She gestured with her pen. "But Victoria couldn't have been the person Annette saw carrying Charlene's body."

He wasn't so sure. Victoria was tall and in excellent physical condition. "Put her name on the list."

"I'll talk to Annette tonight and find out if her 'monster' could have been a woman," Liz said. "Her room is right next to mine."

Again, his concentration slid away from their list of suspects and refocused on the woman sitting beside him. Since her supposed job at the house was as a maid, she would, of course, stay in the upstairs quarters.

In the back of his mind, he'd hoped for a different sleeping arrangement. He wanted her closer to him, preferably in his bed.

As he came around a sharp turn at the foot of a forested slope, his headlights shone on an obstacle in the road. No way around it. He slammed on the brakes.

# *Chapter Eleven*

Unable to come to a complete stop in time, the bumper of Ben's Mustang nudged the object in the road. He threw the car in Reverse, backed up.

His headlights shone on the carcass of a bull elk with a full rack of antlers.

"Did you kill him?" she demanded in the accusing tone of an outraged city girl who thought anything with fur and hooves was Bambi.

"Not enough impact." In a fatal collision between a seven-hundred-pound animal and his Mustang, the car would have been totaled. "He was dead before we got here."

"Hunters," she said in a tone that made it sound like a dirty word.

"They shouldn't be here. This area is off-limits, and hunting season is September."

"How do you know that date?"

"I hunt."

"Yuck."

After her kick-ass displays of karate, he didn't expect her to be squeamish. "What? Are you a vegetarian?"

"I eat meat," she said. "But it comes neatly packaged in the grocery store. Which is the way God intended."

He exited the car and slammed the door. The huge elk had fallen across a narrow spot in the road. On one side, the trunks of ponderosa pine came all the way up to the shoulder. The other side was a steep cliff. If they pushed the rear haunches aside, he could squeeze by on the rocky side.

Liz went to the head of the animal and looked down into the wide-opened eyes. "How could anyone take pleasure from killing such a beautiful creature?"

"For the meat." But this animal had been left behind with no attempt to harvest the venison. Not even the impressive rack of antlers had been taken. Ben couldn't imagine that the animal had fallen in the middle of the road. This carcass had been placed here. As an obstacle. For him?

The hairs on the back of his neck prickled. He sensed that someone was near, someone was watching. This was a trap.

"Get back in the car, Liz."

Fists on hips, she confronted him. "You're going to need my help to move him. He probably weighs a ton."

No time to argue. He started toward her.

The thud of a bullet hit the road near his feet. There was no sound of a gun being fired. Must be using a silencer.

He dived toward Liz and shoved her behind the car. He couldn't hear the shots but sensed them. A bullet shattered the dry bark on a tree trunk. Another tore through an overhanging bough. Close. Too close. Ben heard another whiz past his ear.

Liz's moaning about poor dead Bambi ended. She

ducked behind the car beside him. Her attitude was all action. "An ambush," she whispered.

"The shooter has to be up on the hill. It's a good vantage point."

She glanced over her shoulder into the forested hillside that sloped downhill. "How far are we from the house? Can we make a run for it?"

*Not a chance.* Running through the trees, they'd be easy targets for a sniper with a nightscope. He'd already missed three times. A fourth was too much to hope for. "We're better off in the car."

"Can you go back the way we came?"

"Going in reverse down hairpin turns?" He shook his head. "We'd have to go too slow. We'd be an easy target."

"Then we have to go forward. How can you get around the elk?"

"I'll have to drive over the back haunches on the side nearest the cliff."

She gave a nod. "Let's do it."

"Once you get in the car, stay down."

Moving fast, he climbed through the passenger side and into the driver's seat. If he'd taken the SUV with the higher undercarriage, getting past the carcass wouldn't have been a difficult obstacle. With the Mustang, he had to count on the power of eight-cylinder acceleration. He'd make it. His engine had the juice.

He cranked the ignition and took off. With a sickening bump, the tires went over the back legs. Momentarily out of control, the Mustang skidded toward the rocky cliff. Ben flipped the steering wheel to straighten the nose.

Speed was his forte. Whether in a plane or boat or car, he knew how to go fast. Maneuvering on sheer instinct, he whipped along the winding road.

He heard no shots and felt no impact. None of the windows shattered. They were home-free.

Liz peered up over the dashboard. "Are you okay?"

"Fine. You?"

"I'm good."

Adrenaline poured through him, and his pulse raced. The thrill of making a good escape from a dangerous situation lifted his spirits. They were damned lucky to have gotten away from the sniper without a scratch.

And there was another positive aspect to this incident. Having the murderer come after him ought to alter the suspicions of the CBI investigators.

On the down side…somebody wanted him dead.

DANGER. LIZ HAD WRITTEN THE word on her legal pad when making her decision about coming back to the Crawford estate. A murderer was, by definition, a dangerous person. But she hadn't expected an ambush, a sniper on the hillside and a dead elk. Someone had tried to kill Ben. Or her. Or both of them.

A hint of fear nibbled at her consciousness, but she wasn't really scared as they swiveled around hairpin turns on the narrow mountain road. Ben handled the Mustang like a Grand Prix professional. "You're a good driver," she said.

"I know."

"Any idea who wants to kill you?"

"Not a clue."

When he cruised through the security gates, she noticed a difference in the cedar-and-stone house with cantilevered decks. Though illuminated by moonlight, the shadows dominated. Most of the windows were dark. The house reminded her of a bleak empty shell.

Jerod was gone.

Charlene was dead.

The only people in residence were Patrice, Monte and the staff. It seemed they had all gone to bed and pulled the covers over their ears.

After Ben parked the Mustang near the front door, he reached over and rested his hand on her shoulder. His touch was electric, sparking a sense of tension and exhilaration. "Liz, are you sure you're okay?"

"I'm not afraid," she said honestly. "Maybe a little startled. For a few minutes, things got kind of hairy."

"If you don't want to be a part of this, I'll understand." Sincerity resonated in his baritone voice. "We can arrange for you to ride back into Denver with one of the cops."

"I'm not leaving." She rested her hand on top of his. "Not now. The situation is starting to get interesting."

When he smiled, his blue eyes flashed with excitement, and she recognized a kindred spirit—a man who, like her, never backed away from a threat.

She and Ben came from opposite ends of the social scale. He was an arrogant CEO. She scraped by as a struggling law student and part-time private eye. He drove a Mustang as his second car. She bounced along in an aging Toyota. Their differences were myriad. And yet, at their core, they meshed perfectly. Both of them welcomed challenge. Stubborn and kick-ass, they made quite a pair.

Plucking his hand from her shoulder, she reached for the door handle on the Mustang. "Let's concentrate on finding the killer."

"I'll call the CBI."

"And we need to check on the people in the house. To make sure none of them are moonlighting as a sniper."

Inside the house, they turned on lights and made plenty

of noise. She trailed Ben into the study, where he found the phone number of the CBI agents working the case and made his call.

Rachel Frakes, wrapped in a navy flannel bathrobe patterned with white moose, poked her head through the door. Her usually slicked-back hair fell softly around her cheeks, but her eyes were hard and cold as she stared at Liz. "What on earth are you two doing?"

Ben answered, "Somebody shot at us on the road. I want you to check on the chef, gardener and chauffeur. Make sure everyone is accounted for."

"Yes, sir."

She fired another glare at Liz before turning on her heel and stalking from the room. For such a big woman, she was incredibly light on her feet.

While Ben barked into the phone, Liz moved toward the hallway, thinking that she'd peek into Patrice's room. Though it was hard to imagine that chic, black-clad shrew perched on a hillside with a sniper rifle, her husband might be capable of opening fire on Ben. According to Annette, Monte was an Olympic marksman.

"Wait," Ben said. "Where are you going?"

Over her shoulder, she said, "I thought I'd see what Patrice and Monte are up to."

"Give me a minute. I'll go with you."

While he returned to his phone call, she loitered in the doorway, half in the study and half out. At the far end of the hall, she glimpsed a ghostly form. Who was it? What was it?

Liz rushed down the hall and encountered Annette. With her long, heavy brown hair pulled back in a braid and a flower-sprigged flannel nightgown that fell all the way to the floor, she resembled a Gothic heroine from days gone by.

"What are you doing here?" Annette asked. "I thought you quit."

"Changed my mind."

"Fickle."

Now was as good a time as any to start acting like a real homicide detective. Liz had a lot of questions for this sweet young woman who claimed to have seen Ben carrying Charlene's lifeless body toward its final resting place.

Liz offered an encouraging smile. "How are you doing, Annette? It's been a traumatic couple of days for you."

"As if you give a damn."

Her lower lip pushed out in a frown. Somehow, Liz needed to gain her trust. Empathy usually worked. "It must have been terrifying to see that monster."

"Yes, it was." Still scowling, she folded her arms below her breasts. This hostility was puzzling. Annette had no reason to hate her.

"You were out on the deck. All alone," Liz said. "Why didn't you call for help?"

"How could I know Charlene was dead? I thought they might be playing games. You know, sex games."

Liz glanced over her shoulder toward the study and lowered her voice. "Does Ben do that kind of thing?"

"Well," she huffed, "you ought to know."

"Me?"

"I saw what was going on between the two of you. Sneaking off together. Giving each other little winks and nudges." She waggled a finger. "Mark my words. Ben won't fall for the likes of you. Ben has class."

When she spoke his name, she exhaled a wistful little

sigh. Apparently, Annette was a bit infatuated with the lord of the manor. Even if she thought he was a murderer.

Liz said, "There's nothing between me and—"

"Don't lie. You seduced him. That's why you're really back here, isn't it? To be his mistress."

Liz couldn't believe anyone would think of her that way. The only males who ever had crushes on her were the eight-year-old boys in the karate class she taught at Dragon Lou's.

Ben's mistress, huh? Was that the opinion of the staff? That she was sleeping with the boss, that she had employed her dubious feminine wiles to bag herself a millionaire? *Hah!* Her mother would have been so proud.

"Annette, I'm not having sex with Ben."

"Why else would he be interested in you? You're not especially pretty, you know."

"Thanks." This innocent little maid had a decidedly witchy streak.

"I'm not trying to be mean. But look at your hair. You're a mess."

"I don't bother much with my appearance," Liz said. "And I don't sleep with men I've only known for a few hours. Do you?"

"Never."

Her small face puckered, deepening the fine lines around her eyes and at the corners of her mouth. Though she acted like a third-grader, she might be older than Liz had supposed. She asked, "How long have you been a maid?"

"I've been with the Crawfords for almost a year. This is my first maid job."

"Do you like it?"

"Sometimes. I used to work at a hospital. Dr. Mancini said I should go back to school and get trained as a nurse."

"You'd make a good nurse." Liz slathered on the compliments; she wanted Annette to confide in her. "I've seen you at work. You're very precise. And clean."

Annette's mouth twitched as if she couldn't decide whether to sneer or smile. "Are you sure you're not sleeping with Ben?"

"Not that I recall, and I'd remember. He's a good-looking man, isn't he?"

"Oh, yes." She sighed.

Trying to wheedle her way into Annette's confidence, Liz offered more information. "Somebody's after him. While we were driving up here, a sniper set up an ambush."

"No!" She gasped. "You have to tell me everything."

At that moment, Ben stepped into the hallway. "Agent Lattimer is on his way with a forensic team." He nodded to Annette. "Did we wake you?"

"I was already up."

"You seem to do a lot of wandering around at night."

"I have insomnia." Her hands moved nervously across the flannel of her gown. Feverish color appeared in her cheeks. "Liz said that someone tried to shoot you."

"Yes."

His tone was curt. His attitude, dismissive. Liz couldn't fault him for being cold toward Annette. Her weird testimony about seeing him with Charlene's body had gone a long way toward making Ben a suspect.

To Liz, he said, "I'm going to rouse Patrice and Monte. I want them both present when the CBI is here."

She nodded. "And I'll need to give a statement."

Annette whispered, "Should I stay up?"

Without even looking at her, Ben said, "I don't care."

Obviously, he didn't appreciate the intensity of her infatuation with him. Annette was panting to be noticed. Taking pity on the wistful little maid, Liz caught hold of her arm. "Let's go upstairs together. I need to drop off my stuff."

On the third floor, Liz opened the door and tossed her gym bag into her garret-sized bedroom. Annette paused outside the room next door with her hand on the round brass knob. "Ben is angry with me, isn't he?"

Witnessing this unrequited affection pained Liz. She was fairly sure that Ben didn't care enough about Annette to be angry, sad, pleased or anything else. "Do you want to talk about it?"

"Yes," she said emphatically. "And you can tell me about the sniper."

She pushed open the door and invited Liz into her room. Spotlessly clean, the tiny bedroom sparkled with star-shaped ornaments hung from the rafters by invisible wires. The pine surface of the dresser held a crowd of cut glass figurines, several of which were fairy princesses. A framed poster from *Beauty and the Beast* dominated one wall.

Annette flounced into the center of the baby-blue comforter on her single bed and beamed like a teenager at a slumber party. Had she cast Ben in the role of Prince Charming? Had she named him as the "monster" in a desperate attempt to get his attention?

"Okay," she said. "Tell me what happened."

While Liz described the elk in the road and the sniper, Annette added her own embellishments, various descriptions that made Ben sound like a superhero.

"He's very courageous," Annette said. "And he's always been nice to me. Not like Patrice."

*Amen to that.* "That's why it's hard for me to believe he had anything to do with Charlene's murder. Are you positively sure you saw Ben carrying her body?"

Annette's gaze flickered around the room, resting for a long moment on the figurines before she said, "Charlene was a terrible person. Ben hated her."

"You didn't answer my question."

"I told the detectives that I *thought* it was Ben, but I might have been mistaken."

A cleverly ambiguous statement. She'd given enough of a hint to point suspicion toward Ben while allowing herself deniability. Was Annette that savvy? It occurred to Liz that someone else might have told her what to say.

Liz stood. "I should go downstairs and give my statement to the CBI. Thanks for talking to me."

Annette played with her long braid. "You're not as bad as I thought you were."

"Back at you."

On her way out, Liz studied the figurines on the dresser. Hiding among them was a flower petal brooch that sparkled with unusual fire. Real diamonds? Real rubies? She picked it up. "This is pretty. It almost looks—"

Annette flew across the room and snatched the shimmering piece of jewelry. "Get out. Now."

# *Chapter Twelve*

Standing in the kitchen with a mug of decaf coffee that Rachel had brewed, Ben apprised Patrice and Monte of the current threat situation. His voice stayed calm. His account was as simple and direct as possible. Carefully, he analyzed Patrice's reactions, hoping that his sister wasn't responsible for the dead elk and the sniper, hoping that she wasn't trying to kill him.

"The road isn't technically our property," she said. "It's maintained by the county. So we really can't prosecute for poaching."

"Damn the elk," he said. "This was attempted murder."

"Oh, Ben. Don't be so dramatic."

She raised the coffee mug to her lips. In her black pajamas, she resembled a high-fashion ninja. With her hair still damp from the shower, she didn't look like she'd been running through the forest.

On the other hand, Monte had on black jeans and a cashmere sweater. Ben didn't really think there was time for him to race back to the house. But he could be wrong.

"Someone tried to kill me," Ben said.

"Are you quite certain?" Her eyebrows raised. "Is your Mustang riddled with bullets?"

"Why would I make this up?"

"It's so very obvious." She exchanged a glance with Monte, who sat at the kitchen table and reached for the plate of cookies that Rachel had laid out. In his other hand, he held a cell phone, which he was using to send text messages.

"Why so obvious?"

"You're trying to divert suspicion from yourself. You probably want to make it look like somebody else killed Charlene."

"I don't need a diversion." He struggled to maintain control. His sister had always been able to poke at his last nerve. "I'm innocent."

Liz joined them in the kitchen, carrying her yellow legal pad. As she poured herself a cup of coffee, she said, "I was in the car with Ben. I witnessed the assault."

"Oh?" Patrice's mouth formed a tight little circle. "And why should I believe Ben's new girlfriend?"

"I'm not his girlfriend."

"Then why are you here? You're totally incompetent as a maid."

"Personal assistant," she said. "I'm here to help Ben handle all the details of running the Crawford family business. And, maybe, to help him solve the murder."

"That's right," he said. "She's working for me."

It had never been his intention to use Liz as his assistant. He hadn't gone to her apartment and begged her to return because he thought she'd make a good employee. On the other hand, she was smart, steady and believed in his innocence. With her as a personal assistant, he might pull out of this mess without being charged for murder.

"Quite the promotion," Patrice snapped. "I hope he's paying you well."

"He is." Liz snapped back. "And I'm worth it."

"Perhaps you two geniuses will enlighten me about this supposed sniper. Why would anyone want to kill Ben?"

Liz responded. "The will."

Patrice pulled back. Her confidence ebbed. "What do you know about the will? Are you familiar with the terms?"

"Are you?" Ben asked.

The corners of her mouth tightened. Ever since she was a little girl, that expression had meant she was lying. Further evidence of her uneasiness came when she reached for a cookie. Patrice never ate after dinner.

"I know nothing," she said.

Monte leaned toward her and held out the screen of his cell phone so she could see. "That's a good offer."

She shook her head. "We can do better."

"What the hell are you doing?" Ben demanded.

Monte cradled the cell phone against his sweater. "We're contacting agents who can sell our personal account of the murder. Maybe a book deal. Or a movie of the week."

"Certainly not the tabloids," Patrice added.

Liz laughed out loud. "Yeah, those tabloids are so low class."

"But they pay well," Monte said. "One of them contacted us right after Patrice read that statement to the media. She looks good on television. The camera loves her. She could do talk shows."

"Oh, good," Ben muttered. "That's just swell."

"Why shouldn't I do *Oprah*?" she demanded. "You're just angry because I'm getting the attention."

"Damn it, Patrice. You picked a hell of a time for sibling rivalry."

He'd been disappointed in his sister many times, but never like this. Patrice had been offered dozens of legitimate opportunities to work in the family business. She could have staked out her own career path. But she never wanted to learn the ropes, couldn't be bothered with details.

Now she was choosing to make her fortune through notoriety. Tabloids. Talk shows. Selling the family history to the highest bidder.

Ben grabbed the plate of cookies and headed toward the door. "You might want to put on a fresh coat of lipstick, Patrice. Agent Lattimer will be here momentarily."

He and Liz went to the study, and he closed the door behind them. Still steamed, he set down his coffee on the table and shoved a cookie into his mouth. How could he and Patrice have come from the same gene pool? "She didn't even ask if I was okay after I told her about the sniper. Hasn't once inquired after Jerod's health."

"Go easy on her," Liz said. "Jerod told me—when he thought I was Charlene—that your sister had a rough time after your parents died."

"She's an adult now. There's only so long you can blame the tragedies of the past."

"Then let's stick to the present. It seemed to me that Patrice was lying when she said she didn't know the terms of the will."

"She probably got Tony to fill her in on the details."

"But I don't think she wants to kill you."

"Not with a sniper's bullet. More likely, she'll tear me

apart, one slow piece at a time, and feed me into the gossip mill."

"Have you got a lot of deep, dark secrets?"

"Nothing I'm ashamed of. Sure, I've had my share of disasters. And then, there's my failed marriage." He cringed inwardly, thinking of how Victoria had played him for a fool. It wasn't the kind of story he wanted to see in a tabloid headline. "I don't like to air my dirty laundry in public."

"I get it. You're more of a private person."

She perched on the edge of his desk with her feet dangling. Her running shoes seemed adorably small, almost dainty. She'd changed out of the red blouse into a long-sleeved brown T-shirt that hid her curves, but she still looked cute. "And you? Now you're my personal assistant?"

"Seemed appropriate," she said without apology.

"And you don't have to wear a maid uniform."

"Bonus."

Her grin went a long way toward defusing his anger. "Bringing you on board might be the best hire I've ever made."

"We've got a ton of stuff to sort out. Number one is hiring a bodyguard."

"I'd rather not."

"A sniper tried to kill you, Ben. And there's a good chance that he's a professional hitman."

He had come to the same conclusion but was interested in hearing her reasoning. "Why do you think he's a pro?"

"Unless there's been an outbreak of homicidal mania, there's only one murderer. The person who killed Charlene is responsible for the attack on you."

"Which brings us back to our list of suspects."

Liz consulted her legal pad and read off the names. "Patrice and Monte. Tony Lansing. Ramon. And Victoria."

"A vile woman," he muttered.

"That's a bit harsh."

*Vile* was a mild description compared to what he thought of his almost ex-wife. As far as he could tell, the only decent thing she'd ever done was give birth to Natalie. She'd betrayed him with other lovers and robbed him blind. She was greedy, grasping. Vicious. A pit viper. A venomous She-Beast From Hell. "Don't get me started."

"Somehow, I don't see any of these people getting their hands dirty by dragging a dead elk across the road. But they all have enough money to hire a hitman."

"Good point."

"And you have the dough to pay for security."

"You're right."

Especially since Natalie was scheduled to visit on the weekend. He needed to make sure the estate was safe. He rattled off the name of a company he'd used before, and Liz made a note.

Looking down at her legal pad, she frowned. "This list of suspects is kind of skimpy. Who are we forgetting?"

"All of Charlene's friends who were at the party. There could be a lot of grudges we're not aware of."

She scribbled down a note. "Who else? Don't worry about motive, just give me all the names you can think of. Anybody who was in contact with Charlene."

Sipping his coffee, he tried to remember, to think of all the possibilities.

Setting up their own investigation—parallel to the CBI inquiry—wasn't really much different from running a business. Every detail needed to be considered.

"There's the staff, of course. And Jerod's rotating nurses. Hell, I don't even remember the names of most of them, but they might have known Charlene. And Dr. Mancini."

"How long has he been associated with your family?"

"Twenty years. But he's only been a friend of the family for half that long. He started making regular house calls when my grandmother was ill."

"He told Annette that she could be a good nurse."

As he thought of quiet, little Annette, he frowned. She was another woman who meant to do him wrong. "How did she ever come up with that story about me carrying Charlene's body?"

"Because she's desperate for you to notice her. Annette has a major crush on you."

"She has a strange way of showing affection. Accusing me of murder."

"Nonetheless," Liz said. "I talked to her in her room. Have you ever seen that room? It's a junior high school girl's fantasy land. She thinks she's a princess. And you're Prince Charming."

"Great."

She hopped off the desk and pounced on a cookie. "There might be another reason she came up with that story about the monster carrying Charlene. Among Annette's parade of figurines, there was a flower-shaped brooch. I'm no expert, but it looked like real diamonds and a ruby."

"A bribe," he said. "The killer paid her to tell that story."

"Or she saw who it really was, and he's paying her to keep her mouth shut."

If that were the case, Annette was in danger. "I need to talk with her."

"When you do," Liz said, "be gentle."

There was only one woman he wanted to be gentle with. Gentle and tender. That woman was Liz.

# *Chapter Thirteen*

It was after midnight when Liz finally dived between the sheets on the single bed in her garret bedroom. In her plaid jammie bottoms and mismatched polka-dot nightshirt, she wriggled around, trying to find the most comfortable position. Not that it mattered. She was tired enough to sleep standing up. Tired…and oddly happy.

Finally, she knew what it was like to be taken seriously. For most of her life, she'd been a scruffy little blonde, easily ignored. The exception was Dragon Lou's karate school, where her black belt gave her immediate status. In regular life, she was just one of the herd.

As part of the Crawford estate—Ben Crawford's right-hand woman—she got noticed. The CBI agent in charge—Lattimer—had given her a measure of respect when he'd taken her statement. He'd included her when he and Ben had inspected the Mustang, which was unmarked by bullets. Bits of hair from the elk had caught in the wheel wells, but otherwise the car was fine.

The forensic team had gone to investigate the site where the shooting had taken place, but tomorrow the CBI would return. Lattimer had promised an update on their investigation.

Rolling onto her back, Liz considered questions she should ask Agent Lattimer. Results of the autopsy? Alibis for other suspects? She really couldn't believe that the cops were being so cooperative; they liked to play it close to the vest. But Ben had connections that probably went as high as the governor. Whether or not he was a suspect, everybody—including Lattimer—treated him with deference. Wealth had its privileges.

She closed her eyes, knowing that she ought to sleep, but her mind still raced.

She enjoyed being a *real* detective, looking for a murderer, considering motives, seeking out clues. Investigation stimulated her brain. It was way more fun than her dry, repetitive studies in law school. Maybe she ought to consider a change in career.

*Stop thinking. Go to sleep.*

Or maybe she should sign on permanently as Ben's personal assistant. Remembering the expression on his face when she'd announced her new job made her chuckle. She enjoyed throwing him off guard, shaking up his CEO composure.

As she allowed herself to think of Ben, a whole different part of her anatomy was stimulated. Sometimes, when she looked at him, she felt an electric thrill that started in the pit of her belly and spread to every part of her. And when he touched her? The sexual magnetism between them was growing more intense, harder to resist.

Everyone in the household seemed to think she was sleeping with him. Maybe she should fulfill their expectations.

She heard a sound from the hallway. As if something scratched against her door. Was someone out there?

Listening intently, she heard a faint rustling.

In normal circumstances, she'd roll over and go to sleep. But nothing about this house was normal. The murderer could be lurking in the hall. Her rosy contentment turned a few shades darker. Nothing like a threat to bring a person back to reality.

Liz slipped from the bed and went to her door. Carefully, she turned the knob and peered out into the dimly lit hallway. She heard footsteps on the staircase. Slipping on her moccasins, she followed.

The person on the stairs made no effort to be quiet. Liz matched her footsteps to the sound of theirs, descending at the same pace. In the stairwell off the kitchen, she caught a glimpse of a long flannel nightgown. Annette was wandering again.

Liz stayed in the shadows and watched while Annette bustled around the kitchen, humming to herself. She hadn't turned on the overhead lights; the glow of moonlight through the windows provided enough illumination. She opened cupboards and drawers. What was she doing?

This woman seemed to have a bizarre fantasy life. During the day, she performed her maid duties with silent, invisible efficiency. At night, she took on a different identity. Her humming was interrupted by whispered snatches of conversation. A couple of times, Liz heard her speak Ben's name.

Using the heirloom china and crystal wineglasses, Annette flitted back and forth between kitchen and dining room, laying out two formal place settings at the table— one at each end. She was so caught up in her activity that she didn't notice Liz as she moved through the hallway to get a better view of the dining room.

With the place settings completed, Annette gave a satisfied smile. Holding the folds of her nightgown between her thumb and forefinger as if the fabric were rich silk instead of flannel, she ceremoniously sat at the head of the table. Beaming a smile at her nonexistent guests, she raised her wineglass. Her movements were studied and graceful. In the reflected moonlight from the windows, the oval of her face shone with a feverish radiance.

Her lips moved, but Liz couldn't decipher the words. Sad, lonely Annette was completely consumed in her alternate reality. She wanted this lifestyle so much, with such fierce desperation, that she was compelled to act out her dream of being a princess.

As Liz watched, sympathy welled up inside her. She'd known plenty of other women—including her own mother—who had given up their self-respect in search of an improbable dream. Annette's midnight performance was heartbreaking.

She reached into the pocket of her nightgown and took out the diamond brooch, which she fastened at her throat.

Her mood changed. She covered her eyes with her hands. Sobs shook her shoulders.

Liz wondered if she should step out of the shadows and offer comfort, but she feared that making her presence known might snap Annette's tenuous grasp on reality.

"Damn you all," Annette shouted as she bolted to her feet. "You can go to hell. Especially you, Ben."

She fled from the table and darted toward the stairwell.

A chill crawled up Liz's legs, and she hugged her arms around her waist. Though she still had sympathy for Annette, there was some serious craziness going on in that woman. She could be dangerous.

From the front staircase, she heard someone approaching. The dining room light snapped on. Ben stood there in jeans and a T-shirt. "Liz?"

"Hi there." Her voice was shaky.

He gestured to the place settings. "What are you doing?"

She peeked over her shoulder toward the kitchen, hoping that Annette had fled to her room and locked the door. Telling him the truth seemed like a betrayal.

He asked, "Why is the good china on the table?"

"Annette was wandering again. I heard a noise outside my room and followed her down here, where she laid out these place settings." She paused. This was where the explanation got weird. "It looked like she was having some kind of imaginary dinner party."

"I don't get it."

She picked up one of the plates. "Let's put this stuff away."

"Seriously, Liz. I don't understand what you're saying about Annette."

When he started to stack the salad plates and the saucers, she stopped him. "Take them one by one. Rachel told me we have to be mega-careful with the expensive heirlooms."

"And we don't want Rachel on our ass." He carried one plate in each hand and followed her into the kitchen. "Annette's delusional wanderings in the middle of the night are too much. She's got to go."

"You're going to fire her?"

"First thing tomorrow."

With a quick pivot, Liz marched back into the dining room for another couple of plates. She didn't want Annette to be fired. Certainly not because of something she said.

In the kitchen, she whirled and faced him. "Firing her is an overreaction. Annette was only playing a game.

Kind of like a little girl having a tea party with her dolls. She's harmless."

"She's crazy."

"What if this was an illness? Obviously, Annette has insomnia. That might lead to sleepwalking."

"I'm not running a psychiatric clinic. I don't have time for Annette's delusional behavior."

"Everybody has fantasies." She tried to think of a comparison he could relate to. "Think of sports. Haven't you ever dreamed about being on the PGA tour? Or throwing the winning touchdown in the Super Bowl and having the crowd go wild?" She leaned toward him. This was the clincher. "How about winning the America's Cup? Huh? Ever imagine that?"

"It's not the same thing." He placed two salad bowls on the counter. "How the hell could anybody fantasize about eating dinner?"

"Having dinner served to her. Using the fancy china. Wearing fabulous jewelry." She touched the neck of her T-shirt, indicating where Annette had fastened the brooch on her own neck. "She has this desperate longing to be a fairy princess. To sit at the dinner table with you. Prince Charming."

"Fine. Her next job can be at Disneyland."

The gulf between them had never gaped so widely. He had all the power, the status, the prestige. He was the boss. People like her and Annette were nothing but employees—functionaries whose sole purpose was to make his life easier.

Earlier, when she had gone to bed, Liz had been pleased with herself. And with him. Now she could barely stand to look at his annoyingly handsome face. Some phony Prince Charming he turned out to be. His arrogance picked apart the last of her good mood. And she was angry.

Blushing again. This time from rage and deep-seeded resentment. She remembered every time she'd lost a job or been chastised by an idiot supervisor.

"Why would I expect you to understand?" She glared at him. "You don't know what it's like to struggle. You've always been rich."

"I've worked every job in the Crawford businesses. I started as a roughneck in the oil fields."

"But that was just a field trip for you. Any time you wanted, you could return to luxury. You could have your gourmet chef prepare your dinners. Have your butler brush lint off the shoulder of your two-thousand-dollar jacket."

"I'm not like that."

"But you are." She picked up one of the plates. "You eat off heirloom china."

"That's enough."

His tone was clipped and harsh. His jaw clenched as his anger rose up to match her own. Now would have been the smart time to back down, but her fuse had been lit. She was on her way to total explosion.

"What's the matter, Ben? Not used to being talked back to by one of your underlings?"

"Give it a rest, Liz. I want you to stop. Now."

"Don't tell me what to do." She kept her voice low. Other people were sleeping. "I might be your employee, but you don't own me."

"And you don't know me." He took a step closer to her. The heat of his anger washed toward her. "I don't give a damn about money or the things that money can buy. Like this plate."

He picked it up and prepared to hurl it to the floor. She grasped his arm. "Don't."

"Why not? It doesn't matter to me."

"Just don't," she said.

"Because you're concerned about the cost. Right? You're the one who puts too much value on things. You. Not me."

"Break all the plates you want," she said. "But not in here. You'll wake everybody up."

Without another word, he gathered up the two place settings, stacking them carelessly. He hooked his fingers through the teacups, grabbed the wineglasses. In a few strides, he was at the back door.

Now what? She followed as he stormed out into the night. "You shouldn't be out here. The sniper could still be around."

He circled to the left of the house onto a path that led through the trees. Moonlight cast blue-gray shadows at the edges of towering pines and leafy shrubs. As she ran to keep up with Ben's long-legged stride, she stumbled. The thin soles of her moccasins provided little protection from the rocks and twigs, but she wasn't about to turn back. She had to see this through.

Finally, he stopped in a small clearing. They were out of sight from the house, separated by a wall of pine trees. Squatting down, he placed the delicate china on a bed of pine needles. Then he stood.

Breathing hard from running, she stared at him. In his jeans and T-shirt, he looked like he belonged in this rugged setting. The mountains gave him a stature he would never achieve from a bank account. He looked strong, tall and aggressively masculine. Who was this guy? A hard-driving CEO? A cowboy? A sea captain?

"You're right," she said. "I don't really know you."

"Know this," he said. "Everything I do, every decision I make, is to serve those I love."

"Firing Annette?"

"Day after tomorrow, Natalie will be staying here for three days. I don't want my daughter to be frightened by Annette's delusional fantasies."

Liz hadn't considered what it would be like to have a child on the premises. "This isn't a good time for Natalie to visit. Not with the murder investigation. And a sniper. And Jerod being in the hospital."

"I'll protect her. And Jerod." He picked up one of the salad plates. "And you."

"Me?"

With a flick of his wrist, he flipped the plate like a Frisbee. The edge hit a flat granite boulder. The sound of breaking china echoed in the forest. Ben laughed. "Oh, yeah. That feels good."

She edged closer. "What do you mean when you say you'll protect me?"

He grabbed another plate, hefted its weight in his hands. "I want your trust, Liz. You believed in my innocence when everybody else was ready to condemn me, but you still think I'm some kind of spoiled preppy jerk. I want you to believe in me the way I believe in you."

His words struck her very soul. She'd come to the Crawford estate to find evidence to use against him. She didn't deserve his trust.

He fired another plate against the rock, grinned and said, "If I have to smash every heirloom in the house to prove that money doesn't matter to me, I'll do it."

"You have a strange way of proving your point."

He dangled a fancy teacup from his finger. "This is a hell of a lot more fun than arguing."

The problem wasn't him. It was her. She'd been lying from the first moment they'd met. She'd hidden behind her working class morality. Her assumption that rich people—like Ben—wanted only to take advantage of others was dead wrong. He was a good man.

Moving toward him, she held out her hand. "Give me one of those priceless bowls."

She flung it hard. The sound of shattering china gave her a thrill. "Nice," she said. "Kind of liberating."

"You think?" He threw a crystal goblet. The shards sparkled like diamonds in the moonlight. "I say, the hell with fancy place settings."

"And maids in uniforms."

"And ten-course dinners."

Clearly, they were both behaving badly. Out of control. Wild and crazy. She loved it.

Grabbing the last dinner plate, she lifted it over her head with both hands and threw. Never again would a maid have to carry this delicate piece into the kitchen and carefully store it away.

When they were down to the last saucer, he held it toward her. "Go ahead."

"You take the shot." In a parody of manners, she added, "I insist."

He pressed the saucer into her grasp. She looked up into his face. The night breeze stroked his brown hair. The gleam from a thousand stars outlined the sinews in his muscular arms.

She glided her fingertips along his forearm and felt a slight quiver beneath his skin. The night air between them shimmered, and the glow drew her toward him. She would no longer resist their magnetism. Her arms slipped around him. The saucer fell to the ground, unbroken.

He yanked her tightly against him. His kiss was fierce and demanding. Her body responded with a burst of pent-up passion. All restraint vanished as she threw herself into that long, delicious kiss.

Her breasts flattened against the hard muscles of his chest. She rubbed herself against his erection. His excitement fed her own desire.

Ending the kiss, he drew back, giving her the space to say no. His eyes were fiery sapphires. His lips, drawn back from his straight white teeth, beckoned to her. She wanted him. All of him.

"Yes," she whispered.

Still not kissing her, his gaze heated her skin. His hand slipped under her polka-dot nightshirt and ascended her bare midriff, finding her breast. His fingers plucked her taut nipple, setting off an incredible electric reaction.

She gasped. Her head rolled back, and he nibbled the line of her throat. Tingles shot through her. *Amazing. Fantastic.*

She wasn't sure how they ended up on the ground, but she was definitely prone. And he rose above her on his elbows. His legs spread to straddle her hips.

Arching her back, she writhed against him. She shoved aside the fabric of his shirt and stroked his chest. She wanted more. Her arms pulled him closer. She wanted his full weight pressed against her.

"Liz," he whispered her name.

"Yes, Ben. I already said yes."

"I don't have a condom."

The pressure inside her deflated. Oh, yes, she wanted to make love. But she wasn't about to take the risk of unprotected sex. "Couldn't we ring for a servant to bring one?"

"A condom valet?"

He fell to the ground beside her. They lay side-by-side, panting as they looked up through a tracery of pine boughs to the starry skies. Leftover tremors of anticipation trembled through her.

Maybe they could take this passion inside to his bedroom—make love like normal people in an actual bed. But she wasn't ready for premeditated sex. Too many other issues stood between them.

And the moment had passed.

## Chapter Fourteen

Ben started early the next morning. By eight o'clock, he was showered, shaved and dressed in jeans and a blue workshirt with the sleeves rolled up. He grabbed a cup of coffee in the kitchen and went directly into the study, where he was pleasantly surprised to find Liz sitting behind the desk.

In deference to her new position as his personal assistant, she'd taken more care with her wardrobe. Her scoop neck, short-sleeved T-shirt actually fit. The bright blue fabric outlined her breasts and slender waist very nicely. When she stood, he saw she was wearing gray pinstriped trousers.

He focused on her feet. Her pink toes were visible in dressy, black sandals. "You're wearing heels."

"Hey, I'm a girl." She posed like a model. "It's my power suit. I had to get something appropriate for mock court, and this is it."

"Very powerful." And very sexy.

Given the slightest encouragement, he was ready to throw her across the desk and take her right here. But Liz was all business. She returned to the desk chair and gestured to the computer screen. "You've got lots of e-mails. Several from Crawford Aero-Equipment in Seattle and some from Charlene's friends. Oh, and—"

"Hold it. How did you get into my e-mail?"

"It didn't take a genius to figure out that your password was *Natalie*."

"You might be too smart for your own good."

"There's no such thing as too smart." She stood and relinquished the swivel chair behind the desk. "Before we get into the e-mail, you've had some important phone calls. One was from Agent Lattimer. He'll be here in about an hour to update you on the CBI investigation. The other was from Jerod's doctor."

Apprehension tightened his throat. He forced himself to swallow a sip of coffee. "Did the doc sound positive?"

She nodded. "He wants to operate today."

Sinking into the chair behind his desk, Ben replayed the advice he'd heard from the specialists and neurosurgeons. There was risk in operating. His grandpa was seventy-six years old, and his health had been compromised by the tumor in his brain. He'd lost weight and motor skills. His vision was nearly gone. However, if they didn't operate, Jerod would surely be dead before the end of the year. "It's his decision."

"He wants to be well," she said. "When he's talked to me—thinking I'm Charlene—he's told me how much he wants to be strong again. To see the sunlight shimmering on the lake. He's tired of being sick."

He picked up the phone from its cradle. "We'll head down to the hospital right after we talk to Lattimer."

The hour passed quickly and smoothly. With Liz helping him organize and holding the rest of his demanding household at bay, Ben glided through the workload. His only real stumbling block was coming up with an obituary for Charlene. She had two ex-husbands but no other family that he knew of. No children. She'd been involved in a couple of charities, but he wasn't sure which ones.

When Agent Lattimer entered the study, his attitude was more like a business executive than a cop. His beige suit fit well, and his loafers were polished.

After shaking hands, he took a seat on the sofa and flipped open a small spiral notebook. "I'm afraid we didn't find much evidence from your sniper attack last night. There was a spot on the hillside that he might have used. The sightline to the elk was excellent."

"What about footprints?" Liz asked.

"Nothing but smudges. The soil is too rocky."

"How about bullets or casings?"

Lattimer shook his head. "He cleaned up."

"A professional," Ben said.

"We're the professionals." Lattimer looked down at his notes. "The CBI forensics teams are second to none. Highly trained. Highly efficient. And we found nothing. If Liz hadn't been along as a witness, I might not believe there was a sniper."

Ben was taken aback. So much for the sniper attack's removing him from top spot as a suspect in Charlene's murder.

"But there was a bullet," Liz said. "In the elk."

"From a 12-gauge shotgun. Nothing remarkable. No indication of the silencer you claim he used."

*Claim?* As if he were making this up? Ben folded his arms across his chest and grumbled. Apparently, he had to be shot and bleeding to prove his innocence.

Liz was handling Lattimer with far more finesse. She poured fresh coffee from a thermal carafe and offered him fresh rhubarb muffins baked this morning by the chef. Her smile was sweeter than honey. "Can you give us an update on your murder investigation?"

"There's not much to tell." Lattimer helped himself to a muffin and peeled away the wrapper. "Our forensics are inconclusive. In the log barn—the crime scene—we found a number of fingerprints, including yours, Ben."

"It's my workshop." Being surly would get him nowhere, but he couldn't help being frustrated. "Of course my prints are there."

"What about on the murder weapon?" Liz asked.

"Wiped clean," the agent responded. "Tell me again, Liz. What's your interest in this investigation?"

"I'm Ben's personal assistant."

"The first time we talked, you were wearing a maid's uniform."

"Big promotion," she said with another big smile. She was positively oozing hospitality. "What about footprints? Fibers?"

"We have dozens of footprints—shoes, boots and barefoot—going up and down the hillside. Nothing to clearly indicate the murderer."

Liz continued to ask the questions. "You mentioned that the barn is the murder scene. Was she killed there?"

"Yes."

"So," Ben said, "when Annette said she saw someone carrying Charlene's lifeless body, she was mistaken."

"Not necessarily," Liz contradicted him. "Charlene could have been drugged and then carried. Is that what happened, Agent Lattimer? Do you have autopsy results?"

Lattimer shifted uncomfortably on the sofa but still managed to take a giant bite of the muffin. "It's highly unorthodox for me to share this information. I hope you're aware of that, Mr. Crawford."

"I appreciate your cooperation," Ben said. He didn't need to remind the agent of his many highly placed political friends who wanted to keep Ben as a happy campaign contributor. "About the autopsy?"

"Charlene was drugged. Nothing lethal. A sedative combined with the alcohol in her system to knock her out."

"How about witnesses?" Ben said. "I assume you've spoken to the other people at the party. Did they notice Charlene stumbling around?"

He finished off his muffin and washed it down with a swig of coffee. "I can't talk to you about the testimony or alibis of other witnesses, except to say that no one at the party noticed anything unusual when they went upstairs to bed."

"Ramon left early," Liz said. "Did anyone see him go?"

Lattimer stood. "That's really all I can say right now. If I have a significant break in the case, you'll be informed."

After they showed Lattimer to the door, Ben turned to face the chaos that had already developed this morning.

The first face he saw was Rachel's, her eyebrows pulled down in a ferocious scowl. "Sir," she whispered, "something terrible has happened."

More terrible than murder? Than a sniper attack? Than being suspected of a major crime? "What?"

"Two settings of the good china are missing." She cast dark glances to the left and right. "Someone must have stolen them."

"I took the place settings."

Her mouth flopped open and closed a couple of times like a fish out of water. "You, sir?"

"Is there anything else? I need to see Jerod at the hospital."

"Tony Lansing arrived a few moments ago. He's in the dining room. And there's a gentleman from a security company. He said you called him about bodyguards."

Tony could wait. "Where's the security guy?"

"Front room."

He strode forward, intending to make quick work of these issues and get to the hospital. "Come with me, Rachel. I'll need your assistance."

After a firm handshake with the security guy, whose neck was bigger than Liz's waist, Ben said he wanted full protection at the estate, including someone to monitor the front gate and keep the reporters under control.

"Also," Liz interrupted, "you need a personal body-guard to accompany you when you drive in and out of Denver."

"How many men?" the security guy asked.

"As many as necessary," Ben said. "And as soon as possible. Rachel will give you the identifications for people who work here. Thank you."

Now for Tony Lansing. Ben stalked across the foyer with Liz at his heels. "That was fast," she said.

"I'm a decisive guy."

And there wasn't time for dancing around. He needed things taken care of. In the dining room, Ben didn't bother shaking hands. He circled the table and leaned down to stare Tony straight in the eye. "You want to be the Crawford family attorney, right?"

"Yeah." He struggled to keep his gaze steady.

"Here's your first assignment. I want you here. All

day. Don't let anybody—namely Patrice—do anything stupid. Do not talk to the press."

"You can count on me."

That remained to be seen. "And I want you to put together an obituary for Charlene. Find out when the body will be released and make funeral arrangements."

Again, Tony nodded. He seemed relieved he wasn't being asked to do anything difficult or outrageous, and Ben allowed him to think he was safe until he got to the door leading out of the dining room. Then he turned, "One more thing, Tony."

"What's that?"

"I want a copy of Jerod's new will. And Charlene's."

"Interesting that you mention Charlene's will. I need to do an inventory of her things. Technically, I can't release either of those documents to you without—"

"Make it happen," Ben said.

He caught a glimpse of Annette, who immediately dashed off in the opposite direction. Though he still intended to fire her delusional little self, it would have to wait. He and Liz had almost made it to the front door when Patrice caught up with him. "Where are you going? What are you doing? I have a terrible headache."

"Deal with it," he said.

"I mean it, Ben. My head is killing me. I need something more than aspirin."

"Call Dr. Mancini." The family doctor had been coming here daily for months, might as well pay for one more house call. "I'm going to the hospital, Patrice. The doctors are probably going to operate on Jerod today."

For a moment, he saw a flicker of concern in her eyes. He hoped that—for once in her selfish life—she might be thinking of someone else. Might be worrying about her grandpa, the man who had made her expensive lifestyle possible, the man who had always cared for her.

Just as quickly, her compassion disappeared. She frowned. "Are you leaving me here alone?"

"Tony's here. And a team of bodyguards. You'll be okay."

He hoped he could say the same for Jerod.

ALONE AT A SQUARE TABLE IN THE hospital cafeteria, Liz stared into the depths of her coffee cup and worried. Hospitals always made her nervous. It should have been the other way around; this was a place people came for healing and hope. She desperately wanted to believe that Jerod would recover.

She'd stuck by Ben's side while he'd talked with the two specialists and the brain surgeon. They'd reviewed the results from Jerod's tests; most of what they'd said about micro-lasers and neuro-systems stretched far beyond her comprehension. She wished the doctors would have given odds on the operation, like one in three. Or a percentage—ninety percent sure he'll make it. But neurosurgery wasn't roulette. All they'd say was that Jerod's heart was strong and the tumor appeared to be operable.

One of the specialists had made a point of complimenting Ben on providing the experimental treatment his grandpa had needed. Whatever that meant. She'd ask him later.

Jerod's recovery stayed foremost in her mind, but she had plenty of concerns about Ben. Constant activity swirled around him like a sucking whirlpool. There was the long-distance running of his business in Seattle. And keeping the Crawford estate operational. And the custody battle over his daughter. And Charlene's murder.

Most of all, the murder. Though Agent Lattimer had been respectful, his suspicions still centered on Ben, who had plenty of motive and ample opportunity to slip a sedative into Charlene's drink.

If she and Ben didn't concentrate on solving the murder, he might end up in jail.

Then, there was the sniper. Though the personal body-guard had shown up at the hospital and was—at this very moment—watching Ben's back, the threat remained.

With a sigh, she swizzled her spoon through the coffee. Apparently, it would be her job to think about Ben's safety and to prove his innocence. And, last but not least, to lift his burden of concern about Jerod.

There was one person Liz could always turn to in times of trouble and frustration. She left the table and went outside to use her cell phone.

He answered on the first ring. "Schooner Detective Agency."

"Harry, I need you." She gave him the address of the hospital. "And bring your gun."

# Chapter Fifteen

An hour before the operation, Jerod seemed to be in good spirits. Ben stood beside his grandpa's bed, watching as Liz in her platinum wig gave a strange yet credible performance as Charlene, doused in her signature perfume. Liz modified her gestures to a flutter. Her voice was pitched higher than her normal tone, and she made a conscious effort to start every sentence with *I*.

*Exactly right.* Vanity had been the essence of Charlene. Self-centered to the core. Flighty and thoughtless. Demanding and…pretty damned funny on occasion. He would miss her foot-stamping, hair-tossing arguments.

What if she'd been right to keep Jerod away from the surgeons? What if the operation failed?

His grandpa scowled in Ben's direction. "How come you're so quiet, boy?"

"Thinking." And worrying.

"I'm fixing to do a whole lot of cogitating after I get my brain tuned up. Maybe take up some kind of hobby."

"You used to play guitar," Ben said.

He'd never forget those days. Long ago when his family had been whole and happy, Grandpa Jerod would haul his twelve-string out onto the front porch of the

Texas house after dinner. With daylight fading into night, he'd strum by himself for a bit. Then everybody would gather around to sing cowboy love songs about Clementine and Suzannah. Little Patrice would twirl in time to the music. His parents would sit side-by-side on the porch swing with his mother's head resting on his father's shoulder. His grandma would always sing soprano in a high, clear voice.

Ben missed those family nights. He missed his grandma. His mom. His dad. Damn it, he couldn't bear to lose Jerod, too.

"Sing for me," Liz said. "Come on, bumblebee. One little tune."

"You've never much cared for my singing, honey. I believe you referred to my voice as a rusty hinge."

"A girl can change her mind," Liz said, giving a toss of her platinum wig.

Jerod cleared his throat and rumbled, "Do not forsake me…"

Liz joined in. "Oh, my darlin'."

Ben would have added his baritone to the chorus, but he didn't trust himself to sing without betraying the strong emotions that roiled inside him. His abiding grief. His love for Jerod. His fear about this surgery.

When the song ended, Liz gave Jerod a hug. "Listen up," she said to him. "I have a friend I want you to meet."

"Hell's bells, Charlene. Now's not the time for me to be saying howdy to one of your pretty little pals."

"You'll like this guy," she said confidently. "He's going to stay right here at the hospital and make sure everything goes okay."

He grumbled, "I don't need a babysitter."

"Please, bumblebee. For me. Plee-eeze."

Liz's exaggerated pout—just right for Charlene but so out of character for her—lightened Ben's mood. The pain was still there, but she made it bearable.

When she'd told him her plan to have a friend of hers stay with his grandpa, he'd approved. Jerod's operation could take several hours, and he'd be unconscious in recovery for hours after that. Though Ben had hoped to stay at the hospital, too many other things were happening. Last time he'd checked his cell phone, there had been three urgent text messages from Tony Lansing.

"Oh, look," Liz bubbled. "My friend is here already. Jerod Crawford, I want you to meet Harry Schooner."

Though Liz had told him that Harry was older, Ben expected someone in his forties. Upon meeting this white-haired, heavyset, rumpled man, he added twenty years to his estimate. According to Liz, Harry had once been a cop, and he had the world-weary look of someone who had seen it all. The bulge under his plaid jacket also indicated that he was wearing a shoulder holster.

As Harry shook Jerod's hand, he asked, "How's the food in this joint?"

"Not bad if you're partial to green Jell-O."

"I might have to smuggle in a couple of steaks. You're from Texas," Harry said. "You know beef."

"Damn right, I do." Jerod sat up a bit straighter.

"I'll leave you two to get acquainted," Liz said. "Ben and I need to step out in the hall for a moment."

He joined her in the corridor outside his grandpa's private room. "I like Harry. But why is he wearing a gun?"

"With a homicidal maniac on the loose, it doesn't hurt to have a little extra protection for Jerod."

It didn't surprise him that she was best buddies with

somebody who routinely strapped on a shoulder holster. "What else is on your mind?"

"I checked my cell phone. I have an urgent text message from Tony."

"Me, too." Nothing could possibly be as important as spending these last moments with Jerod before his surgery. "He'll have to wait."

She reached out and took his hands. Though the platinum wig perched atop her head looked vaguely deranged, she was a pillar of sanity. Her green eyes shone with gentle compassion. "How are you holding up?"

"I'm hoping this is the right thing. This surgery."

"It was Jerod's decision to let the doctors operate," she reminded him.

"But he wouldn't be here if it wasn't for me. Or if Charlene were still alive."

She gave his hands a squeeze, and that slight physical contact made him want more. He wanted to wrap himself in her arms and hide from his doubts about Jerod's recovery. He squeezed back and said, "Go ahead and return Tony's call. I'll stay here."

With a wink and a grin, she rushed down the corridor to an area that was okay for cell phones.

When Ben returned to the hospital room, he found Jerod and Harry talking like old buddies. Though they'd only met a moment ago, the two men had shared enough life experiences to make them familiar.

"Tell me about this brain operation," Harry said. "Are they going to shave your head?"

"Ain't going to let them." Jerod raked his gnarled fingers through his thick, white hair. "The doctor said they're going into my brain through my nose."

"Shouldn't be hard. That's a good-sized honker you've got there."

These two were well-matched. It occurred to Ben that his grandpa didn't spend much time with people his own age. Charlene had directed their social life toward a younger crowd. Did he miss his old friends? Was there someone Ben should call?

When Liz came back to the room, she motioned for him to step outside. In a tense whisper, she said, "Lattimer came back to the house with a CBI forensics team. They have a search warrant."

"What are they looking for?"

"Drugs." Her gaze searched his face. "Like the ones they found in Charlene's system."

*Trouble*. They needed to return to the house as soon as possible. Ben had a few secrets that he would rather not share with law enforcement.

As SHE AND BEN LEFT THE hospital, Liz wished she could have matched Jerod's upbeat attitude when the nurses wheeled him off toward the operating room. He'd given a thumbs-up sign and waved. She hadn't been so cheerful as they'd climbed into the back of the SUV driven by Ben's bodyguard—a big, silent hulk of a man who reminded her of the bouncer at the Grizzly Moon, a dance club where beer was free for women on Wednesday nights.

The bodyguard's presence made conversation difficult. She wanted to hug Ben and reassure him, but he had retreated into CEO mode, concentrating entirely on returning phone calls.

When they reached the gates outside the Crawford

estate, they had to drive through a flock of photographers and reporters, some with news trucks and microphones.

Inside the house, they were immediately surrounded. Patrice and Monte. The security guys. Rachel. And Tony Lansing, who was well on his way to being drunk, although it was only noon.

Lattimer and his CBI agents had already departed, but they'd confiscated several items and thrown the already dysfunctional house into chaos.

Liz should have stayed with Ben, should have supported him. But she felt like she was being buried alive under a landslide of stress. Her chest was tight. She needed to breathe.

With a word to him, she slipped away from the crowd and went outside onto the lower deck. Standing at the railing, she looked out on the shimmering lake beneath clear, blue springtime skies. Though she couldn't see the front gate, she heard the distant chatter of dozens of voices. A security guy in a military-type uniform patrolled at the edge of the dock. She should have felt safe, but fear weighed heavily on her mind. Fear for Ben. She knew that he was in possession of illegal drugs; she'd seen him make the buy from the sleazebag dealer in Denver.

Though she hadn't been able to unearth his stash, she suspected that a dedicated team of CBI agents would find it. He'd be in even deeper trouble than he was right now.

Ben stepped up to the banister and joined her. "It's a perfect day for sailing."

"To the ends of the earth," she agreed. Voices from reporters at the gate mingled with the sound of an argument inside the house. "I'd like to be somewhere quiet."

"Sailboats are never silent. There's always the wind

and the lapping of waves." He turned his face to the sun. "Mysterious echoes from the vast blue sea."

The poetic side of his personality captivated her. His brilliant blue eyes gazed into the faraway distance, finding a place where hope thrived and swashbuckling adventure was the order of the day. Easily, she imagined him as the captain of a tallship, standing at the prow with a spyglass held to his eye. Even more easily, she imagined sailing away with him.

Instead, she kept her feet firmly planted on the cedar planks of the lower deck. She asked, "Did Lattimer find anything with his search warrant?"

"He confiscated every pill and capsule in the house, including Patrice's array of Valium and sedatives." He shrugged. "It was a damn good search. Those guys are professional. They even found my drug stash."

Her heart dropped. This was the moment she'd feared. "Your drugs?"

"No big deal. I expect I'll have to pay some kind of fine or something."

How could he be so nonchalant? "You told me that you didn't use drugs."

"I don't." He looked down at her. "This medicine was for Jerod. An experimental drug from Mexico that hasn't been approved by the FDA."

Relief exploded inside her; she felt like singing. "That's what the doctor meant when he mentioned the treatment that you gave Jerod."

"Apparently, the drug helped. It wasn't enough to eradicate the tumor but slowed the growth." He frowned. "You wouldn't believe what I had to go through to get my hands on those pills."

"Oh, yes," she said. "I would."

His late-night visit to the drug dealer made perfect sense. He wasn't a scumbag drug addict; his reason for making an illegal drug buy was heroic. He'd risked his life to help his grandpa.

Unable to hold back, she flung her arms around his neck and kissed him hard on the mouth. Her doubts about his character disappeared.

After returning her kiss, his arms tightened around her. His mouth nuzzled her ear. "I'm not complaining, but what's this all about?"

"You're a good man, Ben."

"Took you long enough to notice."

Though aware that she shouldn't be clinging to him out here in the open where everybody could see them, she didn't let go. Didn't care what other people thought.

Ben was all that mattered.

"We need to find that murderer," she said.

"Damn right."

"You wouldn't look good in an orange prison jumpsuit."

He smiled down at her. "I should get back inside. I want to talk to Tony before he's completely drunk."

She separated from him. "I'll join you in a minute. Downstairs by the bar."

He leaned down to kiss her cheek. "See you then."

After he stepped inside, Liz indulged in a moment of fist-pumping congratulations. *Yes! Yes! Yes!* She'd been right about Ben. He had a perfectly rational reason for consorting with drug dealers. Still not a great idea. But completely understandable.

She couldn't wait to tell Harry.

Liz smacked her fist on the cedar banister, pivoted and strolled toward the sliding glass doors that led into the house.

Hearing a scraping noise over her head, Liz paused. She looked up. One of the long cedar flower boxes shook. Then crashed to the deck.

## Chapter Sixteen

Mangled petunia petals and dirt from the splintered flower box scattered at her feet. If Liz had taken one more step forward, she would have been hit. An accident? A coincidence that she'd almost been brained by falling flowers? She thought not.

Someone had loosened the bolts that held that flower box in place, then had given a good hard shove.

She stared at the upper deck and saw no one. But someone had been there only seconds ago, and she intended to find out who it was. She kicked off her heels and ran. At the side of the house, she raced up the wooden staircase that led to the upper level and Jerod's bedroom.

When she flung open the door to the hallway, she saw Rachel with a stack of sheets and towels piled high in her arms. Her eyes widened at the sight of Liz charging toward her. "What's wrong?"

"Did you see anyone come out of Jerod's room?"

"No." She scowled. "His room will be closed off until he comes home from the hospital. I have changed the sheets, of course, and—"

"Stand right here," Liz said. "Don't let anyone come past you."

"Would you please tell me what—"

"No time." Liz returned to the cedar deck that ran along the edge of the upper floor. If she was in luck, the person who'd tried to kill her with a flower box was still in Jerod's room. She could catch them red-handed.

Circling to the deck outside the sliding glass doors, she took a breath and mentally prepared herself to deal with an attacker. Peering through the glass, she saw no one.

When she whipped open the sliding door, a vase of lilies flew past her shoulder and shattered against the wall. What was it with this person and flowers?

Liz dodged forward, moving fast. Annette stood in the middle of the room. Apparently, she'd been hiding behind Jerod's bed. Her arm drew back to throw another object, but Liz shot out with a quick karate chop, disarming her.

Annette yelped in pain.

"Why?" Liz snapped.

"You were kissing him," she said. "I saw you on the lower deck. Kissing Ben."

She rushed forward with arms flailing. This sort of girlish attack was actually more difficult to deal with than someone who knew what they were doing. Liz hesitated, not wanting to do serious damage to Annette, who managed to land one weak blow on her shoulder, then another on her upper arm.

Enough was enough. Liz caught hold of one of those windmilling arms and flipped Annette to the floor. Immediately, she rolled to her stomach and started to sob. "You promised. You swore you weren't sleeping with him."

Liz didn't bother to deny the accusation. She might not be having sex with Ben right now, but his bed was most definitely in her future plans. Not that her love life was any of Annette's business. She looked down at the weepy little maid and would have felt sorry for her if Annette hadn't been so venomous in her lies. "You obviously care about Ben. Why did you make up that story about seeing him carrying Charlene's body?"

"I didn't make it up." Her fist hammered the carpet. "I saw someone and it *might* have been Ben."

"Who was it?"

Her knees pulled up as she curled into a ball, hiding her face. "I don't know."

Annette's craziness had tainted the murder investigation; the CBI agents took her story seriously and focused their suspicions on Ben. "Tell me. Who was it?"

"Don't know."

Liz's patience snapped. She crouched down beside Annette and turned her so she could see into her watery eyes. "When I was in your room, I saw a diamond brooch. Where did you get it?"

"I don't have to tell you."

"Who gave you that pin?"

Her lips pinched together in a stubborn, sour knot.

Disgusted, Liz released her. "You can lie to me, but not to Agent Lattimer. There's a penalty for lying to the police."

"You won't tell him about that pin."

"Goddamn it." Liz seldom used profanity. In her teens, she'd made a conscious decision to avoid gutter talk. Her swearing was a measure of just how angry she was. "I damn well will tell Lattimer about those diamonds. Why are you so scared? Oh, hell. Did you steal the pin?"

She gasped. "It was a gift."

"And who gave it to you?"

"I promised I wouldn't say."

"It's called obstruction of justice," Liz said. "You could go to jail. So you better start telling the truth."

Annette inhaled a shaky breath. "Ramon Stephens gave me the pin. It was right after I saw the monster."

"How soon after?"

"A minute or two."

"So Ramon wasn't the monster?"

Annette shook her head. "He came out on the deck beside me. I was upset, and he tried to comfort me. He said that he'd seen the monster, too. And it looked like Ben."

Liz took a moment to digest this unexpected piece of information. She'd almost written off Ramon, but he was responsible for planting suspicion of Ben in Annette's brain. "Did he give you the pin as payment? For telling the police that Ben was the monster?"

"Nothing like that." Her ingenuousness was too exaggerated to be real. "But I thought he might be right about Ben."

"Why was Ramon carrying a diamond brooch in his pocket?"

"It belonged to Charlene. Jerod gave her all kinds of expensive jewelry that looked like flowers."

"Right." Flowers fit into that whole bumblebee and honey thing. "If you knew the brooch belonged to Charlene, why did you take it?"

"She must have given it to him." Annette's fingers clenched tightly, desperately. "It was his. And he gave it to me. I didn't steal it."

But she knew who the jewelry really belonged to. On some level, Annette must have known that Ramon was using her, getting her to point an accusing finger at Ben.

Liz tried one last time for a positive identification. "Who was it? Who carried Charlene?"

"He had on a hooded sweatshirt. I couldn't tell." Her

lower lip quivered. "What's going to happen to me now? Are you going to tell the CBI?"

*Oh, yeah.* Liz intended to leave this simpering little witch in the custody of one of the security men to wait for Lattimer.

Ben had been right about firing Annette. Not only was she borderline nuts, but she was also dangerous.

BEN SAT AT THE BAR IN THE downstairs party room beside Tony Lansing, who had managed to perform the task he'd been assigned. His secretary had faxed copies of both Jerod's and Charlene's wills.

For the past twenty minutes, Ben had studied the twelve closely typed pages of his grandpa's new will. The terms were what he expected. The only person who benefited from having Charlene die before his grandfather was his daughter, which also meant her legal guardians. Namely, Victoria and him. "Am I missing something?"

"What you see is what it is." Tony raised a glass of vodka to his mouth and took a healthy swallow. "Unless Jerod changes his mind again, your daughter will be a very wealthy young lady when he passes."

"Why now? Why did he make this change?"

"It's not unusual for someone with a terminal illness. Facing death makes a man think about his loved ones. According to the old will and the prenup, Charlene got five hundred thousand. Jerod wanted her to have more."

Though Tony's words slurred around the edges, his logic made sense to Ben. His grandpa wanted to leave his fortune to the woman who amused him and provided him with companionship. Also, to the next generation of Crawfords, represented by his daughter.

Glancing at his wristwatch, Ben calculated the length of time his grandpa had been in surgery. Just over an hour. Too soon to expect results. "Let's hope Jerod will be around for many more years, and we won't have to worry about the will."

Without looking at him, Tony slid a one-page document across the bar toward him. "The Last Will and Testament of Charlene Elizabeth Belloc Crawford. She doesn't acknowledge any living relations. Leaves all her possessions to a couple of charities."

Ben read the pages. "The Retired Strippers League of Las Vegas?"

"Those were her roots." As he stared down into his glass, the creases near his eyes deepened as though he was holding back tears. "Charlene never pretended to be more than she was. Brassy, demanding and tough. But underneath it all… Underneath, she was a peach."

"You cared about her."

He drained the last of his vodka. "No more or less than any other client."

This half-drunk attempt at professionalism was unconvincing. Liz had caught him and Charlene groping each other in the hallway, and Ben was willing to bet that it hadn't been their first time. Tony might even have been falling in love with Jerod's wife. And that was a motive for murder.

Ben knew from his failed marriage that love could turn to hate in a twist of passion. If Tony had been rebuffed by Charlene, he might have wanted her dead.

Ben said, "Apparently, Charlene had a little something going with Ramon."

"Him? Not a chance."

"Ramon is a handsome guy." Ben hoped his comment

would provoke a reaction. "And passionate. Hell, he came after you with a knife."

"You don't need to remind me."

"Charlene liked him. Liked him a lot."

"He amused her." Tony shook his head, fighting off an alcoholic haze. "Told her some phony sob story. She gave him money." His fist came down hard on the bar. "I told her not to, but she laughed and said it wasn't a big deal. No biggie."

Ben waited for the lawyer to continue.

"That bastard," Tony muttered. "He used Charlene. Even got her to give him some of her jewelry. You know what I think?"

"No, Tony, I don't."

"I think that bastard stole some of Charlene's stuff. We ought to get the CBI to investigate Ramon."

"Why do you think Ramon stole Charlene's jewelry?"

"I was up in her room earlier. Doing an inventory, you know. For her will. I think some pieces are gone."

The potential theft of valuable jewelry shifted suspicion toward Ramon. Ben wished that Liz were here. He could have used her legal expertise in reading the will and her perceptions in reading Tony. When she was around, everything seemed more focused.

But the woman who sidled into the room was his sister. Apparently, Patrice had been eavesdropping because she jumped into the middle of the conversation. "You're right about Ramon. He's a despicable person. And there might have been another reason Charlene was giving him money."

"What's that?" Ben asked.

"Blackmail," she said darkly.

Before Ben could respond to his sister, he heard another

person coming down the stairs. Dr. Mancini offered a genial grin to the group. "It's a bit early to be gathering at the bar, folks."

Ben nodded a greeting. "Doctor."

"How's Jerod doing?"

"Too soon to know. He's still in surgery."

"As long as I'm here," Mancini said as he circled around the bar, "I might have one for the road. That's what we used to say back in the old days before DUIs. One for the road. Didn't seem like too much."

"Not anymore." Tony waggled a finger at him. "Drunk driving lands you in jail."

"Right you are, my friend." Mancini pulled a can of soda from the fridge. "I'll stick to a soft drink. You're all witnesses."

His sociable attitude should have been a refreshing change from the drunken angst of Tony Lansing and his sister's dire pronouncements. But Ben wasn't fooled by Mancini's bow ties and smiles. He'd seen the good doctor's aggressive side when he took fierce delight in destroying his tennis opponents; Mancini was in excellent physical condition for a man in his late fifties.

As Mancini popped the tab on his soda, he glanced toward Ben. "I stopped in to see your daughter a few days ago."

A jolt of alarm went through him. "Is Natalie ill?"

"Just a little summer cold. Nothing to worry about."

For some reason, he didn't like the idea of Mancini treating his daughter. When this was over, the doctor would be cut from all family business. "And you're here to see Patrice?"

"For my headache," she said. "I needed something stronger than aspirin."

"Always happy to oblige," Mancini said as he held up his old-fashioned doctor's bag.

Mancini was a walking pharmacy. Even if the CBI search turned up nothing unusual in the drugs they'd confiscated from the house, the doctor was here every day. And he didn't pay close attention to where he left his little black bag. Anybody and everybody in the household had ready access to those drugs.

Patrice tugged on his sleeve. "Ben, I need for you to listen to me. For once in your life, pay attention."

His supply of sympathy was running low, especially when it came to his sister. "What is it, Patrice?"

"Blackmail." She repeated the word quietly and pulled him a few steps away from the lawyer and doctor. "Like Charlene, I was making payments to Ramon. Nothing huge. Just enough to be irritating."

"For what?"

"An indiscretion." With a wave of her hand, she brushed away his question. "The important thing is that I don't want the CBI questioning Ramon. It would be dreadful to have my secrets known."

Especially while she was embarking on a career as a talk show guest. Her ability to stay completely focused on herself amazed and disgusted him. "How many other people was Ramon blackmailing?"

"Several," she said. "He certainly can't afford his lifestyle on the money he makes as a male model."

He couldn't imagine what Ramon might have on Charlene. The blond bombshell had always been open about her past "indiscretions." She was proud of her past; she'd named a retired stripper's fund in her will.

Glancing over his shoulder at the bar, he saw Mancini push a can of soda toward Tony. If the heartbroken lawyer had been having an affair with Charlene, she'd pay to keep that information from Jerod.

"All right, Patrice. What does your blackmail have to do with me?"

"I heard you and Tony talking. Ramon is about to become central in the murder investigation. You need to see Ramon before the CBI gets there. You have to, Ben. You have to get those photographs from Ramon."

His eyebrows raised. What had she done? "Photos?"

"I was young and stupid," she said. "I posed nude for a photographer."

"So what?" Naked pictures seemed appropriate for her new career as a tabloid darling.

"It was a long time ago, and I was…" She paused, scowling. "I was, well, plump."

Fat, nude photos of Patrice were so far down on his list of priorities that he almost laughed out loud. Being naked didn't bother her. But being pudgy?

He looked toward the door as Liz bounced into the room with her cell phone in hand. She beamed a grin as she came toward him. "Good news," she said.

"I could use some."

"Harry called with an update on Jerod. The operation is going better than expected. Zero complications from anesthetic. All systems are go."

"And the prognosis?"

She glanced between him and Patrice. "I keep trying to get these doctors to give me odds. Like Jerod is a ninety-to-one favorite for a full recovery. But they have their own language."

Dr. Mancini came out from behind the bar to join them. "What did they say?"

"Two words—cautious optimism." She addressed Mancini. "What does that mean?"

"The operation is going well, but they aren't making any promises." He patted Ben's shoulder. "You made the right decision."

It was a course of action Mancini could have supported a month ago, but Ben wasn't about to cast stones. His grandpa's recovery was all that mattered. He asked Liz, "When can we see him?"

"Two or three more hours. After the surgery, Jerod will be unconscious in Recovery."

"Oh, good," Patrice said as she grasped his arm. "That's enough time for you to take care of that other little problem we were talking about. Please, Ben."

His first priority was to be at the hospital. Everything else could wait. He linked his arm with Liz's and headed for the staircase. They were out of there.

# Chapter Seventeen

"She tried to kill you with a flower box?"

"Not necessarily kill me," Liz said. "I think Annette just wanted me out of the way for a while so she could have a straight shot at you. Her Prince Charming."

Ben muttered, "I should have fired that loon first thing this morning."

She walked beside him on the city sidewalk outside Ramon's apartment building, glad that she'd changed out of her power suit and high heels into comfortable sneakers and jeans. "Maybe she deserved firing," she grudgingly admitted.

"Maybe? From what you just told me, Annette lied about seeing me carrying Charlene's body, took a valuable piece of jewelry as a bribe and tried to murder you." He smirked. "With a box of petunias."

Obviously, Annette wasn't a professional assassin. "She's valuable as a witness. And we need all the witnesses we can get. That's why we're here to see Ramon, right?"

"That's one reason. Another reason is Patrice. Another is that I can't stand waiting."

After spending an hour at the hospital, they'd determined there was nothing to be done but pacing and worrying. They'd decided to take action by coming to Ramon's upscale apartment building. The concierge told her that she'd seen Ramon in his running clothes and had assumed he was jogging in nearby Washington Park.

As they crossed the street into the park, she asked, "Why does Patrice want you to talk to Ramon?"

"You saw his apartment building."

"Nice place. Posh."

"And he drives a BMW. Dresses well."

She nodded. "Either Ramon has a trust fund or he's living way above the standard for a male model in Denver."

"According to my sister," Ben said, "his side employment is blackmail."

Given time and a bit of research on the Internet, Liz could have figured this out for herself. As would the CBI. Agent Lattimer would be all over Ramon Stephens after he talked to Annette.

They stood at the edge of the running path in the lush green park, landscaped leafy trees, shrubs and colorful gardens. The two lakes in the center of this acreage attracted flocks of ducks and hordes of waddling Canadian geese that honked aggressively at the many joggers, dog-walkers and young mothers pushing baby carriages.

The soles of Liz's feet itched to join in. She felt the need for speed. Ever since she'd found out that her suspicions of Ben were groundless, she'd been bubbling over with positive energy, and her physical attraction to him had become a palpable force.

Every time she looked at him, her mind went straight to the bedroom. Memories of their kisses in the forest played and replayed. The moonlight on his cheekbones.

The feel of his warm skin. His hard, muscular torso as he'd pressed against her.

She pushed those thoughts to the back of her mind. "Is Ramon blackmailing Patrice? What does he have on her?"

Ben lowered his sunglasses to look at her. "I shouldn't laugh. This is serious stuff to Patrice."

"What?" Liz had to know.

"Nudie photos." He couldn't help snickering. "My uptight sister had a moment of butt-naked wildness. And she wants those pictures back."

Ben's bodyguard stepped up beside them. "I suggest we go back to the vehicle, sir. This isn't a secure location."

"With all these people milling around?"

"Not to mention the geese," Liz said. "I've heard they can be good protectors."

The bodyguard did *not* crack a smile. "Look around. There's a lot of places where a sniper with a long-range rifle could take cover."

"I'll risk it," Ben said.

"It's my job to protect you, sir. I have to insist that we go back to the car."

On the far side of the lake near the boathouse, Liz spotted Ramon. At least, she thought it was him. Sleeveless white T-shirt. Baggy shorts. He ran at a careful pace as if each step was a pose for a commercial.

"You stay here," she said to Ben. "I'll talk to Ramon."

Before he could object, she took off running. Behind her, she heard the discussion between Ben and his bodyguard heating up. Not her problem. Nobody was trying to kill her. Not unless she counted crazy Annette.

Without thinking, Liz fell into her natural stride. Running was her second-favorite exercise. The martial arts, of course, came first. She circled the east side of the lake on the asphalt path, dodging around a very small woman struggling with the leash on a very big dog that apparently wanted to jump into the water.

As Liz approached the guy in the sleeveless T-shirt, she identified Ramon. His exertion showed in the sweat glistening on his chest and upper arms. With a sculpted body like his, she understood why some women found him attractive. He wasn't her type. Too pretty.

When he saw her, he made a quick pivot and went in the opposite direction.

Fine with her. Liz turned up the speed. Her sneakers pounded the asphalt path. "Hey, Ramon. Wait up."

He tossed a look over his shoulder and realized that she was closing the gap between them. To avoid being outrun by a girl, he slowed to a walk as she raced up beside him.

Glaring, he asked, "What do you want?"

"You're in big trouble." She kept pace beside him as they approached the boathouse and the playground on the opposite side. "Annette told me what happened on the night of the murder."

"Annette." He scoffed. "That's one messed-up chick."

"She's prepared to tell the CBI everything."

He stopped at the edge of the path. "That night, she was upset. I gave her a pin to make her feel better. Nothing wrong with that."

"A diamond pin," Liz said, "that belonged to Charlene."

"She gave it to me. As a gift."

"You take a lot of alleged gifts from women, Ramon."

And she was sure the CBI would drag all that information out of him when they investigated. She had a different agenda. "You know who murdered Charlene."

He inhaled, and his chest thrust out. Fists on hips, he

looked down at her with calculating eyes. In stark contrast to his fiery passion when he'd gone after Tony Lansing with a kitchen knife, his manner seemed cold and shrewd, like a con man about to close the deal. "Information like that could be worth something."

She couldn't believe he was suggesting blackmail. "I have no money. I was working as a maid. Remember?"

"Then I got no reason to talk to you."

"One question," she said. "That night at the party, why did you drug my drink?"

"You figure it out. You're the big detective."

How did he know she was a private investigator? That information could have only come from one source. "Victoria."

"Here's some questions for you," he said. "Free of charge."

"I'm listening."

"Who wanted Charlene dead so little Natalie could inherit big? Who wants sole custody of the kid? Who's willing to take a shot at Ben so he won't grab his share of the inheritance?"

She repeated the name. "Victoria."

Ramon sneered. "But we both know that she's not a killer."

She glanced over her shoulder and saw Ben and his bodyguard approaching. "Ramon, tell me who?"

She didn't hear the snap of the rifle. There were no warning reports.

Ramon staggered back. His arms flapped helplessly at his sides. Blood stained the front of his white T-shirt.

His knees buckled, and he sank to the ground.

She whirled and stared, trying to spot the gleam of sunlight on a long-distance rifle. Where was the sniper?

In the trees? In one of the nearby apartment buildings? Leaning out of a car window?

She heard Ben call her name, and her self-preservation instincts kicked in. She dropped to the ground in a low crouch next to Ramon. Blood was everywhere. Soaking his shirt. Staining his hands. Dribbling from the corner of his mouth. As she watched, his chest went still. His eyes stared sightlessly at the blue Colorado sky.

Her mind blanked. All rational thought recoiled. Though she was in the middle of this horrible scene, she felt distant and unconnected.

Ben was beside her. His arms encircled her, pulling her away from the body and protecting her at the same time. Behind him, the bodyguard had drawn his weapon and shouted at others to get down.

The pleasant spring day at the park turned into a nightmare. Joggers reacted with screams. Mothers gathered their babies from carriages and ran. The big white dog broke free from his owner and plunged into the lake. A flock of geese took off in a *V* and arrowed across the sky.

"Liz." Ben shook her. "Liz, are you all right?"

Unable to speak, she nodded dumbly.

"Can you walk?"

Without waiting for her reply, he lifted her from the ground and carried her around the edge of the lake to the boathouse. As they stepped into the shaded pavilion, hidden from the sniper by wide stucco arches, she regained her senses.

Her arms coiled around his neck. "You can put me down now."

When her feet touched the concrete floor, her legs were steady enough to support her weight. Still, she clung to him.

The bodyguard checked them both. Gun still in hand, he instructed, "Stay here. The police are on the way."

Ben leaned back against the stucco wall, and she leaned against him, weakened and stunned. She'd been the same way when they'd found Charlene's body. There was something horrible and shocking about violent death.

"I should be tougher." She had a black belt in karate, could handle herself in dangerous situations. "I think it's the blood. I hate blood."

With a gentle caress, he cupped her chin and turned her face toward his. His gaze examined her, looking for signs of damage. "I shouldn't have brought you here. I wasn't aware of the risk."

"Not your fault." She hadn't recovered enough to smile. "This sniper. Was he the same guy?"

"I didn't hear a gunshot. The sniper must have used a long-distance rifle with a silencer. The same type of weapon as the guy who shot at us."

But he hadn't been aiming at Ben. Or at her. "Ramon was the target."

"This time, he might have blackmailed the wrong person."

From a distance, she heard the scream of police sirens as they converged on the park. She buried her face in the soft cotton of Ben's blue workshirt and closed her eyes, wishing they could be alone, wishing with all her heart that Ramon's murder had never happened.

# Chapter Eighteen

In the relative quiet of the hospital waiting area, Ben sat beside Liz. Waiting. The doctors said Jerod's operation had gone well; they had eradicated the tumor in his brain. But it was taking him a long time to come out of the anesthetic. Possible outcomes ranged from full recovery for Jerod to having him in a coma state.

And there was nothing Ben could do about it. The helplessness was killing him, tying his gut in a knot. When Liz touched his arm, he startled. "What?"

"Do you want coffee?"

"Do you?"

"No." She offered a tense smile. "It seems like the thing to do when you're nervous. A cup of coffee. Or tea. Or a triple shot of Jack Daniel's."

"Spoken like a bartender."

She reached behind her shoulder and patted herself on the back. "Just one of my many skills."

He was glad to see her making jokes again. Her near collapse at the boathouse had scared him. But Liz was resilient.

If he focused on her, he might stay sane in the midst of this endless waiting. He stared at her for a moment, counting the many shades of blond and brown in her choppy hair, noticing the light spray of freckles across her nose. Tonight, he hoped she would sleep in his bed. If she only wanted to cuddle, he'd restrain himself. If she wanted more, he would gladly comply.

"I know what you need," she said. "Close your eyes and think of sailing."

"I'd rather look at you."

"You need to relax. You're so tense."

"Who wouldn't be? Grandpa's hovering between life and death, and I just witnessed a murder. Not to mention being the primary suspect in a CBI investigation."

His whole life was in chaos, and Ben prided himself on staying in control. When ill winds blew, he held fast to the rudder and steered through the storm. In those moments of peril when the waves splashed high and swamped the decks, he held firm.

He didn't blame himself for Ramon's murder. The blackmailing male model had tried to run a scam on a killer and had paid the ultimate price. There was nothing Ben could have done to change the outcome.

Nor was he responsible for Charlene's death.

Unfortunately, he wasn't sure others would agree. Especially not Lattimer.

Ben looked down the sterile hospital corridor and saw the CBI agent stalking toward them. Lattimer's demeanor was nowhere near as well groomed as usual. The knot on his necktie yanked to the left. The carry strap for his laptop computer slipped off his shoulder. His jaw clenched so tightly that he could have been grinding rocks with his back molars.

"He looks mad," Liz whispered. "I can't believe I'm saying this, but do you want me to call your lawyer?"

"I'll handle this." Ben stood to face the CBI agent.

Lattimer spoke first. "Mr. Crawford, I have given you every consideration. Kept you updated. Allowed you to stay in the comfort of your own home rather than taking you to an interrogation room. And what happens? How do you pay me back? You get involved in another murder."

"Didn't plan it that way," Ben said.

"When the CBI is called in on a case, we maintain control of the jurisdiction. I had to spend the last two hours with the DPD, SWAT and NSA-trained officers who thought they were facing a terrorist attack."

That seemed far-fetched. "From snipers in Washington Park?"

"Four people were injured while they fled. Nothing serious. Nothing that required hospitalization." The vein in Lattimer's forehead began to throb. "One woman almost drowned while trying to rescue her dog."

Though Ben regretted the disturbance, he wasn't about to apologize. *This wasn't his fault.* "The next time I run into a sneak ambush from a sniper, I'll let you know ahead of time."

"There had better not be a next time," Lattimer said. "I strongly suggest that you return to the house where you and your family are under the protection of a top-notch security team. Got it? Stay out of my investigation."

Ben wasn't in the mood to take orders. He'd cooperated with the police every step of the way, hadn't ordered his lawyers to block the search warrant. He'd kept quiet...until now. "Your investigation, Agent Lattimer, doesn't exactly qualify as a big success."

"Excuse me?"

"As a businessman, I measure achievement in results. Tangible profit and advances. Far as I can see, you've got nothing." He ignored Lattimer's sputtering objections. "You wasted time and resources by suspecting me, trying to put together a case against me. You skipped over other possibilities."

"Don't tell me how to do my job."

"Did you know Ramon Stephens was a blackmailing son-of-a-bitch? Did you look into his finances?" That should have been an obvious lead. "When Annette started babbling about monsters in the night, you bought it. Instead of poking holes in her story, you believed I was the monster."

"Annette," he said disgustedly.

"You've talked to her. Right?"

His answer was to set his laptop computer down on one of the chairs and flip it open. Liz left her seat and came forward to better view the screen.

"I went to the house to interview Annette," Lattimer said. "She was already gone."

"No way," Liz said. "I left her with the security guard."

"She went up to her room, supposedly to change clothes, slipped out the window and was in her car at the gate before anybody could notify them that she wasn't allowed to leave."

He pressed the play button on the computer. "This video came from the surveillance tape at the gate."

Ben watched the screen and saw Annette lean through the open window of her car and look directly into the camera.

"Should have fired that loon," Ben muttered.

"We'll find her," Lattimer said. "And we'll verify what Liz told me about her change in story."

"About Ramon and the diamond brooch," Liz said. "I

told the policeman who took my statement what Ramon said. About Victoria."

"I have a copy of your statement."

"I can't believe she's a killer," Liz said.

Ben wasn't so sure. He'd seen his estranged wife fly into a murderous rage. It unsettled him to think that Victoria was behind these murders. Thank God, Natalie was coming to stay with him tomorrow.

"I'm stepping up the investigation on Victoria," Lattimer said. "Checking her finances and connections. I'll handle this. In the meantime, I want you both to return to the house and stay put."

"That doesn't work for me," Ben said. "I'll need to be coming in and out of town to see my grandfather."

"How's he doing?"

"We're still waiting to find out."

Lattimer's hostility decreased a few notches. "This is rough on you. I hope your grandfather is all right."

"Thanks."

When he held out his hand, Lattimer shook it. They had come to an understanding.

"One more thing," Liz piped up. "Is Ben still your favorite suspect? Or not so much?"

"The latter." Lattimer packed up his laptop. "Stay safe."

Ben barely had a chance to sit when Harry Schooner came into the waiting room and motioned for them to follow him. "Looks like Jerod's about to wake up."

Ben jumped to his feet. The tension that had been building since his grandpa went into the hospital tightened around his spine. Stiffly, he walked beside Liz. Hoping for the best. Fearing the worst.

Harry shuffled along behind them. "The docs say you can see him for five minutes. Then not until tomorrow."

"Right."

They paused at the window of the ICU recovery room where Jerod was hooked up to IVs and monitors that recorded his blood pressure and heartbeat. His surgeon stood beside him, motioning them to step forward.

"Five minutes," he said.

The moment Ben touched his grandpa's hand, he felt a twitch in response. A good sign. Jerod looked like hell. Every wrinkle deepened to a crevasse. His skin was pale as a sheet of paper. He licked his lips.

"Grandpa," Ben whispered, "do you want some water?"

"Cold beer."

Those two words lifted the darkness. Jerod was going to survive. He'd be okay.

Slowly, his eyelids raised. He focused. Really focused on Ben's face. "You need a haircut, boy."

"You can see me?"

"Hell, yes."

Jerod's gaze shifted. He stared at Harry. Then at Liz. Finally, he looked at Ben again. "Where's Charlene?"

Ben's heart clenched.

"That's long enough," the doctor said. "Jerod needs his rest. We still have a number of tests to run."

Ben leaned down and kissed Jerod's forehead. "I love you."

He'd do anything to spare his grandpa the terrible sorrow of losing his wife. But there was no way to avoid the truth.

NIGHT SETTLED HEAVILY AT THE Crawford estate. As the long shadows of the forest closed in on the tiered cedar house, Liz sat cross-legged in the center of the narrow bed in her garret. Her stomach growled. All she'd had for dinner was a couple of granola bars because she preferred not to sit across the dining room table from Patrice and Monte. Nor did she want to chat with the staff, especially not Rachel. It wouldn't be much fun to tell the housekeeper that her dear friend, Victoria, was likely involved in a murder plot.

As for Ben? He was brooding. In a dark funk, he'd sequestered himself in his workshop with his boat. She understood his pain. Telling Jerod the truth about Charlene would be terrible.

She checked her wristwatch. Nine o'clock. Ben had locked himself away for two-and-a-half hours. She should go to the log barn and see him. As his personal assistant, it was her duty to keep him on track and focused.

But the honest-to-goodness reason she wanted to see Ben had nothing to do with solving a crime or tending to business. After last night's interrupted passion, she wanted a second chance.

She kneaded her fingers in the bedspread, holding on tightly. Making love to him wasn't rational. When this investigation was over, she would return to her world, which was far, far away from the lifestyles of the rich and semi-famous. She and Ben weren't relationship material.

And there was also the matter of her deception. The big, fat lie. When he found out that she came here under false pretenses and was really working for Victoria, he wouldn't want anything to do with her.

But for tonight? She didn't have to tell him. For tonight, they could offer each other the comfort and solace they both needed. They could finally act on the intense magnetism that drew them together.

She should take this night. One night with him.

Before she could change her mind, she hopped off the bed, grabbed her denim jacket and flung open the door. Charging down the staircase, she remembered her first day as a maid and Rachel's comment that she made too much noise. Very true. Liz was loud and abrupt and not very cultured. But Ben wanted her all the same. She knew he did.

At the front door, she encountered one of the security men, clad in a dark gray G.I. Joe outfit with combat boots. "Where are you headed?" he asked.

"Is Ben still in the log barn?"

"The murder scene?" He nodded. "Yeah, he's there."

"That's where I'm going."

"I'll take you." G.I. Joe accompanied her down the hill toward the barn. Though he had a flashlight, it wasn't needed. The waning moon provided enough light to see all the way to the front gate, which was blessedly vacant. At this hour, the reporters had retired.

The closer they got to the log barn, the more she wondered if she was making a mistake. Ben had a right to his privacy. But what about her rights? What about the unspoken promise of last night?

If he didn't want to see her, he'd tell her to leave, and that would be that.

Another security guard was posted outside the log barn. When she approached, he gave her a nod, twisted the knob and opened the door.

Too late to turn back.

She stepped inside. Her gaze went to the spot where they'd found Charlene's body. Instead of a chalk outline of the victim, the concrete floor had been scrubbed clean. Not a single trace of blood remained.

Ben gave her a glance, then returned to his work. With long smooth strokes, he sanded the white oak. "Is there a problem?"

"Not really."

"You could have called me on the cell phone."

But she had wanted to see him. Even if the rest of the night didn't go the way she'd planned, it was worth it. His gray T-shirt outlined his arms and shoulders as he stroked the curved line of the hull. His jeans hung low on his hips. There was nothing like watching a man doing physical labor to remind a woman why the opposite sex was so very useful.

She stepped up beside him and glided her fingers across the satin-smooth wood. "It's beautiful."

"She's coming along." He stepped back to admire his handiwork. "I had hoped to have her finished before Natalie's visit. That's not going to happen."

"You'll have plenty of time. The whole rest of the summer. You and Jerod can both teach her how to sail."

"He's going to be all right."

But she heard the doubt in his voice. He wasn't referring to Jerod's recovery from the operation. The emotional pain of losing Charlene would be hard to bear.

Her gaze fell to the floor where they'd found the body. Cleaning up the bloodstains didn't erase the memory.

Ben touched her cheek and turned her face toward him. "Why did you come down here?"

Her heart skipped a couple of beats. Usually, she was fairly direct with men. Came right out and told them what she wanted. But this was different.

Digging into the pocket of her denim jacket, she pulled out her last granola bar. "I brought you dinner."

A slow grin teased the corners of his mouth, and his eyes took on a sexy glow. "I don't believe you."

"True story."

"I wanted you to come to me. I wished it."

"How much?"

"A lot," he said.

"Show me."

His embrace sent her pulse racing. The pressure of his lips against hers sparked a sensual heat that burned slowly through her veins. In about two seconds, she was ready to tear off her clothes.

Gasping, she asked, "Condom?"

"No."

She wasn't about to go through the same thing that happened last night. "Race you back to the house."

# *Chapter Nineteen*

Holding Liz's hand, Ben ran up the hill toward the house. His armed bodyguard followed, hand on weapon and not amused. By contrast, he and Liz were giggling like a couple of teenagers on a first date. Inside the front door, he aimed for the front stairs, and she followed.

Upstairs in his bedroom, they grabbed for each other. Her arms wrapped around his neck, pulling him close for another deep, fierce kiss. He held her tight with one arm. His other hand cupped her round bottom, anchoring her.

The pressure inside him began to build as her body rocked against him. What they lacked in subtlety, they made up for in passion.

He needed this release, this moment of mind-numbing, heart-pumping lust. But he had to slow down. If he continued at this pace, he'd be done before he got her clothes off. And he wanted more for her. A night for the record books.

Grasping her shoulders, he forced her away from him. Her cheeks flushed a delicious pink. Her lips parted, and she was breathing hard.

He peeled off her denim jacket and threw it aside. In a belated attempt to be suave, he unfastened the first button on her blouse and lightly caressed her creamy skin.

"Too slow," she said.

"Give me time, Liz."

She tore open the buttons on her shirt. The fabric slipped from her shoulders. Her torso was smooth and firm with a feminine curve at her waist. Beautiful as a marble sculpture. Why did she hide this body under baggy shirts? He reached behind her back and unhooked her lacy white bra. Dusky rose nipples tipped her firm, round breasts.

When he leaned down and suckled, she arched her back, trembled and moaned. The sound aroused him. He wanted to feed her hunger, to satisfy her completely. She was more to him than a wild one-night stand. A hell of a lot more.

Liz stood by him when no one else would. She was steadfast and strong. His woman.

He tore off his shirt, and they joined in an embrace. Flesh to flesh, the friction of their bodies sparked a tactile sensation of driving heat that grew more and more intense. Explosive. Combustible.

They fell back onto the bed, shedding the rest of their clothing in a frenzy. He threw back the covers, and she stretched out on the sheets. Her shapely legs moved languidly. With a pointed toe, she traced a line down the center of his chest. He grasped her foot, kissed the sole, then the knee. His fingers parted the delicate folds at the juncture of her thighs. She was hot and wet, ready for him. Waiting for him. But not patiently.

She sat up on the bed, wrapped her arms around him and fell back, pulling him down on top of her in a neat and effective maneuver. She was a demanding lover. He liked that.

Her fingers slid down his body, lower and lower until she grasped his hardness. Slowly, enticingly, she tugged.

Electricity crackled beneath the surface of his skin. He was about to explode, needed for her to stop, wanted her to keep going.

Frantically, he tugged open the drawer of his bedside table. He found his supply of condoms. As he sheathed himself, she caressed his arms, his chest, his shoulders.

"Faster," she urged him.

"I was thinking I might get the whipped cream."

"Later."

Her urgency spurred him to action. He rose above her, positioned himself between her widespread thighs.

For a moment, he paused as he gazed down into her wide green eyes. He caressed her gently, savoring the anticipation of the moment when they would join.

"Now," she said. "Now, Ben."

As if there were any doubt.

He plunged into her, and she closed tightly around him. So tight. So perfect.

She matched the rhythm of his thrusts, taking all of him into her body. Never before had he been with a woman whose hunger matched his own. It took all of his self-control to hold back. Her gasps turned into little yips. He waited. It was impossible. He waited until he felt her convulsing. Then he allowed himself to take his sweet, shuddering release.

He collapsed on the bed beside her. In spite of every other disaster that plagued his life, he was happy. Fulfilled. At peace.

Quiet now, they held each other. As a general rule, he wasn't big on talking after sex, but he needed to let her know how important she was to him. He cared about her, wanted to spend a hell of a lot more time with her. Days and weeks. Maybe even years.

Though he might love her, he didn't dare say the word out loud. It was too soon.

After a contented sigh, she propped herself up on an elbow and looked down at him. Her contented smile was more enigmatic than the Mona Lisa's. "Ben," she said.

"Yes, Liz."

She reached across the covers and picked up his black boxers, which she dangled from the waistband. "Why am I not surprised that these are silk?"

"So are your panties."

"Very true." Liz liked to indulge herself with quality undergarments. "Under our clothes, I guess we're both millionaires."

She dropped the boxers, hoping that he wouldn't bother putting them on. He had one of the all-time best bodies she'd ever seen. A broad, firm chest with exactly the right amount of hair. A long, lean middle. And a tight butt.

She couldn't stop looking at him. He pleased her in every way. Even better, he was a skilled lover who knew when to thrust hard and when to tease.

If this night had been *only* about sex, she would have been coolly, blissfully happy. But there was something more. In the midst of their crazy wild passion, for one special moment, he'd looked into her eyes, and they'd connected at a deep level. More than lovers? That scared her.

He glided his finger through her hair. "There's something I want to ask you."

This could be trouble. "Ben, we really don't have to talk. I'm not—"

"How would you like a promotion?"

"What?"

"You heard me." He kissed her forehead. "I value your intelligence and efficiency. I want you with me on a more permanent basis."

"With full benefits?"

"The fullest." His sexy grin sent a shiver down her backbone.

She didn't know what to make of his offer. "After sex, most guys want to go steady or something like that. But you're offering a job? It almost feels like you're paying me to make love."

"I can't put a price on what happened between us tonight."

"Even with your millions, you couldn't afford me." She rubbed up against his chest. "The only way you get that kind of passion is free."

But there was no way she could accept his offer. She'd intended to return any paycheck he might have cut for her. It was unethical to accept because Liz was already on the job, and Victoria was paying the tab. After she revealed that bit of info, she doubted he'd ever want her around on a permanent basis. "You told Lattimer that you based success on tangible results."

"True."

"We still haven't figured out who murdered Charlene. I mean, we've pushed your name off the top of the CBI's list of suspects, but we still don't know."

"And I need that answer," he said. "Jerod will want to see Charlene's killer brought to justice."

"Here's my proposal," she said. "When I've figured out the crime, I'll have a proven success record. And I'll be worthy of a promotion."

"Fair enough."

He leaned forward to seal their bargain with a kiss, and

she gladly joined her lips with his. His scent intoxicated her senses, and she knew they would be making love again tonight.

But not right now. Though she didn't have the yellow legal pad with her notes, she ran through the list of suspects in her head. Patrice and Monte. Tony Lansing. Dr. Mancini. Victoria. And an array of others who hated Charlene, including party guests and staff at the house.

"Right now, I'm most curious about Victoria," she said.

"Lattimer is investigating her."

"He should be. Ramon clearly implicated her, and I could easily see someone like Victoria hiring a sniper. Still, I don't think she killed Charlene."

"God, I hope not. Not matter what I think of my soon-to-be-ex-wife, she's still the mother of my child."

"She could have talked Tony into the murder. As the family attorney, he'd have a lot of influence in handling Jerod's estate when it passes to Natalie."

"Which," Ben said, "won't be for several years. Jerod is going to recover."

Ironically, Jerod's probable recovery from the tumor changed the motivation for Charlene's murder. The killer had acted within hours of the new will being filed to make sure that Charlene would predecease Jerod. If she hadn't stood in the way of his operation, she might still be alive today.

She finished off a peach and washed it down with a sip of bottled water. "I'll make nice with Agent Lattimer tomorrow. He might have more information."

"That reminds me," Ben said. "He called on my cell while I was working on the boat. The CBI warranted search of the house didn't turn up the sedative used on Charlene."

Which was probably the same drug Ramon had slipped into her drink. She sensed that Ben wasn't telling her everything. "What else?"

"They did find tablets that matched the autopsy report."

"At Ramon's," she assumed.

He nodded. "That particular sedative was also in the black bag Dr. Mancini carries on his house calls."

THE NEXT MORNING, LIZ DIDN'T want to leave his bed. She hated the chirping birds and the morning light that slid over the windowsill. This might be the last time, the only time, she would wake up and find Ben beside her.

She had to tell him about being a P.I., couldn't allow the lie to continue for one more day. Then, he'd hate the sight of her. She'd have to leave him, would never feel his kisses again, would never spend another night making love.

She watched his profile as he slept. Even in repose, he had an intensity that compelled her toward him. She'd tried to shield her heart by telling herself that a relationship between them would never work. They came from different worlds. She'd tried to fight the magnetism, but she'd been swept away. Oh, God, she would miss this man.

His eyelids opened, and a lazy morning grin spread across his face. With a growl, he pulled her close and kissed her forehead. "Glad you're here. Thought maybe I dreamed you."

"I'm real."

He rolled over to look at the bedside clock. "Damn. It's after eight. I need to be at the hospital."

Today, he would tell his grandpa about Charlene's murder. "Do you want me to come with you?"

"This is something I should do alone."

She understood. This was a pain that couldn't be shared. "I wish you didn't have to tell him."

"Me, too."

"If his vision hadn't cleared up, I would have pretended to be Charlene forever. Even if I can't stand that perfume."

"There's no way around it." He stared up at the ceiling. "It's always best to tell the truth."

Not always. When she told him the truth, their budding relationship would explode in a giant fireball. She'd never asked to care about him, never wanted to know how perfectly they fit together. And now, her unrequited dreams would be incinerated.

She decided against telling him now. The emotional devastation of dealing with Jerod was enough for one morning. Instead, she got dressed and went downstairs to the dining room while Ben took his shower.

Breakfast at the Crawford estate was never a formal affair. People wandered in and out of the kitchen, choosing whatever they wanted. Three security guards sat at the table, digging into fluffy omelets and bacon.

In the kitchen, Rachel helped the chef by washing plates. Coldly, she asked, "Did you sleep well?"

"Very." Liz wasn't intimidated. "Looks like you could use a hand."

"Annette had her problems, but she was a good maid. Did as she was told."

"Not like me," Liz said.

"Not in the least."

She pitched in and helped with the household chores while Ben was driven to the hospital by one of the security men.

As she swept the deck outside Jerod's room, Liz turned her thoughts to the murder investigation. Though Ramon hadn't admitted that he'd drugged her and Charlene, she started with that assumption. And the drugs had come from Dr. Mancini's bag.

Mancini could have paid Ramon to make sure that she and Charlene were both knocked out. But why?

Mancini could have also returned to the house and turned off the security camera. Was he the killer?

Her cell phone buzzed. It was Harry, calling from the hospital.

"Wanted you to know," he said. "Jerod's okay. He's got a bad case of broken heart, but all his other systems are working just fine."

"Ben had to tell him about the murder."

"It took courage to talk to his grandpa, but it was the right thing to do."

"It's always best to tell the truth."

No matter how devastating.

## Chapter Twenty

Ben strode through the front door with only one thought in mind. *Find Liz.* He needed her.

In the study, he walked directly into her embrace. In silence, they held each other. He drew warmth from her breath, solace from her touch, strength from her endless supply of spirit. He stood there for several long minutes, reviving himself.

When he loosened his hold, she led him to the sofa and held his hand while he sat.

"Talking to Jerod," he said quietly. "It ripped me apart."

His grandpa was still weak, and the medications made him dizzy. But his vision had returned, and he was clearly on the mend. Then Ben gave him the news. "The light in his eyes went out. I could see his sorrow."

"You had to do it."

"No other way," he agreed. "He's being moved to a private room later today. As soon as he starts watching the television, he'll see all about our high profile murder."

"Did you tell him about me impersonating Charlene?"

"Actually, that was the one bright moment. Jerod's fire came back. He was so damn angry. If he'd been strong enough, he would have climbed out of that hospital bed and kicked my ass."

"Doesn't sound too cheerful."

"I'd rather see him fighting mad than drowning in sorrow. Your pal, Harry, agrees. He's a hell of a nice guy. A good companion for Jerod."

"He likes you, too. He called and told me."

"You never mentioned that he runs a private detective agenda. Maybe we should hire him to investigate the murder."

"There's a thought."

His gaze sank into her jade eyes, and he saw that she was troubled. Who wouldn't be? Together, they had experienced a lifetime in the past few days. Tragedy, fear and pain. On the plus side was Jerod's recovery. And last night's lovemaking. Love? That word kept popping into his head. *Love*. When he was with Liz, no other description applied.

All his life, he'd been running the family businesses and protecting their interests. Sure, he knew how to delegate, but the only person he could count on was himself. And now, there was Liz. He trusted her implicitly.

"We've all got to pull together," he said as he stood. "Natalie will be here any minute."

"It occurred to me that I've never seen her room. I've been all over the house with cleaning and such, but never there."

"I'm sure she'll show it to you."

They went upstairs to the deck outside Jerod's room to watch for the car that would bring his daughter to him. She was only supposed to stay for three days, but he was hoping for a longer visit.

Liz leaned her back against the railing and looked up at him. "I've been trying to figure out the murder. Dr. Mancini looks real guilty to me, but he doesn't have a motive."

Apparently, she was taking her self-imposed task of investigating seriously. "You're focused on Mancini because the sedative used on Charlene was in his possession, but that doesn't mean he used them. He always leaves his bag lying around. Anybody could have gotten hold of those sedatives. Maybe Ramon was acting on his own."

"Not for free," she said. "I don't think Ramon ever did anything without a price. The killer—whoever it was— paid Ramon to drug the drinks and to plant that lie in Annette's mind."

Ben saw the front gates open. Natalie was here.

When the car pulled up, he yanked open the back door and helped his five-year-old daughter out of her car seat. She hugged him and giggled. There was no more beautiful sound in the world than the laughter of a child.

Every time he saw his beautiful daughter, he marveled. She had her mother's thick, black hair, but her blue eyes matched his own.

When he introduced her to Liz, Natalie politely shook hands and said, "*Buenos dias.* I know Spanish. Nanny is teaching me."

"*¿Como esta?*" Liz asked.

"*Muy bueno,*" Natalie said very seriously. "Do you know any other languages?"

"A little bit of Japanese," Liz said. "I teach at a karate school, and some of my students are your age."

"A boy in my class knows karate. He's a big show-off. Can you teach me how to beat him up?"

"Maybe later," Ben said as he stepped in. "Liz has never seen your room. Would you show her around?"

Natalie linked her hand with Liz's and started toward the house. His daughter was chatty and smart, but not annoying. She'd never turned into one of those kids who were like performing seals, demanding attention for all their tricks. Natalie knew how to watch and learn.

He wanted to teach her everything, especially how to sail. When she was a baby, he'd taken her for swimming lessons and she had done him proud. Had taken to the water like a baby otter.

His cares and worries faded in the glow of innocence from his child. She brightened the world around her. Even Patrice and Monte smiled in her presence. Rachel nearly smothered the child in a gigantic bear hug.

Natalie's happiness was the only thing that mattered. Everything else would sort itself out.

After Natalie had showed off her room, Ben escorted his daughter and Liz down to the workshop to check on the progress of the boat. The name of this craft had already been decided by his daughter; it would be christened *Fifi* after her favorite stuffed animal.

He liked the way Liz interacted with Natalie. Not at all condescending or forced. They seemed to honestly enjoy each other. He took pleasure in seeing them joke and talk and flip stones into the lake. For a few sunlit hours, it felt like they were a family. A real family.

Around three o'clock, Natalie had begun to wilt. He picked her up, gave her a kiss on the tip of her nose and said, "Nap time."

"Daddy." Natalie rolled her eyes. "I don't do naps."

"That's not what your mom told me. She said you had a cold and needed to rest."

"She just said that because Dr. Mancini told her to. It's a little cold." She squeezed her fingers together. "Very little."

"When did you see the doctor?"

"All the time." Another eye roll. "He mostly comes to see my mommy. But sometimes, me."

"Dr. Mancini seems nice," Liz said. "Do you like him?"

"Mommy does. She likes him a bunch."

The farthest thing from Ben's mind was probing his daughter for information to use in their investigation. But this revelation could not be ignored. If Victoria and Mancini were having an affair, the doctor had a motive for wanting Charlene dead.

Dr. Mancini with his innocent white hair and bow ties didn't seem like the type to be carried away by passion. But Victoria preferred men with money. Like doctors.

After he told Liz to wait for him in the study, Ben took Natalie upstairs to her bedroom at the top of the stairs, where she negotiated her way out of a nap. This would be an hour of quiet time.

Surrounded by half a dozen stuffed animals, she lay down on her bed, and he told her a story. By the end, she was fast asleep. Her thick black eyelashes formed sweet crescents on her rosy cheeks.

He needed to do a better job of protecting her. If Victoria and Mancini had been plotting murder and hiring snipers, Ben would never allow Natalie to return to his estranged wife's house. He needed to report this information to Agent Lattimer as soon as possible. Get the investigation moving in the right direction.

In the study, Liz stood waiting for him. The afternoon sunlight through the window struck highlights in her hair. Her gaze cast down. "Ben, there's something I need to tell you."

"It'll have to wait." He reached for the phone on the desktop. "I need put in a call to Lattimer."

She caught hold of his wrist. "Believe me, I'd love to wait. But I have to tell you now."

He gave her his full attention. Whatever she had to say was important to her. "I'm listening."

"When I came to this house, I expected you to be a spoiled, insensitive jerk who never did an honest day's work. I never wanted to care about you."

"But you do care."

"God help me, I do. That's why this is so hard."

He saw the pain in her eyes and stepped toward her, hoping to offer comfort. But she braced her arm straight in front of her, holding him back.

"Let me finish," she said. "Posing as a maid was an undercover assignment. I'm really a private investigator, working for Harry Schooner."

His rational mind couldn't accept what she was saying. "What were you here to investigate?"

"You."

The word plunged a knife in his gut. "Why?"

"Credible information that you were a drug user. I was here to get tangible proof that could be used in court." A ragged breath rattled through her. "To prove that you were an unfit father."

He remembered the custody battle. The knife twisted. "Victoria hired you."

"I thought I was doing the right thing, protecting a child from an addict father. On the night you made that drug buy in Denver, I was on the street watching. I saw you give money to that dealer. I saw you take the merchandise."

"Drugs for Jerod."

"I know." A tear spilled down her cheek. "Now, I know."

"You spied on me in Denver. Then you came here to betray me." Everything about her was a lie. "You wanted me to lose custody of my child."

"I couldn't make sense of what I'd seen. I knew you trafficked with drug dealers. But I also knew you were a decent man. That's why I left."

"And why did you come back?"

"I didn't want to. Victoria was offering a lot of money, and Harry really needs a big payoff. He wants to retire, and I couldn't—"

"Why?" he demanded.

"I wanted to solve the murder. Ben, I wasn't lying when I said that I believed in your innocence. I know you're not a killer."

"No more goddamned excuses, Liz." Nothing could make him forgive her. "Why are you back here?"

"Victoria wanted me to return."

"You're still working for her."

"Yes," she said.

The air went out of her, and she seemed to collapse within herself. But he had no sympathy for her and her crocodile tears. He had trusted her, and she paid him back with a heartless deception.

He wanted to hate her, but the rage that surged within him was as much for himself as for her. God, he was a fool.

"I should have guessed," he said. "The way you stepped in and separated Tony and Ramon was too…professional."

"I'm sorry."

"You were too slick when you pretended to be Charlene. Right away, you picked up on her voice and her mannerisms. Just another undercover job for you."

"I wanted to help."

"How about last night? When you went to bed with me, that must have been part of your plan. I hope Victoria pays you extra for that."

"Last night." She lifted her chin. "It was wrong of me to want you. But I did. More than my principles. More than anything. I don't regret one minute."

"Get the hell out of my sight."

Without another word, she walked through the door.

## *Chapter Twenty-One*

Numbly, Liz climbed the stairs to her garret bedroom and gathered her things. She couldn't blame Ben for hating her. She had come here under false pretenses, intending to betray him. There was no pretty way to explain it.

She was in the wrong. And she'd lost everything. The future, which would have been bright with him, had turned into a gaping, dark abyss. She needed to get away from here. To put a million miles between herself and the man she could have loved.

In the third floor hallway with her gym bag in her hand, she paused outside the door to Rachel's room. She probably ought to inform her of what had happened. Though Liz hadn't mentioned Rachel's name, Ben might have questions for the housekeeper.

Liz tapped lightly. "Rachel?"

She pushed the door open to peek inside and caught a whiff of the heavy floral scent she'd come to hate. Charlene's cologne. God, that stuff was strong. She sniffed again. Was she imagining the stink? Liz was so attuned to the guilt she felt for wearing that cologne to

play her role as Charlene, that it was branded in her ol-
factory memory.

She entered the room, which was three times as large
as her own tiny garret. When she opened the closet, she
spotted a pair of sneakers—huge, probably a size twelve.
When Liz held them to her nose, they smelled like
Charlene. Stuffed in the bottom of a laundry bag was a
pair of black slacks and a sweater. On the shelf above the
clothing rack, she found a black knit cap.

Everything became clear.

Rachel had gone into Dr. Mancini's bag and stolen the
sedatives. She must have paid Ramon to slip the drug into
Liz's drink because Rachel had known Liz was an investigator.

Then Ramon had drugged Charlene.

Rachel knew about Annette's night wandering. She'd
arranged with Ramon to poison Annette's mind.

With easy access to all the household keys, Rachel had
gone to the surveillance shed and turned off the camera.
She had gone to Charlene's room. They'd struggled. The
bottle of cologne had shattered, and the smell had been
everywhere.

Big, tall Rachel had carried Charlene's body to the log
barn. And she'd committed murder.

Liz looked up in time to see Rachel barreling across
the room. She'd come out of nowhere. For such a big
woman, she was incredibly light on her feet. She swung
hard with a heavy object. A tool? Though Liz dodged, she
took a glancing blow to the forehead, enough to knock
her down. The inside of her head exploded with pain.

She had to get up, had to defend herself. Couldn't move.

Rachel plunged a hypodermic needle into her arm and retreated, giving her plenty of space. Triumphant, she said, "You'll be unconscious in two minutes."

Enough time to call for help. Enough time to make one assault. Liz staggered to her feet. The room whirled like an insane carousel. She was already light-headed. Struggling, she managed to speak. "Why did you kill Charlene?"

"Because Victoria is my friend. With that bitch Charlene out of the way, our little Natalie will inherit."

"You framed Ben."

"He doesn't deserve custody."

Clinging to the edge of Rachel's bed, Liz sank to her knees. Her black belt couldn't help her now. Her head throbbed with every pulse. A sledgehammer inside her head.

"I hadn't planned on this," Rachel said. "You never should have come back."

"Had to. Ben. Had to help Ben."

"Once again, you've made a mess. You never had any respect for me, for my work. The gardener found bits of those broken plates. How could you destroy those heirlooms?"

"Go to hell."

"Use the proper response. Yes, ma'am."

Her evil smile was magnified in Liz's distorted vision. She saw huge lips and teeth. Rachel's words echoed like she was speaking from inside a well.

"What are you going to do with me?"

"Everybody overheard your argument with Ben. He had a motive to get rid of you. Tonight, I'm going to make it look like you're his second victim."

She was going to die. Tonight. And Ben would be blamed.

Her eyes closed as she tumbled to the floor. Darkness overwhelmed her.

BEN ROSE FROM THE CHAIR behind his desk. He had to make up his mind and didn't have much time. Natalie would wake from her nap at any minute.

What the hell should he do about Liz?

She had come there under false pretenses. She had spied on him and lied to him. She had betrayed his trust.

Damn it, he was right to kick her off the premises. Keeping her around would have been a poor decision. The people closest to him had to be utterly trustworthy. He ran all his businesses that way, delegating to those who would act in his best interest. He needed loyal employees who were hard working and…

He smacked his fist on the hard surface of the desk. This wasn't about efficiency and business. This was about a small woman with wild hair and a great big heart. Her face appeared in his memory with her green eyes blazing. He heard echoes of laughter. He remembered her in that poorly fitted maid uniform, tending bar, posing as Charlene. He remembered her in his bed.

Damn it, he loved this woman. No matter what she'd done, he would not let her leave him.

He burst from the den and strode to the front of the house. She hadn't driven her own car and would have to get a ride back into town.

Near the front door, he encountered one of the security men. "Have you seen Liz?"

"Not recently."

"Check with the front gate. See if she's left."

The guard unclipped a cell phone-sized communication device from his belt and spoke into it. Turning back toward Ben, he shook his head. "The only person to come in during the past hour is Dr. Mancini."

That bastard. Ben knew exactly where to find him. He charged down the stairs to the lower level, where the doctor stood at the bar. As Ben approached, Mancini held up a tumbler of whiskey. "One more for the road."

"What the hell are you doing here?"

"Thought I'd pop in and say my good-byes." He adjusted his bow tie. "I won't be coming here every day. Not anymore."

"You got that right." Ben leaned his elbow on the bar. "Tell me, doc. How long have you been having an affair with Victoria?"

"A beautiful woman can make a man do foolish things. All she told me was that she needed money. Cash money. A lot of it. When I asked her why, she kissed me and I forgot about everything else."

Ben had a pretty fair idea of what he was talking about. "You provided Victoria with the cash to pay for a professional sniper."

"When I figured it out, she said she'd call him off. Then Ramon was killed."

Victoria was clever. If the investigation turned toward her, she could display her bank accounts and show that she hadn't made any sort of large withdrawal. She'd purposely protected herself and betrayed her lover.

Liz was nothing like Victoria. True, she'd come to the house on an undercover assignment, but she'd thought she was protecting Natalie from a drug addict father. Though she should have confided in him as soon as she'd known he was clean, he knew how hard it was to tell the truth when someone else would be hurt.

He wasn't about to give her a medal, but he could forgive.

Mancini straightened his shoulders. "I came here to apologize. I should have been more careful, should have asked more questions. And I promise you, Ben, I never did anything to hurt your grandfather."

"You kept him from getting the operation he needed."

"That wasn't me. I have professional ethics, and I knew I was out of my depth in treating a brain tumor. Time and again, I urged him to get a second opinion. As you know, Jerod is a stubborn old cuss. It wasn't until his vision started to go that—"

"Where's Liz?"

Taken aback, Mancini's eyes widened. "Liz? I haven't seen her."

"Did you know that she was a private investigator? Working for Victoria?"

"No." He downed the dregs of his whiskey. "Victoria is poison. The only thing she's ever done right is caring for Natalie. She loves that little girl."

Small reassurance, but Ben knew it was true. Being a good mother was Victoria's only positive attribute. "Agent Lattimer will be talking to you."

He poured another shot. "I'm almost ready for him."

Ben went back up the stairs to the kitchen, where Rachel and the chef were preparing dinner. "Rachel, have you seen Liz?"

Turning toward him with a chopping knife in hand, the big woman glowered. "I overheard your argument with her. She lied to you. If I were you, I'd want revenge."

"Do you know where she is?"

"I thought she was leaving."

He knew it wouldn't take Liz more than two minutes to pack up her things. Was she still upstairs in the tiny bedroom?

He ran up the stairs, two at a time. This house was too damned big. Liz could be out on the deck. She could have gone back down to the study. Could be anywhere.

In the narrow hallway on the third floor, he faced six closed doors, three on each side. He never came up here. Didn't even know which room Liz had been in.

He heard a faint tapping. It seemed to be coming from the door closest to him. "Liz?"

A whispered response. "Ben."

He tried the handle. Locked. "Liz, open the door."

Silence.

He jiggled the knob again. Something was wrong. Was she hurt? Adrenaline pumped through him. He hit the door with his shoulder. Once. Twice. On the third time, it crashed opened.

Liz was on the floor beside the door. She was bleeding from a head wound, gasping, struggling to move.

He knelt beside her, cradled her in his arms. Her eyelids fluttered. Her lips moved, trying to speak.

"It's all right," he said. "I'm here. I'll take care of you."

"It's Rachel," she said. "Look out."

A sound from the hallway alerted him. He turned in time to see the housekeeper brandishing a knife.

He sprang to his feet and faced her. She was a big woman. Big enough to have overpowered Charlene and carried her through the night. A monster. Rachel was the monster.

She slashed with the knife.

He easily sidestepped. "You know what, Rachel?"

"What?"

"You're fired."

When she raised her knife again, he slapped her hand aside and delivered a sharp jab to her jaw. She crashed to the floor with a loud thud.

He returned to Liz, gathered her close to him. With his free hand, he used his cell phone to call 9-1-1. Liz needed medical aid, and he sure as hell wasn't going to trust her care to Dr. Mancini.

With an effort, she lifted her hand and touched his cheek. "Love you." She forced the words out. "Ben I love you."

And he loved her, too. "I'll never let you go."

They would be together forever. He and Liz and Natalie. And Jerod. A real family.

# *Epilogue*

Liz stepped onto the deck of Ben's fifty-foot yacht as they
sailed the Strait of Juan de Fuca headed for the open seas
beyond Washington state and Vancouver. The brisk
autumn breeze swirled her long, white bridal gown. She'd
never been comfortable in skirts, but this day she was
willing to make an exception.

Natalie, also dressed in white, ran up to her. "You're
so beautiful. Like a fairy princess."

She thought of Annette and her fantasies. "I'm not a
princess. Just a woman."

A very happy woman. They'd closed up the house in
Colorado and moved to Seattle for a fresh start. Ben's
home in Washington wasn't huge or pretentious. No need
for servants or housekeepers like Rachel. Just family.
Their family.

She kissed Natalie on the top of her head and waved
to Jerod, who sat waiting with his twelve-string guitar on
his lap. He'd been practicing and played a version of the
wedding march, mixed with half a dozen other tunes.

She linked arms with Harry Schooner, who looked
very presentable in his black tuxedo. "Ready to give me
away?"

"You're quite the door prize, Missy. Ben is a lucky man."

"Luck has nothing to do with it."

She gazed over the railing at the dark, mysterious waves, unable to comprehend exactly what had brought her to this point.

The inevitable dark thoughts intruded.

Victoria, Rachel and Dr. Mancini had all been brought to justice with varying results. Rachel had pleaded guilty and was serving a very long sentence. Likewise for Mancini, who would be incarcerated for two years for his unwitting part in Victoria's schemes. The lady herself—Ben's now ex-wife—was fighting the charges. Still awaiting trial.

As for Patrice and Monte? Liz began to smile again. Patrice had fulfilled her dream of being a talk show guest, partly because of the plump nudie photos. She'd taken a job as a spokeswoman for a weight-loss program.

Everything had worked itself out.

When they'd first moved to Seattle, Ben had wanted her to work for him, but Liz intended to set up her own practice after she finished up law school. There were a lot of people who needed legal help, people who couldn't afford a fancy law firm. And he'd agreed. He'd already started referring to her as the queen of pro bono.

Not a queen. Just a woman.

And he was just a man. As he stepped onto the deck in his tuxedo, he took her breath away. The most perfectly handsome man she'd ever seen.

She'd never thought she needed a man to take care of her, but she willingly gave herself to Ben. Heart and soul.

When Harry handed her off, she thought she might burst from sheer happiness. Ben's touch on her arm sent shivers through her. He leaned down and whispered in her ear, "Are you ready for this?"

More than ready. "Aye, matey."

\* \* \* \* \*

# MILLS & BOON®

## Why not subscribe?

### Never miss a title and save money too!

Here's what's available to you if you join the exclusive **Mills & Boon Book Club** today:

✦ *Titles up to a month ahead of the shops*
✦ *Amazing discounts*
✦ *Free P&P*
✦ *Earn Bonus Book points that can be redeemed against other titles and gifts*
✦ *Choose from monthly or pre-paid plans*

### Still want more?

Well, if you join today we'll even give you
***50% OFF your first parcel!***

So visit **www.millsandboon.co.uk/subs**
**or call Customer Relations on 020 8288 2888**
to be a part of this exclusive Book Club!